FEATHER HEADS

JF McGonigle

ORIGINAL WRITING

ISBN: 978-1-906018-43-6

A CIP catalogue for this book is available from the National Library.

Published by Original Writing Ltd., Dublin, 2008.

Printed in Ireland.

To
My grandchildren
Michael and Jodie

Acknowledgments

MY LIFE-LONG FRIEND Séamus McCague for his logistical expertise, and technical genius during the process of the novel, and also for his unique creativity in formulating the book cover.

My uncle, Frank Baynes, for his archival Farming knowledge.

Paul McMahon for his original artwork.

Jo Jones for her 'hawk-eye' editing.

To my sister Myra for introducing me to my publishers, Original Writing Ltd. and to Andrew Delany for his valued opinions.

And last, but by no means least, to my loving family—my wife Breda and sons, Shane, Garrett and Emmett who willingly and unselfishly encouraged me to take 'time-out' to fulfil my ambition.

CHAPTER 1

Bad Blood Refreshed

ONE WEEK HAS PASSED since Mammy received a letter from Granny. When Mammy opened the letter she sat down to read it to my brother Mattie and me. I had just began reading it over her shoulder and had only got as far as "*Doiredrum, Portwest Co. Mayo, 26th June 1956, Dear Tessie,*" when she told me to sit down, that she was going to read it out to us.

News in that letter would mean that this was my last day with my pals, Sparks and Vinny, for two weeks.

I met them at the corner of O'Hara's grocery shop to discuss what we were going to do with the old tyres we had taken from the back of Ivor Noble's Garage yesterday evening.

Vinny 'topped' the cigarette he had been smoking and slipped the butt into his pocket as he spoke.

'Let's check out these tyres.'

Sparks and I nodded in agreement and we headed towards the Vicar's field where we had the tyres hidden. The tyres were concealed under some branches we had cut from trees in the surrounding hedges.

We walked three abreast towards our destination. After awhile I got a distinctive odour it smelt like 'rags' smouldering, but I didn't comment. Sparks was twitching his nose as he looked and scrutinised Vinny.

I

I asked my two pals if they remembered where I would be tomorrow.

'Yes Finn, you're going West tomorrow, aren't you?' Vinny spoke downheartedly and then frantically ejected a smouldering cigarette butt from his pocket. He slapped on the outside of his pocket, extinguished the butt properly this time, and replaced it back in his pocket.

'Dead right Vinny, Mattie and me are on our way to Granny's tomorrow morning,' I answered, ignoring the minor drama I had just witnessed—I'd seen it happening to him before.

'And you're going with The Yank in his hackney car, he'll break your heart with War Stories,' Sparks confirmed my mode of transport and profiled the driver.

'Dead right Sparks, and I want to tell you boys right now, in case anything should happen to me in the West, well, that you are my best pals.'

'For "flutes" sake Finn, it's the West of Ireland you're going to, not The Wild West,' Vinny rebuffed my hint of danger and looked at Sparks for his endorsement.

Sparks frowned and spoke profoundly, 'precisely Vinny, no danger there at all.'

I'm not too sure about Doiredrum in the West of Ireland not being dangerous. Mammy had told Mattie and me a lot of stories concerning Doiredrum and what it was like growing up there with her mother and her only brother Frank.

There were cows and horses and mountains and a forest and rivers and if they were there, then there would surely have to be Indians in the mountains—although now that I think again, Mammy never mentioned Indians, maybe she forgot.

It was over a month ago since Granny and my Uncle Frank came to visit us in our house.

'I was expecting you earlier,' Mammy greeted them glancing up at the kitchen clock beside the Sacred Heart Lamp on the mantle piece.

'Mother insisted on another visit on the way here,' Uncle Frank started his explanation for being late but Granny cut him short.

'I'll explain the delay later,' she said walking through the kitchen and following Mammy into the sitting room.

Uncle Frank left the parcel he was carrying in the corner of the kitchen bedside the back door and then went into the sitting room as well. It's only when we have visitors that Mattie and I are allowed to go in there.

Mammy kept sending Mattie and me into the sitting room to talk to Granny and Uncle Frank while she was making sandwiches for them. Granny asked me boring questions every time I went into the sitting room. 'What age are you—what class are you in—are you good in school?' I told Granny that I was eight and a half years old, that I was in third Class and that I was very good in school.

She asked my big brother Mattie the same questions when he came in from the back shed. He told the truth when he said he was nearly eleven, but he told lies when he said he was in fifth Class and that he was good in school—he was still in Fourth Class because he was 'kept back' a year.

Mattie had been very ill with Pneumonia and Pleurisy near the end of Fourth Class and missed the final three months of the school term. Mammy and Daddy went to see the School Principal, Master Kirke, about letting him through to Fifth Class. I sneakily, was listening outside the kitchen door when they were discussing the result of the meeting—'brains to burn,' 'lazy as sin' and 'very disruptive' were some of the comments the teacher had made regarding Mattie—but the end result was, that Mattie was to repeat Fourth Class.

I liked my Uncle Frank. He didn't ask any questions.

My sister Myra came into the sitting room and told Granny that she will be making her First Holy Communion next year when she is seven.

'Isn't it well for you,' Granny commented disinterestedly.

Myra told Granny that she was doing her homework and that she would be on school holidays in a few weeks.

'Well off with you and finish your homework so,' Granny ordered blandly.

Myra asked Granny if she would like to see her new dress but

3

Granny just stared at her and said, 'some other time maybe,' and then added 'haven't you homework to do missie?'

Myra left the sitting room. She had her head stooped and she looked sad. Uncle Frank must have noticed that, as she was leaving.

'You're a good girl,' he comforted her softly.

When they arrived at our house I was filled with curiosity and excitement when I saw Uncle Frank carrying a parcel wrapped in newspapers. Mattie and I left the sitting room when Granny had no more questions to ask. I went over to the parcel in the corner of the kitchen and purposely got in Mammy's way lifting and feeling the parcel. My plan worked and Mammy opened the parcel—no toys, just a dead hen and a big load of meat that had blood soaking into sheets and sheets of newspapers.

I went out to the back shed and told Mattie about the parcel. He was looping fishing line, around and around, a small spiked object that he had shoved into a slit in the arrow he was making. Daddy's fishing bag and toolbox were open beside him.

He never looked up, he just kept on doing what he was doing as he spoke.

'"Country parcels" are no good—it's the American parcels you want; they're the ones.'

'Yes, like the one we got from Chicago with the roller-skates in it, and where are the roller skates now?' I wanted to annoy Mattie because I was disappointed over the 'country parcel.'

'Are you looking for a dig in the mouth?' he asked looking up when he spoke this time.

I stepped backwards to the shed door before I spoke again.

'And if you hadn't done a swap for Ted McMahon's pellet gun, we'd have roller-skates today.'

He had started filing down the arrowhead spike, but I knew by the way he was placing the arrow and the file on the shed floor, that he was going to make a run at me.

'I'm telling Mammy, that it was a lie that you gave the skates to the school jumble sale,' I taunted him further running through our yard and up the back lane.

When I heard his footsteps fading behind me, I stopped running and laughed back him. I was only joking, when I said I wa going to tell Mammy the truth about the roller-skates. My reason was simple; Mammy would have taken it from him and that would have messed things up for me, because I know where he hides the pellet gun in the shed and I use it when he's not around. Anyway I have loads of things to tell on Mattie if I want to get him in trouble.

Seeing as there was nothing worthwhile in the parcel I thought maybe the visitors might have something else for me so I went up to the end of the back lane and around the front way to my house.

On the way down the road Miss Black called me over. She looked determined standing at her gate and was holding a hack-saw in her hand.

'Finn, would you happen to know what this is?' she asked holding up the small hacksaw.

'It's a hacksaw,' I said and then added, 'just like Daddy's.'

'Is that a fact, well some bold, bold person removed a spike from my railing with it, and obviously left it behind, after they had done their nasty deed,' she squinted her eyes at me and continued, 'would you have any ideas who would do something like that?

'Haven't a clue Miss Black sorry,' I said and walked on towards my house.

I would have stayed and talked to her because sometimes she has sweets but I had a job to do—I had to see the visitors before they left.

Granny and Uncle Frank stayed for another hour after the dinner and then they said that they would have to leave because they had stayed longer than expected with Granny's friend whom they had visited before coming to us.

Granny called her "Annie O'Sullivan," and then went on to describe her as 'her oldest and dearest friend.' She said that they both started teaching together many many years ago in Galway but that she was now living with her son who was married and lived here in Clunmon. Granny expanded on her explanation as to why they were so late arriving. She said that there is a sort of a Warehouse Shop beside her friend's house and that she was

5

looking for some carpet-mats for her neighbour Breda Fenlon.

Then it really got boring when Granny went on to say that Breda Fenlon had a new bathroom built onto her house and that the wall tiles were yellow so she thought that primrose coloured mats, would be a nice present for Breda.

'They didn't have yellow or the primrose colour that I wanted but they said that they would be getting them in within the month,' Granny said rising from the table.

I know the place she is talking about it's a brilliant place; it's called "Danny's Cut Price Warehouse" and it's just on this side of the Border. Danny the owner sells carpets, bicycles, cookers, wardrobes, beds, dining room furniture and he has an excellent selection of toys. He used to let us look around the place until Vinny and Sparks started jumping on the beds one day and he told us not to come back. Danny barred me as well and I was only opening and closing the doors of a few glass cabinets in the Antique Section.

When Granny mentioned the name "O'Sullivan" I knew who she was talking about but Mammy said that she didn't know that family. I reminded her that it was the new family that lived at the end of Roslea Road just past The Yank's house and not far from "Danny's Cut Price Warehouse." Mammy kept thinking and wondering if she knew them, but then when I mentioned that they were the people who spoke Irish most of the time, she nodded to confirm that she did know them.

I was watching Granny putting on her black netted-hat. She settled it down on her grey hair and kept in place by pinning it to her hair-bun at the back. Mammy held her long black coat open like a Matador and Granny seemed to vanish into it.

When she picked up her handbag from the hallstand I stood close to her but she didn't open it. She had a Pioneer Pin and a Fáinne Pin, pinned on the front of her coat collar. I knew what these Pins represented because my teacher Master Cullen wore a Pioneer Pin and he never drank whiskey or stout or anything like that and I knew that the Fáinne Pin meant a fluent Irish speaker, because Master McCague wore it and he was always speaking Irish.

When we were all standing in the kitchen Mammy sent m

6

out the back to get Mattie who reluctantly came to say his 'good-byes' and then went back to the shed. Mammy called up the stairs for Myra to come down but she didn't answer or come down and I knew by the expression on Mammy's face that she was furious with my sister.

'I don't know what's keeping Mac,' Mammy frowned looking at the clock on the mantle piece, 'would ye have time to call to the Barracks to see him?'

'We don't have a lot of time, sure we will see him the next time we're up,' Granny said shrugging and settling her shoulders in the coat.

Before they left the hall Granny went over her plans as to how she was going to get the carpet-mats down to her for her neighbour Breda Fenlon. They were brilliant plans and they involved Mattie and me. Granny said that her friend Annie would write to her when Danny got in the carpet-mats she was looking for.

'Annie will parcel the mats up and drop them down to you,' Granny said tilting her hat slightly at the hallstand mirror and added, 'then I'll write to you of course, and give you a date when we are ready for the boys to come on their holidays and they can bring the mats down with them.'

That's why I thought the plan was brilliant; we will be going to Doiredrum on our holidays.

Mammy and Granny and Uncle Frank were kissing and saying goodbye at the car and then at last Uncle Frank took his hand from his pocket and gave me two shilling. He did this when Mammy was looking at him and then he said.

'Share this with your brother and sister and don't tell your mother I gave it to ye.'

That did not make sense to me, as Mammy was looking when he gave me the money, but I like Uncle Frank anyway.

Granny and my uncle were just about to get into their Morris Minor car when I saw Daddy coming down the street in full uniform. I loved to see Daddy walking around the town in his Sergeants uniform because he reminded me of the Sheriff in the cowboy films walking up the dusty town and everybody bidding him the time of day.

7

'Oh! here's Mac now,' Uncle Frank said moving away from the car door and stepping forward to meet Daddy.

Granny just stood where she was at the car.

'Are ye going already?' Daddy said shaking Uncle Frank's hand. 'And how is this young lady?' Daddy said nodding over at Granny. I don't know why Daddy called her "young lady" because she is a very old lady.

'*Tá mé go maith*,' Granny replied in Irish, looking stern faced.

I knew that, that meant in English, that she was "feeling well."

Then Daddy looked back at Uncle Frank and winked as he asked, 'are ye not going over the Border to get yourselves some cheap whiskey or cigarettes before ye go home.'

Uncle Frank shook his head and smiled without answering.

Then Daddy turned to Granny and said with a wide grin, 'how about yourself, butter is real cheap over there too.'

I saw Mammy staring angrily at Daddy.

Granny answered calmly but sternly, 'I make my own butter, thank you, and I'll stay away from those Six Counties, which your short sighted blundering politicians caused,' she raised her head slightly and continued, 'perhaps when they are rightfully re-united with our other Twenty Six Counties, maybe I'll go up that way then.' Granny concluded pulling her coat tightly around her as she gently brushed her Fáinne Pin.

'We can't manage the twenty six counties we have, what do we want another six for?' Daddy answered sharply.

The second or two of tense silence that followed felt like forever until Uncle Frank tentatively broke the impasse, 'no... no smuggling this time...we are running late...we took on too much visiting this time,' and then added as he scurried to the car boot, 'oh God, I nearly forget your spuds.'

'And who else did ye visit?' Daddy asked folding his arms, as his white chevrons gleamed in the early evening sun.

'The O'Sullivans, the new family to the town, the Irish speakers from out the Roslea road,' I said showing off my local knowledge to impress Daddy.

All looked a bit startled at my informative ranting before

Daddy said, 'Ah! yes, the "blow-ins," I hear they do a bit of boasting about their relations being Volunteers at the G.P.O. in the 1916 Uprising...they'll be a great asset all right to a Garrison Town like this,' Daddy said rubbing his solid chin to conceal a wry smirk.

Uncle Frank puffed walking with the sack of potatoes he had taken from the car boot. He left them on the ground beside the front door and stood beside Daddy. He looked nearly as tall as Daddy and Daddy is the biggest man that I have ever seen. I know that Daddy is six foot one and a-half inches tall because he boasts about his height sometimes and sticks out his chest. This only happens when I smell whiskey from his breath. Maybe Uncle Frank only looks as big as Daddy because he has some hair and Daddy is bald. Even though Uncle Fank is at least ten years younger than Daddy I think he has stopped growing and therefore he will never be able to grow as big as my father.

I am dwelling on this when Granny breaks my concentration, ignores Daddy's comments on the O'Sullivan family and speaks softly to Mammy, 'you should get some mats yourself, they have a lovely lilac colour there but I think the primrose will be nicer for Breda's new bathroom.'

'Lilac, Primrose' Daddy said grinning and added, 'by heavens you've gone very posh in Doiredrum since I was transferred from it.'

Mammy's glare at Daddy lessened his grin and he waved, 'well I won't hold ye so, have a safe journey.'

Daddy passed by me and puffed like Uncle Frank as he lifted the sack of potatoes and carried them in through the doorway. I could smell whiskey from his breath. Uncle Frank held the door for Granny before sitting into the car himself.

Mammy and I remained on the pavement until Uncle Frank and Granny drove to the end of our street and around the corner.

'Put that money you got from your Uncle Frank away in a safe place,' Mammy instructed going in the hall door and than added, 'ye will all need new shoes for school.'

My disappointment must have showed in my frown. After all it was only two shillings he gave me for dividing with my brother and sister and I needed it for sweets, but there is no point talking to Mammy sometimes so I just gave her the money.

'Good boy, look after the pennies, 'she said prompting me.

'And the pounds will look after themselves,' I mumbled completing the proverb I had heard so many times before.

Mammy opened her purse and gave me three pence. It wasn't a good exchange but then she was giving me pocket money for my holidays so I didn't mind too much. I went up to my room at the top of our house and lay on my bed. I covered my ears but I could still hear the muffled words of Mammy and Daddy arguing two stories down.

The weeks flew by, Granny's letter arrived and here I am out with my pals in the Vicar's field and looking forward to going on my holidays to Doiredrum tomorrow.

CHAPTER 2

Farewells at the Dead-Chicken Dump

WE TRAIPSED IN single-file through the field until we came to the place where we had hidden the tyres.

Sparks was frowning when he said, 'I calculate it will take the best part of three hours to get from Clunmon to Portwest and then on to, what do you call it?'

'Doiredrum,' I answered sharply and added, 'and that's about ten miles further.'

'Then I calculate that...'

'Will you stop 'calculating,' Vinny cut Sparks short, 'we're on school holidays so no calculating—now a big question, how much pocket money are you getting for your holiday?'

'Five Shillings each, but Mammy said we have to buy presents out of that for Daddy and Myra and a very, very small one for herself when we are coming home.'

Vinny relit the cigarette butt, that he had eventually stubbed out earlier.

'Well what are we going to do with these tyres,' Vinny pointed and held out the smouldering cigarette in my direction, 'want a drag?'

I waved my hand in a definite 'no' sign. I was cautious that Mammy might smell the cigarette smoke from me and I wasn't going to let anything stop my holiday in Doiredrum. We began removing the branches that were covering the tyres.

'I don't think that we should burn them on the railway track this time,' Sparks gave cautionary advice.

'I agree with Sparks,' I said looking at Vinny and then added, 'remember, you caught fire with the petrol and...'

'Okay, okay, I said we are not burning them on the railway track this time,' Vinny interrupted abruptly, throwing and sticking his dagger in a tree trunk.

Vinny rarely goes anywhere without bringing his dagger. I knew by his demeanour that he did not want to talk about our last "tyre burning" escapade so I said nothing else about that incident.

Vinny pulled the dagger from the tree and began paring and cutting one of the branches we had taken off the tyres.

He looked over at me, 'Tell ya what Finn, we'll wait until you get back from the West to see what we'll do with these tyres—right lads cover them up again.'

Sparks threw the final branch on top of the tyres and whispered, 'thanks be to God.'

Vinny wiped the blade of his dagger in his cardigan. We got back out on the road at the part of the field furthest from Noble's garage and headed for our hideout. We were the only ones who knew where it was.

Our hideout was behind the Dead Chicken Dump at the back of Joe McCarville's chicken sheds. There were loads of high bushes and tall weeds between the Chicken Broiler Sheds, the Dead Chicken Dump and the sleeper-fencing at the railway station behind. Sparks said it was as good as the African jungle and that's why we built our hideout right in the middle of it all.

The roof of the hideout was made from sheets of galvanise that we got from Murphy's hayshed. The galvanised sheets were hanging loose at the side of the hayshed and Sparks said that they served no purpose so we pulled them off and took them with us. The sides of the hideout were made from timber.

When we first started to build it there was no bother getting timber and planks but then Mister Woods mended the hole in the fence at his timber yard and we had to gather up bits and pieces of timber we came across in the back lanes of the town and from fences out the country.

Even after that, we were still a bit short of timber so we had to use some of the boards from McCarville's Broiler Sheds. We pulled a few boards from the side of the chicken shed furthest from our hideout to avoid detection. Joe McCarville owned three chicken sheds in total so we felt that he wouldn't miss a few boards.

There were a good few chickens walking around the road and back lane near our house when I was going to school the next morning. I told Vinny and Sparks when I met up with them on their way to school but they already knew because there were chickens near their houses as well. Vinny said that "broiler" chickens are dead stupid anyway.

Sparks said that Joe McCarville and some of the men, that worked in the Broiler Sheds, were running around trying to round the chickens up. I asked Sparks if they used lassoes to round up the chickens, and he said no, but that McCarville was giving out and cursing like mad.

Vinny frowned before speaking, 'what's McCarville getting all mad and excited for over a few chickens, sure he must have millions of chickens in those chicken sheds of his.'

'Well I wouldn't say millions but there are certainly thousands of chickens and anyway it's inhumane to keep chickens in sheds like that,' Sparks said and nodded at the two of us seeking approval of his assessment.

When he explained what 'inhumane' meant, we all agreed and further agreed that, we could not be held responsible for the chickens escaping, because we had only taken a few boards from the side of the chicken shed.

We turned into the back lane at the top our road. Everyone called this lane the 'Gullet.' Nobody knew why, not even Sparks. Half way up the 'Gullet' we slipped in by the first chicken shed and kept looking behind us in case we were seen by anyone. Our house wasn't too far away and if Mammy was to be looking out the top back bedroom window on the third floor she might see us. When we got past the other two chicken sheds without being

13

seen we knew we were safe. Our hideout was a secret known only to Sparks, Vinny and me.

'Quick, quick I need my catapult.' Vinny shouted pointing at a rat that ran across our weedy path. He pushed past Sparks and me and ran through the nettles for a shortcut to the hideout. Sparks and I were waiting by the Dead Chicken dump when Vinny arrived back from our hideout with his catapult.

He had his catapult loaded with a ball-bearing and shouted to us, 'where did the rat go?'

I pointed to the corner of the dump where some dead chicken carcases were rising upwards, 'he's under them,' I said.

Vinny took aim and fired. One of the rotting chickens carcases hopped slightly up in the air from the force of the ball-bearing hitting it. In a split second the rat ran out from just beside it and scurried across the other dead chickens and back into the weeds and nettles.

'Damn,' Vinny said as he spurted into the mass of dead chickens to try and retrieve his ball-bearing.

If it had only been a marble that he had fired at the rat he wouldn't have bothered trying to get it back, but ball-bearings were scarce.

Sparks and I helped Vinny to look for the ball-bearing among the dead chickens for a while but when the smell got a bit much for us we headed for our hideout. We were sorry we couldn't find the ball-bearing as we knew the trouble Vinny had gotten into getting them in the first place.

We had been in the back yard of Ivor Noble's Garage. Ivor and his mechanics had gone home and Vinny discovered that a window at the back of the garage had not been closed properly. We agreed to go in and just have a look around. There would be great peace, not having Noble shouting at you as you examined tools and machines and things. I helped Vinny in the window and all he had to do was crawl across the workbench and on to the floor. But when he jumped onto the garage floor things started to go wrong.

The mechanics or maybe Noble himself had left a metal tray on the floor with oil and ball-bearings in it. Vinny didn't see this and when he landed on the floor he just clipped the edge of the tray and the oil flew all up the side of his trousers and down around his socks and shoes. Vinny was very annoyed and said loads of 'fecks' and started throwing the ball-bearings at the big safe in the corner. I had been helping Sparks in the window but we stopped until Vinny cooled down a bit.

After a while Vinny started looking all around the floor and picking up the ball-bearings he had thrown at the safe. He gave the ball-bearings a quick wipe with an oil rag he had found on the workbench and then threw the oil rag beside the safe and put the ball-bearings in his pocket.

When Vinny looked to be a bit calmer, Sparks and I decided to move again. I told Sparks to hurry up but he told me that he was stuck. I noticed that he had his trousers caught on the notch that clasps the window slide adjuster. The only way I could free Sparks was to try and pull him back out the window but then I heard a tear. Now Sparks was cursing as he pulled and stretched his trousers to examine the tear in his trouser seat.

I know what it is like having a tear in your clothes. Last year I had two rips in my trousers—one on each side of the seat. I got one of the tears from barbed-wire while climbing over the fence at the town dump and the other tear I got when we were going out fishing and I got snagged going through a hawthorn fence.

I didn't mind the tears so much it was the patchwork that Mammy did that brought me the most concern. The trousers were a light brown colour but Mammy patched them with a yellow coloured material. When I was up at the blackboard doing sums Master Kirke told me not to be sitting on butter-flies. All the class laughed but I didn't. I sometimes wonder if Mammy stitched on those patches on purpose, to stop me tearing my trousers.

So I was very careful when I started to climb in the window myself but stopped when I met Vinny coming back out. He said that he was going home to clean himself up a bit, so Sparks and I didn't bother going in then. Vinny showed us the six big ball-bearings and he said it was a 'lucky find' and we agreed with him. They were bigger than the usual ball-bearings we would get from bicycle wheel hubs. That was the lucky bit but the un-lucky bit happened the next day.

Mister Noble rang the Guards and said that his garage had been broken into. I heard Daddy telling Mammy that Noble insisted that Daddy come down to take a look, as this was 'a job for a Sergeant,' because somebody tried to break into his safe. I got a fright when he mentioned the safe, until Daddy started to laugh as he relayed what Noble had said to him.

'"Safe Crackers," wiping off their fingerprints with an oil rag—a job for Sergeant,' Daddy said mockingly shaking his head–'sure a blind man could see where the trail led and they were no "safe crackers" let me tell you—and before you ask Mam, I can't tell you who it was.' Mammy just pulled a face and went into the kitchen.

Daddy turned to me unexpectedly and asked, 'I hope you weren't with him?'

'No I wasn't with Vinny,' I responded immediately.

Daddy rubbed his forehead and looked heavenward before he said, 'you'd make a bad criminal son.'

I didn't know if that was a good thing or a bad thing so I said nothing else.

It was only afterwards that I discovered that Daddy had called to Vinny's father and told him about the 'oil trail' from the garage to his house. Vinny didn't 'rat' on Sparks or me but he was annoyed with Daddy.

'Next time tell your father to bring me to the Garda Station and put me in a cell, or hang me up by the heels or anything—but not to tell my Daddy okay,' Vinny instructed me.

I nodded but deep down I knew that I wasn't going to tell my father the way to do things.

That's why the ball-bearings were very important to us and now we only have five. Vinny said that marbles were okay for breaking light bulbs on poles but useless for killing rats.

'Ball-bearings are the only thing for splattering rats,' Vinny always said when he'd hit a rat. We had any amount of marbles. Vinny used to chase after the girls in the playground, when they were playing marbles and threaten to kiss them, if they didn' give him some.

We held our noses until we left the vicinity of the Dead Chicken Dump and went into the safety of our sacred hideout. Vinny threw his catapult back into the utilised biscuit tin in the corner.

Sparks and I kept our catapults there as well, along with a few model soldier, plastic Indian figures, model war aeroplanes, model ships, loads of marbles and now only five ball-bearings. Vinny sat down and lit up a cigarette. We usually shared the same cigarette but Vinny offered me a whole Woodbine for my-self to smoke, seeing as I was going West for a few weeks. I said 'no' again and for the same reason as before—fear of being found out by Mammy and the inevitable consequences. I had a job to do anyway. I crawled over to the biscuit tin and removed my catapult from it.

'The rat's gone' Sparks said with a frown.

'I know that, I'm bringing this to the West with me,' I told him shoving my catapult down inside the waistband of my trousers.

'Take a good few marbles with you,' Vinny said sounding like an adult; he usually behaves like that when he's smoking.

'How many will I take?' I asked shoving my open clawed hand into the tin.

'Take as many as you think you'll need and take a ball-bear-ing too in case you're attacked by Indians.'

I was really excited when Vinny mentioned 'Indians' and was putting a ball-bearing in my pocket when I heard Vinny and Sparks tittering and saw them pushing one another. I got an-noyed because they were laughing at my excitement when the word 'Indians' was mentioned so I threw the marbles back into the tin but I slipped the ball-bearing into my pocket.

We were really comfortable now in our secret hideout lying down on, the cardboard floor covering, made from flattened cardboard boxes which we had rescued from Mister O'Hara's fire dump at the back of his grocery shop. We were chatting and laughing and pushing one another remembering silly things that we had done but then suddenly our banter and chatting stopped; it was as if a dark cloud ascended on us as it dawned on us to-gether that I was leaving them for a while.

We stood up in silence in the hideout. Vinny stuck his head out of the opening of the hideout and started sniffing the air.

'It must be tea time' he said, 'is there anything better than the smell of a good fry-up?'

'Better than the smell of rotting chickens, that's for sure' Sparks commented.

'What time is it anyway, Mammy told me to be back early for my tea today' I mentioned moving towards the opening too.

Sparks shaded the sun from his eyes with his hand and looked up into the sky before speaking, 'I'd estimate somewhere between 18:30 hours and 19:00 hours.' Vinny looked over at me and pointed at Sparks, 'he's at it again Finn, big words and big figures—is it tea time or not Sparks?'

'Yes, our reminiscing has terminated,' Sparks said going to the utilised Orange Box in the corner.

Sparks and I had found the Orange Box floating at the bottom of the street near Mister Commiskey's Fruit and Vegetable shop after the big thunderstorm last month. The Orange Box suited our hideout for stacking our comics, cap guns and water pistols.

'Here Finn, take these with you,' Sparks said handing me three comics he had removed from the Orange Box as he left the hideout.

'Reminiscing, Terminated, sixteen million hours, fourteen thousand hours,' Vinny mimicked and then shouted after him, 'hey, Sparks if you keep using those big words we will we be calling you Major, Professor Sparks in a few years.'

'None of those things,' Sparks called back over his shoulder,' I told you before I'm going to be a Scientist when I grow up, make a spaceship and fly to the Moon or maybe even Mars.'

'I'm still going to be a stuntman for cowboys,' I said to Vinny checking that I had my catapult with me, 'what about yourself Vinny, are you still going to be a Test Pilot?'

Vinny thought for a while before speaking, 'that or a motorbike racer, but I'll tell you what, I'm definitely not going to work in Daddy's shop selling coats and hats and trousers to 'oul codgers,' that's for sure.'

I took my last look back at our hideout for a few weeks and

followed my pals along the weedy trail past the Dead Chicken Dump, past the chicken sheds and back on to the 'Gullett' lane where the smell of frying sausages and bacon got stronger.

When we got as far as the back of O'Hara's grocery shop Vinny stopped suddenly and said opening his belt, 'sorry Finn I meant to give you this, back at the hideout.' He slipped the sheath and dagger from his belt and handed it to me. 'You'll have better use for this in the West—Sparks and I won't be up to much while you are away—just look after it,' Vinny said buckling his belt again.

'Kill yourself a few Indians with it 'Sparks said.

He wasn't laughing when he said it so I said nothing and put Vinny's dagger and sheath inside my trouser waist beside my catapult and pulled my jersey well down over the top of my trousers.

Nobody spoke until we got to my house and then Vinny asked, 'will you be coming out after your tea?'

'No, don't think so, Mammy wont let me I'd say, we have to have baths and pack and stuff like that,' I said making sure my catapult and Vinny's dagger were well out of sight.

'Well, we'll see you when you get back,' Sparks said holding out his hand.

I shook it.

Vinny gave me a gentle punch on the shoulder 'See you cowboy,' he said walking away.

I watched my two best pals walk up the road for a few seconds and then I went into my house.

CHAPTER 3

Packin' Up and Headin' Out

THERE WAS A LOVELY SMELL of a fry-up in the hall as I headed for the kitchen. I got really hungry but then I heard Mammy scolding, so I stayed outside the kitchen door and listened.

'Don't tell me lies Mattie, sure Miss Black told me she saw you and that adopted "ladeen," from O'Neill Park, what's his name ah, er, Bumper or, or, what's his name?'

I heard Mattie's voice next. 'Towbar,' he said giving the name of his pal.

'Yes, that "corner boy," Mammy continued sharply, 'did you ever hear the like of it, stuffing potatoes into the exhaust pipes of cars.'

I was resting against the door at this stage waiting for the heated conversation to finish but it went on.

'I know now where my potatoes went, now finish up your tea and get up those stairs and have a bath before I break your back, I've run your bath for you so don't use any more water.'

The kitchen door opened suddenly and I stumbled forward. Mattie elbowed me as he passed by. After what I had just heard I knew that Mammy would be in a bad mood, and I knew Mattie was to blame, but we all would suffer.

'Didn't I tell you at dinner time, to be back here early for your tea, where were you 'til now?' Mammy shouted at me.

'Out,' I said.

'Out where?' Mammy snapped back at me and hit me with a flick of the dish towel, 'sit down and have your tea and not a word out of you, I don't care if its burned. Out gallivanting and doing mischief when you should be at home here helping me, do you realise that your going to Granny's tomorrow.' My mother took a deep breath and banged a plate down on the table in front of me.

On the plate was, burned bacon and sausages and a hard fried egg. Mammy continued scolding as she made her way back to the pantry, 'my poor mother and brother, what have they let themselves in for, with you two "feather heads" going down to them?'

When Mammy mentioned the word "feather heads" I thought about Mattie and me going West; we might be taken captive by the Indians, be brought up by "redskins" in their ways, going on the War Path with spears and bows and arrows, have painted faces and headbands with feathers?

I was jerked out of my pensive thoughts, by the jagged pain of my catapult sticking into my ribs, when I sat down. I was trying to move it and the sheathed dagger to the side when Mammy shouted 'What on earth is wrong with you?'

'I'm itchy,' I replied looking innocent.

Mammy came over to me and she was squinting. I thought at first that she had seen the catapult and dagger so I put my hands over my head expecting a slap.

'Sure no wonder you're itchy, look at all those ants crawling on your jumper, get outside and shake yourself off, where on earth do you be when you go out?'

I rushed out and went into the shed. I took off my jumper, gave it a few shakes to rid it of the ants, rapped my catapult and the dagger in it and put the bundle on top of Daddy's paint shelf. I told myself that I was never going to burn or scald or kill ants ever again; they saved my skin today.

When I returned to the kitchen, Mammy asked me what I'd done with my jumper, that she wanted to pack it in the suitcase.

I jumped up from the table and in a nervous voice shouted, 'no, no, it's okay Mammy I'll get it, you just sit down and rest yourself.'

She looked bewildered as I rushed out the backdoor; things were going great.

I made sure that the dagger and catapult were well concealed in the jumper and then came back into the house to go upstairs and hide them again.

'Give me that jumper till I give it a quick rinse,' Mammy said meeting me at the door.

I gulped, and kept walking through the kitchen. 'Don't bother yourself Mammy it will be all right, it wouldn't be dry in time anyway,' I had mumbled entering the hall. I had made it to the bottom of the stairs with my 'bundle' and could hear Mammy talking to herself in the kitchen.

'I don't know what's going on in that fellow's head at times.'

As I passed the bathroom door I heard Mattie splashing and playing in the bath. I gave the bathroom door a rap and shouted to Mattie.

'Have you got my battleship in there with you?'

He just shouted back, 'get lost,' so I knew he had it with him again. I went into the bedroom and straight to the open suitcase on the bed.

I put my catapult under my bed. I did not want to bring it to Granny's now as I was bringing Vinny's dagger and anyway I knew that Mattie was bringing his catapult. I saw him measuring his bow and arrows against the size of the suitcase earlier this morning and I heard him muttering to himself, 'too big, bow and arrows too big, won't fit, it's catapult only, I'm afraid.'

Mattie is not allowed to have a catapult ever since Ivor Noble accused him of breaking the advertising globe on his petrol pump. Noble told Daddy. When Daddy put the accusation to Mattie he denied even having a catapult. After that Mattie had to keep his catapult well hidden and especially when Myra went crying to Daddy that someone had cut the tongue out of one of her school shoes—it was Mattie—he used it for a tongue for his catapult

I hid the dagger in one of my wellingtons in the suitcase. I concealed the ball-bearing at a bottom corner of the suitcase, and covered it with the comics that Sparks had given me. Mammy had done a great job packing for me. I sat on the bed and looked at the vacant space where my battleship should be on the shelf on my bedroom wall.

I was still sitting on the bed when Mattie came into the bedroom. He had one towel around him and he was holding another one in his hand.

'Where's my battleship?' I asked him.

'Stuck in an iceberg,' he said laughing as he dried himself.

I was just about to jump on him when I heard Mammy calling from the bottom of the stairs.

'Mattie are you out of the bath yet?'

'A long time ago Mammy and I'm just trying to get Finn in before the water gets too cold for him,' Mattie lied and giggled.

When I got into the bath, the water was cold and I saw my battleship upside down in the suds. There was no point in waiting for the water to heat up again because I knew that Mammy had only lit a small fire in the 'Rayburn' after the dinner. I just stood in the bathwater and bent down and wet my hair a little. It was just as well that I didn't take a full bath, because when I went to get a towel there wasn't any. Mattie had used the two towels. He had gone downstairs when I went back to the bedroom. I had to get him back for what he had done. I opened his suitcase, dried my hair and feet in his good, freshly ironed shirt, and closed the suitcase again.

We were allowed to come downstairs in our pyjamas after our baths and read for an hour. Mattie was reading one Dell comic and sitting on two more. I told Mammy that Mattie was sitting on the comics and wouldn't give me one.

'If there's any fighting you're both going to bed straight away without your supper.'

I wouldn't have minded no supper because it wasn't that long since my tea but I hated going to bed when it was still bright.

'Here,' he said throwing a sixty-four page War Comic at me.

I knew that it was going to be a waste of time starting to read it because every time Mattie finished a comic he tears out the last four pages and you wouldn't know how the story ended.

I took a quick look at the back of the '64' and right enough there were only sixty pages in it so I threw it back at him. He must have been expecting me to throw it because he ducked and the comic went fluttering through the air and landed in the pantry where Mammy was washing up the dishes. I got two flicks of the dishtowel on the back of the head but Mattie didn't get any because he was first out the door.

When I got to the bedroom Mattie was taking out his bow and arrow from under my bed. He examined the arrow very lovingly. It had a gleaming white feather at the top and the end had a shiny spike.

He used to get the feathers for his arrows from the dead-chicken dump. I knew that because Sparks and Vinny and I were watching him from our hideout one day but he didn't see us. Mattie was talking to himself; 'that's a nice one,' he would say as he sorted through the dead chickens and pulled feathers from some of them.

Mattie pushed up the bedroom window as high as it would go and then leaned half way out, bringing his bow and arrows with him. He used to shoot arrows at Derek Henderson from there, when Derek would be coming home from compulsory study at his High School. I liked Derek and played cricket with him and his brother Basil sometimes, when Vinny and Sarks weren't around. Mattie didn't like him or play with him because he was a Protestant. 'Another "Black Prod" less,' Mattie would shout when he would hit Derek with the arrow.

Mattie did that a few times until Mister Henderson told Daddy. Daddy was furious with Mattie and made him show him where he had hidden the bow and arrows.

'Did you really have to call him a "Black Prod" when you were firing at him?' Daddy asked in anger breaking Mattie's bow in half.

Mattie had made another bow by the end of the next day.

I don't know what Mattie is aiming at this time. He was wriggling a bit reaching out the window. Then I saw him stretching the bow and taking aim down the arrow. With a twanging sound he let go of the arrow. Two seconds later he shouted, 'dead-eye·

24

dick' and pulled himself back in the window. I hoped that he hadn't hit Derek because the point on that arrow looked terribly dangerous. I was very curious and going to take a peep but then I told myself not to have anything to do with this so I didn't even bother looking out the window. Mattie crawled to put his bow back under my bed and then stood up and went back to the window.

'This is a load of "codswallop"—it's still daylight,' Mattie said pulling the bedroom blind down in anger.

I knew by the way he had pulled it, that it was stuck. I didn't say anything because it had happened to me before and Daddy spent a long time trying to free it.

I lifted my suitcase from the bed, placed it on the floor and hopped into bed. I told myself that I wasn't going to be able to sleep as I pushed my head deep into the pillow.

I was wrong; the next thing I heard was Mammy's voice, "Wakie-Wakie, boys, your breakfast is ready.' I was delighted to hear *that* voice; Mammy was in good form again.

It didn't last too long. She tried to let up the blind. She tried it once with a slow pull down but the blind stayed down. She tried a fast pull; nothing. Then she tried a few fast and a few slow pulls in quick succession but still nothing. Then the inevitable question came.

'Who was at this blind last?'

Mattie was too fast for me.

'Well who do think?' he said pointing at me.

I just gave a scream at Mattie and threw my pillow at him.

'Stop it, that's enough from you two,' Mammy ordered and gave the blind one more pull. The blind flipped back into a roll, so suddenly and fast, that it startled the three of us.

Mammy pulled a pair of socks from her apron pocket and asked looking in the vicinity of the bed, 'Mattie where is your suitcase?

Mattie pointed to the corner of the bedroom where he had earlier flung the suitcase. It was lying lopsided against the wall. Mammy shook her head in a disapproving way and lifted the suitcase onto the bed as she spoke.

'Mattie, these are a pair of socks I finished knitting for you last night, wear them in your wellingtons.'

I couldn't get a good look at the socks but I had a good idea what they would look like if they were meant for wearing in wellingtons.

Mammy opened Mattie's suitcase and was about to put in the socks when she gave a loud shriek.

'My God look at your good shirt, it's all wrinkled and damp too, how on earth did you do that?' she said dropping the socks on his bed. 'I'll have to iron this again and look at the time it is,' she muttered leaving the room.

I picked up the socks; I was right, the socks were knitted with loads of different coloured wool and the good thing was, they were for Mattie this time, so I tossed them into Mattie's suitcase and smiled.

Mammy was just finishing ironing Mattie's shirt when we arrived into the kitchen. 'Sit down and have your breakfast,' she said putting the shirt to one side and going to the oven.

She pulled two plates from the oven and placed them in front of us.

'French Toast,' Mattie said pulling a face, 'I was hoping for a fry,' he said reaching for the syrup.

'Now I'm putting this in your suitcase and don't open your case again until you reach Doiredrum.' Mammy ignored Mattie's complaint and left the kitchen with his newly ironed shirt draped over her arm.

As soon as Mattie heard Mammy on the top of the stairs he rushed from the table with the three slices of French Toast spiked on his fork.

'Bird food,' Mattie snarled holding up the French Toast as he opened the back door.

I stretched sideways at the table and looked out the door. I could see him flinging the French Toast up on the shed roof. 'Oops,' I heard him gasping. He came back into the kitchen, ran straight to the cutlery drawer and took out another fork. I know what he'd done by mistake; he had thrown the fork along with the slices of French Toast up on the shed roof. He sat back down beside me and stared into my face as he spoke.

'Keep your mouth shut, if you know what's good for you.'

I just smiled at him as I tucked into another slice of French Toast.

Sparks or Vinny said that they never had French Toast. Mammy had emigrated to America and French Toast was one of the many recipes she had brought back from America with her, when she returned to Ireland for good.

'Good boy Mattie, you're finished. Finn, will you hurry up The Yank, ah, er, Mister Joyce will be here any minute,' Mammy said coming back into the kitchen and picking up Mattie's empty plate.

'Thanks Mammy, that French Toast was really lovely; what can I do now for you?' Mattie asked.

'Oh, go upstairs and bring down your suitcase and leave it in the hallway beside that parcel missus O'Sullivan brought last night, it's for your Granny's neighbour Breda Fenlon, so don't touch it,' Mammy instructed rushing into the pantry.

'Yes I saw that parcel, it's like an Elephant's Swiss Roll,' Mattie said leaving the table.

I remembered seeing that parcel too when I was coming down for breakfast. I had peeped into it but couldn't see much because it was wrapped in brown paper and tied up with so much cord that I didn't bother opening it.

Mammy told me to hurry up again. Sometimes it's hard to fathom Mammy out; most times she says that I'm eating too fast and now she says I'm eating too slowly. Mammy took the plate away from in front of me as soon as I put the last small piece of French Toast in my mouth.

'Good boy, now go upstairs and bring down your suitcase,' she chirped vanishing into the scullery.

When I went into the bedroom Mattie was kneeling down and leaning out the bedroom window that was directly above the front door and two stories up. I wrapped the ball-bearing in a piece of wallpaper I had torn from an old schoolbook cover. Mammy always covers our schoolbooks with leftover wallpaper. I was concealing the catapult ammunition back in the suitcase when I heard knocking on our front door.

I saw Mattie pulling himself back into the bedroom window and squatting down on the floor.

'Damn, I missed,' he said wiping a spit dribble from his chin and hailing me to come over to the window.

'Quick, quick,' he said, 'stick your head out the window and see if you can drop a spit on The Yank's baldy head.'

I wasn't going to do that but I leaned out the window out of curiosity and looked down. Mammy and The Yank were looking straight up at me.

The Yank was wiping his shoulder with a handkerchief saying in a loud voice,

'Goddam birds.'

Mammy tried to restrain her scream, 'get in from that window or I'll go up and kill you, do you want to fall and hurt yourself.'

When we arrived downstairs we went straight out to the car with our suitcases. Mammy handed the parcel to The Yank who was standing beside the open car boot.

'That's a parcel missus O'Sullivan gave to me last night to send down to my mother's neighbour, I hope you don't mind,' Mammy said putting it in the corner of the car boot.

'No bother at all, missus, hold on a second and I'll move over my stuff and give you a bit of room,' The Yank said moving a bulging potato sack.

By the look and shape of the sack, I don't think that it was full of potatoes because there were pointed edges jutting out in places around the sack, and it didn't seem to be that heavy judging by the way he shoved it to one side.

'Be God, but missus O'Sullivan didn't spare the string,' The Yank said lifting the parcel by the wrapping twine as he re arranged the parcel lengthways in the car boot.

'Are you sure now Mister Joyce that you won't have a cup of tea, there's loads in the pot,' Mammy asked again.

'No thank you Ma'am we got a lot of road to cover,' The Yank replied, lifting our suitcases.

Mammy took an envelope from her apron pocket and handed it to The Yank.

'Now that's the fare agreed and there's something small,' she said giving him some coins, 'so you can have a little break on the way.'

'Thank you 'Ma'am, that's darn nice of you,' The Yank said putting it all in his jacket pocket.

Mammy kissed me on the forehead before I could duck out of the way but I looked around fast and nobody saw her doing it except The Yank and Mattie, so it wasn't too bad. Mattie jumped into the back seat very fast before she could kiss him.

Mammy came over to the car door and repeated the same things that she was saying to us all week; 'Have manners down there, call everyone you meet either "Ma'am" or "Sir" and don't be spending all your pocket money on sweets and don't forget your prayers.'

I was checking my pocket again to make sure my two half crowns were still there as The Yank slammed the boot closed.

Daddy came to the door wearing a dressing gown and slippers he had got in a parcel from America. I hadn't seen Daddy for two or three days now. He had been busy like the other Guards from his Station, after the robbery of a very expensive painting from Lord Donaldson Barbour's Mansion a few days before that. Daddy was either out the country looking for the robbers or in bed.

Myra was holding Daddy's hand and she was smiling. She mustn't have realised that she would not be seeing us for a few weeks.

Daddy waved to us holding up his morning newspaper and said, 'have a nice holiday lads, I'll see you when you get back,' and went back into the house with Myra.

The Yank was just about to get into the car when he jumped backwards. A tattered piece of French Toast spiked on a dinner fork landed with a thud on the bonnet of his beloved Chevrolet.

'Those Goddam birds are really out to get me today,' he said, quickly swiping the French Toast debris and fork from the car bonnet onto the ground.

We all looked in the direction of the squawking noise above us. Two jackdaws were still fighting and swooping down in a vain effort to retrieve their fallen French Toast quarry.

'I told you, French Toast is only fit for birds,' Mattie said with a nervous snigger.

I smiled; Mattie hadn't considered the possibility of jackdaws picking up the French Toast that he had thrown on the back-shed roof earlier and dropping it on The Yank's car,

Mammy looked bewildered examining the fork she had just picked up from the ground as The Yank tooted his horn driving up the road.

'Hey guys look at that, we got Goddam' Indians in town,' The Yank said pointing out through his windscreen.

My heart missed a beat, I was going West to see Indians and there were Indians here all the time. Not so. The Yank was pointing at an arrow stuck half way up a telegraph pole beside Miss Black's house.

Then it dawned on me what Mattie was aiming at out the bedroom window yesterday evening. It was the telegraph pole opposite our house. I also know now what he used for an arrowhead.

'Miss Black was asking me about the missing spike from her railing and she was very annoyed,' I said turning back to speak to Mattie in the back seat.

'Sure can't she climb the pole and get her railing spike back if she needs it that badly,' Mattie said pulling a screwdriver from the top of his sock.

I recognised it straight away. It was Daddy's best screwdriver. I looked back once more before we turned the corner. Mammy was still waving from the front door.

Mattie keeps getting in trouble for taking Daddy's tools. I don't believe him that he expects Miss Black to get up the pole because Miss Black must be fifty or eighty years old or something like that and anyway she's too fat to climb up the pole. But she must have great eyesight even with her big age, because she noticed that small spike missing from the top of one of her railings. I'll get Daddy's ladder when I get back from Doiredrum and Sparks and Vinny and me will get it down for her then.

I swivelled in my seat and looked back at my town on the hill; I was viewing the rear of dreary grey buildings that resembled a row of uneven and uncleaned teeth. I turned to my front again as we headed Westward into the country.

CHAPTER 4

The Gasmobile

THE YANK TUNED IN his car radio and kept tapping the steering wheel out of beat to the tune that was playing.

'That "Elvis kid" is going to go places,' he said a few times before the song ended.

I didn't care if this "Elvis kid" was or not; I was waiting for the "War Stories." I had to wait a long time because he listened to more and more songs and then he told everybody to hush when the News came on. I don't know why he said 'hush' to us because he was the only one talking. The man on the radio was boring. He was talking for a long time about the painting that was stolen from Lord Donaldson Barbour's Mansion and that the Gardai suspected IRA involvement.

When the News was over The Yank shook his head and winked at me and spoke with his usual unconvincing American accent, 'by God, 'The Boys' are back in business.'

We were stopped twice at Garda checkpoins within two hours of leaving our town and each time The Yank said the same thing to the Guards, 'clean as a whistle here guys, these are the Sergeant's sons from Clunmon, we're going West.' The Policeman asked us our names at the first checkpoint and when I told him he just said, 'one decent man is your father,' and then waved us on.

At the second checkpoint when I told the Garda our names he stared at us for a while.

'I hope none of ya turn out like your oul' fella,' he said slapping the car roof with his robust hand and hesitated before adding, 'go on.'

We were just about to move off when the same Policeman roared, 'Stop!' 'There's no tax disc on this yoke,' he said pointing to the windscreen.

'I can explain that,' The Yank spluttered,' you see I had it, I had it, shipped in from the United States.'

'Well ya hardly drove it from there did ya?' the Guard interrupted solemnly.

'And, and I'm waiting for those Customs fellas to clear it for me, there, th—they're so slow with the paperwork,' The Yank explained nervously.

The Garda stared at The Yank for a second or two and then said tossing his head backwards, 'I suppose the "good" Sergeant is looking after you anyway, go off with yiz.'

The Guard slapped the roof of the Chevrolet's again as we drove off. I knew that The Yank was annoyed when the Garda hit his car roof a second time because he gripped tight on the steering wheel.

'We won't have a bit of peace on the roads with Guards and checkpoints until they find that shaggin' painting,' he spluttered angrily.

Only when the radio got crackly did he switch it off but then he started talking about Daddy and repeated the same thing after every story that he told about him, 'Best Sergeant Clunmon ever had, if your father doesn't get that darn painting back, nobody will.'

I don't know if Daddy is that good of a Sergeant because I never heard of him shooting a crook or a bank robber.

Then The Yank started talking about Mammy and how much she was loved around the town.

'And I know for a fact,' he blabbered on, 'that your mother will not listen to gossip or say a bad word about anybody, a lady a real lady is your mother.'

32

I just looked at him and thought to myself that he must never have seen Mammy in action with the dish towel, or know about her listening to Miss Black talking 'bad' about Mattie. Just when I thought he might start telling "War Stories" he got back to Daddy again.

'What a brilliant family your Daddy comes from, full of brains, I know that because my brother Seamus is with Government Maintenance and Construction, up in your father's neck of the woods,' The Yank said blasting the horn at a few sheep running furiously along the road in front of the car as if they were being propelled by their tails.

Mattie had been quiet for such a long time that The Yank and I both got a bit startled when Mattie stuck his head in between the seats and declared in a loud voice, 'Do you know my pal Towbar?'

The Yank replied immediately with just as loud a voice as Mattie used, 'Do I know Towbar, that goddam' son of a b-b, yes, what about him?'

'Well, Towbar's father comes from up that country as well and he said that your brother Seamus fills in holes in the road for the County Council,' Mattie concluded bouncing back into his seat.

The Yank thought for a while and then said raising a hand in the air, 'That's what I goddam' said—"Government Maintenance and Construction," now where the hell was I; oh yes your father's people,' The Yank continued.

He knew about my Uncle Jack being a doctor, my Uncle Pat being a priest, my Aunty Rita being a chemist, my uncle Michael being a dentist, my Uncle Thomas being a vet and my Uncle Joe and Aunty Nancy both being school teachers.

'Hang on, I'm missing one,' he said scratching his head before adding, 'ah, yes, your uncle Edward is an Engineer.' He pushed back in his seat and smugly pursed his lips.

I knew that already because Daddy told us about his family a few years ago when he was drunk and said that he was the "black sheep" of the family. Mammy explained what "black sheep" meant when I asked her if Daddy came from a field.

Mattie said that he would hate to go on holidays to Daddy's brother and sisters because you would be either getting injections or taking medicines or saying prayers or doing sums and spellings all day. Mattie is brilliant at working things out sometimes.

'Life is cruel,' The Yank said lighting up a cigarette, 'some families are blessed and others cursed, look at our crowd for example compared to your father's family, my brother Seamus has only one eye, lost it in a quarry accident,' he went on to explain, tipping his cigarette ash on the floor of the car. 'My brother Dan Joe has a stutter and me with my gammy foot, shrapnel—war wound, as I'm sure you know.' He clenched his teeth as if in pain and continued, 'my brother Gerry is the only one who did anyway good in this country, he riz to be a Corporal in the Irish Army and him with only ten years service.'

I saw my opportunity to hear some war stories and took it.

'Did you ever shoot anybody in the war?' I asked.

For an hour my ears were ringing about, Korea, the differences between the M1 and M2 rifle, foxholes, "chinks," hand-to-hand fighting, snipers, bayonets, silencers, booby-traps, culverts. I lost count of how many "chinks" he had killed. I was starting to get bored and feeling a bit sick. I don't know if it was the war stories or the cigarette smoke.

Mattie unknowingly came to my rescue and stopped The Yank in the middle of a war story, when he spoke cold and calculated from the back seat, 'Towbar's father said that you were a cook in the American Army and that the only people you killed were the soldiers you cooked for and that you injured your foot when you dropped a barrel of peeled potatoes on it.'

I saw The Yank's knuckles going white again as he gripped the steering wheel and I heard him muttering just before he switched the radio back on again, 'the next time Towbar goes near my car exhaust with a potato, I'll break his arse with a kick.'

Sparks was right about The Yank's boring war stories. I asked Mattie to change seats but he wouldn't. After about another hour I reminded Mattie again what Mammy had said about changing seats during the journey.

'No, I'm not finished yet,' he muttered.

34

I didn't know what he meant and I could tell by the frown on The Yank's face that he didn't either.

'You can change seats after we call to see my brother Dan Joe in the home place,' The Yank suggested as a compromise.

I turned around to see what Mattie thought about that but he was bent down at the back of my seat with a screwdriver in his hand.

'Did you hear that,' I said to him, 'we're going to The Yan... ah, er...to Mister Joyce's brother's house?'

When Mattie looked up at me I could see a sheen of glazed sweat on his forehead.

'What for?' he asked.

'What would you guys say to some nice grub?' The Yank replied, rubbing his stomach.

Mattie just shrugged his shoulders and went back down behind the back of my seat again.

A half hour later we pulled off the main road and onto a side road that was full of potholes. I thought it was a pity that his brother Seamus didn't live here so he could do something about the potholes. Then after another half hour we stopped at a road cutting about twenty yards past a ghostly looking cottage.

'Home sweet home,' The Yank said switching off the engine and getting out of the car. I looked out the car window.

A small cottage with a rusty galvanized roof was partly hidden by an overgrown hedge. I stayed where I was until The Yank pushed open the rusting front gate of the cottage and waved at Mattie and me to follow him. I still wanted to stay where I was until Mattie spoke.

'This should be good fun, let's go.'

I followed him through the gate and into the cottage.

A middle-aged, unshaven, grey haired man was sitting at a small kitchen table. He had a chipped cup and a bread knife in front of him.

The Yank was bending over an open fire trying to settle a blackened kettle on sods of smouldering turf.

'Pull up a few chairs for yourselves,' The Yank said turning to us.

The man at the table held the cup to his mouth with both hands and slurped from it.

'These are the Sergeant's sons, Mattie and Finn and this is my brother Dan Joe,' The Yank introduced through bouts of coughing caused by the rising ash dust.

Dan Joe just shook his head and gave a despairing glance at the ceiling. Mattie dragged a chair from near a window to the table and sat down beside Dan Joe. Dan Joe looked surprised and sniffed.

I saw a chair over in a dark corner and was just starting to drag it towards the table when a black mangey cat leaped from it and raced out the door. I got such a fright that I flung the chair to one side and it toppled on the floor with a loud clang. Dan Joe jumped back on his chair and tried to turn one way and then the other as he was spluttering, 'What the fu–f–f....'

'Relax Dan Joe, relax,' The Yank said cutting across his brother before he could finish the word.

I picked up the chair and lifted it to the table and sat opposite Mattie who was just twiddling his thumbs and made a poor attempt at whistling.

'Have you any bread, Dan Joe?' The Yank asked opening a cupboard door over a dresser.

Dan Joe pointed to a window ledge where a ginger coloured cat snoozed, resting his head on the crust of a freshly baked soda-bread.

'Scat,' The Yank shouted as he approached the window ledge.

The cat jumped down onto the floor and under Dan Joe's chair.

The Yank grabbed the bread from the window ledge and plonked it in the middle of the table. He went back to the cupboard and took out three cups and a slab of very yellow butter that had chunks dug out of it. He gave the bread knife a quick wipe on the side of his trousers and tossed it on the table.

'Help yourselves boys,' The Yank said moving back to the fire where he poured boiling water into a lidless teapot on the hearth.

He reached up to the mantle piece and took down a tin box that he opened and poured loose tea from it into the teapot.

'I won't be a second,' The Yank said going into a small room at the far end of the kitchen.

'You never changed Dan Joe,' The Yank said with glee as he returned holding three large onions, 'Dan Joe grows the best onions in Longford and he keeps them in his bedroom in case he gets hungry during the night.'

Mattie looked at me and smiled; he knew that I hated onions more than anything else in the world. Then Mattie reached across the table and pulled a cup over beside him. He took the best one; neither of the two remaining cups had handles and each of those had big cracks down the sides.

The Yank ran from the fireplace holding the teapot and dropped it on the table. We all jumped as the tea washed over the sides of the teapot.

'By jingoes that was hot,' The Yank said blowing on his hand and quickly added clipping his brother on the arm, 'where's your manners? Give me your chair and that young *gauson* your cup.'

The Yank frowned as he examined the cups.

'Look at the state of them cups,' The Yank gasped.

'A-hh, F-F.'

'Now, now, Dan Joe, we have "childer" present,' The Yank said nodding at Mattie and me.

Dan Joe just sniffed, grinded his few remaining brown teeth, got up from the table and rushed down to his bedroom.

'That's the best one in the house, it has a handle on it and it's only got one chip out of it,' The Yank said passing over Dan Joe's mug to me.

I just looked at it, smelled the onion that The Yank was cutting into large chunks, slid from my chair and ran out the front door to the car.

I lay down on the back seat for about fifteen or twenty minutes but then I got too hot and was looking for the window winder to let the down the window but I couldn't find it so I just left the door open slightly. I was getting bored then and crawled over into the front seat and let on I was driving the car. I was having good fun doing that but then I heard voices and footsteps approaching the rear of the car. I lay flat across the two front seats.

I recognised Dan Joe's voice by his stutter and even though The Yank wasn't using his American accent this time I knew that it was him when he spoke.

'Who left the bloody door open?' he growled.

I lay still for a while and then peeped back between the seats. I could see them carrying a cardboard box between them as they came towards the car. I heard the sound of bottles clanging over The Yank's grunting and then the boot lid sprung open.

'No, no, take that out first and then put this in,' he was instructing Dan Joe. 'Easy, easy,' he shouted, 'didn't I tell you before, damaged goods loses their value.'

The car was shaking a bit while they were at the boot but I couldn't see what they were doing. The car boot lid closed with a slam and I ducked down again. Then I heard the door that I had left open being closed and when I heard The Yank's voice fading I peeped up again.

I could see that The Yank was looking up and down the road and Dan Joe carrying a bulging sack as he entered the gate to his cottage. I waited until they were well gone inside the gate before I got out of the car and closed the door gently. I walked back towards the cottage as fast as I could and peeped around the hedge near the gate. I could hear The Yank and Dan Joe's voices coming from the back of the cottage so I knew it was safe and ran straight in the door and sat back on my chair at the table.

When I looked around there was nobody there except one cat staring at me from the window ledge and another hissing at me from near the fireplace. I got a fright and was just about to leave when Mattie came in the back door. His face was cringed and he was rubbing his stomach as he slid onto a chair at the table.

'I think that Dan Joe fecker poisoned me—he's a madman,' Mattie said laying his head on the table with a groan.

I was going to tell Mattie about what I'd seen The Yank and Dan Joe doing but then I saw a chunk of onion on the table beside a piece of bread. The smell of onions and listening to Mattie groaning made me feel sick.

'Where's the toilet?' I asked him.

Mattie pointed to the door that he had just come in.

I went out the back door but it just led into a yard. I looked around the yard but all I could see was an open hay barn and a small little galvanised hut with a wooden door. I walked cautiously over to it and pulled at the door. The roar from inside stuck me to the ground for a second or two.

'Wa, Wai, Wait, yo...uur t-t-turn you litt-le, fu, f-,' but I was back in the cottage before I could hear the end of the sentence.

'Ah, there you are, Finn, I was out the front looking for you, we'll hit the road as soon as Dan Joe comes back from the Jacks,' The Yank said looking at me and then turned to Mattie and said, 'by the way Mattie, Dan Joe meant no harm when he pulled you out of the Jacks, he had a bit of an emergency, if you know what I mean?'

'I had an emergency myself, you see I'm not used to eating onions and currant bread together,' Mattie said rubbing his stomach.

The Yank scratched his head and then said slowly, 'What currant bread?'

Mattie looked worn out as he pointed to a small piece of bread still on the table. The Yank picked it up and examined it before speaking.

'Ah, no, no, they're not currants, you see Dan Joe makes his own bread and sometime a few ould flies gets into the buttermilk he has set aside for making the bread, a baked Blue Bottle won't do you a bit of harm,' The Yank said tossing the piece of bread back on the table.

Mattie waited a second and then ran straight out the front door. I ran after him. Mattie got in the front of the car and I just lay face down stretched across the back seat trying to hold in my laughing.

'If you say a word about flies or Blue Bottles, I'll kill you,' Mattie said without turning around.

I believed him so I said nothing but covered my mouth still trying to keep in my giggling. I told Mattie in a serious tone about what I'd seen and that I thought that Dan Joe and The

39

Yank were crooks. Mattie said not to be annoying him and that I watch too many Gangster films.

After about five minutes The Yank and Dan Joe came towards the car. I saw Dan Joe peering into the car and then focusing on me lying in the back. I thought he was going to give out to me for disturbing him in the toilet but I was wrong.

'U–up–pp, th–the IRA,' and gestured with a two finger victory sign holding his hand high in the air.

I sat up then and looked back at Dan Joe through the rear car window. Dan Joe held his victory sign until The Yank had turned the car and headed back for the main road and The West.

The Yank tuned on the car radio again and tried whistling to the songs. In the middle of one of the songs he stopped whistling.

'Oops,' he grinned raised himself from the seat, 'better out than your eye, there was a silencer on that one, a burner, better open your window, guys,' he ranted, smiling, and lowered himself back down on the seat.

The stink in the car was overpowering and obnoxious. I saw Mattie grabbing the window winder and turn it very fast until his window was all the way down.

'That's a real stinker,' Mattie shouted stretching his head and neck out the window.

The Yank turned his window down as well and I got the full blast in the back and started choking and coughing.

'Goddam it Finn, turn down your window before you die on me,' The Yank chuckled and then continued, 'onions have that effect on me, make me very gassy.'

'I can't wind down my window,' I said holding my nose with my fingers.

'Of course you can, Goddam it, just turn the window winder,' The Yank hollered turning around.

'There isn't any window winder,' I screamed from behind my hands now covering my mouth and nose.

I was lucky to have had my face covered because The Yank stopped the car so fast that I was thrown against the back of his seat. He had hardly the car stopped when he was out on the road and opening my door.

'There's…the window winder…where the…' The Yank said stuttering like his brother Dan Joe as he examined the door on my side first and then the other, looking for window winders.

He lay his head and arms softly on the roof of his Chevrolet's and pined talking to himself.

'Who would do this to my beautiful baby?'

Then his mood changed to one of anger. 'Who was in my Hackney last?' he asked himself moving away from the Chevrolet's and scratching his head.

He walked a little circle and began talking to himself. 'The "Skiter" Donnelly and his pals, brought them to the dance at the Starlight on Saturday night.'

The Yank sat back into the car and slammed his door closed.

'I'll break Skiter's arse with a kick,' The Yank said with a quick shake of his head and then continued, 'if they did that in the States, they'd get the Gas Chamber,' he said driving off at high speed.

'If you could get them back into your car and then eat more onions, you'd have your own Gas Chamber,' Mattie said looking into The Yank's face.

I knew that Mattie was happy that The Yank was going to get revenge on Skiter because Skiter beat Mattie up last week for taking the wheel of his bicycle when he had it parked down the side of the cinema.

The Yank thought for a while about what Mattie had said, about eating onions, to make his own Gas Chamber and then chuckled laughing.

'You're a gas man young fella,' The Yank said reaching over and punching Mattie lightly on the shoulder.

'No, no, you're a "Gas Man,"' Mattie said punching The Yank hard on the shoulder and laughing.

They kept punching one another until Mattie started feeling his arm and then they both stopped. I was glad when we reached the main road again.

'Look at that sign pointing to Portwest, it won't be long now until we're in Doiredrum,' The Yank said pointing to a road sign.

I hoped we were finished with the potholes now and stretched out on the back seat again.

The Yank tuned in his radio and said with glee, 'Ah! Ceilidh music, you can't beat it.'

Then the Irish Ceilidh music stopped suddenly and a voice on the radio called attention to a Newflash. The newsreader announced that the charred remains of a picture frame had been identified as the one from the stolen painting and that it had been found in a field at the rear of a Warehouse near Roslea Bridge.

'Did ya hear that, did ya hear that?' The Yank spurted out, 'Those robbers past by my own front door; a dollar to a dime, it was your father that found that picture frame,' The Yank said, shaking his head in agreement with himself.

I don't know why they put that on The News as it was only the painting frame that was found and not the actual painting— and as well as that, it was all burnt. The Irish Ceilidh music came back on the car radio. I hate Ceilidh music and pushed one ear deep into the car seat and covered the other with my hand.

I heard tapping. I opened my eyes and struggled sitting upright. A gush of fresh air hit me as the car door opened.

'You're verra, verra welcome,' a voice said. I looked out the open door. It was Granny.

We had arrived. By the time I had got out of the car Granny had gone around to the car boot and Uncle Frank was shaking my hand and welcoming me.

'Good God woman, don't take out the wrong stuff,' The Yank complained as Granny was pulling a parcel from the open car boot.

'Well don't worry your little head, sir,' Granny said holding up the roll shaped parcel, 'isn't that Annie O'Sullivan a great woman to send this down; now everybody come on in and have something to eat,' she said heading for the open front door of the bungalow.

'Now that's everything out, I'll have to make tracks' The Yank said closing down the boot with a bang.

'Ah, will you not come in for a bit to eat, it's all ready.' Uncle Frank said holding The Yank's arm.

'Couldn't eat another thing, we had a big feed on the way, but thanks anyway, I hate driving in the dark,' The Yank said jingling his keys and sitting back into his car. 'Have a great vacation you guys,' he said before closing the door.

'What big feed?' I asked Mattie as we lifted our suitcases. Mattie nudged me and briefly pulled two car window winders from his pocket before slipping them back in again. I smiled.

'Come on lads, follow me,' Uncle Frank said with a broad smile. Two sheepdogs barked all the way after The Yank's car until it went out the gate at the top of the lane.

Mattie and I stood in the open farmyard. I looked up at the high mountains. I saw cows and horses in fields. I followed the course of the river as it meandered along the forest's edge and pondered—look out Indians here I come.

CHAPTER 5

A Curtain Raiser

As soon as I walked into the hallway I could smell onions. I thought that Mammy had told Granny, that I don't eat onions, and that they make me sick. I'll just have to remind Granny again.

'This way lads,' Uncle Frank said as we followed him along the hallway to a room at the back of the house.

There was one large high bed in the middle of the room. Mattie ran to it first and threw his suitcase on it. I waited at the door and hoped that my room would have just as big a bed.

'Come into the kitchen when you are ready and have a bit to eat,' Uncle Frank said, leaving the bedroom door.

I followed him and he stopped.

'Put your case in the bedroom and then come to the kitchen,' he said with a bit of a frown.

I told him that I didn't know where my room was. He laughed briefly and then hugged me as led me back to the bedroom I had just left.

'You're sharing with your brother, did you think it was a hotel you were coming to?' he said with a broad smile and gestured with an open hand.

I couldn't see Mattie but I heard him grunting at the far side of the bed. Uncle Frank looked a bit surprised and asked Mattie if he was okay.

Mattie put his head up from the far side of the bed and said, 'I'm fine, I'm just putting away my things.'

'Put them in the wardrobe,' he said pointing to a large timber wardrobe. Uncle Frank shook his head and smiled as he left.

'This has to be the biggest and heaviest mattress in the world,' Mattie said grunting again as he heaved at the mattress and pushed his catapult under it.

He got up off his knees and opened the poorly fitted wardrobe doors that squeaked like a coffin lid in the horror films. He went back to the bed, lifted his suitcase and just flung it from there straight into the wardrobe making a loud bang as it landed on the wardrobe floor.

I heard Uncle Frank shouting, 'Is everything okay?'

'Yes, yes,' Mattie called back, 'it's just Finn falling into the wardrobe, but he's okay.'

I hadn't got time to go to the door and shout out that Mattie was telling lies as I was in the middle of hiding Joe's dagger under the mattress on my side of the bed. Mattie sniggered at me as he was s leaving the bedroom. I caught up with him in the hallway and gave him a punch in the back as I passed him out and went into the safety of the kitchen.

I went to the end of the kitchen and looked into the scullery. Granny was coming in the back door wiping her hands in her apron.

'Ye must be starving, I had to put that parcel away, it's for a friend of mine,' she said brushing past me and going to the large stove in the kitchen. She used her apron to cover her hand as she lifted the lid of a black pot on top of the stove. I could smell the onions again.

'Sit down, sit down,' she said putting two large plates on the table.

Before I could tell her that I don't like onions she was heaping mashed potatoes onto the plate. I could see the onions glistening in the lumpy mash. I looked at Mattie. He was grinning. I shook my head and looked up at Granny who was pouring a cup of tea for my Uncle Frank who had left the armchair by the fire and joined us at the table.

'Now tell me all the news from home,' Granny directed her enquiry at Mattie.

'There isn't any,' Mattie muttered, stretching to the centre of the table and slicing off a big chunk of butter from a slab of butter on a butter dish.

The chopped onions embedded in the mash potatoes were staring teasingly out at me.

I took a deep breath and uttered my complaint, 'Granny I don't like onions.'

'Arah, sure there is only a few in it, they won't harm you!' Granny replied dismissively.

'I like brown bread,' I bartered.

'Well go on then have some bread but look what a good boy your brother is eating up his dinner.'

Mattie smiled, purposely crunching a diced piece of onion as he moved his face towards me.

'I get sick if I eat onions,' I explained looking at my uncle who was vigorously slicing more brown bread.

Uncle Frank handed me a slice of brown bread that he'd just cut. I gladly took it from him and buttered it holding it on my hand.

'Here you might as well get some nourishment into you,' Granny said putting a cup of what looked like lumpy milk in front of me.

I put my head down close to it and sniffed.

'It's buttermilk,' Uncle Frank said observing my mistrust.

I took a bite out of the brown bread and froze with disgust as my stomach heaved. I leaped from the table and ran into the hallway. I had opened two wrong doors before I found the bathroom. I don't know if the onion flavour that I tasted came from the butter, or the bread, or was it or the knife that cut the bread, but it was sufficient to empty the contents of my retching stomach.

When I got back to the kitchen Mattie was relaxing in Uncle Frank's armchair at the stove. Uncle Frank was leaning on the mantlepiece as he shoved his feet into his wellingtons.

'Are you okay?' he asked with a half laugh.

'I don't like onions,' I mumbled slumping onto the chair I had vacated a few minutes earlier.

'I can see that,' Uncle Frank said rubbing his chin.

'I think you took after your father's side; spoiled,' Granny muttered vanishing into the scullery.

'Come on, a bit of fresh air will do you good,' Uncle Frank said moving towards the hallway, and added, 'I have to check on a few sheep up the hill.'

I was glad to get away from the smell of onions.

As we were following Uncle Frank out the front door Granny called after us.

'Make sure ye wear old clothes going up the hills,' she ordered.

'I'll wait until you change,' Uncle Frank said before he gave a loud whistle and picked up a crooked stick that was left against the corner of the open porch.

Two dogs scurried into the farmyard from a hay barn.

'These are our old clothes,' Mattie said holding his leg high to protect himself from the speeding dogs coming towards him. I looked at Mattie in disbelief. I remembered Mammy distinctly cautioning us, as she packed our wellingtons, to wear them at all times on the farm, but the thought of going back into the house and smelling onions again I decided to say nothing.

'If you say so,' Uncle Frank said, swiping his stick playfully at the dogs.

Mattie kept kicking stones in front of him as we walked up the lane from the house. The dogs barked every time he did this.

'Will you stop you *ceolan*, you're driving the dogs mad,' he said looking back at Mattie.

'What's their names?' Mattie asked kicking another stone.

'Will you stop that,' Uncle Frank said in a sterner voice and then added in a friendlier tone, 'Shep and Toss, that's their names.'

'What breed of mutts are they?' Mattie enquired.

'*Mutts*, is it?' Uncle Frank repeated, sounding offended at

Mattie's description of his two working dogs and then continued, 'these dogs are thoroughbred Collies I'll have you know.'

'Are they any good at biting people? Mattie continued with his questions.

'Only bold boys who don't do as they are told,' Uncle Frank said winking over at me.

I looked behind at Mattie. He was sticking out his tongue and twisting his ears behind Uncle Frank's back.

As we went out the gate at the top of the lane the dogs sped off across the narrow road and up the side of the rocky green hill. I noticed that there was no hedge or fence between the roadway and the hill. I asked Uncle Frank why this was but all he said was 'commonage, commonage.'

'What are we going up here for?' Mattie asked pressing on both his knobbly knees to speed up his effort to climb up the side of the hill.

'I brought sheep down from the mountain a few nights ago for shearing and I just want to keep a check on them that they don't stray off on me, that's all.'

'Ah, is that all?' Mattie said jumping across a narrow mountain drain.

He stumbled as he landed on the far bank.

'Careful, careful,' Uncle Frank called to him.

'Don't worry about me, Uncle Frank,' Mattie called back pulling his foot and shoe free from the boggy turf earth where he had landed and got stuck.

'Mushrooms, mushrooms, I love mushrooms,' Mattie's exciting roar startled my uncle and me as he ran pointing in front of him. He pulled up what looked like toadstools to me.

'They're not mushrooms, they're blooda cock-bos,' Uncle Frank said dismissively.

'They're what?' Mattie exclaimed sniffing the cream, dark brown objects in his hand.

The words *poisonous, poisonous* from my uncle worked like an emergency release valve as Mattie flung the fungi from his hands.

'If you want to pick real mushrooms why don't you come

48

down with me in the mornings when I'm bringing the cows in for milking and there're as many mushrooms growing around the fields than you would ever want to eat.' My uncle leaped over another stream and continued, 'a bit of salt in the centre and they'll cook on a smouldering turf sod for you in less than a minute, lovla, lovla,' my uncle enticed.

'What time of the morning, what time?' Mattie asked enthusiastically.

'Seven, around seven in the morning.'

'Seven o'clock in the morning?' Mattie gasped at my uncle's reply, and quickly added, 'I'm not that fond of mushrooms.'

Suddenly Uncle Frank roared, 'Way off wide before them, way off, way off well before them.'

The two dogs brushed against me on either side as they as they ran off at high speed. As Uncle Frank was shouting he was moving around in random motions and then in an even louder voice roared, 'Toss get back you bloody *coelan*, good dog, good dog Shep, away off wide.'

The dogs were looking back at him from a distance and changed direction at every roar from Uncle Frank. Now the dogs were heading straight towards a flock of sheep that were scattered on the side of the next hill.

Uncle Frank gave another roar and then whistled as he moved backwards and to the side, shouting the same thing, 'way off wide, way off wide.' The next movement was continuous; Uncle Frank going sideways and then downwards. He looked aghast in a seated position for a second before struggling to his feet from the boggy wet surface. He brushed the seat of his trousers with both his hands and shouted at the dogs again, 'way off wide, way off wide.'

'You went a wee bit too off wide there yourself Uncle Frank, be careful,' Mattie called leaping across another mountain stream.

I glanced over at Uncle Frank and he looked very angry. His dogs must be really annoying him. I thought that it was a good idea to get my uncle's mind away from his confused dogs so I asked him what sort of Indians were up on the mountain beyond

49

the boggy hills where his sheep were scattered. He mustn't have understood my question because he looked even crosser. I thought I'd better help him out so I just asked were they, Sioux or Cherokee or Apache. I think that I scared him because he just shrieked at the dogs.

Mattie was tittering and hopping around in a small circle flapping his hand to his mouth as he mimicked Indians dancing around the totem pole. After a while the dogs were herding the sheep closer and Uncle Frank looked pleased. I could see red around the necks of the sheep and questioned Uncle Frank as to what he thought caused it.

He looked a bit puzzled so I gave my answer first as to what I thought the red marks were before he could answer. 'I think it's blood from a spear or an arrow or a dagger wound,' I said looking up at him for a show of approval at my suggestions.

My Uncle only grinned and shook his head and spoke in a low voice, 'Blood? you're looking at too many cowboy films, 'and then added scratching his head, 'sure how else would I know my sheep if I didn't mark them?'

I don't think I really understand his answer. My uncle gave two loud whistles and the two dogs raced back to him. Their dribbling tongues were flapping at the side of their mouths as they panted and looked up at their Master for praise that did not come. We headed back to the farm.

As we neared the bottom of the hill before crossing the narrow road Mattie pointed as he spoke, 'what do you keep in that thatched shack beside your house?'

'We call that the Old House, that's where your mother and I was born,' he said with a gentle shake of his head and continued, 'in fact your mother lived there until she was married and your Granny and me lived there up to seven or eight years ago until we moved into the new bungalow.'

'What's in the Old House now?' Mattie spurted out.

'Ah, bits of this and some of that, fodder for the cattle and other sort of junk and stuff like that.'

Mattie's eyes seemed to sparkle and he asked another question, 'what's in that galvanised shack up through those fields,'

Mattie looked at Uncle Frank and pointed more precisely, 'past your barns and across the stream.'

Uncle Frank focused for a second to see what Mattie was referring to and then answered smiling.

'That's not a shack, that's where our good neighbours and indeed very good friends of your mothers live, yes, yes, Agnes and Stephen, you'll have to visit them.'

'That's for sure,' Mattie said smiling up at Uncle Frank.

Then Uncle Frank's humour changed as he shouted, 'Shep, Toss, away off down before you.' The two dogs sprung into action. 'Those blooda asses of Walter Delaney, look where they are again, at my blooda gate.'

I could see now what he was shouting about, as Shep and Toss whimpered furiously speeding towards the two donkeys.

'He won't feed them and let's them roam to get something to eat, I'll get the Guards for Mister Delaney, that'll soften his cough.' Uncle Frank threatened as the dogs barked and avoided the wild swinging kicks of the donkeys calmly trotted down the road.

'A penny to a pound, I'll bet Walter Delaney is perched, half asleep in the corner of O'Toole's Pub, there for most of the day, praying for rain so he won't have to do any farm work at all, at all,' Uncle Frank said with a shake of his head going towards the roadway. I opened and then closed the gate at the top of the lane and followed my uncle and brother down to the bungalow.

'Take off your shoes and leave them in the porch till they dry,' Uncle Frank said pushing the hall door open.

'And will you be leaving your trousers to dry in the porch as well?' Mattie said pointing to the two wet patches on the seat of Uncle Frank's trousers.

'Just do as I tell you,' Uncle Frank said sternly going in the door. I could see what uncle Frank meant when I looked at my shoes. They were wet from just walking on the boggy turf but Mattie's shoes were completely soaked and his legs were all splattered from all his stream jumping.

Mattie and I headed straight to our room. Mattie tried to slide on the rubber-like tiles in the hallway in his stocking feet but

51

he just seemed to stick to the floor and he stumbled forward and muttered, 'could do with a bit of polish around here.'

My suitcase was gone from the bed and my wellingtons were left nice and tidy beside Mattie's at the end of the bed. They looked very nice. Mammy's hard work cleaning them before putting them in our suitcases was well worthwhile. I opened the squeaky wardrobe and my jumper and shirts and underwear and socks were put in shelves inside the wardrobe. All Mattie's clothes from his suitcase were on the other side of the wardrobe shelf. I looked at the top of the wardrobe and I could see both our suitcases. I was glad I had hidden Joe's dagger before going out.

'Who was messing with my stuff?' Mattie asked putting on his wellingtons and looking into the wardrobe.

'Who do you think, Granny of course, 'I said putting on my second wellington. I was looking at the bright orange coloured curtains on my bedroom window and I was trying to think where I'd seen them before when Mattie pushed me up against them.

'It's visiting time,' he said. I thought that my head was going to hit the windowpane so I grabbed at the curtains to stop.

The next sound was like the noise of the string on my bow as the arrow was released. Then there was a flop and I was in darkness. I panicked and started waving my hands around. When I saw brightness again I was holding the bright orange curtains in my hands. Mattie was lying back on the bed laughing and kicking his legs in the air so vigorously that his wellingtons nearly flew off his feet. I studied the damage I had done.

Only one cup-hook had come out from the window frame and I looked around the floor until I found it. I picked it up from the floor and climbed up on the window ledge and screwed the cup hook back into the same hole as tightly as I could. My finger and thumb were red from the pressure I used tightening the cup-hook. Then I threaded the curtains back to the way they were on the springy wire curtain cord and hooked the end eye-hook on the cup hook. I started breathing normally again, and in disbelief, I examined the repair job I had just done.

'Finn you'll have to be more careful or we'll be sent home,' Mattie giggled pulling his catapult from under the mattress.

He stuffed the catapult inside his trouser waistband and pulled his jumper down over it before leaving the bedroom. I didn't bother bringing the dagger. We were only going as far as Agnes and Stephen's house and that was a long way from the mountains and any Indians.

I followed Mattie into the kitchen. Uncle Frank wasn't there but Granny was and she was twisting the handle on what looked like a rounded wooden box on a stand. We just stood there staring at her and said nothing.

'Don't tell me you never saw anybody churning before,' she asked smiling over at us and then added, 'come on, give it a churn, it's for good luck.'

She stood up and lifted the lid of the churn and gestured to us to take a look inside. Small yellow lumps of butter were partially submerged in rich cream between wooden paddles. I remembered then the drink she had given me earlier with my brown bread. Granny removed the floating bits of butter with a net strainer and placed them on a dish with other lumps of moist yellow butter. She replaced the churn lid and I took hold of the handle. I twisted the handle a few times and I could hear the splashing from inside the churn.

I was getting a nice rhythm going and enjoying it when Granny said, 'now give your brother a turn.'

Mattie grabbed the handle with both his hands and twisted furiously. The lid of the churn was rising up and down before Granny shouted. 'Stop will ya, before you turn it over on me.'

'We were thinking of going visiting, is that okay with you Granny?' Mattie interrupted Granny's scolding and moved away from the churn.

'And who are ye thinking of visiting?' Granny enquired sitting back to the churn. 'Friends of Mammy's, Agnes and eh, er, Stephen,' Mattie replied and stood there waiting for an answer.

'Well that would be nice but don't be late, tea will be in an hour or so.'

We turned to move towards the door but we stopped in our tracks at Granny's tone of voice changed, 'wait a minute you two, come back in here,' she sounded like a teacher giving orders, 'I thought ye said that they were your old clothes ye were wearing going to the hills for the sheep.' I nodded slowly as Granny pressed on with her inquisition. 'Well if that's the case how come I found those in your suitcase when I was unpacking,' she said pointing at the wellingtons on our feet.

'We were saving them for going to Mass on Sunday, do you not see how clean they are, Granny?' Mattie replied meekly.

Granny smiled and returned to her churning saying in a low voice, 'well aren't you the innocent little "creatureen."' I know that Granny used be a teacher and therefore could read into boys' minds then, but not anymore; Mattie had fooled her.

We were crossing the yard when I heard Uncle Frank call out from the side of the Old House, 'do you want to give me a hand filling the Dipping Box?'

I took a few steps backwards and I could see my uncle carrying a bucket in each hand. A stream gurgled and splashed nearby. I was going to help him when Mattie exaggerated a sigh and answered for both of us.

'God, we'd love to Uncle Frank but Granny said that we had to go and visit Agnes and Stephen, you know Mammy's friends.'

'Okay, off with you so, I'll see ye later, tell them I was asking for them,' Uncle Frank called aloud vanishing back behind the Old House.

I couldn't help worrying all the way to Agnes and Stephen's house; I have a gut feeling that Mattie is going to get us into trouble with his lies.

As we approached the stream before the field in front of Agnes and Stephen's house Mattie grabbed me and said that he 'bet me' two sweets that he could jump across a wider part of the stream than me without using hands when landing on the far bank.

I picked out a fairly wide part of the stream and took a few steps backward before starting my run and jump. My wellingtons sunk deep into the boggy soil as I landed safely on the far bank but I had to struggle to keep my balance and not put my hands on the wet grassy bank and loose on the bet.

'Ah! That's only a "baby jump," Mattie declared taking a much shorter run to the stream than I did.

Even though his longer legs still carried him across the stream his right wellington lodged deep in the bank on landing and when he tried to run forward his foot came up out of his wellington and he stumbled and fell. I heard Mattie utter a curse word under his breath as he stretched backwards to retrieve his embedded wellington.

'That's two sweets you owe me, when are you going to pay up?' I asked.

Mattie just glared at me, looked back at the stream, muttering more curse words and then ran off in front of me. Mattie never pays his bets.

CHAPTER 6

Woolly Tails and Wildcat Tales

I COULD SEE AGNES and Stephen's house now just behind a winding stonewall that was toppled in parts. There was a trickle of smoke coming out of the chimney and the galvanised roof was rusty at the ends. I thought about the galvanise sheets we had on our secret hideout beside the Dead-Chicken Dump at home.

I was a thinking of Sparks and Vinny and how they were getting along when Mattie shouted, 'Quick, quick get me a stone.'

He rummaged through the wall-rocks that had tumbled on the grass, until he found a stone. As I approached Mattie I could hear the croaky sounds of a dog's bark. I looked over the wall and saw an old overweight sheepdog standing in the doorway of an off white cottage. Mattie had loaded his catapult with the stone and was aiming at the dog. The twang of the released catapult was quickly followed by a sickly yelp as the stone hopped off the dog's dirty thick matted coat. The dog turned and waddled back through the open front door.

We climbed over the highest part of the stonewall beside a small slumped wooden gate. Mattie had just scaled the wall when a large rock tumbled to the ground and bounced and rolled behind him. He danced out of its way and holstered his catapult to its previous position. Mattie and I went in the door where the frightened dog had retreated earlier. The dog was now cowering behind a very fat woman who was sitting in an armchair beside a smouldering turf fire.

The fire nestled nicely in an open concrete hearth. The woman looked a bit like Granny but her hair was greyer and she seemed to be sleeping.

'And who are ye?' a voice from behind startled me.

I turned and saw a weary unshaven balding man emerging from a door at the end of the house.

'I'll give you a clue,' Mattie said shoving his hands deep into his pockets and continued, 'do you know a woman called "Tessie"?'

'Ah, are ye Tessie's lads?' The man asked passing by the two of us going to the fireplace.

'You got it in one, you're a genius,' Mattie said.

'Aha, beGod I wouldn't say that I'm a genius now,' the man chuckled with pride.

'You two must be Agnes and Stephen?' Mattie asked moving nearer the fire.

Mattie must have forgotten Mammy's instructions; Call everyone you meet "Ma'am" or "Sir" she had warned us.

'That's us,' Stephen replied shaking and swirling a lidless teapot before throwing the contents into the fire.

Ash and steam rose like an Indian's smoke signal as wet clods of used tealeaves tumbled onto the smouldering turf. The ash dust engulfed a large pair of pink knickers and a pair of thick woollen socks that were hanging on a cord clothesline under the mantlepiece.

'Who did they say they were?' Agnes asked, barely waking from her slumber as she stirred in her chair.

'Tessie's lads, from the city.' Stephen answered in a raised voice.

I don't think Mattie was right when he called Stephen a genius because our town, Clunmon, isn't a city—there couldn't be more than three thousand people there and that's counting the people out our road as far as the Border. I know this from one of Sparks' "brain waves" when he got the three of us to count everybody in the town. I don't think Vinny's headcount was too accurate in the section of the town allocated to him because I know that he didn't want to do it in the first place.

'How is your mother?' Agnes asked closing her eyes and slumping even deeper into the cushioned chair.

I didn't answer because I think that she has gone back to sleep and I'm afraid to waken her.

'Are ye here on a bit of a holiday?' Stephen asked pouring steaming hot water into the teapot from a black kettle that was hanging from a hook over the fire.

'No,' Mattie replied, 'we are here to help Uncle Frank on the farm.'

'Good boys, will ye have a bit to eat?' Stephen asked measuring a handful of loose tea from a battered tin canister he had taken from the top of the mantle piece.

He funnelled the tea from his cupped palm into the teapot. He is using the same recipe as The Yank did in Dan Joe's house. Hardened welts became visible as the dried tealeaves disappeared from his hand.

'No, we're not hung...' was all Mattie could say as he held his mouth with one hand muffling a titter and pointed with the other hand to the pink knickers hanging on the line under the mantlepiece.

I wished he hadn't done that because I was trying not to giggle when I first saw the knickers but now it was even more difficult with Mattie pointing to them. We were saved by the dog. It gave a wheezy sneeze as the ash dust from the fire settled around him. Mattie and I burst out laughing. The dog gave another sneeze and moved away from the chair as Agnes struck out with her hand and hit the dog on the head without saying a word or opening her eyes.

'Isn't it easy to make ye laugh,' Stephen said giving a small chuckle himself.

He then went over to a cupboard and opened a door in a press underneath. A few bluebottles buzzed around him as he pulled out a basin, containing what looked like wool, with red coloured splattering. He reached into the basin with a clawed hand as he spoke.

'Are ye sure ye wouldn't like a few lambs' tails?'

Mattie's cringed faced answered for both of us. Stephen replaced the basin in the press and moved towards the fire.

The blood on the lamb's tails in his fist was obvious to me now. He threw the fistful into the open fire and pulled his head backwards from the ensuing gush of burning wool.

I got a similar smell before one time when we were smoking in our hideout. I accidentally knocked the top of a lighted cigarette onto my lap and couldn't find it until it had burned a hole in my woollen jumper. But this smell was much stronger.

Stephen moved from the fireplace to the table where he opened the table drawer and took out a long knife. The knife was wafer thin and worn away in the middle. Stephen pulled a loaf of soda bread to the centre of the table and began slicing it. He gathered up the bread slices then aimed and threw them into a bowl-sized hole in the concrete floor beside the table. I looked back at the frizzling lambs' tails in the fireplace.

'Do the lambs' tails fall off themselves?' 'Mattie enquired.

'They do with a little help from this,' Stephen answered with a croaky chuckle as he dropped the knife on the table.

He poured milk from an enamel jug into the hole in the floor until the bread was floating. Then Stephen went back to the fireplace and grabbed the long blackened tongs resting against the hearth and began removing the now cremated lambs' tails with it. They looked like little black burned sticks. He threw two of them into the improvised feeding bowl and slung the rest onto the table in quick succession as he spoke.

'Wouldn't that smell make a dead man hungry?'

I didn't answer him.

The dog waddled over to the food eyeing Mattie and I as he passed.

'That's a great watchdog you have,' Mattie said moving away from it and asked, 'what's his name?'

The dog chewed, gulped and swallowed from his 'feeding bowl.'

'His name is "Dog," that's what we call him.' Stephen replied.

'That's the best name for a dog I ever heard,' Mattie said laughing.

'You're full of the oul crack, what's yeer names anaways?' Stephen enquired picking two eggs from a dish on the kitchen windowsill.

'I'm Mattie and this is my baby brother Finn and we're at your service.' Mattie replied with a wide grin.

'Has the cat got Finn's tongue, there's not a word out of him,' Stephen said looking back at me as he rolled the two eggs into the ashes surrounding the burning turf.

'He's a bit shy, doesn't say too much,' Mattie answered and put his head down giggling.

'Well you sure make up for him,' a voice mumbled.

We all looked in the direction of the voice. We were looking at Agnes who had one eye half open as she continued in a slurred voice, 'I can't get a wink of "shleep" with the yapping.'

Stephen pushed the teapot further into the fire and gave a slight groan as he straightened up again. The dog went back to its place beside Agnes and lay down on the floor. Stephen walked over to a dresser near the table and took an enamel mug out and left it on the table and then scattered cutlery around in the table drawer until he choose a spoon which he flipped onto the table.

He grabbed the tongs again from the side of the open hearth and gently poked the eggs around in the ashes for a few seconds. He picked them out of the ashes one by one in the clasp of the tongs and purposefully placed them on a wide crack at the side of the hearth. He replaced the tongs, spat on his hands, picked up the eggs and steadied them against the enamel jug on the table.

One of the eggs had hard egg-white bursting from its shell but the other appeared to be in perfect condition. In one sweeping movement he returned to the hearth, spat on his hands once more, pulled the teapot from the fire and returned to the table where he filled the mug from a height with black treacly tea. He picked up a black crispy lambs' tail from the table and scraped off the cindery surface with the knife before popping it into his mouth.

'I'd get up in the middle of the night to eat lambs' tails,' he said chewing with dribbling satisfaction.

I was watching Stephen delving into the egg with a spoon and scooping into the hard yellow yoke when I heard a fumbling sound near the fireplace. Mattie had picked up the tongs and was trying to manipulate them to pick up sods of turf from a cardboard box beside the hearth. Agnes still had her eyes closed but Dog was wide eyed staring at Mattie who was struggling with the tongs to place a sod of turf on the fire. He smiled with delight when he managed it and returned to the turf box for more.

His confidence grew and he attempted to lift a larger and longer turf sod but it sprang from between the tongs and tumbling along the floor in the direction of Agnes. He stretched his foot out fast in order to stop it rolling towards her but instead of blocking it, he had kicked it forward and it cart wheeled onto Agnes's lap. Agnes's legs were wide apart and her apron acted like a safety net for the turf sod. Her eyes shot open as she shrieked, 'Mother of sweet Jesus!' Dog crawled under Agnes' armchair with a weak whine.

In three long strides Mattie was over at the window. He made out that he was examining the eggs in the dish on the windowsill. Agnes examined the missile that had woken her from her slumber and then slung it into the fire sending sparks dancing up the chimney. She was cringing as she brushed the turf mould dust from her apron and stared at me and spoke, 'phat are you at, at all?'

I looked over at Mattie but he turned his back to me even more and started looking out the window. I looked back at Agnes with my hands out and mouth open but nothing came out. Then she closed her eyes and peacefully slouched back into her previous position and belched.

I moved over to Stephen at the table. He was slurping the dregs from the mug. Empty eggshells were strewn in a heap on the table beside a few tiny bones and black cinders of what was once lambs tails. Stephen wiped his mouth with the back of his hand, picked up a galvanised bucket from under the table and walked towards the door.

'Where're you going?' Mattie asked following him.

'I have to feed an oul' calf and milk a cow,' Stephen said going out the door.

'I'm with ya,' Mattie called increasing his step.

61

I took a quick look at Agnes and the dog before I followed. I had the feeling they were glad to see us go.

I heard on the wireless that ye had a big painting robbery or something up there in Clunmon last week,' Stephen said pushing open the decaying door of a small shed in the yard and continued to talk in the dark shed as we followed him inside, 'isn't yeer father a Sergeant up there in Clunmon?'

'He's a Superintendent, but he deals mostly with murders,' Mattie lied again.

'A Superintendent is he? I'm not surprised, 'cause all his family are verra clever, Doctors and Teachers and Priests, I met them at yeer parent's wedding, grand people, lovely people verra clever,' Stephen said shaking his head with emphasis.

Stephen reminded me of The Yank the ways he was praising Daddy's family but he hadn't as many details as The Yank.

I couldn't make out Mattie's face in the darkness but I knew by the way he was shaking his head that he was holding in a giggle.

'I know only too well what Cities are like for murders,' Stephen continued, 'myself and Agnes were in Manchester for a lock o' years in our young days,' Stephen divulged as he dipped the bucket into a sack standing in the corner.

'What do want the sawdust for?' Mattie enquired looking into the bucket.

'That's far from sawdust,' Stephen said with a shake of his head and added, 'that's the best of Indian meal,' putting a few more handfuls from another sack into the bucket. My ears pricked when I heard the word 'Indian' at last. I wondered what he had traded with the Indians to get the meal.

As we came out of the shed I could hear a mooing cry from another shed at the end of the yard and we walked in that direction. Stephen dipped the bucket into a barrel of water under a water spout at the corner of the shed. He picked up a seasoned sally stick that was resting against the barrel and vigorously stirred, mixing the water and the meal.

When we got to the shed door where I heard the mooing, Stephen opened the top half of the door. A calf with snorting wet nostrils, pushed at the half door as its neck stretched over it. Stephen hit the calf on the nose with the bucket and when it backed a little he leaned in over the half door and lowered the bucket of mixture to the floor.

We followed Stephen back across the yard to the first shed where he picked up another bucket and closed the shed door.

'Bad sest to you.' Stephen roared running from the door as he swung his empty bucket in a threatening manner at a large furry animal chasing chickens and hens across the yard.

At first I thought it was a fox and then a big cat but if it was, it was definitely the biggest ginger tomcat I had ever seen in my life. The animal stopped, humped its back and spat, showing white fangs before it cleared the wall.

'That bloody wild yoke hasn't a chicken or hen left alive around these parts.' Stephen said staring after the frenzied animal as it leaped and zigzagged at high speed down the field towards Granny's house.

'Where did it come from?' Mattie asked still staring after the wild animal.

'They say that blooda Dutchman,' he pointed with his free hand at a house on the base of the mountainside near the edge of the pine forest, 'who smuggled it in somehow and...' Stephen didn't get finishing his story because Mattie butted in.

'How much would it be worth to you dead?' Mattie asked tapping his concealed catapult.

'Are you a bit of a bounty hunter?' Stephen chuckled as he opened the slumped gate, picked up a three-legged stool just inside the gate and directed his question toward Mattie, 'you'd want to be a dead-eye-dick to kill that thing, manys the good-shot in this parish has tried and failed.'

'I'll give you the head, if you give me the money, a Pound note is that a deal?' Mattie bargained walking backwards staring up at Stephen.

Stephen chuckled even louder as he said, 'be God but you're the wild buckeen.'

'I take it that's a deal so,' Mattie said rubbing his hands.

I hope Mattie wasn't expecting me to use my dagger for the

job. The only thing that I ever cut the head off was a fish that I'd caught, when I was out fishing with my pals.

I began thinking of Vinny and Sparks when we would catch a fish. Vinny would give me his dagger to gut the fish. We would remove our sandwiches from the newspaper wrapping and wrap the gutted fish in it instead. After that we would make a cake of the wet blue riverbank mud. Then Vinny would plaster the newspaper all over with the wet mud and throw it on the open campfire we'd have lit. We'd leave it in the fire until the wet mud had gone hard and cracked. Vinny would sniff lovingly as he broke the caked mud away and tore open the newspaper. Even Sparks said that he preferred Vinny's way of cooking trout to his mother's recipe.

I was surprised to hear Stephen mention 'bounty hunter' and 'dead-eye-dick' and wondered does he read comics. Maybe the next time we're visiting I'll ask him has he any 'swaps' for my Roy Rogers comics.

We kept in step with Stephen going through the field. I wondered what Sparks and Vinny were doing just now and what sort of question they would ask Stephen if they were here now.

'Does you and your wife Agnes have many children?' I ventured my question.

Stephen and Mattie stopped suddenly and Stephen gave a startled look at me.

'Wife, children,' Stephen gasped, 'sure me and Agnes are brother and sister, be God when you do say something, you make it good.'

We moved on again and I felt free to talk now once I had started. I could see horses galloping at the foot of the mountain beyond the river.

'Are those horses yours?' I asked pointing.

Stephen shaded the sun from his eyes before looking.

'Yarra not at all,' he said shaking his head, 'those are wild horses, useless yokes, good for nothing,' he qualified.

"Wild Horses," I gleamed inwardly; can the Apache be far away?

Mattie kicked at every clump of rushes that came in his way.

'Do you like football?' Stephen asked watching Mattie's antics.

'Do I like football? I love it, best in the school team.' Mattie said making a wild kick at a hardened piece of cow dung that whizzed up in the air, turned in mid-flight like a Frisbee and landed with a clang in the bucket that Stephen was carrying.

'Be God you're a good shot, anaways,' Stephen chuckled emptying out the caked cow dung.

I knew that Mattie hated football and only played when he was forced to do so by the teacher to make up a team, but I said nothing and walked on.

As we crossed over the brow of the hill I saw a bony looking cow wandering up towards us. It was mainly brown with a white face.

'Good girl,' Stephen called as the cow hastened its step.

I was fairly sure that it wasn't a bull because I could make out its milk filled swollen udder swaying but I stopped walking towards it anyway.

I stayed at a safe distance until the cow stopped beside Stephen and Mattie. Stephen plonked the stool down near the rear of the cow, leaned under it near the udder and stretched and pulled each of the teats in turn. When I joined them I heard Mattie pleading.

'Go on Stephen, give me a go, I'll fill that bucket in no time for you.'

I hoped that Stephen would let him milk the cow because I knew that Mattie never milked in his life and if Mattie got on okay maybe he'd give me a go too.

'I'll make a start anyway,' Stephen said nestling the bucket between his legs and grabbing a teat in each hand.

Twanging sounds echoed as the milk sprayed against the inside of the bucket as Stephen's rhythm increased. Mattie and I watched Stephen's technique as the bottom of the bucket disappeared under frothy fresh milk.

Stephen grunted a few times when the cow swished its matted tail. The marauding flies that buzzed around Stephen's head and the belly of the cow were the intended target for the cow's swishing tail but Stephen's head was in the way a few times and roared his discontent at the cow—'Sthop-it-cannot-ya.'

When the milk spray from the teats was splashing into the filling bucket I knew by the way that Mattie was going from one foot to the other that he had decided that there was no more to learn and bent down beside Stephen.

'Take a break there Stephen and I'll take over,' Mattie said in an anxious voice. Stephen looked sideways at Mattie, broke his rhythm and stopped milking. Stephen was no sooner off the milking stool when Mattie had occupied it. Stephen handed Mattie the bucket which he grabbed by the handle and began manoeuvring it into a comfortable position between his knobbly knees.

The milk splashed and swayed around the insides of the bucket for a while but then settled as Mattie reached under the udder and grabbed a teat in each hand. I don't think that Mattie had been paying too much attention to Stephen's masterful hands because what he did next was not the way that Stephen had been milking. Mattie seemed to twist, wrench and squeeze the teats with all his strength.

The cow's eyes bulged as like in a cartoon film and then simultaneously looked back at her torturer and kicked forward with her back leg. In synchronised motion, Mattie, the bucket and stool all rolled for a second or two and then lay motionless on their sides in the grass.

I knew there and then that my chances of milking that day were nil so I didn't even ask.

'What made him do that?' Mattie asked with a startled face kneeling on the milk soaked grass before staggering to his feet.

'Well that's the end of that,' Stephen said picking up the bucket and added, 'I'll be lucky if I can squeeze a few drops of milk from her into my tea-mug tonight.'

'We better be off,' Mattie babbled into an explanation, 'Uncle Frank will be looking for us but sure who knows, if we get finished early with him we'll pop over and give you a hand tomorrow.'

'There's no need,' Stephen rushed his reply, 'your uncle Frank has plenty to keep you going with the hay and the shearing and dipping, I'll go over visiting some night and I'll see ye then.'

Stephen concluded with a wave of the stool as he headed back to his house.

'The next time Mister Cow and me meets I'll have my catapult in my hand,' Mattie said in a low, threatening voice as I followed him down the field. I did not know where he was going but it was not towards Granny's house.

'Where are you going? I asked.

'We are going to see what that river has to offer,' Mattie said pointing past a couple of fields to a valley where a silver river meandered.

'Don't forget we told Granny that we wouldn't be long,' I reminded Mattie as he grunted tumbling over another stonewall into another field.

The river was further away than I thought. An optical allusion, as Sparks used to say when he and Vinny and I found ourselves coming back late from another one of Spark's mysterious fact-finding expeditions, through Clunmon's roaming hills.

'Get me "ammo" quickly,' Mattie shouted several times drawing his catapult as he chased after a sprinting hare.

I looked around the boggy soil peppered with bunches of rushes, but there was no sign of any stones so I didn't bother to look anymore. When we got to the riverbank there were plenty of stones but no hares.

Mattie leaped on to the pebbled basin of the riverbank shouting and pointing to a pool that was continuously being filled by water manoeuvring its way through slippery rocks and stones, 'look, loads of baby fish.'

'They are called "Fry,"' I informed him of the knowledge imparted to me by Sparks.

'"Fry" is right, frying on the pan,' Mattie yelped wading into the water 'til the flowing water level skimmed the top of his wellingtons. The minnow brown trout scattered and vanished as Mattie grabbed and splashed with his trawling hands. He looked disillusioned as he examined his dripping wet empty hands.

I was aware why this happened since the day Sparks and I were out at the river near Murphy's farm. I was sure that my aim was accurate to spear a small trout but Sparks explained that the refractive light had distorted my calculation of the depth. He explained this to me at least three times and I still wasn't sure, so there was no point trying to explain to Mattie. I left him wondering why he hadn't managed to grab a fish.

After a quick turn of his head he stopped momentarily and then moved cautiously as he spoke in a low voice, 'That's a biggie, that's a biggie.'

He was moving sideways towards the slippery inlet to the pool. I could see what he was moving towards. It was a sleek silvery salmon basking motionless except for its gills wafting in the water and was just a few feet away from where the river bottom darkened.

It all happened suddenly. The vision of the salmon became distorted as the still water of the pool rippled with Mattie's slip and splash into the edge of the pool. He sat bewildered in the shallow water between the large rounded stone he had just slipped off and the slimy green waterweed that swayed and weaved with the water flow. His wellingtons filled in seconds and he struggled with his water weighted wellingtons to get to his feet and splash his way to the riverbank.

He sat on a large bolder and poured the water from each of his wellingtons in turn before he muttered, 'I think we'll head back for Granny's.'

The only sound to be heard from Mattie on the way back was the squelching of his wet socks in his wellingtons.

Mattie opened the gate leading into the yard at Granny's house, 'close this behind you, we don't want to get in Granny's bad books,' he said marching towards the house.

I gave my wellingtons a quick wipe in the tufts of grass beside the gate and then ran to catch up with Mattie. The front door was ajar and he just pushed it and quick stepped it down the hall to our room.

I was going to go straight into the kitchen but when I heard Granny call out, 'What kept ye?' I changed course and followed Mattie to the bedroom.

Mattie was sitting on the bed and he cringed red-faced as he forced off his wellingtons. He pushed his catapult into its usual hiding place under the mattress before he leaped towards the wardrobe. He was putting on dry socks when I relayed what Granny had asked.

'I heard her,' he said putting on the second sock.

'What will we tell her?' I asked anxiously.

'Let me do the talking,' Mattie said calmly pushing his feet back down into his wellingtons. I could still see a wet patch on the seat of his trouser from his encounter in the river but it wasn't very noticeable so I said nothing.

I followed him sheepishly into the kitchen. I could still get the smell of onions. Then I saw the reason why. Uncle Frank was sitting at the kitchen table spiking pieces of tomato, ham and onion onto his fork.

'Well ye were a great help to me,' he said with a grin as Mattie and I slid into the two chairs at the kitchen table.

'What kept ye?' Granny repeated her earlier question placing two plates in front of us.

I did not want to believe it; but there on the plate beside the ham and tomato were slices of onions.

'We were shockin' busy,' Mattie said before picking up an onion slice with his fingers and biting into it.

'Busy at what?' Uncle Frank enquired buttering a slice of bread on his hand.

'We were helping Stephen with the feeding and milking,' Mattie answered reaching for some bread.

Uncle Frank gave a loud laugh and spurted out, 'that was "shockin' busy" all right—feeding and milking for Stephen, sure he has only one cow and one calf.'

Granny smiled pouring our tea.

'I'll get another drop of milk,' Uncle Frank said moving away from the table towards the dresser.

Granny turned to replace the teapot on the stove. I saw my opportunity and took it. With one gathering swoop I had picked up all the onions from my plate and shoved them into my pockets. I was more relaxed now and would have really enjoyed my tea except for the slight hint of onion odour all around the kitchen. I even got involved in the conversation that Uncle Frank had with Granny about his plans for tomorrow.

'We will be able to help you with the hay and the sheering and dipping,' I said remembering what Stephen had suggested we should do rather than go over to him.

'Ye had a long journey and ye must be tired, so off with ye to bed and we'll see tomorrow what God sends,' Granny responded to my offer.

I didn't think of it up to now but I did feel tired.

'We'll get into our pyjamas anyway and see what happens from there,' Mattie said getting up from the table.

When we got to the bedroom Mattie started mimicking me, '"we will help you with the hay and the sheering and the dipping"—you're a lick-arse Finn, do you think I have nothing better to be doing than that oul stuff,' he scoffed grabbing his pyjamas from the wardrobe.

I looked at the curtains in the bedroom; they were still up and I blessed myself in thanksgiving, but I still couldn't remember where I'd seen them before.

I got into my pyjamas and folded the clothes I'd taken off and put them in the wardrobe. Mattie just threw his on the bed and headed out the bedroom door. I caught up with him and we both entered the kitchen together.

'Yeer just in time, did ye bring your beads with you?' Granny asked taking a Rosary beads from a hook at the side of the mantlepiece.

'No, but I'm just as good with the fingers,' Mattie said spreading his fingers and holding up his hand.

Granny knelt with her elbows embedded in the seat of the armchair. Uncle Frank took the other Rosary beads hanging on the small nail at the side of the mantle piece and knelt at a kitchen chair. Mattie and I had just knelt at the other two kitchen chairs when Granny began the Rosary in a melodic voice in Irish.

I knew the Our Father and Hail Mary in Irish but I just mumbled the rest. When it came to Mattie's turn to say a decade of the Rosary he sounded very devout but the rest of the time he looked really bored and was fidgeting. When it was my turn to say a decade he was pulling funny faces at me but I just had to look over at Granny and I never once felt like laughing.

When Uncle Frank was starting to say his second and final decade I was looking at Mattie wriggling his head through the rails at the back of his chair. The rails at the back of the chair were wider at the top than the bottom. By the time the decade was finished Mattie's face looked very flushed as he tried to force his head back out. He was moving his head up and down to see if could find a wider spot but it wasn't any use. When he started dragging the chair and making noise Granny and Uncle Frank looked around at him.

His face was even redder now. They both blessed themselves, got up of their knees and rushed over to him.

'Just stay as you are, and don't be pulling anymore,' Uncle Frank said rushing to the cupboard.

He came back to Mattie with the butter dish and began rubbing lumps of butter into the back of Mattie's ears, neck and head and on the inside of the chair rails. Mattie made a wailing scream as Uncle Frank pushed Mattie's head back as he pulled the chair forward.

'I must have fallen asleep and slipped through the rails,' Mattie said collapsing onto the chair.

'Sure of course you're tired *a grá*, off to bed with ye,' Granny said wiping Mattie's buttery head with a dishcloth.

His face was pale now but his ears were bright, bright red. I was going to tell Mattie that he looked like a hedgehog with his hair all sticking up but he is in such bad humour I know well that he'll start fighting with me and I am just too tired to fight back.

I partially closed the orange coloured curtains on our bedroom window. We both got into bed but Mattie told me to go back and switch out the light in the hall. It was a little bit brighter in the hallway but I still couldn't find a switch so I just peeped into the kitchen where there was better light.

'What do you want?' Granny's question startled me.

'The light switch,' I answered immediately.

Uncle Frank spoke getting up from his chair, 'here's your light,' he reached and pulled down a large lamp that was suspended from the ceiling, 'and here's your switch,' he added twisting a small knob under the globe as the light dimmed.

He looked at me for a response and when it didn't come he

released the oil lamp gently and it recoiled back towards the ceiling. Granny smiled and faded into the scullery.

'Good night,' I muttered turning back for the hallway. I can't believe that I hadn't noticed the oil lamp earlier. I closed the bedroom door and the room got darker but I'm sure the room would be pitch black only for the bright moon shining through the curtains.

When I got back into bed I asked Mattie what was the most thing he was looking forward to tomorrow. I asked him again and looked down at his face. His mouth was open and his breathing was deep and slow. Even when I pushed him over to make more room for myself he just snorted but his eyes remained closed.

A statue of the Virgin Mary on the window ledge stood as if on guard, between a gap in the curtains, and slightly hindered my view of the moonlit silhouetted landscape. The robust mountains looked threatening and I wondered if the Indians were planning a raid to night. I turned on my side, slipped my hand under the mattress and groped until I felt the dagger. I eyed the gentle wafting of the now darkened orange coloured curtains.

CHAPTER 7

The Witch and the Scam

WHEN I SAW THE CURTAINS again they were back to their usual glowing orange. Mattie had woken me by his jumping on the bed to put on his trousers.

'It looks like a nice day for hanging around that river,' Mattie said looking out the window, 'I might even go for a dip.'

'Are you going to take your clothes off this time?' I said giggling.

Mattie grabbed one of his wellingtons and swung it at me as I leaped from the bed. It slipped from his hand, bounced off my back and glanced off the Virgin Mary statue on the window ledge.

The wellington landed upright and began wobbling in sequence with the statue. I knew that the statue was going to topple but just before it did I grabbed it.

I kissed the statue lovingly and whispered as I replaced it, 'thank you for not falling and breaking.'

'Come on you weirdo, kissing statues, you're weird,' Mattie called back leaving the room.

When I was putting on my trousers I got the smell of onions. I looked over at the statue that I had just saved and prayed, 'Please not onions for breakfast.' My prayer was answered in a funny sort of way.

When I put my hands in my pockets I found the cause of the

onion smell. It was coming from the onions I had concealed in my pocket yesterday evening. I waited until Mattie came out of the bathroom. I locked the bathroom door behind me and emptied the contents of my pocket into the toilet bowl. I had to wait for two flushes to get rid of the slimy smelly vegetable. I scrubbed my hands with the red carbolic soap until all the scent of the onions was gone.

'Come on slow coach, do you know that I have the cows milked and back in the fields and yeer not even up,' Uncle Frank declared proudly as I entered the kitchen.

Mattie ignored the boast and was making faces at the bowl of porridge in front of him.

'I'm going to hitch up the horse to the mower and I'll meet ye in the yard then,' Uncle Frank said getting up from the table.

'Where is your horse?' I asked.

'Where else but in the stable,' he replied with a frown heading out the door.

I rose from my chair to look out the window and watched him going across the yard and down behind the hay barn.

I remembered seeing a shed there yesterday when we were going to Stephen and Agnes. I would have preferred to have spent my time with the horse if I had known it was there rather than messing about with Mattie at the river.

'Did you sleep well?' Granny asked and added without waiting for a reply, 'now sit down and have your porridge like a good boy.

I was buttering my bread when I heard a loud voice echoing in the front yard. 'Hold up, hold up cannot ya,' Uncle Frank was roaring.

I rose from table and looked out the window again. He was harnessing a beautiful Chestnut horse into a two-wheeled machine. The machine had a raised arm with a row of shiny blades like pointed metal teeth sticking up on one side. This has to be the mowing machine that Uncle Frank was talking to Granny about last night. I crammed the last piece of bread into my mouth and ran from the table. Mattie followed me into the yard as Uncle Frank was tightening a leather belt under the horse's belly. He gave it one more tug and buckled it. He held the reins as he sat up on a metal basin-shaped seat.

74

'Right lads, there's a couple of rakes I got ye,' he said pointing to two hay rakes resting against the hedge and wall that surrounded the house, 'follow me up to the meadow,' he added giving a quick chuck on the reins.

I ran over and grabbed the two hay rakes and handed one of them to Mattie.

He hesitantly took the rake from me and muttered, 'what's this all about,' before he ran up beside Uncle Frank who was bouncing along at a slow pace on the mower.

'What do you expect me to do with this?' Mattie asked holding up the rake.

'Just follow me and you'll soon find out.' Uncle Frank said gently flapping the reins on the horse's rump.

I walked beside the horse and watched as it dug hoof and metal shoe into the earthy lane.

The chain across the straddle jingled as the turning metal wheels crunched the stony dry earth. I thought of Uncle Frank as the driver of a covered wagon leading the wagon train into the prairies of the Wild West.

I was excited too about getting my first taste of real farm work. I looked back at Mattie. He was dragging his rake behind him as he furiously kicked at the stones unearthed by the horse's hoofs. I slowed my pace and turned to speak to Uncle Frank.

'What's the horse's name?' I asked.

'Name?' my uncle chuckled, 'it's not a race horse, it doesn't have a name.'

'Roy Rogers has a horse nearly like yours and he calls his Trigger,' I informed him hoping he'd think it was a great idea to call his horse the same name.

'Is this "Roy Rogers" fellow from Clunmon?' he said pulling on the reins and half standing on the foot rests of the mower.

I could tell by the expression on his face that he had never read a Roy Rogers Dell comic or saw a Roy Rogers film. I was wondering if there was any point in telling him how Roy Rogers shot an arrow in half just before the arrow hit Trigger, when Uncle Frank abruptly interrupted with a roar.

'Shep, Toss,' he shouted at the top of his voice.

The horse jibbed at the roar but Uncle Frank calmed him with a tug on the reins. 'Look at those bloody asses at my gate again.' Uncle Frank said in an angry voice. I could see them now too. I don't think these donkeys are as stupid as other ones because just as soon as my uncle roared the dog's names and before Shep and Toss went whizzing past us, the two donkeys turned away from the gate and moved slowly away.

Uncle Frank turned into a field just before the top of his lane and we followed him in. I thought that the meadow would be like Murphy's meadow at home with high dense hay but this only looked like a field with bits of long grass in it.

'Now its as simple as this,' Uncle Frank said stretching his arms before grabbing the reins again, 'I go around the meadow mowing the hay and you two just rake away the cut hay back from the hay to be cut on the next round, okay,' he concluded dropping the blade shaft to the ground and slapping the horse with the reins.

He had hardly moved twenty yards when he looked back at Mattie and I who were happy that we were carrying out his instructions. He stopped the horse, tied the reins to the mower seat and walked back to us at a fast pace. I could tell by the way he was biting his lower lip that he wasn't happy about something. He grabbed my rake from my hand and began raking the hay he had just cut. The way he was doing it was the complete opposite to way Mattie and I had been doing it.

'Like that, okay?' he snapped forcing the rake back into my hand.

'May I ask you a question Uncle Frank?' Mattie said resting on the rake handle. Uncle Frank just cocked his ear but didn't say anything as Mattie continued, 'how long is this "lark" going to last?'

'Until this meadow is cut and the other three,' Uncle Frank replied before pounding back to his mower.

The horse had been curtailed from grazing by its reins being tied to the seat of the mower. The cumbersome horse collar shifted up and down its neck with each effort the horse made to stretch its head towards the grass but it was all in vain. Uncle Frank untied the reins, sat back on the seat and got the horse back to work.

76

Mattie stood for a second or two but then burst into a run after Uncle Frank. I didn't know what Mattie was going to ask now, but I knew that he was about to really annoy my uncle.

'I thought you said last night in the kitchen that you were going dipping sheep to day?'

Uncle Frank looked bemused.

'Did you ever hear the expression "Make hay while the sun shines"?' Uncle Frank said calmly before returning to his mowing.

Mattie walked back to me muttering, 'did you ever hear the expression "I'm out of here."'

I knew by the way Mattie was talking that he intended going down to river the first chance he got.

'I'll bet Uncle Frank is only joking about the other three meadows,' I said in attempt to humour Mattie.

'He better be joking.' Mattie threatened.

The more laps we did following Uncle Frank the hotter and more bored we got. But the most annoying thing was the millions of flying ants that hovered around us. Some of them would land on Uncle Frank's white sleeveless vest but he paid no attention to them. This is more than could be said about Mattie and I, and we spent a lot of our time swiping at our attackers. They were more prevalent at the bottom part of the sloped meadow.

When we got to the top part of the meadow Mattie began to lag behind and said that he had an idea to put to Uncle Frank. Mattie eventually stopped and said that he was going to wait there until he was lapped by Uncle Frank. I just kept raking behind the mower; and praying that Mattie would keep his mouth shut and keep us out of trouble.

Uncle Frank pulled up slowly as he approached Mattie who was resting on his rake with both hands. 'What's wrong?' he asked Mattie with a puzzled face bringing the horse to a complete standstill.

Mattie took a deep breath and then with cocked head and squinted eye he delivered his proposition.

'I was thinking that maybe we should take turns, you know, everybody gets a go driving the mower.'

I looked at Uncle Frank with an expression that said that I wanted no part of Mattie's plan. It went unnoticed.

'You're doing just fine as you are, keep going, keep going.' Uncle Frank laughed with a flick of the reins and moving off on his mower again. It was the first time I'd seen him laugh today.

Eventually the last row of the hay fell limp at the butt of the slashing blades of the mower. I felt that it was the longest day that I had ever put in but then when Uncle Frank called merrily, 'Perfect timing, all done before dinner.' I realised it was only half a day. We threw our rakes in the air and ran for the gate.

'Bring those rakes with you,' Uncle Frank bellowed after us.

I saw a thin grey haired person going into the house as we rambled down the lane.

A goose and few goslings met us near the bottom of the lane and Mattie swung the rake in their direction. The goose hissed as the goslings scattered, and one by one scurried into a drain-pipe near the entrance to the field just up from the stable. The goose flapped her wings and stretched her neck hissing at us even more. We increased our step and kept looking behind us to keep a check on our surprise attacker. Just before we reached the safety of the house the goslings reappeared at the far end of the drain-pipe and were gaggling merrily flapping their fledgling wings. I told Mattie that they were laughing at him.

'We'll see who has the last laugh,' Mattie retorted pushing the hall door open.

'Go and wash up, dinner is ready,' Granny greeted us from the kitchen.

Dinner ready and not a hint of a smell of an onion; the stress of my hard morning's work in the meadow was forgotten. Mattie pushed me out of the way and rushed into the bathroom first. I went into our bedroom. It was lovely and tidy and both my shoes and Mattie's were polished and placed beside the wardrobe.

When I went into the kitchen Mattie was shaking hands with the thin grey headed person I had seen at the door when we were coming down the lane. 'Mammy is doing just grand and this is my baby brother Finn, who I am looking after,' Mattie said breaking off the handshake.

78

The person Mattie was talking to was sitting at the table having dinner. I couldn't see if the person was wearing trousers or a skirt and the grey hair was cut very short. I held out my hand but I still didn't know if I was being introduced to a man or a woman. Just in time I thought of Mammy's advice; "Call everyone you meet "Ma'am" or "Sir.""

The hand extended to me, consisted of stretched skin pulled over thin brittle bones, all tied together with a mass of bulging blue veins. I immediately withdrew my hand in fear that I would either break the fragile bones or burst the swollen veins and spluttered out, 'Hello, Ma'am Sir.'

Mattie quickly shoved a potato into his mouth and was silently shaking with laughter.

'So you're Tessie's youngest lad, are you?' The voice gave the gender away. I was talking to a woman whose tone of voice told me she was not at all happy.

I sat on the chair furthest from the woman I had just insulted, but immediately had to vacate my seat when Granny said that, that was Uncle Frank's spot and placed my dinner beside the woman. Her eyes glared at me through her bushy eyebrows, as she bent over the dinner plate gobbling her food, with speedy repeat movements of her fork.

I didn't like her and she scared me. I tried not to look into her eyes and concentrated instead on a large black wart just to the left side of her upper lip. A dangly hair sprouted from the growth which quivered with each munch she made. Granny came and went from the kitchen a few times and commented on how quiet everyone was. I had to get back in the 'good books.' This person had to be a very good friend of Granny's otherwise she wouldn't be having dinner in her house. I came up with an idea and spoke it aloud.

'If you turn the handle of the churn you'll have good luck,' I said directing my advice towards the woman.

The woman immediately stopped eating and raised her head from the plate. Mattie sprayed masticated boiled bacon and cabbage across the table as he jumped from his chair holding his mouth. He sent Uncle Frank backwards as they met at the kitchen door.

'Hello Sadie-Tom,' Uncle Frank greeted the woman going to his chair. I gulped my milk to hasten my speed at finishing my dinner. I was still chewing as I excused myself from the table and took sanctuary in my room.

I threw myself on the bed and consoled myself that to call someone whose name was "Sadie-Tom," "Mam Sir," was not too wrong at all. I'm going to ask Mattie what he thinks when he comes out of the bathroom. I didn't get a chance to ask Mattie what he thought because when he came out of the bathroom he raced over to me and spoke in a whisper.

'I'd hate to be you, she'll put a curse on you, she's a witch you know.'

He had a frightened look on his face as he spoke. I told him that I didn't believe him. I told him that I still didn't believe him when he said that he saw her arriving at the gate on a broomstick.

'If you see her riding the broomstick, will you believe me then?' Mattie said moving close to my face.

Now I wasn't too sure.

'Come on we'll hide behind the wall at the meadow and watch her leaving,' Mattie said pulling his catapult from under the mattress.

I heard a clanging noise and looked on the ground. Daddy's screwdriver and The Yank's window winders were on the floor. I had wondered where he had hidden them. Mattie pushed them back under the mattress.

'Come on let's go Witch Hunting,' Mattie said stuffing his catapult down the back of his trouser waist leaving the bedroom. He pressed his finger to his lips and pointed to the kitchen as we sneaked out the hall door.

'We better not go too far, Uncle Frank will be looking for us.' I advised Mattie as we headed up the lane.

As we went into the freshly cut meadow I could hear voices back at the house door.

'Don't worry I'll make it, I'll run between the drops.' I recognised Sadie-Tom's crackly voice as she sped from the house and up the lane.

I could feel drops of rain on my head.

'Just look at that big black cloud up there,' Mattie said before pushing me to the grass near the wall, 'what more proof do you want that she's a witch?' he finished in a whisper.

I wanted better proof than that; there had to be a broomstick ride.

We didn't move again until we heard the gate open and close at the top of the lane. Mattie was biting his lip as he silently instructed me with a wave of his hand to stay down. He slowly moved up the wall and then peeped over it. He immediately flopped back down beside me and with wild staring eyes cried in a low voice.

'Quick, quick, look now, look now, she's getting up on her broomstick.'

I could hear my heart beating in expectation as my head rose over the wall.

Everything else seemed to happen all at once.

'Ground control to Sadie-Tom, you're clear for take off.' Mattie bellowed at the top of his voice before running down the meadow.

I was left staring at a speechless frightened old woman looking back at me. Her long frock flopped around her skinny legs as her laced boots bounced at a speedy pace along the road. She was clearing the road in spots but I don't think that Sparks would classify it as a clean takeoff with or without a broomstick.

With the rain falling I headed down the meadow, sad, angry and worried. I felt sad for the old lady, angry at Mattie and worried that Granny and then Mammy would find out. I saw Mattie running from under the trees at the bottom of the meadow. He was shouting and screaming and waving his hands around. As I got closer to him I could make out a swarm of flying ants above his head. I steered my course away from the trees and kept well back from Mattie until I saw that he had stopped running. When I got close to him he was swatting a few remaining flying ants on his sleeve. I was happier now than I had been earlier.

'The witch must have put a curse on you before she flew off on her broom,' I said expressing my delight at his encounter with the ants.

'Fecking things,' he cursed before aiming his hand and splattering a colourful ladybird on his leg.

The rain was beginning to ease off as we headed through the last field before the river and had completely stopped as we jumped onto the pebbled river basin. 'Let's go down to the salmon pool,' Mattie said crunching the pebbles as he leaped along.

I let him run on and then I caught up with him at the dark pool. I asked him what we would do if the big wild cat that we had seen at Agnes and Stephen's house were to show up.

'I was thinking about that, I will kill it now with my catapult or if it shows up later with my bow and arrow,' Mattie said trying to skim a stone on the still water of the salmon pool. The stone just plonked and sank.

'You haven't got your bow and arrows with you,' I reminded him.

'I can make one can't I,' he snapped.

I picked up a slim stone and got it to do several skips on the water before landing on the far bank. I was surprised at how well I'd done.

'It's as simple as that,' I taunted Mattie.

He was about to make another attempt at skipping a stone on the water but instead aimed at me and hit me on the wellington. I screamed and roared. It didn't hurt at all but it stopped Mattie throwing any more at me.

Two cows wandered up the field towards us on the far bank.

'That cow on the left looks like Stephen's cow, the one that tried to kick me when I was milking it,' Mattie said loading his catapult with a stone from the river basin.

I knew that it couldn't have been Stephen's cow because it was on the other side of the river but I said nothing. He aimed his catapult across the river and in a sweeping movement released the stretched rubber. The flying stone hit the cow on the chest which jerked back a pace and snorted. I screamed at Mattie and told him he was cruel.

'I'm practising for the monster cougar kill,' Mattie giggled.

'That cow is about a hundred times bigger than the wildcat and easier to hit, and anyway it's not a cougar it's only a big wild cat,' I corrected myself.

'When I get my Pound from Stephen you wont be so smart will ya?' Mattie said reloading his catapult.

He started sneaking down the bank towards a flock of sheep further down from the two cows. I started shouting and shushing at the sheep but Mattie had fired two shots at them before I got near enough to frighten them out of Mattie's range.

'Did you see that, did you see that?' Mattie came boasting towards me, 'I hit that lamb smack on the head and that's about the same size as the cougar.'

'The same size Mattie but a lot quieter,' I criticised Mattie for his cruelty again. 'What are you going to do for pocket money, you know how stingy Mammy was with her five shillings and just think a Pound going-a-begging for just killing a big old cat.' Mattie tried to justify his target practise on the animals.

I was annoyed and I glared at Mattie.

'Ah don't worry about it I'll get you money some how,' Mattie said obviously thinking that I was annoyed over our lack of pocket money. I was about to tell him that it was his cruelty and not the money that was annoying me when he raised his hand and gestured to me to be quiet. I looked in the direction where he was pointing.

'Here's a dopey looking eejit,' Mattie said squinting at a man coming towards us on the far side of the river. 'I want you to look ga-ga, and don't open your mouth no matter what happens, have you got that? 'Mattie said in a threatening tone.

'What do you mean "look ga-ga"?' I asked.

'Just twist your eyes inwards and move your jaw to one side,' Mattie said holding my head and pushing my jaw sideways.

'What's this all about?' I enquired making a poor attempt at turning my eyes. 'Look, just do as I told you, Towbar and me got away with this trick once, so just do it,' Mattie rushed examining my face and then continued, 'ah! that's no good, forget about twisting your eyes , just close one eye and look stupid.'

I don't know what Mattie's plan was but when he mentioned Towbar I know that I wouldn't like it.

And anyway it was easy for Towbar to look stupid. He's long and skinny; has a "soup-bowl" haircut, a haircut given to him by his father because he can't afford to bring him to the barbers; has goofy teeth and is "froggy-eyed."

Mammy hates Mattie hanging about with Towbar and Daddy said that he is "bad news."

The man was getting closer and I knew by the way he was looking in our direction that he wanted to talk to us.

'Remember, not a word,' Mattie reminded as he straightened up and put his two hands behind his back.

I was getting worried. I wondered if the man saw what Mattie had done to the cow and lamb. When the man came directly to the opposite bank I could see why Mattie called him dopey. His teeth were protruding. His left eye was bulging and turned sideways. I was glad that I hadn't managed twisting my eyes in case he would think that I was mocking him. The fastener on his cap peak was missing and the front of the cap bulged upwards. He wore a tatty jacket over a badly ribbed jumper and the collar of his shirt looked like solid grease.

'How're ye?' the man said in a friendly voice.

'Couldn't be better sir and how is yourself.' Mattie replied.

'Grand, grand thank God,' he said taking a pipe from the torn pocket of his jacket.

He took a few sucks from the pipe and spat before talking again, 'and who are ye?' he asked.

'I'm Joseph and this is my poor brother Peter,' Mattie said nodding sympathetically at me and then asked, 'what's your own name sir?'

'McGinn, Micky McGinn.' The man replied cautiously looked over at me. I did not know which eye was focused on me.

He struck a match and put it to the pipe and sucked. Smoke hung around him and then rose as he blew out the match and flicked it into the river.

'Ye're not from these parts are ye?' he said before putting the pipe back in his mouth.

'God no, we're from Manchester, we're Stephen and Agnes's nephews,' Mattie said in a convincing tone.

I glared at Mattie and my jaw straightened a little but I wrenched it sideways again. Then I realised that I had both my eyes open. I closed one eye again and wondered if it was the same one as before. I wasn't too sure so I closed the other one and switched back again.

'What's wrong with your brother?' Micky McGinn asked pointing his pipe at me. 'Deaf and dumb, Sir,' Mattie replied devoutly looking heavenward.

'God bless the mark,' he responded resting his elbow on one arm as he gently sucked his pipe.

I slowly opened the eye I had been keeping closed as my jaw straightened slightly again. I looked over at Mattie.

'People give him money for luck,' Mattie spurted out as if he'd sprung his trap. 'Be God is that a fact?' Micky McGinn said looking concerned removing the pipe from his mouth.

'Some people give two and six for a little luck and some give a lot more for a lot of luck.' Mattie pushed on with his now evident plan.

Micky McGinn's jaw began moving back and over. He said nothing putting his pipe back in his pocket and leaving his hand there.

'How much would you be thinking of giving?' Mattie enquired moving into the shallow river.

'Be God now I'd be thinking of giving very big,' he replied nodding his head.

Mattie increased his pace stepping onto rocks that barley cleared the gently flowing water.

There was a big gap before the next rock which made Mattie stop and steady himself.

'How big is "very big" Mister McGinn?' Mattie asked readying himself for a leap onto the next rock where the water looked deeper.

'Tell me how long has your brother been deaf and dumb?'

'Since birth, since birth,' Mattie snapped, anxious for closure on his plan.

'Be God then I witnessed a miracle here today,' Mister McGinn said as Mattie landed on his intended target.

'What miracle?' Mattie asked wobbling getting his balance on landing.

'You asked me how big I was going to give, well I'm going to

85

give you the biggest boot in the arse you ever got,' he said moving nearer the bank, and continued to spurt out, 'I'm watching you two for the last while, and not just today, and the shouts and screams out of that buckeen,' he pointed at me, 'would deafen the Lord.'

Mattie had just got his balance but then in one sweeping movement did an about-turn and leaped back ballerina style from rock to rock. He bypassed the last few remaining stepping stones and splashed through the shallow water to the safety of the shore.

'And what's more if get that machine you used to shoot stones at my animals with, I'll stuff it up along with my boot,' was left ringing in our ears as we vacated the river bank heading back up the field.

CHAPTER 8

Free Baba

I DON'T KNOW HOW TOWBAR and you got away with a stupid trick like that,' I said coyly.

'We got a shilling from a "Boghopper" coming out of Grady's Pub, he was mad drunk,' Mattie muttered.

'Maybe if that "Boghopper" McGinn had been mad drunk too, we might have got away with it,' I said trying to pacify Mattie.

'Shut up,' he snarled through grinding teeth.

I stayed a few paces behind him as we continued back through the fields. A few hens and chickens were taking shelter under the hedge near the barn until Mattie kicked a stone at them and they squawked scattering. A horse neighed from the back of the barn but I couldn't see it.

'Ah shut up you too,' Mattie shouted in its direction.

He gave a short chase after a rooster who accepted Mattie's challenge with raised wings and ruffled feathers. Mattie lost his nerve and ran at a couple of ducks instead as we crossed the yard. It started to drizzle rain again. I could see Uncle Frank peeping out at us through the kitchen window.

'And where did ye go?' my uncle called as we entered the hallway.

'Not too far,' Mattie answered entering the kitchen.

I followed him in.

'We wont get verra much more work done with the hay today with that blooda rain,' Uncle Frank said looking through the window again.

'You better unbridle that horse so,' Granny called from the scullery.

'I think you're right mother, I'll open the pen gate and gather up a lock of sheep so,' Uncle Frank said with a frown and then asked, 'was it ye I saw talking to Micky McGinn abroad at the river?'

I let Mattie answer.

'It was him all right, a lovely man,' Mattie replied taking the vacant seat at the fire.

'Had he any news?' Granny asked putting a pot on the stove.

I sat on a kitchen chair and when I realised that it was the one that Sadie-Tom had been sitting on I moved to the next one.

'Not a lot,' Mattie answered pressing back into the armchair and then sat up as he spoke again, 'oh he said that he caught a few buckeens throwing stones at his cows and sheep.'

Uncle Frank looked a bit startled and then asked, 'did he know who they were?'

'I can't remember the names but he said that they were Agnes and Stephen's nephews from Manchester,' Mattie replied with a frown.

I did remember the false names that Mattie had given to Mister McGinn and I knew that Mattie was getting us into a tangled mess so I said nothing. Granny put her head back from the scullery.

'Agnes and Stephen's nephews?' she repeated looking puzzled, 'it's a wonder Agnes never said they had visitors coming when I was talking to her last Sunday at the shop.'

Mattie's red herring was obvious to me when he asked, 'where is the shop?'

Uncle Frank replied unaware of Mattie's ploy, 'it's a couple a miles back the road, beside the church,' and then added as he lit up a cigarette, 'ye would have passed it on the way here yesterday.' I stared at him because I didn't know that he smoked.

'A couple of miles,' Mattie said looking horrified, 'let me know when you're going again and I'll get a lift with you in the car.'

'A seat, in the car, going to the shop is it, do you know the cost of petrol?' Uncle Frank spluttered out between bouts of a chesty cough, 'there's a few ways of going to the shop, you can go by horse and trap, by ass and cart, by bicycle, or like most do; walk it,' Uncle Frank informed wiping a tear from the side of his eye.

Granny smiled coming into the kitchen from the scullery, 'sure we get anything we need from the shop coming from Mass on Sunday and then we have the Travelling Shop, Pat Tobin calls regular every two weeks, so we're not too badly off,' she concluded with a breathy whistling tune before going back to the scullery.

Uncle Frank leaned on the table and looked through the window once more before speaking, 'Right so, I'll unhitch the horse and put things away,' and then turned and looked at each of us in turn, 'don't leave the house 'til I get back, we'll bring down a few sheep for shearing and dipping tomorrow,' he said leaving the kitchen.

Mattie got up from the chair and was heading for the door when I pointed to his catapult on the chair cushion. It must have come up from his trouser belt with all his wriggling and moving on the chair. He grabbed it and had shoved it up his jumper just in time before Granny had returned from the scullery. I followed him into the bedroom.

'Work, work, work, that's all you hear around here,' Mattie said hiding his catapult under the mattress again.

I got my suitcase from the top of the wardrobe and opened it on the bed. I pulled out a few comics I had put in the pocket of the suitcase and rummaged around the bottom until I found the ball-bearing. It was still wrapped in the piece of wallpaper that once was part of my schoolbook cover. I turned my back on Mattie as I unravelled it. He took immediate interest and moved in front of me. He picked up the comics, took a quick look at them and threw back on the bed.

'What have you there?' he asked curiously.

I smiled as I held up the big bright ball-bearing that Vinny had given me. Mattie held out his hand demandingly.

'Give,' he said.

I placed it in the palm of his hand. He sat back on the bed and fondled the bright silvery ball-bearing between his fingers as he spoke with glee, 'A definite Cougar killer.'

'That's what I was thinking,' I said.

It was great to be able to agree with Mattie on some thing. I took up the comics and picked out a Roy Rogers one and was putting the rest back in the pocket of the suitcase when Mattie raised his hand suddenly.

'Leave them there,' he snapped at me.

I pulled away from him and told him that they were comics Sparks had given me for a loan on my holidays.

'I'm on my holidays too,' Mattie protested.

'Yes but Sparks said that you were not to get them because he knows about you pulling out the last few pages when you read them,' I reminded him.

'No I don't,' Mattie said giggling and reached for the comics again.

We started wrestling on the bed until my suitcase fell on the floor with a thud. Then the ball-bearing banged on the floor and seemed to roll forever until it came to rest at the foot of the wardrobe. We stopped and waited for any response from the kitchen—nothing—then Mattie jumped from the bed and gave my suitcase a kick walking towards the window.

'It's too hot in here,' he said pushing the window up.

The window stopped quarter way. He moved the statue of the Virgin Mary to one side. He tried pushing the window back down a few times and then back up again.

'Jammed,' Mattie puffed stating the obvious. Mattie is not very lucky with windows or blinds or most things really.

He took a few steps back from the window and froze. His mouth quivered as he pointed out the window.

He spoke before moving again but I didn't know what he said, 'Ah-th-cata…quick,' he muttered.

I moved in trepidation towards the window and looked out. Between the wide spaces of a shirt, our underwear and a pillowcase flapping on the clothesline I was staring out at the monstrous wildcat with the Bounty on his head.

It looked even more like a Cougar now than it did before as it stretched itself and clawed its long nails deep into the bark of the sally tree in the hedgerow about ten yards from our window. I turned slowly and saw Mattie coming from his side of the bed with his catapult and picking up the ball-bearing from the floor. He was tiptoeing in my direction loading the catapult. He eased me out of his way and crouched down taking aim. The intended target was now hunkered down and it appeared to be dozing. There was plenty of room between our underwear and the pillowcase on the clothesline but I wasn't too sure about the window space opening.

My premonitions were scaring me. Was Mattie going to break the window pane, the Virgin Mary statue, or worse still, would the ball-bearing bounce of the window frame and hit one of us? I was wrong on all three counts. The twang of the released catapult was quickly followed by the sound of a muffled thump outside. A puff of dust rose from the furry neck of the startled wildcat. It sprang to its feet, gave a twinge and stared in our direction. I turned and checked my intended escape route. Yes the bedroom door was still open. I looked back out the window. The wildcat sneezed before it slipped into the hedgerow and disappeared.

Mattie was standing silently with his jaw dropped and catapult by his side. I nudged him.

'Did you see that?' I asked.

Mattie looked aghast as he shook his head and spoke softly, 'We're going to need bigger and better ammo than an oul' steel ball-bearing, it just bounced of that wild yoke,' Mattie exclaimed finishing with a yelp.

I made an effort to close the window but it was still jammed. 'That Cougar could get in the window to night and eat us up,' I cautioned Mattie.

'Don't be such of a 'scardycat,' Mattie jibed from the far side of the bed replacing his catapult.

'All right lads, let's head for the hill,' Uncle Frank called from the kitchen.

I was happy to hear him talking like a cowboy. I popped my suitcase back on top of the wardrobe before joining Mattie in the kitchen.

'Are we right?' My uncle said getting up from the armchair. I didn't know if Mattie had said anything about shooting out through the window at the wildcat with his catapult so I said nothing.

As we were going across the yard towards the lane I could see the goose poking its head into the grassy dyke further up the lane. The goslings were merrily splashing and foraging in the drain beside her. I got on the other side of Uncle Frank.

As we got closer Mattie shouted, 'look,' pointing to the goose that was trying to lift a shiny lid top with its bill.

I was glad it was doing that and not chasing me.

'I think there's a bit of a Magpie about that oul' goose, it's always mooching around looking for shiny things,' Uncle Frank said as he slapped the side of his leg with his stick and gave a short whistle. The two dogs galloped up beside him.

'Shouldn't there be a gander with that goose?' Mattie asked and then went on to give an explanation for his question, passing the goose who was still contending with the lid top, 'My friend Towbar, well his granny has a goose and a gander.

'So had we up to a few weeks ago,' Uncle Frank interrupted quickly, 'I found the gander dead at the back of the house, I thought at first that maybe the fox killed it but I don't think so now,' he took a deep breath, 'there's a blooda wild yoke knocking around these parts, some say it's a baby lion and the local papers call it, "The Doiredrum Bobcat"' He gave a short chuckle and continued, 'and I'd swear it was him that killed the gander because it was only half eaten and left there; the fox would have taken it away; I don't know.' He finished with a sigh opening and closing the gate behind us.

Mattie looked at me and pressed his finger to his lips in such a manner that I knew he demanded my instant silence.

Mattie spoke casually as we crossed the road and began our hill climb, 'I suppose this wild yoke, eh the Bobcat, would be worth a few bob to you dead?'

Uncle Frank gave a loud laugh before speaking, 'Are you going to do something that the best of men in this parish have being trying to do for the past two years?'

'I will for money,' Mattie said with wide pleading eyes.

'Where did it come from?' I asked.

My Uncle scratched his head and took a deep breath, 'Well it only appeared in these parts around the same time as that blooda Dutchman arrived here. I put a bit of chat on Shane Freeman, he's the local Sergeant, and he told me that all they know about this Dutchman is what's on his Canadian passport, would you believe that, a man claiming to be a Dutchman, has a sort of a foreign or English accent and produces a Canadian Passport.' Uncle Frank gave a little chuckle. 'He claims to be Irish as well, when he has a few pints on him, but that's another story,' my uncle cleared his throat and continued.

'According to the Sergeant he worked his passage on a cargo ship from Canada to Ireland, he's an "Art Expert," whatever that is,' my uncle shrugged his shoulders, 'the Guards thinks that he probably brought the wildcat with him from Canada, according to the Sergeant these yokes are called "Bobcats" in Canada, anyways it looks like it escaped on him, but he denied knowing anything about it when the Guards questioned him,' he finished with a gentle warning, 'keep well away from it, it's a vicious yoke,' and then shouted 'heel' at his straying whining dogs.

As we reached the top of the first hill I looked back and had an idea why the dogs were restless. I could see two donkeys slowly strolling up the road. They were passing a house beside an incline on the road near Granny's house. Shep and Toss looked to their master for a command but Uncle Frank had more pressing work for them to do.

'Why don't the donkeys stop at that house with the big metal gates?' I asked pointing to the house on the bend.

Mattie stopped and looked behind him.

'Because they know they can't kick in big metal gates, that's why, cute ould buggers' Uncle Frank answered glancing behind him too.

'Who lives there?' I enquired casually.

'That was doctor Galligan's house, God be good to him, he died last year,' he blessed himself and continued, '*Teach an Dochtúra*, as he named it. Ah, he loved the Gaelic and his traditional Irish music, great man to knock a tune out of "the box."'

I knew that 'the box' was a musician's term for an Accordion because Mammy plays it for our visitors sometimes when they pressurise her with words like, 'Ah come on Tessie give us an ould tune on the box.'

'No, no, those asses are cute oul yokes, they know they can't get into the doctor's place,' Uncle Frank continued and then he pointed his finger at me, 'they are after my hay, ever since they got into my meadow last year, they tried kicking in my gate again not long ago, and would have done so only for the dogs,' he said with a shake of the head.

'Kicking in your gate?' I exclaimed.

'Yes, kicking my gate and that's not all they've kicked, last week they kicked the side of Pat Tobin's van. Pats' our "Travelling Shop" man,' he explained and added, 'and they have also kicked at Dan McShane on his bike, he's our postman—buckled the front wheel, they're the greatest nuisances of yokes ever.'

'Does anyone at all live in the doctor's house now?' Mattie enquired catching up with us.

'Nobody now, his only son Bernard came home from America a few months ago, cleaned out the surgery, sold off the lovely stallion,' he continued with his story after he jumped over a small bog-hole.

Mattie jumped over it too, splattering Uncle Frank's trousers as he landed on the soft wet edge of the bog hole. Uncle Frank gave a disapproving look at Mattie before speaking again.

'Bernard the son dumped and burned a lot of stuff, said he would be back again near Christmas time and auction off what's left and sell the house,' he stopped and looked high towards the next hill and then continued walking again as he spoke.

'There are some fine antiques there that will fetch a fair oul price. Bernard asked me to go in around the house and keep an eye 'til he gets back.' He paused as he came to a very wide bog-hole, hesitated and walked around it, 'Doctor Galligan did all his housecalls in the horse and trap, you know, Lord rest him, ah! times are changing,' he finished with a long sigh.

I heard quick squelching footsteps behind me. I looked it was Mattie coming at speed towards the big wide bog-hole. His legs

94

and feet were flopping in his wellingtons. A pace or two before the bog-hole's edge he staggered to a halt, regained his balance and then went the same route around the bog-hole as my uncle and I.

'They're some powerful looking spikes on those wroth iron gates at that doctor's house, massive spikes on them, massive,' Mattie drooled catching up on us again.

'God bless your eyesight, but I don't know why he bothered because those gates were never locked,' Uncle Frank said taking a quick glance back.

'What did the doctor call his house again?' I asked stumbling on a sod of turf.

'It hasn't changed since the last time I said it,' Uncle Frank replied shaking his stick jovially and continued, 'do you not learn Irish at school? *Teach an Dochtúra, Teach an Dochtúra,* The Doctor's House,' Uncle Frank repeated and translated, starting up the second hill where a scattered flock of sheep were in sight.

'You don't have a name on Granny's house, would you like me to give it one?' I asked excitedly looking into my uncle's face.

'And what name would you be thinking of giving it?'

'How about Granny's House,' I suggested.

'You know Finn you have great imagination,' my uncle said looking away and whistling for the dogs.

I heard Mattie sniggering. He was probably jealous that I thought of the name first. Then I thought of a great idea and kept it to myself; I will make a sign for Granny's house and I will write it in Irish, just like that doctor did.

Uncle Frank shouted furiously at the dogs in the beginning, when they had misunderstood his directions to roundup the sheep on the hills. After a few more bellowing roars, the dogs began to obey his commands, which he backed up with his own movements, simulating the direction that he wanted his dogs to go in.

'That I'll be enough to keep us going tomorrow,' my uncle said as we formed a line behind thirty or so sheep and headed back down the hill.

The drizzly rain had stopped completely as we got nearer base. I saw the two donkeys trotting back the road. They were nearing the doctor's house. I had forgotten the name of the doctor's house in Irish so I asked Uncle Frank again but he didn't answer me and just told me to go ahead of the sheep and open the gate at the top of the lane.

The sheep hesitated when they saw me standing at the open gate. I stepped out a little and beckoned them to come through. When I waved my hand furiously and pointed to the yard they stopped all together.

'Get out of the way cannot ya, ya *ceolan*,' I heard my uncle shout.

He gave a short whistle and the dogs swung left and right at the back of the confused sheep. At first only two sheep sped past me but then the rest tried to squeeze in the gate at the one time. There was a stampede coming towards me and it was too late to run to the side.

I thought of what Roy Rogers had done when a herd of buffalo charged at him; he jumped on the first one and grabbed it by the horn and stayed on until the stampede had run its course. After the film Sparks said that in reality it was impossible to do such a thing due to the law of "opposite forces meeting." Vinny and I disagreed even though we didn't know in theory what Sparks was talking about.

I was now convinced that Sparks was right. I got spun around with the first wave of sheep but then the rest just parted and thundered past me down the lane to the yard. The sheep looked bewildered as they bunched in the yard. Before we got to the bottom of the lane Uncle Frank gave a sharp whistle and the command word "Pen" to the dogs.

The dogs zigzagged and yelped at the sheep until both dogs and sheep flowed from the yard around the back of the Old House. When we arrived there, all my uncle had to do was close the gate on the penned sheep. The panting dogs looked at their master for an expected further command, which came immediately. 'Way off wide well down before them,' my uncle roared moving to the gate at the end of the yard. It was obviously a routine for the dogs at that part of the day, as Uncle Frank issued no further command until the dogs started rounding up cows in a field by the river.

I watched with keen interest the single line of cows passively walking in front of the dogs all making their way through gaps in fences towards the farmyard. 'What's happening now?' I asked.

'It's milking time,' my uncle said, opening the gate he had been resting on as the cows entered the bottom of the last field before the yard. 'Now follow me to the byre and the cows will join us in no time,' he said with a hint of pride in the work unfolding.

'Milking time,' Mattie exclaimed with a cringed face as he moved in the opposite direction to Uncle Frank and me.

Uncle Frank went to the corner of the byre and pulled out an armful of hay from a hay-pile there. He told me to stretch out my arms as he loaded me with the dry dusty hay. He got some more and began dropping it in front of stalls in the byre. I saw my uncle smiling as I followed suit.

'You might take up farming yourself yet,' he said broadening his smile.

'If I can't get a job as a Stuntman I wouldn't mind being a farmer,' I replied dropping the last of my hay in the end stall.

'Sthuntman, and what does he do?' Uncle Frank frowned.

He had to be joking so I just smiled at him as the cows strolled into the byre where they each occupied a stall.

The byre filled with a crunching noise as the cows to be milked munched the hay in front of them. Shep and Toss disappeared from the byre door as soon as Uncle Frank put a tattered rope around the neck of the first cow and tied it to the side of the stall. My uncle lifted a bucket from near the door. He plonked a stool at the rear side of the cow and began spraying fresh milk into the bucket. He milked exactly the same way as Stephen. I'd seen it all before so I left.

When I went into the yard I saw Mattie rushing across the yard holding a few rocks tightly to his chest. He went to the same drainpipe that the goslings had run into yesterday. I saw him dropping the rocks at the end of the drainpipe and pushing them with his foot. He rubbed his hands together and then wiped them in his jumper. As I passed by I could see more rocks and stones at the other end of the drainpipe.

'You're going to cause a flood,' I said heading for the house.

'Is that a fact,' he muttered and stuck his tongue out at me.

I was just going in the door when Mattie roared.

'Quick Finn look, one of the sheep has escaped from the pen,' he was pointing around the side of the house.

When I looked around the corner I saw what Mattie was referred to, contentedly grazing along the hedgerow of the embankment at the rear of the house.

Mattie came up beside me and dragged me towards it saying, 'You grab the sheep's horns and I'll grab it by the wool.'

I don't know how Mattie is going to do his part because its off-white coat looked patchy and loose.

It had its back turned to us as we approached but then it looked around at us and stared momentarily. Mattie and I stopped and it went back grazing. We both tiptoed as Mattie pushed me in front of him until we were directly behind the feeding animal. I was wondering if maybe we should get a lasso instead, when Mattie gave me a hard push from behind and sent me head first over the top of it. I grabbed its long thin horns as I landed.

Our intended 'prisoner' bent down and shook its head violently. I tumbled to the side but still held onto the horns for fear of being thrown to the ground and stamped on.

Mattie was now standing in front of me shouting 'that's it Finn, bring the sheep down, bring it down.'

I screamed at Mattie for help but he just kept running around after me and the animal, as we stumbled around in circles. All of a sudden it stopped bucking and I fell to my knees panting beside it but still holding on to the horns.

'Good sheep, good sheep,' Mattie said coming closer with his hand held out. Mattie coyly got a grip of the horns, just slightly below where I was holding them. It shook its head slightly and Mattie let go and jumped back.

I gradually stood up and was about to let go when the hitherto disgruntled animal, suddenly bleated and licked its nose. I laughed. Mattie smiled coming back towards us.

'See I told you there was no danger,' he said reaching and gently grabbing the horns again.

I didn't remember him saying anything about 'danger' in the first place but I was happy now that there wasn't any. The two of us led the subdued animal down the embankment and onto the yard. It stopped and moved when it pleased and all we had to do was steer it towards the sheep-pen at the back of the barn.

We were just passing the front of the house when Granny came around from the side carrying a basin and calling out, 'Chuck, chuck, chuck, chucky.' She took a handful of mashed up food from the basin and scattered it on the ground in front of her as she walked. Hens, chickens and ducks seemed to come from everywhere as they pecked and bumped of one another jostling for the best position to be first to get the tumbling food.

As she moved around in a circle dispensing the food she stopped and looked at us leading our capture across the yard.

'What are you two doing?' she frowned calling over at us.

'This sheep escaped from the pen and I ran after it and caught it,' Mattie called back as he let go one of the horns and wiped his brow.

I cringed as I looked at Mattie but was glad that I didn't contradict his version of the story just then. Granny shook her head as she spoke.

'Will you let Baba go, he's not for dipping or shearing, that's a pet goat we keep, let it go you pair of gooseens,' Granny finished with a smile and then with a frown looked around the yard and asked solemnly, 'talking of gooseens, did any of you see the goose and goslings?' Granny's breathing was intermittent and wheezy.

I looked at Mattie and let go of Baba. Mattie made an innocent gesture with his hands as Baba rambled over beside Granny. The goat made threatening movements with its horns at the unconcerned feeding fowl.

Granny upended the basin and emptied the remaining food particles onto the ground and then patted her pet goat as she spoke, 'Where on earth could the goose and goslings be?'

'They were up the lane when we were going for the sheep,' I said pointing.

'Will ye take a look so, I have a few more potatoes left over from the diner, I'll make up more feed for them,' Granny said heading back for the house.

'Mattie, what did you do with them?' I asked when Granny had gone out of earshot.

'I might just have an idea where the goslings are but there was no sight of that goose when I was…' Mattie finished abruptly.

'When you were what?' I pressed.

'You go and look for the goose and I'll see if I can find the goslings,' Mattie ordered walking towards the drainpipe I had seen him blocking earlier.

I was walking towards the house and then I stopped and looked back. Mattie was standing still and apprehensively looking after me.

'Go on and start looking,' he shouted at me.

I went behind the house and stayed there for a second or two before peeping out. Mattie was walking again and took a few more looks behind him but he didn't see me. He went to one end of the drainpipe and started pulling away the small rocks and stones from it. Then he went to the other end and did the same. He bent down and shouted 'sca' a few times. Within seconds yellow fledglings waddled out flapping their murky wings before running across the yard. I came back around from the side of the house and watched.

The goslings stopped near the centre of the yard and gathered in a tight group gawking aimlessly around them. The rooster that had challenged Mattie earlier flew from its perch on the gate pillar and scattered them landing in their midst. Mattie walked past the rooster but when it flapped its wings he gave a quick jump and increased his step going towards the house.

'I found them, I found them,' Mattie bellowed outside the kitchen window.

'Good boy Mattie,' Granny said opening out the window, 'and where were they?'

'There's no sign of the goose though,' Mattie quickly evaded giving an answer.

'No sign of the goose, well that's strange,' Granny concluded pulling back from the window.

'Will I feed the poor little cratereens for you?' Mattie offered moving nearer the window.

I moved up beside Mattie.

'Well that will be great for me, I can take in the washing, and do a bit of ironing, there's no drying outside in this weather,' I heard Granny say from the kitchen. Then Granny put her head out the window again and said, 'come on in the back door Mattie, I'll make up some feed for those goslings.'

I was furious with Mattie getting praised by Granny after what he had done.

'I know what you did,' I said keeping a few paces behind him, 'you blocked one end of the drainpipe and chased the goslings into it and then blocked the other end so they couldn't get out, didn't you?' I waited for a response. Mattie turned and wriggled his finger at me.

'You stop spying on me if you know what's good for you,' he threatened.

I didn't see him doing it but I had guessed right.

'And what did you do with the goose?' I asked keeping further back from him.

He stopped and turned as he spoke, 'I don't know anything about that blooda goose.' I looked suspiciously at him like the detectives do in the gangster films.

'You don't think I'd try to get a big fat goose like that up that skinny drainpipe, do you?' he said walking off in front of me.

CHAPTER 9

Rodeo in the Dyke

WHEN WE GOT TO THE BACK of the house Mattie jumped and grabbed at a vacant part of the wire clothesline near the scullery door. The long thin poles at either end of the clothesline bowed to each other. When Mattie let go of the clothesline it quivered as the rain soaked shirts, pillowcases and socks dangled and danced clinging to the weather-eroded clothes pegs. One white shirt was now just barely hanging by the sleeve end.

Mattie twisted the door handle and we stepped into the scullery.

'Any sign of the goose?' Granny asked mulching lumpy bits of potatoes and meal in a basin.

I recognised the Indian meal from the time we were in Stephen's. I wondered if Granny did deals with the Indians too.

'I could only find the little goslings, Finn couldn't find the goose,' he boasted taking the basin of feed from Granny.

'And did ye try over at the bottom of the lane, sometimes she rests there on the step down to the well?' Granny quizzed.

'I looked everywhere,' Mattie lied and nodded to me to open the door. When I did he pushed me aside but I followed.

When we reached the yard the poultry that had been there earlier gathered again but this time around Mattie. They were gaggling and chirping seeking advantageous positions for second helpings. He scattered small handfuls of food all around at first but then he placed the basin on the ground and took two handfuls of the feed from it.

He pressed the feed together in his hands and made a sort of a pie the size of a snowball. He stood up, aimed and threw it hard at the rooster now pecking below him in the basin.

'Got ya,' Mattie yelled as the potato feathered rooster jumped and flew up in the air and back to its perch on the gate pier. Mattie emptied the remainder of feed in a heap on the ground. He threw the empty basin high in the air and when he went to catch it coming down a gust of wind took it and it landed in the hedge.

I tried hushing the other fowl away so that the goslings could have all the food but it was in vain as all feasted on the second course. Mattie was reaching into the hedge to retrieve the basin when Granny came from the side of the house with her arms raised shouting, 'Frank, Frank, get Frank, quick get Frank!' She looked very upset and was ringing her hands in her apron. Mattie and I ran to the byre.

'There's something wrong with Granny,' we both shouted in an attempt to convey granny's request.

The cow Uncle Frank was milking backed sideways into the side of the stall and pulled on its tether as my uncle leaped up from the milking stool and gasped, 'what's wrong with mother?'

'We don't know but it sure doesn't sound good,' Mattie spurted out as we both looked to him for instructions.

He clanged the milk bucket on the floor at the end of the stall and brushed us aside going out the byre door. We were either side of him as he sprinted across the yard. 'Mother are you okay?' he called seeing Granny at the centre of the yard.

'I'm okay, it's the goose, I think it's dead,' she said turning back towards the house.

'Sod the bloody goose, I thought there was something wrong with you,' he said giving a perturbed look at Mattie and me. He exhaled deeply stepping behind his mother as he looked heavenward.

Granny led the way and we followed three abreast behind her. She pushed through a pillowcase hanging on the clothesline and stepped up on the green embankment between the back yard and the hedgerow.

Granny began to slow her pace as she pointed and spoke, 'I went over there to get a shirt that had blown off the line and then I thought I saw a pillowcase there by that sally tree but it wasn't a…a…pillowcase.' She stopped and nodded towards the white fluffy object beyond the sally tree and spoke through open fingers raised to her mouth, 'It's, it's…the goose.' Granny was finding it difficult to catch her breath.

Frank put his hand on her shoulder as he passed her. Mattie and I followed him but now we were a step or two behind.

'It's dead all right,' he said feeling under the goose, 'but not verra long, it's still warm' he continued as he turned the goose over.

'We better bleed it so,' Granny sighed and went back down the embankment towards the house.

The goose's eyes were glazed and its limp neck lay motionless in the grass.

'Did the wild cat kill it, the, the, The Doiredrum Bobcat?' I spluttered out taking a step closer, 'we saw it today, it…' I didn't get finishing what I was going to say as Mattie got beside me and pinched my arm.

'I don't know,' Uncle Frank said turning the goose over again, 'there doesn't appear to be any cuts or wounds on it.' He stood up and rubbed his chin as if in deep thought. Then he turned solemnly to me and asked, 'You saw what today?'

'We saw the goose,' Mattie replied sharply, 'remember when it was trying to lift the tin lid in its mouth.'

'Ah!' Uncle Frank said dismissively.

'Mattie,' Granny called from the scullery door, 'give this to Frank.' She was holding a carving knife.

Mattie ran and took it from her. 'Careful, careful,' she called after Mattie as he sped along the embankment to deliver the knife to his uncle.

'It looks like goose for dinner for the rest of the week,' Uncle

Frank said bending the goose's neck and bringing the sharp knife to the bend he had created. Mattie closed one eye and put his hand to his mouth. I realised what was about to happen and turned my head away closing my eyes tightly.

'What the blooda hell?' I heard Uncle Frank exclaim. I opened my eyes and turned. Mattie had his hands pressed to his face bending down beside Uncle Frank.

Uncle Frank was examining a large ball-bearing coated in blood. 'She chocked on a ball-bearing; but where the blooda hell did she get it?' he asked wiping his bloodied hands and ball-bearing in the grass. 'Would it have come from the mower?' Uncle Frank questioned himself quietly.

Mattie reached and took it from him and looked at it and nodded. 'From a mower I'd say all right,' Mattie said biting on his lower lip slipping the ball-bearing into his pocket. My Uncle looked at Mattie and frowned but said nothing.

My uncle grabbed the blood-dripping goose by the legs, stood up and we followed him to the back door. He flopped the goose onto a small forum just outside the door and dropped the carving knife beside it. Its slit neck dangled lifelessly to the side. Shep and Toss came as far as the corner and looked curiously in our direction. Uncle Frank let out a resounding roar at them and they turned with a whimper and with bushy tails tucked tightly between their legs they vanished from sight.

'Are ye any good at plucking and cleaning out a goose?' my Uncle Frank asked with a big grin. We both looked at him with mouths open. 'Thought as much,' my uncle shook his head, 'we'll leave it to your Granny so,' he said dipping his bloodied hands in a half barrel under a drainpipe at the corner of the house. 'Well I'm off to finish the milking,' he said shaking his hands dry. We followed him as far as the front yard but Mattie dragged me to one side and nodded in the direction of the lane.

I kept walking behind him until he stopped at the steps leading down to the spring well. He jumped from the top step to the middle one and sat down. Then he gave a commanding nod to the step below him. I brushed past him and sat on it.

'We need a wee chat,' he said throwing a handful of clay

and pebbles into the crystal clear water in the well and continued, 'now today, when I took a shot at that wild, wild bobcat thing, with my catapult and with your ball-bearing,' he patted his pocket, 'and which is now my ball-bearing,' he pointed his finger threatening at me, 'that never happened, got it?

'I don't understand why you don't want Uncle Frank to know that we just saw the bobcat,' I said, staring at Mattie as he moved to the step in front of me.

He used the heel of his wellington to kick and loosen the flagstone on the last step at the well's edge as he spoke in short intervals dictated by each kick, 'because you're a blabbermouth... and you'd only...tell about me and my catapult...taking the shot from the bedroom...that's why,' he said with a grunt as the long flat stone tumbled free and gently dipped into the crystal clear surface barely causing a ripple.

'No I'm not a blabbermouth, anyway I was only going to say that we saw the bobcat at Stephen and Agnes's house, I wasn't going to mention that you took a shot at it with your catapult through the window,' I protested, hastily going back up the steps.

'I know you, you're a blabbermouth,' he shouted after me. Then I heard a loud splash.

As I went into the byre, Uncle Frank was milking the cow in the third stall. 'Are you nearly finished Uncle Frank? I asked.

'Oh, I'll be a whileen yet,' he replied and asked without turning, 'are you enjoying your holidays so far?'

I didn't think it was a great question because we were doing a lot of farm work and no holiday stuff like we do when we are on holidays with Mammy and Daddy, like going on bumping cars, chair-a-planes, the cinema, plenty of ice cream and sweets but I decided to reply to his question anyway to put him in good form after the goose episode.

I took a deep breath and blabbered a continuous response, 'yes, we are having great fun we caught Granny's pet goat because we thought it was a sheep that had escaped from the pen and Mattie fed the chickens and when the rooster landed and was eating the food that should be for the goslings Mattie made a food pie and...' I felt a burning pain at the back of my arm. I turned. Mattie was baring his teeth as he pinched me.

Uncle Frank laughed as he spoke, 'Be God, you better not do anything to that pet goat, mother treats Baba like a baby, even when it chewed her washing on the line, and destroyed the ends of her good tablecloth,' he glanced towards us, 'all she said was that I should have higher poles, so Baba won't be able to reach, ah, it's her pet all right,' he puffed standing up moving to the next stall.

'I think we'll go and give Granny some help,' Mattie said pulling me by the jumper.

'Good boys,' Uncle Frank called after us.

When we got to the yard I was heading for the house but Mattie steered me towards the lane again.

'Let's take a squint at the doctor's house,' he said in a low voice.

Then he started giggling trying to impersonate Uncle Frank, 'Teach an Dochtúra, Teach an Dochtúra.'

'I thought you said we were going to help Granny,' I reminded him what he had just told Uncle Frank.

He stopped and looked at me before speaking, 'do you want to be putting your hand up dead goose's bum and pulling out guts and smelly stuff?'

I didn't answer him.

As we passed the path to the well I looked down and I could see a dark space in the last step where a flagstone used to be. I knew then what the splash was that I had heard after leaving the well and where the flagstone is now; at the bottom of the well. When we got to the top of the lane Mattie pulled me and wide eyed pointed furiously towards the gate.

I could just see the ears of a donkey protruding over the gate pier and as we sneaked closer. Then I could see the tail end of another donkey reversing towards the gate.

'Will we give them some hay?' I asked.

'Yes good idea, are you thinking what I'm thinking?' Mattie asked, putting his face close to mine.

I was just thinking of feeding them some hay but I knew

Mattie had other ideas so I just shrugged my shoulders and asked what he was thinking.

'You remember Frank said if we want to go to the shops we would be walking it?' Mattie said pulling me with him to the meadow fence.

I nodded and climbed the wall along with Mattie into the meadow.

'Well now we have our own transport looking at us; if we treat them right,' Mattie said pointing to the two donkeys now looking at us over the stone fence between the road and the meadow.

We each gathered a bunch of hay and scaled the stone fence onto the grass verge along the road. The two donkeys jerked their heads and moved away as we landed beside them.

'Chuckie, chuckie, chuck, chuck,' Mattie said shaking a hand-ful of hay in front of them as he moved cautiously nearer our intended transport.

'Wait a minute Mattie,' I said moving back, 'remember what Uncle Frank said about how dangerous they are?'

'Big deal, kicking a gate and a van, they don't have spikes on their feet, do they?' Mattie said dismissively edging slowly closer to the hay sniffing donkeys.

'And he kicked the postman's bike,' I added.

'He probably deserved it,' Mattie said softly putting the hay to the mouth of the smaller of the two donkeys.

Mattie doesn't like our postman at home. His name is Donald Dooley and he is sort of deaf. Mattie shouted "Donald Duck" at him one day we met him on the road but he must have heard him and unknown to us he turned his post bike and came back up behind us. Mister Dooley got off his bicycle, caught Mattie and beat him around the head with his postman's cap. 'I thought he was supposed to be deaf,' Mattie said rubbing his head as the postman cycled away.

When I saw the small donkey nibbling and then munching the hay I moved closer to the bigger donkey as it tried taking the small donkey's hay. In a short while the two donkeys had all the hay finished.

'See, they are our friends now,' Mattie said gently touching the small donkey's ear. It shivered its ear and Mattie moved back his hand.

I moved to the front side of the other donkey and patted its mane. It shook its head and I moved back. I patted it again and then gently held its mane and the donkey stood still.

'You're a born cowboy Finn,' Mattie quietly encouraged. I slid my hand down its neck to its back. It gave a quick glance back at me and then looked in front again. 'See that Finn, it's asking you to get up on its back for a quick spin,' Mattie said moving towards me.

'Who are you, Doctor Dolittle?' I chastised Mattie for taking me for a fool.

'Doctor do what?' Mattie muttered with a confused frown and then called out loud, 'look you can get up on him down there.'

He was pointing down the road to a deep wide dyke between the road embankment and the meadow wall. It seemed like a good idea because we had no stirrups to mount the donkey and if we could get the donkey into the dyke and have its back level with the road I could slide onto from there. I put my hand back on the donkey's neck and held its mane nearer the head. I walked slightly in front and gently pulled. The donkey was walking with me.

Mattie and the other donkey followed behind at the start but then they went ahead of us on the roadway as I led my donkey into the dyke.

'Hold him right there, no up a bit, that's it, now you're level,' Mattie said waving his hands in front of the donkey and me.

The donkey stopped in the dyke. Its back was nearly eye level with the roadway. I climbed up on the road and looked down on my prize capture that had now moved sideways to the meadow wall.

The donkey looked up, then bent down and started munching the wild grass at the bottom of the meadow wall.

'Now or never,' Mattie said in a half whisper pulling me towards the edge of the embankment. I raised my leg to slide on the donkey's back. I hesitated when the donkey shook its head stooped deep in the dyke. My hesitation was overruled as Mattie pushed me off balance and onto the back of the unsuspecting animal.

Its reaction was instantaneous. I could hear the thud of its violent kick against the meadow wall before its clumsy attempt to climb up the embankment. I was slipping backwards so I threw myself forward and reached in front for something stable to keep myself on. I was grabbing the donkey's ears. A shuddering shake of the head loosened my grip as we parted company. I tumbled backwards into the dyke. My head thumped onto a tuft of wild grass and I lay prostrate and breathless at the base of the meadow wall.

My shortlived mount dug deep with its curled up hooves into the side of the embankment and heaved, stretched and pulled itself onto the roadway. I looked up and could see a hazy figure looking down at me from the roadway. I heard a voice.

'Huh, you're some stuntman.' It was Mattie. 'Come on, let's take a look at this house,' I could hear him say as the hazy figure vanished from sight.

I felt pain in my head, in my neck, in my arm and shoulder and the view of the caked mud on my legs and trousers made me feel even worse. Mattie had a stone in his hand and was aiming it at a blackbird that was perched in a bush across the road when I climbed the embankment and wobbled onto the road. He fired at the bird, missed, cursed and then turned to me.

'You know what Finn, we are going to have to "break" those donkeys in like Roy Rogers does in his paddock,' he said sticking his hands in his pocket waddling up towards the bend in the road.

'Where did they go?' I asked slowly catching up with him.

'Ah you should have seen them take off, the "buck-leps" out of them was magic to watch galloping up the road,' Mattie said between raucous belly laughs.

CHAPTER 10

Alladin's Bin

WHEN WE TURNED THE BEND Mattie spread out his hands and quickened his step towards the spiked wrought iron gates. The name *Teach an Dochtúra* was engraved on the topping stone of the two gate piers.

'What sort of spear would you like Finn?' Mattie asked, running his hand along the arch shaped gates, 'long, short or medium?' he added turning with a sparkle in his eye.

'I don't know what you mean,' I said rubbing my aching head.

'Look, look,' he said grabbing the rounded wrought iron bars, 'ready made spears, definite wildcat killers.'

I wasn't really interested and my arm was beginning to hurt even more.

'Those bars are part of the gates, they're welded,' I hinted at the futility of his intensions.

'A half hour with a good hacksaw,' he chuckled, 'weld or no weld and we are in the ammunition business.'

I was too sore to argue with him so I said nothing more about his idea.

He pressed down the handle lever on the gate and pushed. The gate squeaked open. He took a few cautious steps onto the crunching gravel into the yard and I followed. I checked that the gate was still open behind us. Mattie stopped and reached back, pulled me closer and began easing me out in front. I could read *Teach an Dochtúra* on a hanging sign positioned between the grey stone pillars adorning the large varnished front door. The three steps leading up to the porch were patched with bright green moss. Tall red roses stood guard, edging the overgrown lawn like the plumage feathers on soldier's berets. We steadily and slowly moved forward until two cut stone outhouses came into view at the rear of the house.

One of the outhouses had closed doors but the other was more of an open shed. I could see the ends of two shafts resting on the turf-mould floor of the shed. Mattie moved slowly past me and looked in.

'It's a fancy cart,' he said, going as far as the shed entrance.

'It's a horse trap,' I corrected him, surveying the interior of the dimly lit shed from outside.

'That Sparks fellow is going to make a nutty professor out of you yet,' Mattie jibed me for correcting him.

The horse trap had a black leather seat with a matching studded leather back rest. The spoked wheels were varnished and had rubber rims and apart from cobwebs stretched across some parts of the framework the trap looked like new. We were becoming less fearful now on our self invited tour and we moved to the next outhouse.

The door had two sliding bolts. Mattie slipped the top bolt backwards and pulled. Only the top half the door opened just like the door on the shed where Stephen housed his calf. Mattie stretched on his tiptoes and gawked in. He quickly pulled his head back and held his nose, 'Pew! The pong!' he uttered behind his hand. I grabbed the top of the door and pulled myself up to take a look.

As light filled the interiors I began to realise that it was a stable. I strained my eyes to identify the things hanging on the back wall. I could make out a coil of old rope, a bridle and straddle and other things like the tackle that I saw on Uncle Frank's horse when it was harnessed to the mower. The pain in my arm became unbearable and I let go.

'Anything worth while in there?' Mattie questioned me as I landed on the ground. I told Mattie what was in the stable but he just muttered, 'rubbish, no good,' as we causally made our way towards the back of the house from the stable. Mattie quickened his step and before I reached him he had his hands cupped to the back windowpane of the house and was peering in.

I noticed a bench against the surround sidewall like the one Mammy saved up to buy for our back yard at home. I wondered how Mammy was and was she missing me. If Mammy was here now she would be able to put my sore arm in a sling like the time she did when I fell off an apple tree one day Sparks and Vinny and me were out the country 'progging' apples from an orchard. Mammy made the sling out of two flashy multicoloured ties she had got in a parcel from America. I took the sling off before my arm was fully better because Sparks and Vinny were laughing at it and doing a mock war dance around me chanting 'How Big Chief Rainbow.'

'Same rubbish like every other house,' Mattie said moving away from the window and rounding the corner.

A part of the house jutted out there and it looked like it was a new extension to the existing old-fashioned house. I could make out the writing on a plastic sign tilted inside the frosted glass window of the extension. It read SURGERY. I heard clanging sounds behind me.

It was Mattie throwing stones and hitting a barrel situated in the corner near the bench. He threw three more stones but he only hit the barrel once more.

'Why are there holes in that barrel and why is it black burnt around the top?' I asked.

'Roy Rogers probably uses it for target practice,' Mattie said giggling and then stopped suddenly and pointed his finger at me before racing over to the barrel, 'Finn I didn't think I'd ever say this but you're a genius,' he called out as he ran.

I slowly followed. He rocked the barrel back and forth a few times and spoke with a tremor in his voice.

'This is a fire dump barrel, and you know what that means,' he grunted pushing against the barrel until it tumbled, 'that means not all the stuff that you want to burn gets burned, Towbar told me that,' he said with glee upending the barrel into a cloud of ash. Mattie wrapped his outstretched arms around the bottom end of the barrel as best he could and dragged and rocked it in front of his reversing movement until assorted scorched items puked from the blackened barrel mouth. 'And how right Towbar was,' Mattie said staring at his booty.

Some of the burned items were fused together and unidentifiable but some small boxes, packages and assorted bottles had only been scorched by the fire. Mattie knelt down beside the burnt debris and poked through the best of the remaining items. He picked up, identified and sorted his array muttering, 'tablet's no good but hold onto, medicine no good but keep it, bandages maybe, oh brilliant a very large injection needle, cough bottle don't need it, more pills okay, castor oil yuk,' he aimlessly threw the cod liver oil bottle over my head and it bounced onto the soft unkept lawn.

I got tired bending down watching him arranging and rearranging his selection so I sat on the verge of the lawn near the discarded castor oil bottle with my feet on the gravel. He stuffed the bottom of his jumper inside his belt and began dropping the smaller items inside the V of his jumper. He reconstructed a crunched cardboard box and filled that with the rest of his find.

'What do you want that rubbish for?' I asked as I yawned.

'Never mind, remember what Towbar said—never pass a bin or a dump without checking it out, now you take the box.

'No,' I said emphatically and then coyly added, 'my arm is sore, I want to go back to Granny.'

'Just wait a minute will ya,' he ordered struggling to his feet.

'You can't bring that back to Granny's,' I cautioned him.

'Who said I was?' he said crunching past me on the gravel.

I watched him rest the box on top of the wall beside the bench. He stood on the seat part of the bench, then onto the back rest and from there was able to straddle the wall without crunching the contents inside his jumper. He eased himself down the far side of the wall and then he vanished.

'Fecking nettles,' I heard him cursing and then the box on the wall vanished with a quick swoop of his hands.

I studied the back door of the house. It looked bleak compared to the front door and the green paint was cracked and chipping revealing bare weather beaten timber that had rotted in places. I was thinking that if Daddy was here he would sandpaper and fix it and paint it lovely, when sudenly Mattie grabbed my sore arm and plonking himself down beside me on the back lawn.

What are you going to do with the stuff?' I asked rubbing my arm.

'What am I going to do with it, none of your business, is it, you didn't help me did you, so it's all mine isn't it,' Mattie spurted out creating trenches in the gravel with the heels of his wellingtons.

I didn't bother answering his rambling questions so I just said, 'let's go.'

'No, not yet we have to make plans for tomorrow,' he began by fingering his index finger. 'Now the first thing is...' is all I paid attention to.

I started wondering if Sparks and Vinny saw any new Cowboy and Indian film or War ones. I was thinking of the last great Roy Rogers film we saw when all of a sudden I felt hot air gently blowing on my hair. I rubbed my head and heard a gentle snort. Mattie stopped talking and I glanced at him. He was wide eyed staring at something behind me on the lawn. I slowly began turning around. Mattie used my shoulder as a launching pad as he sprang across the gravel yard leaving deep footprints in his wake.

As I completed my turn I first focused on a castor oil bottle then one hoof and then another came into my view about two feet away in the deep lawn grass. I don't think that I was breathing as I forced my eyes upwards from the turned up hoofs to the grey and white hairy legs. I could feel the blast of hot breath again, this time on my neck.

Mattie leaped onto the bench and would have cleared the wall with his hand vault only for the heel of his wellington clipping the top of the wall and he tumbled over it.

I remember nothing in between the time when I stood up and when I was panting beside Mattie who was rubbing his legs and his neck and his arms and cursing nettles again. The deep pain in my shoulder was gone but the soreness in my neck and arm was still there. We slowly peeped over the wall and into the yard of Teach an Dochtúra.

One donkey was still standing where I last saw him and the other had its back to us nibbling on a multi thorned rose bush in the centre of the lawn.

'Quick, quick, corral them, corral them,' Mattie hollered leaping over bunches of nettles and scrambling through briars as he ran around the wall to the front gate.

I walked at a quick pace behind him but avoided nettles and briars. I noticed that there was a wet patch on the seat of Mattie's short pants and that the inside of his leg appeared to be wet as far as the top of his wellingtons. I yanked and pulled the back of my pants around to see if I had sat on something wet too but it was only a very small bit of dampness which I probably got from sitting on the grass.

Mattie had the front wrought iron gates closed when I arrived beside him.

'Two donkeys corralled,' he announced. I got a toilet smell. It must be the donkeys I thought to myself.

'Yes this is the one I've picked,' Mattie said caressing a long bar in the wrought iron gate.

'Picked for what?' I asked.

'Have you been listening to my plans at all?' he snarled, 'Our plans for tomorrow of course.' He put his hand on my shoulder and spoke into my face, 'I'm going to get a hacksaw and cut that spear from the gate,' he pointed, 'and all you have to do then is catch a chicken or a gosling and tie it under the tree where we saw the wild cat bobcat thing this morning, are you with me so far?'

I shook my head first of all but Mattie looked cross so then I nodded and stammered, 'yes.'

'Good,' he said and took a deep breath, ' then I climb up the sally tree and when mister wild cat comes to take the bait,' Mattie made a wild swing with his hand, 'whacko, spear through head, dead bobcat and money for Mattie.' He smiled broadly at me looking for approval.

'I don't want any part of this plan.' I gulped.

'That's the thanks I get for saving you today,' he said moving away from me.

'Saving me today, when?' I frowned.

'Only for I warned you in time, that donkey was about to start eating you hair, your head maybe, you'd be dead now only for me,' Mattie said through gritted teeth.

I decided to change the subject a little, 'What are you going to do with the donkeys anyway?

Mattie gave an impatient look and spoke, 'They're corralled aren't they, break them in of course, remember it's a long walk to the shops.'

I just gulped again and said nothing. The two donkeys raised their heads and glanced at us from the back lawn of Teach an Dochtúra and then went back to enjoying their newly found rich pastures.

Mattie pulled at the back of his trousers as we headed back for Granny's house. I got the toilet smell again. I was glad to be moving away from the donkeys. When we got to the bottom of the lane the rooster flapped its wings and danced close to us until we had passed by a hen. Mattie bent down while still walking and grabbed the back of a resting duck but it flew a short distance leaving Mattie with a fistful of feathers. A few chickens moved away as we crossed the yard and Baba stared blankly and bleated at us from the gable end of the house.

Uncle Frank was going around the side of the house with two milk buckets when he stopped and hollered at us as we approached the front door.

'Where were ye, I thought ye said that ye were going to help your Granny?' 'Those donkey's came back and we chased them away up the road nearly as far as the church.' Mattie called exaggerating breathlessness.

'Ah good boys come on in, tea's nearly ready,' he shouted in a friendlier tone going by the side of the house.

Mattie was pulling at the back of his pants again as we went entered the hallway. I got the toilet smell again and looked back out the door to see if the donkeys got out the gate and were following us. They weren't.

As we passed the kitchen I saw Granny walking towards the scullery with a blackened clothes-iron in her hand. There were some ironed clothes stacked at the end of the table. Mattie went straight into the bathroom and I heard him locking the door. I went into the bedroom and sat on the side of the bed. I decided to wait for Mattie so we could have our tea together and he could answer any awkward questions from Granny or Uncle Frank.

I heard the bathroom door unlocking and I stood up from the bed. Mattie rushed past the bedroom door and I called after him and asked if he was ready to go for his tea but he didn't answer me. By the time I got to the bedroom door Mattie was going out the front door. I saw what looked like a large white rag, that was elasticised at the top, hanging out of his bulging trouser pocket. He turned left outside the front door.

When I came out of the bathroom I couldn't hear any talking in the kitchen so I went back into the bedroom. I was just going to sit back on the bed when I heard Mattie's voice calling out, 'Chucky, chucky, chuck, chuck.' I was curious to know what he was going feeding. I put my head out the window a small bit and looked left and right. Mattie's voice appeared to be coming from the gable end of the house and he was still calling, 'Chucky, chucky, chuck, chuck,' but this time he added 'Baba' to the end. I moved the Virgin Mary statue further to one side. I stretched out a little more and I could see the back end of a goat and its tail was twirling around. Then I heard Mattie's voice in a lower tone say, 'Yum, yum, Baba.'

The next voice I heard was not Mattie's and it was coming from behind me in the bedroom. It was Granny's voice.

'What are you doing hanging out the window?' I pulled myself back in so fast that I hopped my head of the window fame. When I looked around the room I saw Granny putting some underwear and socks in our wardrobe.

'Stay away from that window in case it closes down on you, now come and have your tea,' she said leaving the room.

Then I heard her talking in the hallway.

'Good boy Mattie, your tea is ready.'

Mattie came into the room and went straight to the wardrobe.

'Don't disturb anything there,' I called at him, 'Granny is just after bringing in some ironed clothes.'

'Did she bring in any underpants?' he muttered pulling out a vest and socks.

The socks he pulled out were the wellington socks Mammy had knitted for him before we left home.

'I'm not wearing them stupid things there must be ten colours in each sock,' he protested throwing them back in the wardrobe.

'Mammy said that they are for wearing in your wellingtons.' I reminded him with glee.

Mattie was exaggerating when he said that there were ten colours in each sock because there were only about four or five different colours of wool in each sock. 'Don't worry, I have a way of getting rid of them sock yokes too,' Mattie said with a wink rushing to the bathroom with an underpants in his hand.

I had two boiled eggs for my tea. One was too soft and the other was too hard but I said nothing; at least I didn't get onions. When Mattie was asked about the red nettle rash on his arms face and legs, he calmly said that it happened when he fell chasing the donkeys through bushes and then added that 'a little hard work never killed anybody.' Granny said that, 'he was a good boy,' and I felt like getting sick.

During the tea Granny and Uncle Frank were talking about work that had to be done tomorrow. It all depended on the weather. Uncle Frank cut two chunks of bread and opened the kitchen window as he whistled. The two dogs bounced off one another racing to the tumbling bread. They gulped and swallowed at once and looked for more. Uncle Frank closed the window again.

Granny said that she would clean and pluck the goose after the Rosary this evening that she hadn't time with doing the ironing and getting the tea.

'I suppose it will be goose for dinner for the next week,' Uncle Frank said with a smile.

Granny turned and looked at him in such a way and with such an expression that he stopped smiling. Just for a split-second

I thought that it was Mammy that I was looking at. It was the same way Mammy would look at me when I had done something wrong.

Then they started talking about people I didn't know, so I started thinking about Vinny and Sparks and where they might be coming from or going to now. Mattie kept well away from the rails at the back of the chair during the Rosary. I didn't pray for an onion famine as I usually do at the 'special prayers' after the Rosary; I prayed instead that the goslings would be okay without their mother.

I thought of Mammy as I was getting into bed. I was just dropping off to sleep when Mattie pulled me on the shoulder and was staring into my face in the semi-darkness.

'Ouch, my neck is still sore,' I complained.

'So was the goose's neck when it choked on your ball-bearing and did it complain? No,' he answered his own rhetorical question and continued, 'now forget about your neck and forget about breaking in those donkeys,' he said sitting up in the bed.

I was happy to hear that but then what he had to say next made me unhappy, 'We'll tie the donkeys into that fancy cart-trap yoke and off with us to the shops.' He looked closer into my face awaiting a response.

'I'm not interested,' I said turning away.

'We'll be like cowboys on a stage coach,' he said in a low voice beside my ear.

I still wasn't that much interested.

'The Indians will come down from the mountains and chase after us but we will be too fast for them,' he whispered closer in my ear.

Maybe I might be a bit interested I thought to myself, pulling the bed cover over my head.

CHAPTER 11

Raddle and Roar

WHEN I WOKE UP THIS MORNING I was very happy that it was only a nightmare I had about me driving a stagecoach and the Indians catching up on me. Then I wasn't that happy when I realised that it wasn't all a nightmare.

'It looks like a day for dipping sheep,' Uncle Frank said forcing his foot into his second wellington as he looked out the kitchen window. His mother checked for herself and spoke softly, 'With those clouds low on the mountain I think you can forget about the hay for the morning time anyway,' Granny agreed with him as she wiped the table after breakfast.

Mattie and I followed him across the yard and around by the Old House to the sheep-pen.

'Are you going to give them a bath?' I asked looking into the rectangular concrete structure that was half full with water.

'Don't let anybody hear you calling it a "bath," it's a "dipping box",' Uncle Frank said with a grin.

'I'll chase them into it for you,' Mattie volunteered examining the walkway from the sheep-pen to the dipping box.

'Will you wait until they're sheared and the dip mixture is made first.' My uncle was smiling walking towards the back door of the Old House but then he frowned.

'Who put the wire around this?' Uncle Frank asked, untangling wire from around the bolt and the receiver on the door before sliding the bold back. I didn't answer because I didn't know. Mattie was impatiently going from one foot to the other and was looking from the bolt to Uncle Frank's face in sequence.

Uncle Frank pushed the door in and threw the wire aside. It was nearly dark inside, gloomy and smelled of dampness. Mattie was doing so much gawking all around him that he stumbled on the front wheel of a gents bicycle that was resting against a barrel and fell into a wheelbarrow beside it. The wheelbarrow had one handle completely missing and a broken support leg. The unsteady barrow capsized and Mattie tumbled with it to the grimy floor.

'Will you watch where you're going!' Uncle Frank shouted at Mattie and then grunted as he lifted up a large drum container. He slung the drum bearing the label "Young's Sheep Dip" onto his shoulder and went outside.

He eased the drum from his shoulder to the ground beside the dipping box and returned to the Old House. I followed him and kept in step with him going back inside the grim building.

'Get down off there,' Uncle Frank hollered suddenly from the doorway. I jumped in fright.

He was roaring at Mattie who had one foot on the window ledge while his other foot dangled free. He was holding onto a rafter with one hand and was shaking the handle of a scythe with the other to wriggle the long, curved blade free from between the thatch and the rafters. He leaped forward as he let go his grip and landed in a tea chest half filled with what looked liked sliced potatoes. He put his foot on the top edge of the tea chest to leap out but this only resulted in him tumbling to one side along with the tea chest spilling the contents onto the stone floor. He was rubbing his knees and cringing as he rolled away from the sliced potatoes.

My uncle was watching Mattie's actions silently and in amazement at first but then suddenly snapped.

'Gather up those shallots and put them back in the tea chest. Finn, give him a hand,' Uncle Frank ordered.

Uncle Frank went to the other window and started lifting up bundles of old magazines and dropping them on the floor. I recognised the names of two of the magazines; 'The Messenger' and 'Irelands Own.' Mammy gets them every month.

Uncle Frank was getting angry and talking to himself, 'where the blooda hell are the shears,' he muttered going on his tiptoes to look into a shelf on a lopsided dresser. He pulled out two squeaking drawers and slammed them closed again. He stared into a cabinet that had both its doors hanging off. He paused and looked behind in a frenzy in the direction of the door and quickened his step towards a window there.

'Ah-ha, I knew I'd left them on a window ledge,' he praised himself squeezing the shears to and fro to a grating rhythm and then ordered, 'out, the two of you,' pointing at the door.

He picked up a bundle of sacks by the binding cord and threw them out the door in front of him before pulling the door closed saying, 'Pick those up and bring them over to the pen.'

Mattie nodded to me so I picked them up. I struggled carrying the weighty sacks as Uncle Frank opened the gate and pulled it behind him locking himself inside the sheep-pen. He took a deep breath and rolled up the sleeves of his white shirt.

'Pull me a sack from the bundle,' Uncle Frank said squeezing the shears a few times and grabbing a sheep that was huddled amongst other fretting sheep in the corner of the pen. The rest of the sheep scattered and bunched into another corner of the pen. He upended the sheep and started cutting the fleece. He made it look as simple as Mammy peeling a well massaged orange.

When he had finished shearing the sheep he flung the fleece over the pen wall in my direction and just said, 'Sthick that in the sack.'

The sacks for the wool were at least four times the size of an ordinary potato sack. Mattie put a few fleeces into the sacks and compressed them in with his wellington. His foot came out of the sack without his wellington on two occasions and I heard him mumbling curse words .

One by one the freshly sheared sheep whitened the inside of the pen as the sacks outside filled up with white fleeces. When he had shorn the last sheep in the pen my uncle left the shears on the stone walled pen and wiped his brow. His white shirt was completely saturated with sweat.

'Will one of you go inside the Old House and bring out my tool box,' he said between short intakes of breath, and then continued as he lit a cigarette, 'it's near the cartwheel over beside the fireplace.'

Mattie was going in the door of the Old house before my uncle had finished his sentence.

I remembered seeing the cartwheel with the broken spokes at the fireplace when I was in there.

When I went in Mattie had his hands on the spokes of the cartwheel and was rolling it from side to side and calling out, 'All passengers, all passengers, this is your captain speaking, men and boys to the life boats, women and girls go overboard.'

I was picking up the toolbox near the fireplace when Mattie gave a short yelp and then started dancing on one foot and trying to reach the toe of his wellington. The cartwheel kept rolling and only stopped when it crashed into a stack of blackened cooking pots.

Mattie's voice was barley audible over the resulting clanging noise. 'That feckin thing rolled over my toe,' he cringed.

The next very audible voice was my Uncle Frank's, 'What the blooda hell are ye at? Come out of there!'

I took a quick look at the scattered pots. Mattie grabbed the toolbox from my hand and began rummaging in it. Just then I noticed a brown paper parcel under the cartwheel. I recognised it by all the string on it. It was the parcel that Mammy had sent with us from missus O'Sullivan for Granny's friend Breda Fenlon.

Granny must have put it behind the pots for safety but it wasn't very safe now with the cartwheel on top of it. I was trying to pull it from under the cartwheel when it got stuck. I chucked it harder and I heard a tearing noise. When I examined it closer in the dim light I noticed that a nail protruding from the broken cartwheel spoke had pierced the parcel and was snagged on a piece of string.

I stood on the parcel and was just about able to raise the heavy cartwheel enough to un-snag the nail from the parcel and I kicked it free from under the old cartwheel. The string had prevented the nail from tearing any further. I examined the damage and was able to squeeze and iron the ripped paper back to its near original position with my finger.

'Uu-ups,' Mattie tittered watching my repair efforts before responding to Uncle Frank's second barking command, 'get out of there.' Mattie closed the toolbox and hastily limped out the door with it.

I brought the parcel over to the window and was relieved that the tear wasn't very noticeable even in the better daylight. I was cross with myself putting the parcel back behind the pots that I had to restack. I was cross because I nearly always end up covering up for Mattie and he never does for me.

When I went outside Uncle Frank flicked a lighted cigarette butt through the gate rails and turned towards the sheep in the pen. 'Now where's that blooda sheep?' he said, going into their midst with a hacksaw in his hand.

Mattie was wide eyed staring through the gate rails. Uncle Frank suddenly reached and grabbed a sheep by the horns. He threw his leg over it and raised the hacksaw.

'Uncle Frank please don't!' I screamed.

'Don't what?' Uncle Frank called back with a frown.

Mattie was now standing on the bottom rung of the gate and looking over it. 'Please don't cut the sheep's head off, please don't,' I pleaded.

Uncle Frank held the hack saw by his side and smiled. It was the first time I had seen him smiling in a while.

'I'm not cutting the sheep's head off you *ceolan*, I'm cutting this broken bit of horn off, before the blooda sheep goes mad with maggots in its brain,' he said, sawing into the cracked horn on the sheep.

'Ah, is that all!' Mattie gasped with disappointment.

I climbed over the gate and when I got closer I asked my uncle how it got cracked.

'Probably from getting caught between rocks on the mountain or maybe from fighting with another sheep,' he said, finishing the amputation.

The cut part of the horn tumbled to the ground as maggots

crawled and rolled from inside it. I jumped back as Uncle Frank kicked it towards the end wall of the pen.

'There's a bottle of Jeyes Fluid on the window ledge where I had the shears, will you get it for me?' he said tightening his grip on the terrorised sheep.

When I was walking out of the pen I could see puffs of smoke rising from behind the pen wall and when I went out the gate Mattie was sitting on the ground with his back to the wall. He was grinning as I crossed the yard to the Old House. He held up his hand and waved at me as a trickle of cigarette smoke wafted from his hand. When I was in the Old House getting the Jeyes Fluid I noticed a roll of netting protruding from between the top of the wall and the roof rafter.

'Pull out the cork as quick as you can and give me the bottle, this yoke is getting restless,' Uncle Frank said to me as I approached. He poured a drop onto the stump of the horn, gave it a quick rub and as he eased his knees apart the sheep sprang from between his legs and back into the midst of the newly shorn sheep.

'Do you play tennis?' I asked following him to the pen gate.

'Play what?' Uncle Frank asked, stopping to ponder my question.

I heard Mattie giggling from behind the wall.

I rephrased the question. 'Are those tennis nets up near the rafters in the Old House, they're like the nets doctor Walsh has on his tennis court at home? '

'Be God but you're like your father all right, you don't miss a thing,' Uncle Frank said patting me on the head.

'What are they for?' I pressed.

'Let's just say I play a wee game with the salmons at night in the river, do you understand?' Uncle Frank said closing the pen gate behind us.

I nodded but I didn't understand.

Mattie was now standing on the sheep dip drum beside the dipping box wall.

'Get off that,' Uncle Frank called at him.

When Mattie jumped down and ran towards the stream. Uncle

Frank loosened and removed the screw cap lid on the drum. I got a smell like Jeyes Fluid. He grunted raising the container onto the top of the dipping box wall and tilted it on its side. The contents gurgled and splashed into the water in the dipping box as he rolled the drum along the top of the wall. When Uncle Frank had shaken the last drop from the drum he flung the empty container back towards the wall of the Old House.

'Right lads, it's dipping time,' he said opening the pen gate again.

Mattie ran towards us from the stream nearby where he had being building a small dam and we followed Uncle Frank into the pen.

'What happens now?' I asked.

'Just watch,' he said catching a sheep by the leg and turning it upside down.

He dropped the sheep into the dipping box and it disappeared under brown coloured water. The sheep frantically turned itself upright again and bleated tumbling up and out the opening at the far end which led to a similar type pen where the shearing had taken place.

Uncle Frank stretched his neck as he spoke, 'Just check will ye that the gate is properly close in the draining pen.' Mattie and I looked at each other and stayed where we were.

'The pen the other side,' Uncle Frank explained realising our lack of sheep dipping knowledge. The gate was properly locked so we just climbed over it and watched another sheep coming through from the dipping box.

Some of the sheep ran wild when they came out into the draining pen but others just stood at the opening and coughed and bleated. Mattie tried to push one back in again from the draining pen end but Uncle Frank roared, 'blooda ceolan,' at him and he stopped.

'What ever happened to "good boy, good boy",' Mattie muttered trying to mimic Uncle Frank as he climbed over the draining pen gate and back to the stream. I stayed at the draining pen until the last sheep arrived.

'We'll put the Raddle on them when they dry out a bit,' my

uncle called over to me from the pen as he dropped the hacksaw into the toolbox and picked up his shears.

I climbed over the gate and met him at the door of the Old House.

'What are we putting on them when they dry out?' I asked for a repeat of what my uncle had just said.

'Raddle, it's the red markings we put on them, I thought I told you that before,' he said going in the door, 'each Sheep Farmer puts the Raddle on a different part of the sheep so he will be able to know his sheep, mine are marked on the left side of the neck, do you understand?' he said pulling the door closed having left his toolbox and shears inside the Old House.

'What are you at there?' my uncle called, passing Mattie at the stream.

'I'm making a swimming pool for the goslings,' Mattie called back dropping another large rock on his self made dam.

'The goslings don't kneed a swimming pool, come on it's dinner time.' Uncle Frank responded going around the corner and heading for the house.

Mattie didn't follow until we were near the house and then he came running and passed us out shouting, 'A snake, a snake, a black snake!'

I looked at my uncle for a reaction but he just shook his head as he spoke, 'It's not a snake, it's probably an eel, they come down in the stream from the mountain lakes, but let him think it's a dangerous snake, it might keep him quiet for a while.' Uncle Frank smiled going in the scullery door.

'What's wrong with that Mattie fellow? He nearly knocked the basin of cream out of my hand.' Granny said pulling a white net from the top of a basin.

'Where did you get all the cream?' I drooled.

'Well where do think but from the milk,' she replied as she expertly skimmed cream from the top of another basin into the first basin. I stood staring at her actions and she responded to my curious look.

She spoke like the teacher as she once was, The milk is milked from the cow into the bucket, as you've seen your uncle do, some of that we use ourselves or for feeding calves, the rest goes into the basins until the cream forms on the top, we collect the cream as you see,' she pointed at the basins, 'we churn it into butter, some of which we sell and from the buttermilk left over we make bread.' She stooped and looked at me when she had finished talking.

It was that 'teacher' look. I thought for one horrible second she was going to ask me to repeat what she had just said or worse still get me to write it out.

I wanted to show that I was really interested which I wasn't really so I just asked, 'What's the nets for?'

'Keeps the flies out of the cream,' Granny replied knowingly.

I was going to tell her that Dan Joe, The Yank's brother, doesn't use nets but I asked another question instead, 'When do you put the milk in the milk bottles?'

Granny pulled the white net over the basin and walked into the kitchen without answering me.

Mattie was sitting in the fireside chair when I went into the kitchen. Uncle Frank winked at me as he took a glass jar of salt from the cupboard and he appeared to be restraining a laugh.

'Did you see the snake too?' Mattie asked anxiously

It just dawned on me in time before I answered what was amusing my uncle. 'Yes, Uncle Frank said that it's a poisonous snake.' That's a small lie I have to tell in Confessions I thought to myself going to the bathroom.

Just before I came back out I heard a voice call out, 'God bless all here!'

'You must have smelt the spuds.' I recognised Uncle Frank's voice responding. Then I heard the voice again, 'Make it a small one ma'am, it's not long since I had the oul breakfast.'

When I went into the kitchen a lanky elderly man was standing in the middle of the kitchen. He was wearing the same type of Donald Duck cap that Donald Dooley our postman wears.

'And this is Finn, Mattie's brother, Dan McShane our postman,' Uncle Frank introduced us.

'Be God but you're the spit of the father,' the postman said shaking my hand, and then asked, 'how is your mother.'

Before I could answer he gave a chuckle of a laugh and continued, 'Be God, I was mad about Tessie, a great dancer, but she went for the policeman instead.' He cleared his throat removed his cap and flipped it onto the window ledge and asked, 'Is your father still chasing after people with no lights on their bikes and decent men making a dropeen of poteen? Don't get me wrong now, he was a nice man in his own way, but to be honest I was glad to see the back of him from these parts when he was transferred.' He took a breath and then looked at Mattie and I as he added an explanation, 'You see they had to transfer your father because he married a local girl,' and then with a grin that showed yellow crooked teeth, he turned to Granny, 'and the authorities would be afraid that he would show favouritism to the in-laws.' His grin vanished as Granny dropped a dishful of potatoes hard in the centre of the table and gave the postman a stern flashing glance.

'Are we not having the goose?' Mattie asked looking at the boiled bacon and cabbage in front of him.

'You have a nice head on you for goose in the middle of the week. Sunday, please God,' Granny said giving the postman the same size dinner as the rest of us. Granny doesn't listen to people about dinner, she still gives me onions and I'm sure I heard the postman asking for a small dinner.

'Choked on a ball-bearing be God, tragic, tragic,' the postman said when Uncle Frank told him about the goose. 'Indeed I saw the self same goose trying to swallow a damn big sized white stone from the drain one day last week when I was coming down your lane, anyways.' The postman hesitated and then continued, 'You know the damndest thing, on the way here, near the doctors house, God be good to him, I heard donkeys braying.' Then Dan McShane put a full potato in his mouth and we had to wait until he chewed that before he continued with his story. Mattie didn't swallow while he waited to hear the rest from the postman.

'Anyways,' the postman continued after taking a slug of milk, 'I stood up on the bike as I peddled and looked all around but not a sign of a donkey anywhere.'

'Maybe a ghost,' Uncle Frank joked and Mattie went back to eating his dinner.

'Were ye down at the river last night?' Dan asked rescuing a piece of cabbage dribbling from his chin.

'Ah just myself and Garr went, Emmett, Maurice and Noel stayed in the pub,' Uncle Frank answered softly taking a quick look at Granny to see her reaction.

'Any luck?' the postman questioned.

'Just a few,' Uncle Frank murmured with a flippant toss of the head.

Mattie had kept his head moving back and over in sequence with the questions and answers. I knew by the way that he put down his knife and fork that he was very interested in the conversation and that he was going to ask a question but my uncle beat him to it and changed the subject. 'Have you many deliveries today Dan?' Uncle Frank enquired as the postman spiked another potato from the potato dish.

'Yarra not a lot Frank, that one there, from that nun your mother writes to in the orphanage in England,' he said nodding to the letter on the window ledge and added, 'she must be a good old age now.'

'Not much older than yourself Dan,' Granny snapped looking back from the stove and then added demurely, 'in fact Sister Bernadette is now in charge of the Orphanage in Ilford...' she hesitated and looked flustered going to the scullery as she muttered something incoherently about Baba.

'A new pension book for Stephen,' Dan continued his list of deliveries with less enthusiasm, 'a letter for Tim Herrity from his brother in Chicago, a letter from the Forestry for Tommy O'Leary, a small parcel for Breda Fenlon from her friend who works in the drapery shop above in Dublin—nylons I'd say,' he spiked the biggest of the three potatoes left in the potato dish, 'and another blooda Arts Catalogue for that blooda Dutchman— hard peddling over to that blooda mountain just for an oul catalogue,' he concluded wiping his brow.

I was amazed how he could read through the envelopes and packaging. I looked at the postman's eyes to see if he had the same sort of deep blue x-ray eyes like Superman. Dan McShane's eyes were green and a stye had begun filling on his left eyelid.

'The kettle's boiled Dan if you'd like a cup of tea,' Granny offered.

'Well just a drop in my hand so ma'am,' he said stretching his arms and yawning.

Mattie nodded at me to follow him as he left the table. 'Don't be going far you two, we have to mark the sheep and a few other jobs,' Uncle Frank called after us as we slipped out the door.

CHAPTER 12

Surface Mail

MATTIE WAS SHAKING HIS HEAD and waving his hand furiously at me to join him at the gable end of the house. By his actions I knew he had a plan and that I was going to be involved in some big way. I approached him slowly despite his impatient looks and further repeated actions.

'We have to silence those donkeys,' he said walking in a small circle.

'Why?' I asked showing no enthusiasm.

'Did you hear that long string of misery of a postman talking about hearing the donkeys bawling?'

'Braying,' I corrected,

'Bawling, braying, who cares, they are going to mess up our plan if we don't shut them up,' he said scratching his head and then pointed his finger at me, ' I got it, I got it, were those donkeys shouting after we gave them hay, well, were they?' He looked at me for a response.

I just shrugged my shoulders.

'No they weren't, so let's go and give them more hay,' he answered his own question jumping onto the small wall that surrounded the house and then leaped into the front yard.

'Mattie,' I called after him, 'Uncle Frank said that we were not to go far, remember?'

'But we wont be long, look,' he said pointing to the postman's bicycle resting against the small wall that surrounded the house.

By the time I got over the wall Mattie was scooting on a peddle on one side of the bicycle. After a few skips he threw his leg over to the opposite peddle. Even with his toes doing the peddling he was barely able to reach the pedals when he sat on the raised saddle. There were a few ducks and chickens in the yard at first but now they had suddenly disappeared. He kept shifting his tongue from side to side as his balance improved.

Then he pulled up in front of me with a hard pull on the front brake that sent him half way into the metal basket in front of the bicycle.

'Right, get on, let's go,' he said taking a cautionary look at the front door of the house.

'Get on where?' I asked with a puzzled look.

'Where do think, look, made for you,' he pointed to the metal basket that formed part of the bicycle.

'There's a post bag in that, I don't want to sit on the bag and crease the letters and stuff,' I searched for an excuse not to take a 'crossbar' with him.

I don't like taking a 'crossbar.' I have bad memories of an incident that occurred with Vinny. One day after school he gave me a 'crossbar' on his father's bike.

Vinny decided to hold onto the ladder at the front side of a passing petrol truck to get more speed up but when the truck braked suddenly we both tumbled off the bike and the rear double wheels of the truck crushed the bicycle wheels.

Misses Haren had been watching us from her summer bench at the front of her shoe shop. She said that I was very lucky only to have a cut on my forehead and Vinny only to have two scraped knees.

Vinny whispered to me as he wiped the blood from his knees, 'That sort of luck I could do without.'

And here I am now about to take a 'crossbar' from Mattie and it wasn't even on the crossbar; he wanted me to get into the basket on the front of the bicycle.

Mattie spoke as he removed the postbag from the basket, 'Put the strap around your neck and hop in, you can put the hay in the postbag for the donkeys,' he concluded throwing the postbag at me.

I reluctantly and slowly I wriggled the straps of the postbag around my neck. 'Remind me to let the air out of the tyres when we're finished with this yoke, did you hear what "lanky" said about Daddy?' Mattie said inhaling and exhaling fast as he angled the bicycle back as far as the small gate in front of the house and aimed the bicycle towards the lane. I clumsily waddled myself to a seated position in the carrier basket. I was onboard.

My legs were dangling over the front of the basket frame as Mattie launched the postman's bike.

'Will you stop moving and shaking,' Mattie grunted and peddled as the bicycle wobbled. We were just getting good synchronised balance when I heard a loud roar from behind us. Mattie and I both looked behind together.

I had a sensation of a sudden change in direction. I got a glimpse of somebody looking out the kitchen window and movement at the front door. When I turned around I was bobbing down the steps to the well in the front basket of the postman's bike. I turned sideways to get off. I saw Mattie grabbing the front brake as the front wheel crunched into the earth where a paving slab used to be.

I thought that I was breathing but I wasn't; I was gulping. Ice-cold pain filled my head as bubbles raced past me and my ears and mouth flooded with thunderous gushes. I could see the faint outline of a paving stone embedded in the sandy bottom of the well. Then a bubbling postbag blocked my view as I groped and swung my hands in front of me. I felt a grip on my neck and then I was breathing air again at last.

When I wiped my eyes I was looking into the face of Uncle Frank who was on his hunkers and hugging me closely.

'Are you okay you little *ceolan*?' he consoled, gently patting my head and then shouted at Mattie, 'get up you.'

Mattie was entangled between the fork of the bicycle and the front basket. I was shaking and my teeth were chattering.

The postman was holding on to the side stonewall that

surrounded the well with one hand as he reached and pulled the leaking post bag from the water. He threw it to one side and reached back into the well where one letter and a package were floating but partially submerged. He pinched the package by an end and carefully placed it behind him on the ground and reached again to retrieve the letter.

Mattie pulled himself free from the bicycle and tumbled forward. There was a squelching bursting noise as he trod on the package on the ground. The postman was right; the parcel did contain nylons.

Granny had come to the top of the well steps and was starting to come down when Uncle Frank told her to go back that everything was okay. The postman took the remaining mail from the soaked postbag and then shook it upside down until the emptying water came to a dribbled before he put the sapping post back into it.

Uncle Frank dragged the bicycle back up the steps and we went back to the house together with Mattie taking up the rear. Granny told me to get out of my wet clothes and get into my pyjamas. Uncle Frank told Mattie to sit on the chair at the top of the table and not to move. The postman and Uncle Frank started a frantic discussion on the best way to dry the post out. Only the top half of me was really wet but I got into my full pyjamas anyway. When I came back into the kitchen the post was lying flat on the table in the sunlight.

Uncle Frank was smoking and the postman had a glass of whiskey in his hand. They were saying nothing sitting and staring at the ground. The dripping postbag hung on the clothesline suspended over the stove.

Granny broke the silence. 'Frank,' she said lifting a saucepan of milk from the range, 'I'm not happy with Baba, I don't think she's eating and she wouldn't even take milk form me this morning.'

Uncle Frank looked disgruntled and responded in a low voice, 'I'll take a look at her later.'

Mattie looked worried as he shifted his eyes from Granny to Uncle Frank.

Granny poured hot milk into a mug and gave it to me saying, 'when you finish that go into bed like a good boy.'

Mattie was resting his head on his folded arms on the table and then suddenly he slammed his hand hard on the Arts Catalogue envelope drying on the table. A spray of water squirted from it as a bluebottle easily escaped the descending hand and flew away.

I thanked Granny handing back the empty mug and went to my room where I took a comic from my suitcase. I jumped into bed and started to read Roy Rogers. I was half way through the comic when I heard Granny and Uncle Frank saying their farewells to the postman.

'Thanks for the salmon,' I heard the postman say in a self-pitying voice.

'It's the least I can do Dan,' Uncle Frank said before closing the door and then in a loud voice called out, 'Mattie come with me we have to mark those sheep.'

I smiled turning the page; Mattie was going to do some work. I had finished Roy Rogers and getting a sixty four page war comic from my suitcase when Uncle Frank put his head in the door. 'Did you dry out yet? He enquired caringly.

'Yes,' I said jumping back into bed.

When Uncle Frank was leaving the bathroom I heard him calling out, 'Mother, where did you see Baba last, I have a drop of de-wormer here I'll try on her.' I didn't hear what Granny said but I did hear my uncle's reply, 'okay, I'll try up the lane so.'

The war comic wasn't that good and as usual the German Huns were all killed by the Tommies. I was coming to the end when I heard shouting in the distance but I couldn't make out what was being said. As I turned to the last page I heard footsteps thumping fast towards the back window. Then I heard the shouting getting nearer and this time I could make out what was being said, 'come back here you blooda ceolan.'

It was Uncle Frank who was shouting. Footsteps and a shadow went past the window very fast. I put the comic down and stretched across the bed.

I was just in time to see Uncle Frank race past as he hollered, 'I'll blooda kill ya.' He sounded very angry. I heard the scullery door rattling and opening fast. 'What's all the commotion about?' Granny demanded.

Uncle Frank returned past the window and was panting as he spoke, 'That blooda fecker,'

'Frank mind your language,'

'Sorry mother but that, that Mattie yoke,' Uncle Frank apologised and continued, 'he's after putting the wrong markings on the sheep, he has the Raddle everywhere, even Toss got a dollop.'

'Why didn't you show him the correct way and stay with him 'til he knew what he was doing,' Granny said in her 'teacher' voice.

'For God's sake of course I showed...'

'Don't raise your voice to me young man.' It was Granny again.

'Mother, I showed him how and where the sheep were to be marked,' Uncle Frank said in a slower and calmer voice, 'then I went off to dose Baba. When I eventually found her and when I went back to the pens I discovered what he had done.' Uncle Frank coughed hoarsely and added, 'Of course no sign of himself 'til he comes running out of the Old House, honest to God mother that fella...'

'He was in the Old House on his own?' Granny interrupted abruptly.

'Mother, mother will you take it easy or you'll trip and fall,' was the last I heard as footsteps faded.

I finishing the last page of the comic but I wasn't really concentrating when I heard 'pssst, pssst' from outside the window. I stretched across the bed and looked out. Mattie was peeping in the window.

'Where did he go?' he asked in a whisper.

'Mattie you are in big trouble,' I whispered back and then answered his question as best I could, 'I think he's gone back to the pens.'

'Good,' Mattie said crawling head first in the window and then gave a whinge as he stopped. He put his hand down the front of his trousers and moved something to one side. Whatever it was, was protruding through his jumper and catching on the base of the open window.

The statue of the Virgin Mary wobbled at the side of the window but didn't tumble. He flopped onto the floor hands first and immediately did a stooped walk to his side of the bed. Mattie pulled a hacksaw from the front of his trousers and pushed it under the mattress.

I recognised it straight away. It was the one Uncle Frank used to dehorn the sheep's maggot infested horns.

'What do you want that for?' I asked.

'To cut out our spears from *Teach an Dochtúra* gates this evening, of course,' he answered dismissively.

'I don't think we'll be going anywhere for the rest of the day,' I suggested.

'Why not? Sure there's nothing wrong with you that a bit of fresh air won't cure,' he said flopping onto the bed beside me.

'I hope that stuff is dry,' I pointed to the red Raddle on his wellingtons.

'Dry as a bone,' he said kicking off his wellingtons and lying flat out on the bed.

He squirmed taking the 'goose choker' ball-bearing from his pocket.

'Now here's the plan,' he said throwing the ball-bearing up in the air and catching it, 'I cut out the spears from the gate and you start getting those donkeys used to the horse tackle stuff trotting around the doctor's lawns before we take to the road and on to the shop.'

'Where are we going to get the tackle?' I asked nervously forseeing all sorts of dangers.

'Didn't you see all that sort of stuff on the wall in the back shed up there? So you told me anyway.'

'That tackle was probably for the doctor's stallion, it's too big for a donkey,' I protested.

He immediately followed with another question. 'Are there ropes there?'

I thought for a second or two before answering. I heard a small thud as Mattie cried 'Ouch.' He had failed to catch one of his ball-bearing throws and it dropped hitting him on the cheek.

The closing of the scullery door echoed gently in the back yard.

'Well, are there ropes there or not?' he asked rubbing his cheek.

'I think so,' I said meekly, realizing that I was now involved as an unwilling participant in Mattie's plan.

'Good,' he said sitting up and throwing the ballbearing at the wardrobe. Mattie just went 'Oops.' I held my breath. The ball-bearing whacked into the solid timber boards of the wardrobe door and clattered to the floor where it began its tiresome roll. The ball-bearing came to a halt and rested at the skirting board in the corner of the room as the bedroom door opened.

Granny stood there with her hand on the door handle as she peered into the room with staring eyes.

'Granny, do you know where the nearest postbox is?' Mattie calmly posed another of his red herrings sitting upright on the side of the bed. It was to no avail.

'What was that noise?' Granny said moving slowly into the room.

'Did you hear it too?' Mattie responded with a puzzled face. He moved around the bed and towards the window as he spoke, 'I think it came from that direction,' he pointed through the window.

Granny just glanced out the window and then turned towards Mattie as she spoke, 'Your Uncle Frank is looking for you, you gave him a lot of extra work to do cleaning the sheep and re-marking them.' She looked even more solemn as she continued, 'Now this rule applies to both of you, you are not allowed in the Old House unless Frank is with you, its too dangerous in there, is that understood?' We both nodded.

Uncle Frank must have told Granny about Mattie falling trying to get the scythe down from the rafters.

Mattie lowered his head as he said remorsefully, 'I'm sorry about the sheep marking but I did try my best.'

Granny stared at him silently and then asked, 'What was your enquiry about a postbox?

'I wrote a letter to Mammy and I'd like to post it, that's all,' Mattie said looking up at her under his eyebrows.

She stared at him for a few more seconds taking deep wheezy breaths before speaking, 'The postbox is at the Post Office.'

'And is that far?' Mattie's sign of remorse changed to one of interest.

'The Post Office, the shop, the pub, they're all the one, over near the church,' Granny responded cautiously.

She gave one lingering glance at Mattie as she stood by the door and opened it wider. She bowed her head slightly and slowly flicked her index finger towards Mattie as if she was about to say something, but Mattie interrupted.

'I think I'll go and help Uncle Frank first, sure there's plenty of time to post the letter,' Mattie said picking up his wellingtons and passing her in the doorway.

'I think that would be a good idea,' I heard Granny say pulling the bedroom door closed.

I finished another Roy Rogers comic and saved the last one for another time. I felt tired. I woke up to Mattie bursting in through the bedroom door.

'Worst day of my life, worst ever,' he grunted and panted, pulling off his wellingtons and flinging them in the corner.

'When Frank finished putting that red stuff on the sheep he brought me back to that field, you know where we were shaking it around the place yesterday and guess what?' He stared wide eyed at me, 'Well mister slave keeper Uncle Frank had me raking the same scattered hay into big stacks.' Mattie flung himself on the bed and continued, 'And do you know what he did then?' Mattie asked and then answered with a half squeal, 'He made ropes out of hay, to tie the haystacks down.'

I was curious. 'How did he do that?' I asked.

Mattie's mood changed to a less hyper state as he answered, 'Well all you have to do is keep twisting around a bit of tough wire that is shaped like the starter handle for a car and keep feeding the hay to the twisting wire. I'll show you sometime, they're called Sugans,' he concluded smugly.

He lay silently on the bed for a few moments as if welling in his new found knowledge and then suddenly leaped from the bed chirping, 'Oh! yes, the tea is ready! Granny said that you were to get dressed.' I was a bit drowsy but when Mattie relayed Granny's instructions I was wide awake.

I was looking in the wardrobe for a dry change of underwear when Mattie pushed me aside. 'I'll swap you these lovely colourful socks for an ordinary pair of yours,' he said holding up the multicoloured wellington socks Mammy had knitted for him.

I wasn't falling for his cunning proposition. 'No deal,' I said with a grin.

'I was thinking of bringing Finn for a walk with me to post the letter,' Mattie said as I appeared in the kitchen after him. Granny looked surprised to see me.

'I wasn't expecting you to be up after your ordeal. I'd have brought your tea down to you, are you sure you'll be able for the walk?'

I glared at Mattie and shook my head but Granny was over at the stove now and didn't observe my visual show of indignation at Mattie's devious lies.

'A bit of fresh air will do him all the good in the word,' Mattie said.

'What's this about "walk" and "posting letters," haven't we had enough of letters for one day?' Uncle Frank said sugaring his tea and continued, 'After the milking I was thinking of bringing down more sheep and might need a hand.'

'Arrah, let them off, they have enough done for one day, Mattie has a letter for posting to his mother,' Granny tactfully pleaded.

'He's written a letter to his mother?' Uncle Frank frowned nodding at Mattie and then said through his laughter, 'I'd love to see that letter.'

'It's private and it's sealed Uncle Frank,' Mattie said looking straight into my uncle's face. Granny smiled cutting the cold chunk of bacon on her plate.

Mattie was very convincing and only because I didn't see him writing any letter I would have believed him too. I think Mattie is going to be a long time in the Confessional Box when he goes to confessions the next time.

'I have the letter with me and we're off,' Mattie called into the kitchen and pulled me with him to the front door. I could see the bulge in the back of his jumper going out the door. I think it's the hacksaw but I know for definite it's not a letter for Mammy.

'Bless yourselves and don't be late, I'll wait for you to come back to say the Rosary,' Granny called from the kitchen.

I don't think that Mattie heard her. He had gone through the small front gate and was heading across the yard.

He slowed his pace and turned to wave me on at a faster speed. My interest in the intended operation hadn't increased any. When we got to the top of the hill on the lane Mattie pointed over the wall at the meadow.

'Go fetch, as much hay as you can carry. We have to be best friends with the donkeys.'

I shook my head as I passed him out and partially opened the gate.

'What's wrong with you?' Mattie enquired squeezing out the gate with me.

'I'm not going in there, Uncle Frank might see me when he's bringing in the cows.'

Mattie stared at me and looked angry.

'I'll go into the meadow nearer the doctor's house,' I said going onto the road.

Mattie nodded. As we approached the gates at *Teach an Dochtúra*, Mattie unholstered the hacksaw. I cautiously climbed the stonewall and crept into the meadow.

'Will that be enough?' I enquired throwing an armful of fermenting hay over the wall.

'No,' Mattie said taking a quick look back as he sawed out his improvised spear in the wrought iron gate. I repeated my hay run but didn't ask for any more approval from Mattie. I scaled the wall and dropped to my newly created hay trough in the deep ditch between the wall and road embankment. I gathered up the hay, crossed the road and prepared myself for entering the grounds of *Teach an Dochtúra*.

CHAPTER 13

Arena of Terror

THERE WAS NO SIGHTING OF my four legged would-be recipients. Mattie changed his hands positions on the hacksaw and began sawing again. I took a quick glance at his labours. There was little evidence of any major impression on the ironwork. A drop of sweat dangled at the end of Mattie's nose. The red mark on his cheekbone, caused by the falling ball–bearing earlier, looked brighter.

'Where are the donkeys?' I asked.

The reply I got was a painful short yelp. Mattie danced away from the gate with his hand lodged up under his armpit. He lowered his hand and slowly examined it. I could see a smear of blood on both of his knuckles. The hacksaw dangled on the crossbar of the gate with the broken blade warped viciously to one side.

'Now look what you made me do,' Mattie cringed flicking the wounded hand.

'I don't see them,' I said softly looking for the donkeys through the bars of the gates.

Mattie looked through the bars also as he spoke quietly, 'Me neither.'

We remained static momentarily and then he pressed the lever to open the gate. We stepped in together and I gently lowered the lever on the closed gate. I settled the hay more comfortably under my arm as we moved from the crunchy gravel to the soft overgrown lawn. We slowly made our way towards the back, stretching our necks and peering wide eyed as we went.

I heard cloggy steps nearby but their exact location was undeterminable. We had reached the back and still no sighting. I grabbed at Mattie's arm and pointed. The back door had badly damaged panels. It was hanging by its top hinge with diagonal corners jammed at the top and bottom of the doorframe.

'Burglars,' I gasped, dropping my armful of hay.

Mattie pushed me to one side to make the first move for retreat but I was ahead of him this time. We both panicked scrambling to open the gate and Mattie got in front of me as we reached the road.

He stopped suddenly and turned waving his raised hands shouting, 'Stop, stop, stop,' he gulped for breath as he spoke, 'how would it be burglars, steal the donkeys and come back to break in, are you mad?'

I panted beside him as I digested his reasoning.

'What do you think?' I asked hoping for an explanation and decision that would take me far away from there.

'Let's go back,' he said releasing his pursed lips.

That was neither the explanation nor decision that I wanted to hear from Mattie. I was eased in the gate first, with Mattie's hand resting on my shoulder. We retraced our steps but stayed on the gravel stopping at intervals to review our position. I saw my reflection in the side window of the house but could not see into the house. I changed course and cautiously stepped in a straight line towards the window. I could see Mattie behind me in the reflection as I moved forward and then a donkey's head appeared.

I jumped and ran sideways in one movement. I glanced behind me as I raced towards the gate. I came slowly to a halt when I realised that no donkey was following. Mattie passed me out and swung the gate wide open running out onto the roadway again.

'Wait!' I hollered.

Mattie eventually peered over the wall at me as he spoke, 'Did you see a ghost?' 'No,' I said exhaling with relief, 'but I did see a donkey.'

'Where?' Mattie said in a half whisper as he stretched his neck over the wall like a scanning periscope.

'In the house,' I answered with a giggle and then frowned seeing the serious side of the situation. Mattie jumped to one side and entered the gateway skipping, jumping and laughing loudly. Two donkeys brayed out of sequence a few times and then stopped.

Mattie ran to the window and hopped his head off the windowpane peering in. He cupped his hand and pressed them to the glass. He jumped back and laughed even louder.

'He has…he ha, he has,' Mattie spluttered and then fell to the ground pointing. 'You sound like a donkey,' I said impatient to find out what was amusing him so much.

Mattie wiped his laughter tear and pointed again, 'He, he, has the place wrecked inside.' Mattie stood up and was still giggling as I approached the window.

The donkey was now sniffing the inside of the window and licking the glass. A second donkey came into view and both jostled at the window for better viewing positions.

'How did they get in?' I asked as we both ran to the back of the house.

'They knocked on the front door and the ghost let them in,' Mattie said shaking his head dismally and then pointed at the battered back door. 'How do you think they got in, they kicked the door in dumbo, that's what they're good at isn't it?'

I had to agree with Mattie's theory. 'But why didn't they come back out?' I asked peeping between the split door panels.

'Because they're donkeys, dumbo, they got in and when they tried to get back out they probably pushed the door closed and then being donkeys they started kicking the hell out of it and it got jammed like you see it now, doors only open one way, got it?' Mattie spoke authoritatively and gasped coming to the end of his breath intake.

'In the bar saloons in cowboy film the doors open both ways,' I corrected.

Mattie pushed me aside peeping through a split lower down the door as he giggled and said, 'Well they didn't come here for a drink in the saloon, did they?' He jumped backwards as a snort was quickly followed by a nose and tongue appeared through a wider split in the panel above him. 'It's make friends time,' Mattie beamed picking up a handful of hay from the bundle of hay I had abandoned a short time earlier. He dangled the hay at the crevice opening between the door panels and it disappeared with the scoop of a tongue.

'More, more,' Mattie cheered getting more hay and watched it vanish in the same way. 'Now that they trust us we can move to the next stage of the plan,' Mattie grunted and pushed at the jammed door. The door squeaked and moved slightly.

The sound of scattering hooves moved away from inside the door. Mattie stood a few paces back from the door this time and made a run at it. There was a crashing sound as he collided with the door which became free at the bottom and swung in-side still suspended by the remaining top hinge. Mattie vanished inside too but returned back just as fast as two donkeys tried to squeeze through the space created. Eventually the bigger of the two claimed supremacy and trotted into freedom. Mattie and I moved further back as the second inmate followed suit.

'Is the gate closed?'

'Yes,' I confirmed after a quick glance towards the road.

'Right let's see what these two hairy burglars have been up to,' Mattie said linking me with him as far as the door.

He looked in, released me and then stepped over the thresh-old. He began with a little titter which increased to howls of laughter as he went further inside Teach an Dochtúra I cautiously followed and peered around the kitchen and cautiously sneaked into a living room area.

A long mahogany table had three chairs pinned to a side wall. Two more chairs were overturned on the manure-soiled Persian Rug. One had the back rest cracked and partially separated from the chair frame. The cushioned seat on the other chair was burst and a mahogany leg dangled from a splintered dowel. Polished pieces of carved and engraved timber were scattered at random on the floor.

Large and small chunks of glassware sparkled and crunched

under my feet as I passed an ornate mahogany glass case, now with jagged glass pieces pointing outwards from the door frames. I was making my way through the hallway as Mattie sprang up the stairs taking steps two at a time.

'They never made it to bed,' Mattie chuckled from the doorway of one of the bedrooms at the top of the stairs.

Part of the stair's bannister, cracked and broken, was collapsed on the carped stairs surrounded by, gnawed, and spliced stair rungs.

'Right nothing more to be seen here,' Mattie's voice echoed in the stairwell as he rumbled back down the stairs. His feet rolled on the broken stair rungs before he leaped into the hallway where he landed on a fresh pile of donkey's manure. Orange coloured flies rose from the smelly pile and buzzed over our heads as we ran through the ransacked house towards the back door.

Mattie was still giggling as he went back outside. ' I can't wait to tell Towbar about the best housewreckers ever, ever, ever,' he took a breath after a bout of laughing and added, 'if you want to wreck a place, a couple of donkeys is your man.'

I thought about the damage and destruction. I had seen furniture like that in the antique section of Danny's Cut Price Warehouse at home and it was expensive but this furniture was much, much older so maybe it won't be too costly to replace.

'That's enough, that's enough,' Mattie said as he cautiously pulled the remaining hay away from in front of the munching donkeys and then turned and spoke to me as he walked towards the stable, 'where did you see the ropes?'

The donkeys followed the hay and us. 'See that, they're not just our friends, they're our pets,' Mattie said gently stroking the smaller donkey as it pulled and chewed the hay from his other hand.

'If they're our pets we have to give them names,' I declared taking some hay from Mattie and feeding the bigger donkey.

'That's your department Finn,' Mattie chirped going towards the stable.

'Ok, let me think so, this is "Neddy" and the small one is "Noddy."'

'What ever you say Finn, we'll baptise them some other day,' Mattie sneered pulling at the bridle hooked on the wall in the stable. He jumped up a few times pushing the bridle high until it became unhooked.

'Look, that's not too big at all for eh…eh…Noddy,' Mattie pointed at the big donkey.

'Neddy,' I corrected him.

'Ye, ye, Neddy, who cares, try it on him,' he said slinging it towards me.

Neddy shook its head and took a few steps backwards as the bridle landed between us.

'Stop it Mattie, you're frightening Neddy,' I protested picking the bridle from the ground. I picked up some more hay in one hand and slowly walked towards Neddy dragging the bridle behind me. I stuffed some hay up through the lower part of the bridle until it held on its own and then pulled the straps apart as wide as I could at the top.

My trap worked first time as Neddy sunk its head into the bridle for the hay. Neddy pulled back a bit when the blinkers hit its ears as I pulled home the complete bridle and buckled it. When the hay was finished Neddy shook his head vigorously and although the bridle flopped sideways it remained on its head.

'What do mean too big, it's perfect fit, perfect,' Mattie praised my work coming from the cart house with a coil of old rope. It was dirty brown and had cobwebs and leaves dangled from it. 'Now just so that Nedd…er…Noddy doesn't get jealous, this is for her,' Mattie said dropping the rope on the ground.

I looked at Mattie and shrugged my shoulders.

'Wrap the rope around, Ned…ah, eh, Nodd…eh that donkey there,' Mattie pointed to Noddy, 'and around that one and then tie it onto the leather straps on that bridle yoke.' He reached cautiously and flicked the side of the blinkers. I increased my cringe of bewilderment as Mattie continued, 'That way the two are tied together, got it?' He looked at me, 'Then wrap it around the linking ropes and bring the rest back to the cart, ah er trap, and I'll tie it to the front of the trap and we're in the Wells Fargo business,' Mattie concluded with pursed lips and widened eyes awaiting my actions. I made no movement except stare at him in disbelief.

'What's wrong now?' he enquired with disgust.

'For starters, Neddy and Noddy won't fit together between the shafts, and there is only a reins for one,' I said straining my eyes into the cart shed to see if I could see the reins I saw there yesterday.

'Don't get all "know-all" with me Finn,' Mattie scratched his head and spoke as he was thinking, 'there's no need for any reins, this is only a trial run around the grounds here, so we'll slot one shaft between the two of them so the little donkeys can get used to pulling a—a trap, that's all Finn, a trial run, got it?' He raised his hands as if he had simplified thing.

He may have thought that he had made things sound less complicated but they didn't sound any less dangerous than before. I had just enough hay left to pacify Noddy while I looped the rotting rope around him and brought the remaining part of the rope to the rear of both donkeys. All that was left to do now was a linkup with the horse trap.

When we rolled the trap into the yard Neddy and Noddy were strenuously trying to move away from one another. I became anxious as the strain on the tethering rope tightened on the two donkeys. I pulled some grass from the lawn and coaxed them to a position where they were standing adjacent to each other again.

Mattie stopped and studied the situation unfolding, 'I think that it would be better if we put one of them in front of the other rather than the two together,' he said rubbing his chin, and then changed his mind again. 'No, no his way will do 'til we're out on the road,' he said nodding his head slowly and then as if he had a sudden burst of knowledge and spurted out, 'all I want you to do now is get more grass and keep them happy eating.' I was glad to pull more grass from the lawn in the hope that this would be my final part played in the looming fiasco.

When I came back Mattie was standing between the two raised shafts of the horse trap.

'Start the feeding,' he said.

I divided the fresh grass into each hand and stood in front of the donkeys. Mattie moved in slowly from behind as Neddy and Noddy sniffed and munched the grass from my hands. I limited the two donkeys to small handfulls of grass at a time and peered between them in disbelief as Mattie's plan developed behind them.

His arms were at full stretch as he pulled the trap by the shafts up to the rear ends of donkeys. Then by holding one shaft only, he tugged and steered the trap forward until the other shaft went in between the tethered donkeys. He managed this with one attempt. I think it was more of good luck than good horsemanship.

He kept manoeuvring until the shaft protruded slightly past the heads of the donkeys and rested on the lower part of the looped ropes. Noddy looked unsettled as the shaft appeared beside its head but Neddy was oblivious to it due to his blinkers.

Mattie was giddy and delirious as he picked up the remaining part of the rope and whipped it into the seating area at the front of the horse-trap. Both Neddy and Noddy stopped chewing and froze as Mattie climbed into the trap. He grabbed the rope and began looping it in between the varnished upright laths, near the front footrest.

The donkeys began munching again, but slower than before, as if anticipating a pending catastrophe. Mattie kept wrapping and looping the rope until it was just long enough to tie and knot to the centre wooden lath. He leaped down from the trap with a crunching thud to the gravel and with a frantic beckoning wave ordered me to join him at the horse-trap.

'Right cowboy, your stagecoach awaits,' Mattie whispered with a hand gesture. I studied the entanglement presented to me and tried to make sense of what I was looking at.

One bridled donkey was tethered on the inside of a single shaft and was linked to another donkey on the outside of the same shaft by a looped rope. This same rope was drawn back along the shaft between the donkeys and tied to wooden laths on the frame of the trap. The remaining free shaft pointed ominously forward like a warped missile. The combination of two donkeys and a horse-trap, linked together by a rotting rope meant only one thing to me—imminent danger.

I was distracted from my terrorising thoughts by barking dogs in the distance who appeared to be getting closer. Mattie nudging me forward and my grip of fear returned. I hesitated.

'Do you want to be a stuntman or not?' Mattie encouraged.

'I want to be a Stuntman not a Test Pilot,' I whimpered.

I was going to ask him why he didn't get on first but from past experience I knew that it would be a waste of time. The barking dogs sounded nearer. The donkey's ears twitched and pointed. I put my foot on the protruding metal step-up at the front side of the trap. Another step and I will be in the "pilot's seat."

A clambering sound to my right got my attention and I turned in that direction. I gulped focusing at a monstrous wildcat regaining its balance on the top of the wall. It was the 'Doiredrum Bobcat.' I felt a rush of air at my knees as the trap wheel whisked past me.

The Doiredrum Bobcat leaped wild-eyed into the yard and spat through snarling fangs as it landed. Blood-soaked lambs wool garnished its arced tongue and razor sharp teeth. It leaped forward and hugged the inside of the perimeter wall speeding towards the road at the surgery side of the house. I was still frozen to the spot as I saw the two donkeys and trap speed towards the road on the other side of the house.

As the donkeys and their 'carriage' reached the front of the house from one side, the wildcat arrived there too at the same time from the opposite side. The trap spun one wheeled in an about-turn motion, propelled by terrorised donkey power, as the wildcat leaped and disappeared over the front wall.

The trap bounced back on both wheels as it thundered back towards me. A door slammed behind me and I turned and looked. Mattie had just slammed the bottom half of the stable door and taken refuge in the stable. Dogs were whinging and barking behind the back wall.

I ran to the gaping door at the back of the doctor's house and stumbled inside as the donkeys and trap rumbled past me continuing their lap in the opposite direction from where they had set out. I heard a crashing thump outside in the vicinity of the surgery as I crunched on broken glass and chinaware on the floor inside. I rushed to the dining room window and looked out onto our 'Chariot Arena.' The galloping hooves were coming closer again. Neddy and Noddy swung past the window, tirelessly pulling in opposite directions to one another. They were still bound together by a now shredding rope, but without a horse-trap at the end.

I sat on the window ledge and gasped foul-smelling air. My eyes focused on a large gold-framed painting hanging over the fireplace. It was a portrait of an elderly man with an accordion resting on his lap. A cold shiver went through me as I came to the conclusion that it was probably a portrait of the deceased doctor Galligan. In a few seconds I was outside moving around the back yard breathing fresh air again.

All was calm again except for the fading sound of barking dogs on the hills at the back of us.

'Is that you Finn?' I heard a subdued voice coming from the stable.

'No,' I snapped back and then added mockingly, ' I'm the wildcat b-o-o-o-o' Mattie shoved open the stable door .

'Oh my God, what a mess,' he giggled looking out from the stable.

We conducted a closer inspection of the aftermath.

A one shafted horse-trap, lay static and collapsed on its one wheeled axle, beside the surgery wall. A detached broken shaft rested on weeds under the surgery window. The plaster at the corner of the surgery extension was freshly scraped and cracked. Splintered and broken trap-wheel spokes were scattered around the badly dented barrel which was once used as a fire dump.

Two donkeys grazed near a bridle and short piece of rope discarded on the lawn. Neddy and Noddy raised their heads and glanced at us. Neddy spluttered and both went back feeding.

'It's an awful pity that I wasn't able to cut that spear from the gate, one dead Bobcat and money in Mattie's pocket,' Mattie said with raised hands to heaven. 'What were you going to do Mattie, fire the spear through the stable door at him?' I mocked him again.

Mattie stared wildly at me and then spoke, 'Can that

153

contraption be seen from the road?' he asked pointing to the disintegrated horse-trap.

I stepped away from the surgery extension and took a quick look towards the road before answering.

'No, I don't think so, why?'

'Because we have to hide all the evidence.'

He looked around sharply and added, 'Open the gates, dumbo, and let those two dumbos out,' he concluded moving towards the donkeys

I was just opening the gate when the two donkeys galloped towards me with Mattie shouting and yelling behind them. I swung the gate open and leaped to one side. The galloping donkeys increased their speed as they neared the gate and bounced of each other squeezing through. They whipped their hind legs high in the air like a triumphant sign of freedom as they galloped up the road.

'Dump that bridle yoke around the back as well as that,' Mattie said pointing to the broken hacksaw still hooked on the gate rails. 'Close the gate behind you and let's get out of here,' he called back at me as he exited the gate.

By the time I had carried out Mattie's orders I had to run very fast to catch up with him pounding along the roadway back towards Granny's house.

CHAPTER 14

Net, Trap and Poison

I SLAPPED HIM ON THE BACK passing him out. 'All done sir,' I mocked with a salute and then asked from a safe distance, 'were you in time for the post?'

'That letter was posted,' Mattie threatened with his finger and then examined his hacksaw sliced knuckles.

Before we reached the gate at the top of the lane I could hear dogs barking again. I looked up to my right and saw sheep, two dogs and a man coming down the last hill before they would reach the road.

He was making signs to us by waving his stick and pointing in the direction of the lane.

'It's Uncle Frank,' I said running to open the gates.

'I know it's him, more torture, blooda sheep.' Mattie grumbled.

I stood well to the side this time and rested on the open gate. Mattie walked ahead and had reached the yard by the time Toss and Shep had guided the sheep through the gate. Toss had red markings on the back of his neck; compliments of Mattie I presumed. I waited until Uncle Frank arrived.

'Good boy, did you get your business done at the post office?' he asked closing the gate behind us.

'All the business done,' I answered crossing my fingers in my pockets. Sparks said that it's not a sin to tell small lies if you cross your fingers.

'You haven't as many sheep with you this time,' I estimated taking a red herring trick from Mattie's book.

'Ah! don't talk to me, that blooda wild cat was devouring a lamb when I got up there.'

One of your lambs?' I enquired with excitement.

'No, no, one of Stephen's I'd say, well one of Stephen's yews was standing by it, so I'd say its one of Stephen's all right, most of the sheep were scattered everywhere, then the dogs took off after the wildcat, huh,' he flung his head back, ' they were as well off chasing a flash of lightening.'

'We saw it today...' I began and then stopped suddenly wondering if I should say anymore when I was relieved from my quandary by a frightened boy running in our direction.

Mattie was out of breath trying to relay his message. 'It's that wild, wild cat thing outside our window near, near,' he gulped, 'near the hedge at the sally tree,' he pointed, stopped and waved at us to follow him.

'Stay quiet, 'til I get my gun,' Uncle Frank shushed us running in front.

'You have a gun?' Mattie bellowed running after him.

'Will you shush!' Uncle Frank snapped going in the small gate, panted and added, 'Finn said ye saw it today,' he said pushing in the hall door.

Mattie glared at me.

'Coming back from the post office,' I spluttered out crossing my fingers again. Mattie exhaled with a sigh of relief.

Mattie and I were impatiently waiting in the hallway when my uncle returned from his bedroom carrying a double-barrel shotgun. He was loading a second cartridge going out the front door.

We crept behind him like two of the posse behind the sheriff. Mattie tripped on the spout of the down pipe at the corner of the gable and Uncle Frank turned and stared at him with gritted teeth. He moved on taking every step with caution, his gun at the ready. Uncle Frank peeped slowly around the corner and then pulled back again. He raised his gun and jumped out bringing the staff to his shoulder.

He lowered it again with a gasp, 'Blast it to hell anyway, he's too fast and too bloody cute,' Uncle Frank said with utter disgust.

'Where did it go? I asked.

'Slipped through the hedge at the sally tree,' he responded ducking down and peering through the hedge.

'I'll carry that for you Uncle Frank,' Mattie said putting his hand on the barrel of the gun as we retraced our steps back to the house.

'Get away, will ya!' my uncle shrieked pulling the gun closer to himself and cautiously unloaded it.

Mattie looked subdued as he spoke, 'Where do you keep the gun?'

'You don't need to know that,' Uncle Frank said warily.

'Ye're back,' Granny called from the kitchen.

'Not for long, I'll have to go over to Stephen, that blooda wild thing killed one of his lambs, I better let him know I suppose,' Uncle Frank spoke exiting his bedroom minus the gun.

'According to Mattie it's around the back, I heard him shouting and screaming a while ago,' Granny informed us with a wry smile.

Mattie bowed his head with a look of shame.

'It was too, sure I went around the back to take a shot at it but it got away again.' Uncle Frank sighed entering the kitchen.

'I was wondering what all the shushing and commotion was about,' my Grandmother commented.

'Well I'm off to do the milking, I'll call to Stephen later on,' Uncle Frank said moving towards the kitchen door.

'Frank, I don't see the dogs, did you close the sheep-pen?'

' Ah! I forgot about the blooda sheep with all the commotion,' Uncle Frank responded, gently slapping his forehead.

'And when you've finished milking we'll have the Rosary and then you can go to Stephen,' Granny's instructions resounded through the kitchen.

I saw Uncle Frank bearing his teeth as he left the kitchen.

Mattie looked happy enough as Uncle Frank headed out the door. In about three seconds Mattie was in the hallway looking at Uncle Frank's bedroom door when the front hall door swung open.

'Don't even dream about it,' Uncle Frank said putting his head in the doorway and disappearing again.

Mattie shrugged his shoulders and muttered to himself turning for the hall door, 'Who needs your gun? I have my own plan.'

With a shake of his head he beckoned me to follow. I was weary and exhausted but I followed him anyway. We responded immediately to a tap at the kitchen window.

'Where are ye going?' Granny called from inside.

'Just checking on the sheep, Granny,' Mattie pointed in the direction of the pen. 'Good boys, don't go any further.'

Shep and Toss careered at high speed from the back of the Old House. Uncle Frank followed at a dreary pace. I had a sense of uneasiness going across the yard. I also had a sense of trouble as Mattie veered away from the sheep-pen towards the rear of the Old House. I could hear Uncle Frank roaring instructions to the dogs.

'Wait 'til you see what I found here today,' Mattie said with glee untangling a piece of wire from around the bolt on the door of the Old House.

'I hope you didn't touch that parcel?' I questioned in fear.

Mattie frowned. 'What parcel?

I sighed with relief but didn't answer as I watched him throw the wire on the ground and sliding back the bolt with a clang.

'Will you be quiet, or Uncle Frank will hear you,' I cautioned Mattie.

He ignored my instructions swinging the door wide open.

'Look,' he said, pointing to nets between the thatch and the top of the wall.

'Is that all, sure that's what I was asking Uncle Frank about today,' I said showing no surprise.

Mattie scratched his head before speaking, 'Are they what you were calling "tennis nets"?' I nodded. 'You dumbo, don't you know what they are?' I shook my head. 'They are for fishing, look they are still a bit wet,' Mattie jumped and tipped them, 'and how else do you think he got the salmon for that long string of a postman today?'

I didn't actually see Uncle Frank giving the postman the salmon but then I remembered hearing the postman thanking Uncle Frank when he was leaving. Mattie looked around him and in a half whisper continued, 'But they have a better use than catching a few oul fish.' He looked at me for a response. I shook my head again.

Mattie sighed before explaining, 'Did you ever see the jungle film where the hunters dig a hole somewhere along the animal's regular track, then they drag the net over it and cover it over with branches and leaves?' I nodded. 'And when the tiger or lion or wild boar falls into the hole it gets tangled up in the net and then, whack, a spear through the head.'

'But we don't have a spear,' I responded with a frown. Mattie rubbed the wound on his knuckle as he snapped,

'I know that, dumbo, but take a look at this,' he rolled a barrel to one side and picked up a short broom handle with a spike attached to one end that was pointed like a straightened-out fish hook.

'What's that? 'I asked reaching out to hold it.

'A short spear, I suppose,' he said releasing his grip.

I had seen a drawing like it in my history book but I think that they are meant to be bigger. They were called Pikes and were used by the Irish farmers to fight the invading Normans.

I was imagining Uncle Frank's father or grandfather killing Norman soldiers with it when Mattie spoke yanking it from my hand.

'Not as good as one of those in the doctor's gate, but if the Doiredrum Bobcat is tangled in the net it will do to kill him,' he said imitating a throw. He slipped it back behind the barrel at the sidewall. Then it dawned on me. I had an idea who would be digging the hole.

My premonition was proved correct with Mattie's next instructions. 'Finn I know where you can get a spade,' Mattie spoke to me leaning into a tea chest and began rummaging in it. I could hear the sound of glass clanging together. 'Nothing worthwhile there,' he grunted waddling his lower torso to pull himself back up out of the tea chest and then continued, 'do you know that field with the long weeds in it, beside the meadow we just cut?' he said pulling himself back up fully. I shook my head. 'I'll show you,' he said moving towards the window.

I took a quick look behind the stack of black cooking pots near the cartwheel without Mattie noticing me. The parcel was still in the same position where I had put it after the cartwheel spiking incident. When I turned around Mattie had the shears in his hand. 'Anyone for a haircut,' he giggled, snipping some wool protruding from one of the wool-sacks stacked in the corner.

'Mattie, put those down,' I ordered.

He did some mock hair cutting actions at me with the shears before flinging them back on the window ledge. I put the wire back on the bolt as best I could and followed Mattie across the backyard of the Old House.

He stopped a safe distance from the stream and picked up a stone. He shook his fists in the air, 'Come on mister snake, let's see how good you are,' he shouted throwing the stone into the stream. The stone glided once on the water and then lodged in the thick grass in the embankment on the far side as a hen squawked and fluttered out.

Mattie kept running until he came to the middle of the front yard. He slowed down his pace and kept a watch on the kitchen window as he headed up the lane. I took my time passing the window and even made some noise kicking stones in the hope that Granny would call us. It was not to be and I followed Mattie into a field beside the cut meadow.

A spade with a chipped and weather-beaten handle was imbedded and tilting in a half dug potato ridge. A garden fork was spiked in the ridge beside it. Mattie kicked at the potato stalks as he made his way to the spade. So this is Mattie's 'field with the weeds'—I am too tired and have no interest in explaining anything to him at this time. Mattie flaked at the green potato stalks with the spade as he made his way up and across the ridges. When we were going out the gate he shushed and pushed me back in as he pointed.

'Frank with the milk,' he whispered. He peeped a few times and then said, 'Run!'

We squeezed through the same part of the hedge that the wildcat had used and found ourselves in an overgrown briary field. I got Mattie to take his turn digging beside the sally tree. Every time he hit a tree root he flung the spade on the ground and shouted at me to dig in another spot beside it. After both our patience had run out we only had a few holes dug and not one capable of even resembling a hole deep enough to be called a wild animal trap.

In the end he grabbed the spade and swung it into the air. The spade twirled and tumbled into the large bunch of briars nearby. I glared at Mattie. He flopped down on the flattened long grass and freshly dug clay. He stared up at the sally tree and made some wild swipes at the swarm of midgets accumulating around his head before speaking. 'We'll get the nets anyway,' he said rolling sideways in the clay and grass to get up.

'What use are the nets without the trap hole?' I protested.

'Follow me,' he said walking out past the sally tree, 'I have another plan.'

I don't know what it is but I know I won't like it.

We had barely gone out through the hedge at the sally tree when Mattie pushed me backwards and ran back through the hedge again. It was my uncle with the milk again. 'Run,' Mattie said as soon as Uncle Frank had gone in the scullery door. Mattie removed the wire from the bolt and I followed him inside the Old House.

He went straight to the nets and started jumping up to grab them but he was unable to get a good enough grip to pull them down. He gave a quick scan around and then ran to where the one handled wheelbarrow with the broken leg was. He dragged it over and toppled it on its side under the nets.

'Hold it steady,' he panted standing on the side of the barrow. I got on my hunkers and kept the barrow pressed to the wall.

He wobbled a bit and shouted at me, 'Put your back into it!' I only moved a bit closer because the ways he was stretching made me nervous that he was going to fall on me. I was right but not alone did Mattie fall on me but so did the roll of netting. The barrow tumbled once and came to rest upside down on the floor.

Mattie didn't wait for me to get up before he began bundling the nets into a sort of a roll. He pulled a stick with fishing line wrapped around it from the net and stuffed it down the back of his trousers. When he realised that he was unable to lift them on his own he unrolled them again and told me to grab an end. The nets got entangled on the leg of the upturned wheelbarrow but apart from that we had a clear run to the door.

When we were outside I shouted at Mattie to wait until I would put the wire back on the bolt but he snarled to keep going that he wasn't finished in the Old House. I traipsed behind him out the back yard of the Old House and into the front yard until we bungled our way back through the hedge at the sally tree. We had arrived there unnoticed by either Uncle Frank or Granny. Mattie pulled the nets further into the filed and swung them in a heap beside the briars. 'Open the nets as wide as you can Finn, I'll be back in a minute,' Mattie said pointing to the nets and then vanished back out through the opening we had widened by our activities.

The nets were as long as tennis court net but were twice as wide. I had just finished unravelling them when Mattie reappeared holding the Pike which he had discovered behind the barrel earlier. He was wielding it around and making fake throws until at last he launched it through the air. It sunk slightly into the bark of the sally tree, lilted downwards and then flopped to the long grass beneath.

'Not bad,' he said glumly striding over to retrieve his new weapon, 'but we need something sharper.'

Mattie was biting his already badly stumped nails as he lifted the compromised spear and began walking in circles. When he bit his nails and walked in circles it was a sure sign that he was in an intensive thinking mode. In the middle of his third circle he stopped and jumped in the air, 'I have it, I have it,' he gritted his teeth with glee, 'now here's what you do.'

My heart sank when I heard the words 'you do' but when he

revealed the whole plan my inclusion in his plot wasn't as bad as I had assumed 'You see those hanging branches?' He pointed up at the sally tree. 'Well hang the net from them with this stuff,' he yanked the reel of fishing line from the back of his trousers. 'Have it done when I get back,' he said before charging through the briar field in the direction of the road.

At first I tried climbing the tree and pulling the nets behind me but they were too heavy and I broke a branch and a couple of twigs in my effort. Then I pushed one end of the nets up the base of the tree in front of me and managed to hook the net mesh on the stump of a branch I had broken with my earlier attempt. I climbed the tree and began pulling the net up to me as a fisherman would, pulling his fishing net into his boat. I climbed out along the branch balancing myself by holding an upper branch and hooked the rest of the net on every twig and branch within range. I had to break some of the branches when they were too big to hook the small mesh of the net. As I neared the end of the sally branch it began to sag enough for me to drop safely to the ground.

I examined my work from the ground. Some of the net was still in a fold on the ground and the rest was dangling about a foot above the ground. The worst part of my work was the obvious fact that only part of the gap between the sally tree and the hedge was covered in any way by the hanging net. None the less I was happy enough with the job I had done, even though I knew that Mattie wouldn't be; but I didn't care. I had just noticed the fishing line that Mattie had told me to use to tie up the net on the tree branch when I saw Mattie coming down the field. He pounded through the briars, long wild grass and weeds and plonked down beside me on his knees.

'That net looks useless,' he cringed looking up at my labours before he dropped a silver object from his hand into the grass. His jumper had an array of bulging shapes in the front. He pulled the end of his jumper up from inside his trousers and I watched as packets, small bottles and small boxes tumbled in front of him. I leaned over and looked closer. He had retrieved the dumped medicines from his hiding place in the field at the back of Teach an Dochtúra.

I picked up the mysterious silver thing. It was a large injection needle with a glass tube and plunger attached. There were two silver coloured looped finger grips on either side of the tube and a circular lug for the thumb at the top of the plunger shaft. The glass tube had short lines with numbers beside them. It looked bigger than the injection needle our doctor uses and even bigger than the needle the clinic dentist used to freeze your mouth before filling a tooth.

Mattie had unscrewed the caps of small jars and bottles and was tearing open small packages when he ordered me to hand over the injection needle. It looked too dangerous to hand directly to him so I threw it on the grass beside him.

'Easy,' he scolded with a loud whisper picking it up. I could see the sheen of sweat on his brow as he unscrewed the plunger cap. 'Get me two rocks,' he instructed sitting on the grass and then called after me as I moved away, 'one flat and one round.' I had a few scratches on my hands from the briars before I could fulfil Mattie's specific order. Mattie had separated the plunger and cap from the tube and needle.

He put the flat rock between his knees and emptied a few tablets from the packets onto it. Mattie had poured so many different kinds of pills from the other bottles that they began falling off the side and into the grass. He reached for the round rock and rolled and ground it on top of the muddled prescription. When he threw the round rock aside the flat rock was a mass of white and coloured powder.

I usually have an idea of Mattie's plans once he starts but nothing was becoming clear so far so I had to ask him. He pulled a long dock leaf from the weeds beside him and made it into a sort of funnel before answering me. 'Just watch,' he said scooping a half fistful of the ground tablets and emptying it into the dock funnel which he had squeezed loosely into the top of the tube of the injection needle. He gently taped the dock leaf and his newly created substance poured into the tube. The tube was half full before he stopped.

'Now do you get it?' he asked with a wide grin. I shook my head. 'I'm making poison you dumbo,' he snarled.

'Will I get some onions,' I offered with delight.

'Don't be stupid Finn, I want kill something not make it healthy, give me that bottle there,' he pointed at a small bottle out of his reach. I handed it to him. There was a liquid in it but the name on the label was too long to pronounce. He pulled the cork from the bottle with his teeth and aimed and poured the contents into the tube until it overflowed.

'Ah Mattie tell me what you are going to do,' I snapped losing my patience. He smiled screwing back the plunger and extended shaft onto the tube which he vigorously shook before speaking.

'Get me that spear,' he nodded towards the implement which I called a Pike.

I reluctantly handed it to him as he still hadn't told me the plan.

'Now the fishing line,' he ordered holding out his hand, 'and I hope you haven't used it all tying the net up the tree.' I was glad now that I hadn't used any of it. The plunger shaft was extended to its full length when he placed the metal spiked head of the Pike head beside it. Then he forcefully and repeatedly wound the fishing line around both. He checked the rigidity of his binding a few times, knotted it and then gasped, 'solid as a rock,' when he looked satisfied that the plunger shaft and Pike head were bound firmly together.

He tried cutting away the rest of the fishing line with his teeth and when this proved too difficult he rested the line on the flat rock and with a few bangs of the round rock the line was cut. He rested his newly created missile on his open hands as if presenting it to me. 'Made to kill,' he gloated in a low voice.

The plan was sort of clear, but when, where and how was the missile to be launched I needed clarification.

'What's next?' I pressed glumly. Mattie looked to the dusky sky before speaking, 'Tomorrow I will do a proper job on that,' he said nodding at the hanging net, 'and you will find a nice fat gosling and tie it by the leg to the tree.' He stared wildly at me before further plan disclosure, 'I will be up the tree with this baby waiting for the wild cat, and then...' he said pressing the plunger of the needle slightly.

We both watched as a gooey white liquid oozed out through the capillary at the top of the needle.

'Oops, mustn't waste the good poison,' he said raising his contraption to stop the flow, 'see it's a simple killing machine, I throw this like a spear into the "Doiredrum Bobcat" and the spear head pushed the plunger down and out comes the poison, one dead wildcat and one rich Mattie.' He bowed as if had performed on stage.

'And what's the net for?' I asked glumly.

He looked impatiently at me as he spoke, 'That is to tangle the wildcat up, just in case he tries to run away after I spike him with the poison.'

I didn't like my part of the plan any more than I liked his part so I tried to discourage the whole idea. 'Supposing the Doiredrum Bobcat,' I watched his eyes flicker and I continued, 'goes up the tree after you and eats you up.'

He tried to conceal his frightened gulp and answered, 'Let's see him try it.'

I could tell by the tone of his voice that he was faking his brave threat. I smiled walking behind him as he squeezed by the net and the sally tree. He listened and hesitated before rushing across the back yard to the open window of our bedroom. He carefully reached in the window with both hands outstretched and lowered his primed missile to the bedroom floor and then wriggled himself back out. Mattie's timing was impeccable.

'Where were you?' Uncle Frank asked coming around the corner of the house carrying a bucket of milk.

'I hope we're not late for the Rosary,' Mattie said opening the scullery door.

'Just in time,' Granny's announcement gave Mattie another reprieve from an awkward question. I stayed in the scullery with my uncle until he had poured the fresh milk into a basin.

Mattie wasn't in the kitchen when I went in but Granny already had her Rosary beads in her hand and was resting on the arms of the fireside chair to lower herself to her knees. Mattie reappeared and was grinning. I knew his weapon was in a safe place.

After the Rosary, Uncle Frank sprang to his feet and stamped his boots loudly on the floor as he spoke, 'Anyone for a visit to Stephen and Agnes?'

Granny answered for us, 'They have enough for one day and you know well that it will be late when you come back from there.'

'Whatever you say mother,' Uncle Frank replied with a slight shake of the head going out the kitchen door.

'Have a drop of milk and off to bed with you,' Granny said placing two cups on the table, 'you could have a busy day tomorrow and you'll need your sleep.'

'It could be busy all right,' Mattie said winking at me over his raised cup.

The moon shone brightly through the bedroom window and I studied the curtains again to see if I could remember where I had seen them before. I went to sleep again not remembering where.

CHAPTER 15

The Lethal Weapon Launch

I WOKE TO THE USUAL farmyard noise but the squawks of a hen sounded louder and nearer than the other familiar sounds. I could hear Uncle Frank talking to Granny in the kitchen. Mattie was still asleep when I was fully dressed so I pushed him.

He swung out at me and then opened one eye. 'Ah no don't tell me we're still here,' he mumbled sitting up in the bed, 'I was just dreaming that myself and Towbar were after finding a new dump that nobody knew about.'

'Well he's not here and it's time for work,' I goaded him with the reality of the situation.

Uncle Frank was crunching up the eggshells of boiled eggs he had just eaten when I went into the kitchen.

'Good morning sir, are you all ready?' he greeted me with a smile.

'Where's you brother?' Granny asked placing two boiled eggs in front of my bowl of porridge.

'He's coming now Granny,' I replied subduing a yawn.

'Some of the hens must be "laying out," I collected very few eggs this morning,' Granny complained going into the scullery.

'What's "laying out"?' I asked my uncle in a whisper.

He frowned before answering with a wry smile, 'Sometimes

the hens don't want their eggs collected from the hen house so they lay them in secret nests for hatching.'

'I think I know where there is a secret nest beside the bank at the stream,' I exclaimed with delight and awaited praise.

'That's a usual place for them alright, get a basket from your Granny and collect them after breakfast,' he said stretching back and yawning.

'You didn't stay long with Stephen and Agnes last night,' Granny said entering the kitchen.

'Ah, stop will ya,' Uncle Frank yawned again and continued, 'they were arguing like cats and dogs when I went over.'

'What about this time?' Granny enquired showing little interest.

Uncle Frank gave a little chuckle before answering, 'well Stephen decided that he was going to whitewash the whole place and in order to save time and what did he do, he made up the whitewash in Agnes's clothes bath.'

'You mean he made a full bath of whitewash?' Granny frowned.

'To the brim, it's a wonder the handles didn't break off with the weight, I saw it myself, a bath full ready and waiting outside the house,' Uncle Frank laughed again and added, 'and the funniest part of all is that he said he wasn't going to whitewash anything now and is leaving it there, well I suppose until the two of them cool off anyway,' he concluded standing up.

I was finishing my second egg when Mattie strolled into the kitchen, sat down at the table and said nothing.

'And a very good morning to you too,' Uncle Frank said sarcastically.

'Yup,' Mattie said reaching for the sugar to sprinkle on his porridge.

'We'll start with the sheep, and with the help of God if the day keeps good we should get a bit of hay cut too,' Uncle Frank pronounced studying the sky through the kitchen window.

Mattie gritted his teeth plunging his spoon with a clang into the porridge. I smiled at him as I rose from the table and following Frank out of the kitchen.

'I'll manage for a while myself, get a basket from your granny and yourself and Mattie collect the eggs from that hedge you were talking about,' he said going out the front door.

'What eggs, what hedge?' Mattie called from the table.

I put my head back in the doorway, 'It's farm talk, you wouldn't understand, get a basket from granny, I'll explain later,' I said putting my hand to my mouth to stop my giggling going up the hallway to the bedroom.

Movement in the hedge beside the sally tree caught my attention as I passed the bedroom window. I stepped closer and looked out. A hen was squawking and flapping its wings going back and over by the gap at the sally tree. I looked closer. It looked like it had its claw entangled in the net mesh and was trying to free itself. It's going to be another bad day; how am I going to free the hen without Granny catching me and then uncle Frank is going to ask who put the nets there, I tormented myself flopping on the bed.

I was sitting up and thinking hard when Mattie arrived in the bedroom. 'I'm fed up of boiled eggs,' he muttered taking two eggs from his pocket as he walked towards the open window. He stopped suddenly and stared out. The eggs seemed to drop free flow from his hand. One of the eggs cracked on the floor and began leaking egg yolk, the other just crunched and stopped on its own indentation.

His right hand came up slowly and loosely and wriggled in a pointing motion towards the window as his jaw dropped. He looked over at me as if looking for advice or help.

'I know,' I said, 'I'm just having a rest before I go out to it.'

His jaw dropped lower as he stared at me. He moved in a jittery way and sort of flopped on his hunkers beside my side of the bed. He reached under the bed and raised himself up with a hand on the bed. The other hand had his spear contraption in it. I looked bewildered at his whitening face.

The squawks of the hen got louder and more frantic. He held his weapon out towards me as he straightened himself.

'I don't need that, I'll do it with my hands,' I protested getting up from the bed.

He grabbed me and forced it into my hand. His mouth was moving but he didn't utter a word. I was going to refuse to take the lethal weapon again but then I thought that I'd bring it with me and hide it in the hedge because if Granny found it under my side of the bed she would only blame me.

I grabbed it from him and went into the hallway. I met Granny coming out the kitchen door with a basket in her hand. I stopped, glanced at the spear contraption in my hand and leaped forward into an even quicker walk. She cut short her puffy whistling tune and stared after me going out the door. I was right; it was going to be another bad day. My head was muddled as I ran towards the back of the house. What was going to be worse; my explanation to Granny about the lethal spear or how her hen got trapped in the net I had erected yesterday. When I turned the corner of the house I came to realise that those problems were the least of my worries.

The Doiredrum Bobcat leaped into a stride towards me with a lifeless hen in its mouth.

My speed lowered to staggering halt. Toss and Shep yelped and raced around the opposite corner near the scullery.

I raised my only protection and aimed as I turned to flee. In one frenzied and terrorised throw, I released the weapon at my presumed attacker, and then closed my eyes. The bellowing shriek resounded in my ears. A furry wallop at my legs, buckled my knees and I stumbled sideways and downwards. I opened my eyes as I hit the ground beside a gutted hen.

I saw the back end of Shep and Toss disappearing around the corner where the wildcat had headed. I was in a running motion getting up from the grassy earth under the clothesline. The shrieking howl of the wildcat drowned out the yelping of the dogs as they ran and jumped in half circles around the terrorised animal in the front yard.

The weapon was lodged high on the neck of the wildcat—the injection needle imbedded to the butt. The spiralling contraption, dangled, swirled and swung with the animal's every unpredictable movement.

Hens, chickens, ducks, goslings and a rooster, scurried and

bounced of each other as they fretted clearing the front yard. Birds chirping frantically flying from and through hedges, as crows squawked rising from trees. Baba bleated, released an inordinate amount of droppings and froze, frightened in the centre of the yard.

The wildcat gave another bawling howl completing a cartwheel motion. The weapon swung free and hurled into the air and landed with a splat in Baba's droppings. Baba took one rigid step forward and froze again.

Uncle Frank was striding towards the centre arena of the show. Granny and Mattie gawked from behind the front gate of the house. The wounded animal suddenly stood still, humped it back and gave a threatening snarl as its wild eyes scanned the yard.

The two dogs barked and danced at a safe distance from it. It prowled slowly towards the wall and in one leap cleared the wall barely touching the top and landed in the field on the far side. We all seemed to move in slow motion towards the wall and watched as it hopped and sprang down the field towards Stephen and Agnes's farm.

The Doiredrum Bobcat zigzagged and did a few more cartwheel movements before vanishing through the hedge at the bottom of the field. Shep and Toss followed only as far as the hedge and returned wagging their tails We all strained our eyes along the lower hedgerow but when there was no further sighting of the wild animal we turned back towards the centre of the yard.

Uncle Frank was first to speak as he moved towards the weapon, 'What the blooda hell is that?' he said pointing and picking the manure stained spear, from an equally stained rag, on top of Baba's droppings. Baba moved in beside granny nearly knocking her over.

'There, there,' she said tenderly rubbing Baba's back.

'Where the…what the blooda hell did you do to my fishing spear?'

For a split second I educated myself, it wasn't a Pike it was my uncle's Fishing Spear, whatever that was. Uncle Frank seemed puzzled as he shook free, what looked very like a wet greenish-brown elasticised rag, hooked on the spear head. I was looking at it as it flopped to the ground. I was wondering could it be underpants that I was looking at when the words, 'Get into the house,' resounded in my ears.

Mattie and I followed my uncle's direct order and sheepishly strode towards the house. Granny said nothing gently preventing Baba from following her in the gate. Uncle Frank was still studying the apparatus when he went into the kitchen and threw it on the table.

'Right,' he said clearing his throat, 'I'm only asking questions once and I want an answer every time, is that understood?' We both nodded. 'Right, how did this all come about?'

Granny collapsed into the fireside chair wheezing, taking deep intakes of air.

I looked at Mattie but he lowered his head; he was leaving it to me to clean up anther one of his messes. I took a deep breath and crossed my fingers in my pocket before speaking.

'We didn't want the Doiredrum Bobcat killing your lambs and hens so we made a spear to kill it.' I looked at Uncle Frank's frown of puzzlement and I continued, 'and then I saw it going past my bedroom window and I ran out and fired the spear at it.' I gulped and waited.

'Spear? 'he said and then his voice pitch increased as he continued. 'Were ye rummaging out in the Old House?'

We nodded again, as Granny left the kitchen and went into the scullery.

'That's my fishing spear,' he said in a half cry pointing to the object on the table.

I heard the scullery door closing.

'And what else did ye take?' I looked at Mattie but he still had his head down.

'Well?'

'Your fishing net Uncle Frank,' I spluttered out responding to his roared demand.

'And where is that now?'

'Hanging on the tree,' I said softly, still eying Mattie for help that was not forthcoming.

'What blooda tree?'

'The sally tree,' I barely uttered concealing a sob.

Uncle Frank must have noticed that he was upsetting me because he lowered his voice issuing an order, 'Will you go and get it down from the sally tree and put it back with my fishing spear where you found it,' he said lifting and studying his improvised fishing spear.

He frowned and looked closely at the broken injection needle unit and spoke hesitantly, 'What sort of a bottle is that you have tied to my spear?'

Mattie looked up for the first time. With the needle missing and the plunger concealed with the reels of fishing line, the tube did resemble some kind of bottle. Some of the mixture was gone from the tube, which was coated white on the inside. I looked at Mattie to answer but we didn't have to say anything as Uncle Frank switched to his cross mood again and hollered, 'And is that my fishing line too?'

We were back to the 'nodding' as answers.

'Get out the pair of you and put everything back where you found it, and meet me at the sheep-pen when you're finished.'

Mattie grabbed the wasted 'lethal weapon' and I followed him out the scullery door. Granny was coming around the corner and she just smiled as I held the door open for her. I couldn't wait to scold Mattie for letting me out, to tackle the Bobcat with his stupid invention. I didn't get a chance; he spoke first, giving me a complimentary slap on the back.

'You were going to take on that wildcat yoke with your bare hands, wow?' he exclaimed and then giggled, 'did you see the wild cat pawing at that hen that was tangled in the net, and then snap, straight into his mouth?'

'No,' I said meekly.

I was dumbfounded at his praise and rather than spoil his heroic image of me, I let him believe, that I was aware of the bobcat's presence. The truth was, that when I looked out the window, all I saw was just a hen tangled in the net.

'Look he has most of the poison in him,' Mattie said with delight examining the tube and then continued as he leaped playfully into the hanging net, 'he won't live for long.'

The net flopped down around my brother and he fell to the ground laughing. He rolled and tumbled himself free and stood up.

'Destroy all evidence, get that hen' he said pointing at the dead hen under the clothesline.

I picked up the blood-matted feathered hen by a leg. The head and other leg flopped as I walked back to the gap at the sally tree. I stumbled through the long grass and dropped the fresh carcass near a growth of briars. Mattie hadn't thought out his, evidence cleanup operation, too well. It should not have necessary to hide the dead hen as I'm sure Granny would never have known that it got caught in our net trap, before the wildcat got it, but I dumped the carcass anyway.

We had the net folded in a short time, but Mattie had to bite at the knots of the fishing line a few times, before he eventually unwound the line and separated the remnants of the injection needle, from the fishing spear. He aimed the poisonous tube at the spade in the briars and threw it hard. The glass tube shattered on the metal spade head and sprinkled broken glass into the weeds and grass beneath the briars. We made one trip back to the Old House with the net and then returned to bring back the spear and reel of fishing line. I replaced the wire on the door bolt as I had found it and walked with Mattie to the pen gate.

Uncle Frank was in the pen, chasing another sheep to be sheared.

'Did you get those eggs you were talking about?' he directed his question at me rubbing his perspiring brow with the back of his hand.

We left him without saying anything. I meekly asked Granny for the basket and told her of the possibility of a nest at the back of the stream. Granny called after us that we should also search along the embankment on the way to the well as we set about our quest for the nests of 'outlaying hens.'

Mattie stood well away from the stream holding the basket while I leaped across the stream. He was obviously conscious of the 'poisonous snake' in the stream. I found the nest exactly where the hen had flown from, the day before, when Mattie threw a stone and challenged his imaginary snake to a fight. The nesting hen made several attempts to peck me as I outwitted her and managed to retrieved five eggs from under her warm body. I cradled them in my arms jumping back over the stream and watched helplessly as one tumbled from my clutch and floated in the current and vanished into the drainpipe under the farmyard.

'Sloppy Finn, very sloppy,' Mattie giggled as he tried to conceal his visual search in the stream for 'poisonous snakes.' I carefully lowered the remaining eggs into the basket and we headed for the embankment near the spring well.

'Try and stay dry this time,' Mattie sniggered throwing an egg up in the air and catching it in the basket as it fell. I heard the splatter and grabbed the basket from him to examine the result. Just as expected, one egg was completely smashed, and the one it had collided with, was splattered with egg yolk and cracked. I dumped them in the long grass along the lane and wiped my hands in a dock leaf.

'I found a nest, I found a nest!' Mattie hollered holding an egg in each of his raised hands, running out from the hedge at the embankment, as a hen with ruffled feathers flapped its wings after him. The hen stopped and squawked. Mattie turned and in quick succession fired the eggs at the disgruntled hen. Two separate egg yolk stains, on the stony lane marked the final destination of the hen's labours. The rest of our labours proved negative and we returned to the scullery with just two eggs.

'Well is that all ye got?' Granny said grimly lifting the two forlorn eggs from the basket. She shook each egg individually close to her ear and then dropped them in the rubbish bucket behind the door as she spoke, 'Ye found these too late, the hen was hatching them, they're rotten now.'

She must have noticed my look of curiosity, because she followed up with an explanation for her actions, 'If you hear a sort of a rattle, or if an egg floats, then that egg is either hatching or rotten.'

I didn't feel too bad now about the one I dropped in the stream, but Mattie's breakages could be presumed 'fresh.'

'Ah, I'm out of flour,' Granny said looking into a press.

'Do you want us to go to the shop for you?' Mattie asked pleadingly.

'Ah, I don't think so, the travelling shop will be here tomorrow.'

Mattie frowned, but then he smiled as Granny had a rethink.

'No, no, I think I'll have to bake tonight, Johnny Byrne will be expecting something, I'll get some money.'

Mattie followed Granny into her bedroom and was still walking close to her when she returned to the kitchen with her handbag. She opened her purse and took out a shilling. Granny looked at the calendar at the back of the door and then the clock on the mantelpiece as she spoke pondering.

'Paddy Cassidy usually goes to cash his War Pension about this time—he might give ye a lift, if you tell him who you are,' and then in a sterner voice continued, 'and ye should be back by dinner time, if ye go straight there and back.'

'As quick as you like granny,' Mattie said holding out his hand and taking the money from Granny as she spoke.

'Get me two pounds of flour.'

'What section in the shop will I get the flour in?' I asked wanting to show that I was going to play my part too help.

'Section?' Granny frowned and then continued, 'Pauric or Ann will serve you, or sometimes Ann's sister Maura gives a hand if the post office is not busy,' she concluded breaking into her usual puffy whistle.

We were barely out the small gate at the front of the house when Mattie divulged another one of his plans, 'We have to find the body and collect the money,' he said running off in front of me.

As soon as he got to the top of the lane he climbed over the gate and leaped into the meadow. I walked past him and was opening the gate at the top of the lane when he shouted over the wall at me.

'Where are you going?'

'To the shop and nowhere else,' I responded in a determined voice.

'But unless I show Stephen the dead wildcat he won't give me my bounty money,' he pleaded from the meadow side of the wall keeping in line with me as I walked up the road. 'So you're not going to search with me, right so,' he said in a threatening tone, 'I was going to split the bounty money with you, but now you can forget it,' Mattie muttered climbing over the wall and tumbling onto the road behind me.

I didn't believe him so I felt free to say what I wanted without fear of loosing out on any deal he might offer. 'Anyway you don't know if it died, it looked very much alive the last time I saw it,' I called back over my shoulder at him as I increased my pace passing Teach an Dochtúra.

CHAPTER 16

Flourbag Secrets

'I WONDER WHAT SORT OF A CAR this Carson man has?' Mattie asked kicking at loose stones as we plodded along the road.

'Who's "Carson"?' I quizzed.

'The man that's giving us a lift, dumbo,' Mattie snapped.

'His name is "Paddy Casidy," and there was no mention about a car,' I corrected as we walked up the incline passing the vacant doctor's house. I strained my neck and looked back to check if the wrecked horse trap was visible over the perimeter walls of Teach an Dochtúra and was relieved that it wasn't. Before I turned around again I saw a donkey-and-cart trotting along the road behind us. A small man with a cap was holding the reins close to his chest. I nudged Mattie and pointed.

'Wells Fargo comes to town,' Mattie said with a laugh.

I stood to the side on the grass verge to let him pass as he approached. Mattie stood out in the middle of the road and raised his hand like a policeman stopping traffic.

'What are you doing?' I shrieked.

'This will do until our real lift arrives and then we can jump off,' Mattie responded in a low calm voice.

The man pulled on the reins and stopped the donkey in front of Mattie.

'Good afternoon sir,' Mattie said lowering his hand. The man pushed his cap up slightly from his forehead and looked at both of us in turn. Mattie walked to the side and placed his hand on the shaft near the front of the cart as he spoke.

'A Mister Carson…'

I exhaled deeply in disbelief at Mattie's memory retention and just looked at him as he continued to lie.

'…well this Mister Carson was supposed to pick us up but he drove by and just left us here,' Mattie's voice faded out as he shook his head with a faked look of disappointment.

The man pushed his cap further back and his frown became visible.

'I don't know any "Carson" around here but if you want a lift…' he said moving over on his improvised seat that was really a board which rested on either side of the cart.

Mattie had jumped up on the ass-cart so fast that the donkey raised his head and moved backwards.

'Easy will ya!' the man roared pulling on the reins and moving further along the board. I don't know if he was talking to Mattie or his donkey. Mattie had moved close to the man and was sitting down by the time I had climbed on the cart.

'Who are ye anyway?' he asked flicking the reins. The donkey moved with a sudden jerk.

'I'm Mattie and this is my brother Finn, Uncle Frank is our uncle,' Mattie explained pulling at the tartan rug that was covering the man's lap.

'Are ye Tessie's lads?' he asked looking over at us.

'That's us, and who is yourself sir?' Mattie asked tugging at the rug again.

'Paddy Cassidy,' he replied retrieving the piece of rug that Mattie had tugged from him as he held the reins with the other hand.

I was glad now that Mattie had got the name wrong after what he had said about being abandoned on the side of the road.

'Do you want some cover?' Mattie asked me as he jerked the rug towards me with both hands.

The rug sprung free from Cassidy's hand and most of it landed on the floor of the cart. I looked at him and I could see fire welling in his eyes. I bent down and stretched to grab the rug but my face was sideways on the front board of the cart and couldn't see exactly what I was lifting. As I grabbed the rug I could feel a long rounded solid object underneath it.

'Uncle Frank always lets me drive his cart,' I heard Mattie lie as I rose up struggling with the rug and its attachment.

Mattie pulled the rug from me and left me grabbling with what fell from underneath it. It was a crutch.

Mattie looked puppy-eyed as he spoke, 'Uncle Frank says that I am the best...'

I cut across him in mid sentence as I exclaimed with a shriek and spluttered out, 'You only have one leg!'

I was clumsily pointing with the crutch at Mister Cassidy's folded and pinned-up trouser leg. Paddy Cassidy wrenched the crutch from my hand as Mattie pushed me. I just about got my balance as I landed to the ground but lost it again. Mattie had tumbled onto me, yelping 'ouch' and we both rolled into the side embankment along the road. The donkey got spooked.

Paddy Cassidy struggled to gain control of his transport as the donkey swerved towards a field gate and tried to either go through it or jump over it. I followed Mattie as he got to his feet rubbing his head and ran back most of the way we had only just covered in the ass-cart.

Mattie slowed his pace to a halt as he looked back over his shoulder.

'Hay, Ho, Hopalong Cassidy away,' Mattie bellowed through cupped hands in the direction of the man desperately trying to control a fretting donkey as it now galloped frantically along the road.

I looked after them until they had careered and vanished around the bend before speaking.

'It's "Hay, Ho, Silver away,' I corrected Mattie in relation to the Lone Ranger's chant and not Hopalong Cassidy's.

'Never mind "Hay, Ho" Finn, did you really think that Carson ah eh Cassidy, whatever his name is didn't know he only had one leg until you told him, dumbo, and thanks to you I got a whack of his crutch on the head,' Mattie cringed rubbing his head as we walked the roadway we had been transported on a short time earlier.

Every so often Mattie would jump up in the air and peer down fields and say in the same disappointing tone, 'No sign of my bounty.'

I could read the sign over the shop as we rounded a bend— 'O'Tooles Grocery and Bar' was written in green letters over the door at one end and 'Doiredrum Post Office' was written in smaller letters at the other end of the two story whitewashed building. Doors lay invitingly open under each of the signs. A petrol pump appearing to have been newly installed gleamed in its newly set concrete base in the forecourt.

As we got closer I noticed a new looking bench near the shop and bar entrance door and another bench in poorer condition propped against the Post Office wall.

The spout on a rusty pump hung drearily over a dried up stone water trough at the side of the shop.

The heavy foliage on chestnut and oak trees practically blocked out a stone crucifix mounted on the gable end of a church, as crows and jackdaws squawked and fought viciously flying in and around the church and trees.

Handlebars and front wheel of a bicycle were turned deep into a hedge at the post office side of the building.

'Is that where you posted your letter to Mammy?' I jibed Mattie pointing to the green postbox embedded in the post of-fice wall.

'Never mind the postbox, does that bike belong to that lanky postman,' Mattie stopped suddenly and squinted towards the bicycles.

'No, it has no front carrier,' I said putting Mattie at ease.

'Is this the pub entrance or shop entrance?' Mattie asked out loud going in the open door. I shrugged my shoulders.

'The one door does both,' a chirpy female voice called from inside. I followed Mattie as we moved into a hallway that had doors practically facing one another half way down the dark hallway.

The smiling face of a petite young woman greeted us leaning

over a bar counter as I looked into a barroom on the right side of the hallway. She remained smiling as we came into the pub. Mattie took a quick glance at the woman as he walked past her and kept walking until he came to the end of the bar. I followed him. I looked left into a corner section at the end of the pub where a tattered dartboard hung on the end wall. I don't know why I am following Mattie because I don't think that he knows where he's going.

Mattie frowned and looked back at the woman, 'Where's the shop?'

'You mished it, tiz on the other side of the hall,' the woman lilted in her western dialect.

I hadn't noticed a middle aged man slouched over the counter just behind the pub door entrance until we had turned and were walking back. He appeared to be sleeping on the counter-top using his arms as a pillow. He is broad shouldered and his balding dishevelled black hair just grazed the glass in front of him. The pint glass was partially filled with stout with a stale looking yellow froth on top.

'Do you know if they have flour in the shop?' Mattie asked as he came level to the female who appeared to be holding in her desire to burst out laughing.

Mattie mustn't have been listening to Granny when she told us that it was a husband and wife that owned both the pub and shop and that her sister ran the post office.

'Flour is it you want, I'd say they do, would you like some?' the woman just about uttered before she began giggling. Mattie looked at me but I didn't know why she was giggling either.

'Who are ye? she asked lifting the counter hatch and coming into the public part of the bar.

Mattie just kept walking towards the hallway and didn't answer. She stopped giggling and looked at me for an answer.

'Finn and Mattie, Uncle Frank is our uncle,' I answered nervously at first but then was confident enough to ask, 'are you missus Anne O'Toole?'

'I am,' she relied pleasantly and added, 'God but your verra posh, call me Ann,' she introduced herself and then with a raised finger continued, 'ah, I know who ye are now, Tessie's lads, isn't it?' she said skipping past Mattie.

'Have they "gobstoppers"?' Mattie asked looking up at her.

'We have,' Anne answered as a smile lit up her face.

'Have they "liquorice ropes"?' Mattie queried again standing close to her at the door.

It still hadn't dawned on Mattie that Ann was the shop owner.

'We'll take a look and see,' Ann said turning a wobbly black knob as she pushed open the door to the sound of clanging bells.

The agitating smell of soap power pierced my nostrils. Mattie went straight to the sweet section stand in front of the till and I followed Ann to the other end of the shop.

She spoke as she went inside a small counter that had weighing scales on top of it, 'how much flour does your Granny want?'

I had to think for a second or two but then answered quickly, 'two pounds please.' 'I think I have a bag weighed,' she said stretching to a shelf situated over a white sack that was upright on the floor. The sack which appeared to be bursting at the seams had blue print on it—RANKS PURE FLOUR— and further down the sack was written in smaller print '1 hwt.'

'You're in luck, two pounds of flour weighed and ready for you,' Ann smiled taking down a bulging paper bag from the shelf.

I followed her to the till at the confectionary counter. Mattie was waiting there and placed two toffee bars on the counter as Ann went behind it.

'Are ye paying by cash or cheque?' she asked sternly and then burst into laughter when I looked at Mattie with a puzzled face. 'Will there be anything else?' she asked at the end of her laughter.

'That depends on how much the flour costs,' Mattie replied looking up at Ann with a pleading face as he slid the shilling across the counter towards her.

'Ah, I see,' Ann said pressing her finger to her lips as if in deep thought, 'let me see so, did your Granny tell you to get sweets with the change?'

Mattie nodded a definite 'yes' as my eyes widened with disbelief; Granny had most definitely not said to get sweets with the change.

'Well then,' Ann said taking her finger from her lips, 'how about two gobstoppers as well, not that ye need them for all the chatting you do, but anaways that will kill the shilling, okay?'

She placed the two toffee bars and two gobstoppers in a small white paper bag. Ann held the bag by the two top corners and gave it a twirl before placing the now semi-sealed bag on the countertop.

Mattie had put the bag in his pocket before Ann had clanged down the shilling button on the cash register. He went out the shop door, crossed the hallway and back into the bar. I picked up the flour and closely followed behind Ann.

'Great,' I answered her question as to how we were enjoying our holidays, stopping behind Mattie who was now struggling to climb onto a barstool at the counter.

The man in the corner was still slouched in the same position at bar counter. The drink in front of him had a small black fly struggling for its life in the yellow froth on top. A man bending down inside the counter was clanging bottles as he wiped them before placing them in a row on a shelf. He stopped to watch Mattie balancing himself on the wobbling barstool.

'How are ye?' he asked straightening up. His broad smile revealed white teeth as a trickle of sweat ran down the side of his black hair locks.

'Very well thank you sir,' I replied bearing Mammy's instructions in mind and answering for Mattie as well who was now wriggling and twisting his hand in his pocket.

'Be God ye're not from around these parts talking like that,' he said studying his two new customers as he wiped his hands in the dishcloth and introduced himself, 'I'm Pauric, and what can I get you?'

'They're Frank's nephews,' Ann informed him going back behind the bar.

'Ah Tessies lads, from Clunmon, you're verra welcome,' Pauric said discarding the dishcloth on the sparkling glasses at the sink.

'Get me a...' Mattie said peering along the shelves.

'Did anyone see Paddy Cassidy yet?' a young woman interrupted entering the bar.

'No Maura, he hasn't called in yet,' Ann answered.

'Well I wish he'd hurry up because I want to have my dinner and you know what he's like if there's nobody in the post office to cash his war pension postal order,' the woman said going towards the door.

'Maura, Maura, hold on,' Pauric beckoned the woman, 'I did see him, but he was travelling like lightening, and flew past here.' He took a breath and chuckled before adding, 'I was coming down from the top field when I saw him galloping along the road at speed, well, the little cart was hitting the road in spots, he must be half way to Portwest by now.'

'I'll have a...' Mattie began his order again but stopped and leaped from the bar stool as a half crown coin sprang from his pocket and clanged and rolled along the concrete floor. Mattie went on his hunkers as soon as he landed from the bar stool and chased the rolling half crown. It collided against the bottom of the counter and then spun a few times before eventually flopping to a stop under the sleeping man's stool in the corner. Mattie had no hesitation in grabbing the man's trouser leg for balance as he reached under the stool to retrieve his holiday pocket money. The man sprung to life and flaked out with his hand. The pint glass and stale contents toppled and splashed over the counter as Mattie scurried away on his hunkers with the half-crown firmly gripped in his hand.

'Don't move Walter, don't move,' Pauric roared at the man swinging and wobbling as he stumbled from his bar stool and sprawled himself against the wall.

A choking pungent smell engulfed and swallowed up the air in the bar. Ann grabbed her nose and pressed herself back against the bar till. Mattie cancelled his movement to get back up on his recently vacated bar stool. I cancelled my next intake of breath as I rushed to the door.

'Bad shest to you any ways, what did you disturb him for, you broke the crust on him, he'll stink us out of it now,' Pauric spluttered lifting the bar counter hatch with one hand and covered his mouth with the other.

Mattie pushed me aside getting out the front door and into the sweet country fresh air. He was gasping in air sitting on the edge of the water trough under the disused pump as I plodded towards him with the bag of flour.

'And Delaney leave your bike where it is before you kill yourself, you can throw yourself in the river for a wash if you like,' Pauric said leading the smelly man by the scruff of his collar at arms length as he ushered him onto the road.

'Delaney, Walter Delaney,' I said looking at Mattie for confirmation.

Mattie stared blankly at me as he swiped at two wasps circling over his head.

'He's the man who owns the donkeys, remember Uncle Frank said the name "Walter Delaney,"' I said in a half whisper.

Mattie didn't reply as he stood up and used his two hands to crank down the rusty handle on the pump. The pump handle squeaked and jammed. Mattie tried pushing it back up. A few extra wasps had gathered now and were buzzing around his head.

'Keep away from that oul pump, it hasn't worked for years, there's a wasp's nest in it now,' Pauric called from the door before he went back inside his premises.

Mattie ducked down scampering away from the pump but I kept in front of him as he ran. The wasps had returned to the pump when Mattie panted to a halt beside me at the hedge.

'Are you thinking what I'm thinking?' Mattie asked kicking the back wheel of the bicycle lodged in the hedge.

I knew instinctively what he intended doing. I was hoping that Mattie had had enough of 'bicycles' since our episode with the postman's bike but I was wrong. 'No I'm not thinking what you're thinking,' I replied jerking the flour up under my arm, 'and anyway I don't like carrying a bag of flour when I'm having a "crossbar,"' I objected to Mattie's imminent plan.

'Look,' Mattie said drawing my attention to a rusty carrier over the rear wheel of the bicycle, 'and a lovely low saddle as well,' he enticed pulling the bicycle completely free from the hedge.

'Mattie I'm going walking back,' I said going past the petrol pump.

'We'll bring it back tomorrow, we'll hide it at ,tig, ah, teachha, ah what do you call the doctor's old house,' Mattie called after me.

'Teach an Dochtúra,' I muttered but kept moving.

'Do you want another lift on the ass-cart with "Hopalong"?'

I stopped walking, looked back and conceded to his powers of his persuasion and my fear of meeting again the one legged man on the ass-cart.

Mattie was lining up and studying the bicycle as I walked back towards him. A single wasp was hovering and buzzing around the back of his neck as if searching for a landing spot.

'Give me that,' he said turning and taking the flour bag from me. He stretched the top of the carrier upwards until the spring hinges twanged to their full capacity.

He placed the bulging flour bag lengthways on the base frame and lowered the top part of the carrier onto it.

'That's going to spill out,' I cautioned him pointing to the top of the paper-bag facing outwards. 'Sit it straight on the carrier and against the butt of the saddle,' I instructed pulling up the spring loaded part of the carrier, as Mattie removed the bag.

He reluctantly took my advice and jammed the flour bag the way I had advised. He faced the bicycle back towards the road and mounted it.

Mattie had one foot firmly on the ground while the other rested on a raised peddle. He lowered one hand from the handle-bars so I could slip up onto the crossbar. 'Don't move,' he whispered with a startled look raising his free hand and then with swiping speed slapped his open hand on the back of his neck with a victory cry, 'die fly, die.'

He gasped and cringed as he flicked his hand rapidly and re-peatedly. A wasp tumbled to the ground and then rose again in a staggered flight. Mattie straddled the bicycle now with both feet on the ground while still sucking and licking his finger web.

'He stung me, it wasn't a fly, it was a bee, he stung me,' he whimpered and then pointed to the disused water pump yelling, 'I'm going to kill you all dead, dead, do you hear me, dead.'

'What's all the shouting about?' Maura the Post Mistress called from the post office doorway as she removed her spectacles and frowned, 'and what are ye doing with Mister Delaney's bicycle?'

'He asked us to bring it home for him,' Mattie spoke through his fingers still held near his mouth.

'Who are ye anyways?'

'Stephen and Agnes's nephews from Manchester,' Mattie answered as he closely examining his hand and returned to sucking and licking the area around his wasp sting.

Maura stared at us for a second or two. I thought that Mattie had been found out in his lie but then I remembered that Maura wasn't in the bar when Ann introduced us to Pauric. She replaced her spectacles low on her nose and dubiously muttered 'good boys' as she went back inside the post office. I just know that it wont be long until she finds out who we really are but there is no turning back now on the lie or the bicycle.

I grabbed the handlebars and pulled myself up onto the crossbar. We wobbled for a while getting our balance in the forecourt but once on the open road Mattie got into a steady stride and all was going well. I remembered the last time I was getting a 'crossbar' when carrying flour. All didn't go so well.

Usually when Vinny and I went to the border shop to get butter we would smuggle it into the South by going along the railway track adjacent to the road. The Customs Hut was visible from the railway track but all the customs men could do was shout at you to come over to the hut for inspection but we always ignored them and ran along the railway track. That was the usual routine until Sparks said that he had a great idea how to avoid all that walking and running.

It was legally permissible to purchase flour in the North and bring it into the South because there was no price difference. However butter was a different matter. It was half the price North of the border and was regarded as contraband when brought South. Spark's plan seemed foolproof; there would be no long walk involved, no running and I will be getting a 'crossbar' from him on his father's bicycle.

The next time our mothers needed butter we put his smuggling plan into operation and began our half-mile cycle North. We were delighted to see that it was Pascal Reidy who was on duty at the Customs Post because Pascal never bothered to check people on bicycles. When we reached the shop just north of the border Sparks put the second part of his plan into action.

He instructed Jimmy Bohan the owner of the shop to place the butter on its ends in the centre of the paper bag and fill the space left at the sides and at the top with flour until it concealed the butter completely. I got Jimmy to do the same for me.

He smiled broadly putting an extra piece of sellotape, as requested by Sparks, on top of the folded creases on the paper bag. We pooled our change and bought our usual Spangles and Cartwheels as those types of sweets were not on sale in the South.

'You're some bootleggers all right,' the shop owner chuckled as we were leaving and then added in a serious tone, 'remind me to charge you for that bit of flour the next time your "across."'

We put one bag upright on the back carrier and I held the other close to me sitting on the crossbar. On the return trip we were cruising along calmly as we approached the Customs Post but then Sparks whined, 'look,' and took a wobble on the bicycle. We both gasped together. Pascal had gone and was relieved by George Kelly who was standing in the doorway of the Customs Hut.

The word on Kelly was that he would 'do his own mother.'

'Stay calm, stay calm,' Sparks muttered.

I did until I saw Kelly stepping onto the roadway in front of us. He fluttered his hand to the side like a bird with a broken wing.

'He wants us to stop,' Sparks stated the obvious applying the brakes.

I stayed on the crossbar as Kelly calmly removed the bag from my hands.

'And what have we here?' he smirked.

'Flour,' I said and then pursed my lips.

He shook the bag as if guessing the weight and then spoke in a mocking tone, 'Say what you like about Jimmy Bohan, but he gives great value in flour weight.'

His Donegal accent grated my eardrums and I gulped as he slowly removed the two strips of sellotape. He opened the folds and widened the bag at the top as he peered in. After patting the sides of the bag with open alms he glanced at me and peered into the bag again. Flour dust settled on his dark tunic. His wry smile turned to a sneer as he slowly drew a pencil from the top pocket of his tunic and poked it into the flour at the top of the bag.

'Uh, uh, ups,' he said smiling as the pencil pushed back up through his fingers. He had struck the butter still concealed in the flour.

He took two military-like steps to the rear of the bicycle.

'Same here?' he questioned pushing his face close to Sparks.

Sparks nodded and frowned.

'Next time I take the bike as well as the contraband,' he said yanking the other bag from the carrier.

Mattie interrupted my silent reminiscing.

'We have plenty of time now to look for that dead Bobcat, and I can collect my bounty,' he said raising himself on the peddles as we neared familiar fields.

I knew by his next actions that my emphatic response had both annoyed and scared him, 'You can go looking for it if you want to but I am going back to the house, and anyway how do you know that it died, it might only be wounded and more vicious.'

Mattie conceded and peddled furiously ahead until we reached Teach an Dochtúra. I jumped off as soon as we stopped and went around the back of the bicycle.

The flour bag was listing to one side and it didn't appear to be as full as it was when we were leaving the shop. I examined it more closely as Mattie pushed the bicycle through the large gate he had just opened. The rear tyre and wheel spokes were coated in white. A small tear near the top of the bag was still leaking its powdered contents.

Mattie parked the bicycle inside the wrought iron gates and I began my forensic examination to determine the cause. I removed the bag in trepidation. A broken spring under the saddle seemed to point leeringly back at me. I meekly placed my finger to the hole in the flour bag. I felt that I was in just as much danger as the brave Dutch boy Hans who had held his finger in the leaking dyke.

'What's wrong with you?' Mattie asked observing my deathly stare.

I thought of something else that was going to add to my woes and posed my question. 'As well as this,' I pointed to the leaking flour, 'what are you going to say to granny about having no change to give her?'

'What's the big deal?' my brother said calmly folding the bag down to the holed part and scratched his head before speaking slowly, 'let me think so…lost a bit of flour okay, no change okay, eh, the price of flour has gone up and what the woman in the shop gave us is exactly one shillings' worth.'

'You can say that if you want but I am not,' I said dismissively presenting Mattie with the flour.

'Ok, missy Finn but remember no gobstoppers or toffee bars for you,' Mattie grumped grabbing the flour. I don't think that I was in line for any of the tuck anyway so I don't feel that I lost out on anything.

The horse shackled to the mower, was tied by the reins to the gate at end of the front yard as we walked down the lane.

'Ye made good time did ye get a lift?' Uncle Frank called to us from his bedroom as we passed in the hallway to the kitchen.

'Yes, Mister Carson ah, eh Mister Cassidy gave us a lift, a lovely man, told us all about his missing leg,' Mattie called back.

'What!' Granny exclaimed.

My uncle frowned as he spoke coming into the kitchen. 'Are you sure it was Paddy Cassidy you were talking to, sure it's like waving a red rag at a bull to mention his war wound, he goes into shell shock at the mention of it.'

'The people who sent those young lads into the trenches in that War have a lot to answer for,' Granny sighed lifting the flour bag that Mattie had left on the table. She stopped half way to the scullery and asked the inevitable question raising the bag to eyelevel.

'Well wasn't Ann badly off, doesn't she know well that I'd pay her later for the full amount of flour,' Granny said smarting, having listened to Mattie's explanation as to how she had not got the full two pounds of flour.

I went to the bedroom to avoid any further questioning.

The bedclothes were pulled back. Faded lettering in blue print was barely recognisable on the sheets airing on our bed. The early afternoon summer breeze was lapping in the open window. I tried to make sense of the letters and after some time squinting was able to read RANKS PURE FLOUR in the larger print and '1 hwt' in the smaller print. As I return to the kitchen for dinner I'm hoping that Granny doesn't think that it was Mattie or me who wrote on the bed sheets.

CHAPTER 17

Pig Block

AFTER FINISHING THE DINNER we left the table and followed Uncle Frank with his horse and mower to another meadow. This particular meadow wasn't as big as the previous one and not as many flying ants to plague us.

'You're getting good at this,' Uncle Frank said inspecting our hay raking in the meadow he had just cut. He was smiling as he turned the horse and mower towards the gate.

'Are we finished for the day now?' Mattie grumped following him closely.

Uncle Frank gave a mocking laugh and then spoke back at us as he headed back down the lane, 'Ye are when you shake out the hay you turned yesterday in the big meadow.'

Uncle Frank had issued each of us with a pitchfork to shake out the drying hay but he took Mattie's away from him when he saw him throwing it around the meadow like spear and told him to shake the hay out with his hands now.

I had to agree with Mattie though when he complained that it didn't make sense to shake and scatter the hay this way one day and then rake it back to the same place in small stacks the next day.

I was tired when it came to teatime.

The aroma of freshly baked bread filled the air as I entered the yard. We sat down to a meal of fresh brown bread and cheese.

Granny told us that she had a pleasant surprise for us if finished what was on our plates. Raisin scones with jam turned out to be the treat. Mattie picked out the raisins from the scones and heaped on the strawberry jam over the butter. Granny wanted to know if there were many people in the shop. I told her that we think we met the man who owns the straying donkeys. I knew by Mattie's stare that I had said enough about our trip to the shop.

'Does that oul Delaney ever leave the pub?' Granny scorned shaking a baking tray of freshly cooked scones onto the table.

Uncle Frank just tossed his head backwards but said nothing. One scone was rolling off the table but Mattie caught it and tossed it back but it rolled off the other side and onto the floor. Granny kept staring at him until he crawled under the table and retrieved it. He placed it gently on top of the pile of scones this time.

'If ye're not too tired will ye bring these few scones and this cake of bread over to Johnny Byrne for me,' she said coming from the scullery with a basket in her hand.

I recognised the basket; it was the one we had collected the eggs in but this time it had a tea towel draped over it.

'Where does he live?' I asked enthusiastically.

'The next house past Tim Herrity's.' Uncle Frank became more precise noticing my frown, 'Go left when you go out the gate,' he added and pointing behind him.

'Did Tim's sow have her bonhams yet?' Granny called from the scullery amidst the distinctive clanging sound of dishes in water.

'I don't know, but it shouldn't be long now,' Uncle Frank answered sinking into the fireside chair.

I was waiting at the front porch when Mattie joined me wildly swinging the basket.

'Will you be careful!' Granny's voice echoed into the hallway. Mattie handed the basket to me when we were going out the gate at the top of the lane.

I could see the roof of Tim Herrity's house as we walked up the small incline on the road but as we reached the top we both stopped abruptly. A rotund sow stood facing us in the middle of the road just over the incline. Mattie looked at me as we cautiously made our way towards her. The sow was sniffing the air between snorts. Her hairy pink body was dirty in patches and two rows of teats hung heavy and robust under her floppy belly. It made no effort to move off the road as we slowed our pace towards it.

I moved to the right to ease past it and balanced myself on the edge of the road embankment so as not to tumble into the deep ditch below. Mattie followed my actions but the sow snorted and with two short steps had blocked our path to safety.

We changed direction and attempted to pass out on the left side of the roadway. The sow seemed to be pivoted on its hind legs as it did a bouncy dance on its two front legs to face us going left. The air-sniffing, grunting and snorting increased as her pale pink eyes squinted and stared. We made one more attempt to pass on the right hand side but once again the bovine animal threatened our approach.

Mattie had been holding my arm during the manoeuvres but when we stood still contemplating some other way to pass I glimpsed the tea-towel moving on the basket. I looked down to see his skinny hand remove a freshly baked scone from under the cloth. His aim, throw and contact resulted in a 'bulls eye' shot except it was a pig's eye that he hit.

The scone disintegrated on impact leaving the narrow road-way strewn with large and small scone crumbs. The animal leaped in a cumbersome fashion with a deafening squeal and tumbled into the deep ditch on the side of the road. I took a quick look as I ran past. The sow was on her back and made in-termittent snorts and squeals as it struggled to right itself in the bottom of the drainage ditch. I pushed the tea towel down into the basket and ran behind Mattie.

As we were passing Tim Herrity's, I saw a grey bearded man resting on a crooked walking stick peering from the doorway of the house. The barking of the sheep dog inside the gate was only just audible over the squealing sow in the background.

At last Johnny Byrne's house came into view. Mattie had al-ready opened the door of the house when I was only arriving at the front gate.

'Come in ye're welcome,' a voice called out from inside the poky house. 'Ye're Tessie's lads aren't ye, and this is something for me from your granny, am I right?' the man said taking the basket from me.

Both Mattie and I stood staring at his pinned up shirt sleeve but said nothing. I recognised the distinctive looking man—he had only one arm. It was the same man who was calming the Canon's horse along the ditch, the day we were coming back from Portwest.

'I'll bet ye're wondering how I know all that, well there's no mystery, I was talking to your Granny at Mass last Sunday and she said that she was expecting you,' he finished with a mucus cough.

Mattie looked at me as Johnny Byrne removed the contents from the basket and placed them on the table which had a bright oilcloth covering. He tapped the centre of the crusty soda bread as he lowered his ear to it.

'Ah your Granny has the knack for the baking,' he said with a deep intake of breath. He made a nest of the scones near the end of the table.

'Will ye join me?' he asked merrily.

He withdrew his hand from a drawer under the table, wielding a carving knife. We shook our heads in silence. He wedged the soda bread loaf firmly on the table with his stumped arm and cut vigorously with the other until a crusty fresh slice flopped onto the table.

'Were you in the war too?' I asked.

Mattie looked wildly at me before heading for the door.

'Ah-ha, be God I wasn't in any war, there's no mystery,' he answered willingly, plastering a lump of butter on the slice of bread he had just cut.

Mattie stopped short of the door and returned to sit on one of two chairs at the table beside the stacked scones.

'I lost this,' Johnny said nodding to his arm stump and sunk his solitary yellow top tooth in the bread before continuing, 'well it happened in the coal mines in Arigna—have you ever heard of them?' we shook our heads again, 'Ah, there's no mystery,' he said acknowledging our silent response and continued, 'indeed you're not missing much, and let me tell you, nothing any good ever came out of there, not even the coal.'

He paused while he poured tea into a tin mug and sat down.

Mattie propped his elbows on the table and rested his chin on his open hands. I stood by the table with my arms folded waiting to hear the gory details of the missing limb.

'Anyways this day I was told by my gaffer to free one of the drilling machines that was stuck...' He stopped telling his story when Mattie's elbows slipped forward on the oilcloth covering on the table and ploughed into the scone stack.

Johnny concentrated on the tumbling scones and then spoke slowly gathering them up, 'There's only five here, she always gives me the half dozen.'

'There's no mystery,' Mattie said sitting back on the chair, 'you see the price of flour has gone up and that's all Granny could bake you, and she also said that you weren't to give us too much money for bringing them up to you, a shilling should cover everything she said,' Mattie concluded with a deep intake of breath and stared without blinking at the dumbfounded man.

'A shilling,' he gasped steadying himself at the table before getting up.

I gritted my teeth and stared wildly at Mattie but he just smirked.

'I don't have a lot of money but I never owed anybody anything in my life and I'm not going to start now,' the weakened one-armed man said drawing coins from his pocket and slapping them with fury onto the table. He picked a shilling from the scattered coins and slid it along the table towards Mattie.

'Tell your Granny if she has a bill for all the other times, give it to me and be God I'll pay it,' he spurted out with rage.

Mattie lifted the shilling as he spoke, 'We'll leave you in peace to get on with your lovely buns and bread.'

I grabbed the empty basket and was out the door first.

'Mattie how could you do that to that poor man, and give Granny a bad name?' I shrieked at him going out the gate.

'Missing a bun,' Mattie said dismissively and then attempted

198

to explain his actions, 'that miserable old fool was hinting that we ate one of his buns.'

'No he wasn't Mattie,' I answered angrily and then pointed my finger at him, 'and anyway you did take a scone, the one you threw at the sow, remember.'

Mattie stopped and pondered as he spoke, 'maybe we should have held on to another one,' he said turning to me to emphasise his concern, 'we'll need it if that pig got out of the drain.'

We went to and fro with our opinions of Johnny Byrne and I told Mattie that no matter what way he looked at it, that he had in fact stolen a shilling on an old helpless man. Mattie was about to reply again but stopped as we both focused on the movements of a man in the drain, where the sow had fallen into earlier.

We walked in silence towards him. I knew this had to be Tim Herrity. The dog that had been barking inside the gate as we passed Tim Herrity's house was now sniffing and eating the remaining scone crumbs on the road.

'Hey lads will you get me some help, the sow has gone into labour,' Tim Herrity called frantically from the deep ditch. He bent down again and the sow squealed pitifully.

We didn't stop running until we reached the house.

'Tim Herrity wants help now,' I screamed entering the kitchen

'His sow is gone in "favour,"' Mattie gave his interpretation from behind me.

'Will ye slow down, what are ye talking about?' Granny enquired rushing from the scullery.

'The sow is in pain in a ditch at the side of the road,' I gasped out.

'Frank is milking, go and tell him immediately,' she ordered excitedly after deciphering our urgent message.

As Uncle Frank listened to our story unfolding he gradually moved away from the cow he was milking, left the bucket at the byre door and strode in long strides up the lane. We ran to keep up with him. He immediately jumped into the drain beside Tim and the moaning sow. Mattie jumped in also and collided with Tim on landing who had to use his walking stick to regain his balance. I was about to follow when I noticed the slimy blood on Tim's hands and remained on the roadside instead rubbing the thick coat of the contented sheep dog.

I heard a choking cough and looked back into the ditch. Mattie was vomiting as he climbed the embankment. I forced myself to look back where the action was taking place. Three lifeless piglet's were left in a line on the grass verge. The sheep dog was edging his way towards them when Uncle Frank roared at him and the dog scampered.

I followed Mattie back the road towards Granny's house.

'I never want to see that again,' Mattie said wiping his tongue with the back of his hand and then continued, 'it was like watching the butcher's sausage machine pushing out sausages, except instead of a sausage machine it was a pig squirting out loads of baby pigs, aah.'

He stopped at the gate at the top of the lane and pondered, 'I have a shilling and we have a bike just up there,' he pointed towards Teach an Dochctura, 'what do you say we go to the shop for sweets?' I opened the gate, shook my head and walked down the lane without giving him a verbal answer.

'Was it as bad as they say with the sow and the bonhams?' Granny asked nodding at us, when Uncle Frank came back from the bathroom and strode into the kitchen.

'Worse,' he sighed still drying his hands in a small hand towel, 'saved seven but lost three and Tim'll have to get the vet for the sow,' he slumped into the fireside chair, 'it looks like it took an awful tumble into that "shuck." Oh yes,' he turned and looked at Mattie and I, 'Tim told me to ask you, was the sow in the "shuck" when ye were on yer way to Johnny's house?'

'Drinking and eating away as happy as could be,' Mattie replied.

Uncle Frank frowned.

Granny shook her head as she spoke, 'We'll have the Rosary after you finish the milking.'

'I won't be long, I'm nearly finished,' he responded, springing to his feet.

I don't think that I want to be a farmer.

Even though I went to the toilet before going to bed I still had to go again just as I was dropping off to sleep. Raisins and currants affect me like that and I had had another one of Granny's raisin scones with milk after the Rosary. When I was coming back from the bathroom I stopped to look out the bedroom window before getting back into bed. Mattie wheezed in a deep sleep.

The moon shone bright on the back yard. The curtains still taunted me as to where I'd seen them before as they fluttered in the gentle breeze wafting through the open bedroom window. My eyes widened, my mouth dropped open and my body went cold.

CHAPTER 18

The White Furry Ghost

I WAS STILL SCREAMING and shaking when Uncle Frank and Granny came running into the bedroom in quick succession. I was pointing out the bedroom window and trying to speak.

'You're okay *a grá*,' Granny said bending down and cuddling me.

Uncle Frank was on his hunkers holding my two hands. My screams lowered and a whinging cry took over.

'You're all right it was just a bad dream,' Uncle Frank repeated.

'What were you dreaming about?' Mattie asked sitting on the side of the bed.

I gasped for air between my cries and got a few words to come out, 'the ghost, the, the ghost.'

'What ghost? Mattie asked sliding from the bed to a standing position beside Uncle Frank.

I tried again, 'The ghost, the Wildcat Ghost,' I gulped my words, trembling and staring out the bedroom window.

'The what ghost?' Granny asked moving her face close to mine wheezing as she caught her breath.

'What's he saying?' Uncle Frank asked.

'Will you let him talk,' Granny interrupted.

All were silent as I took a deep breath and spoke each few

words with a definite pause, 'I looked out the window; the white ghost; red eyes; looking in at me; a red hen in its mouth; the wild cat that I killed today.' I burst out crying and then everyone else began with a giggle that erupted into laughter.

My cries got louder as their laughter began to wane. Granny and Uncle Frank each put their head out the window in turn and each grinned standing up straight again. Mattie stayed where he was on the floor.

'Okay, okay, what you probably saw was Baba,' Granny hushed me consolingly.

I shook my head woefully. 'It was the Wildcat Ghost, it looked white and scary,' I protested and sobbed.

'Tell you what so, why don't you come into my bed or Granny's bed and we'll talk about this in the morning,' Uncle Frank proposed rising from his hunkers.

I looked at Granny's combed-out grey hair resting on the shoulders of her long white nightdress. I grabbed Uncle Frank's hand tightly and pulled him to his bedroom.

I was under the blankets with my head covered before I felt him sliding under the sheets. I couldn't stop myself shivering until I felt Uncle Frank's strong arm resting over the blanket on my exhausted body. I slowly drifted into a sleep as his snores faded.

My deep sleep pattern was broken with Uncle Frank's movement and whisper, 'There's hardly enough room for myself in the bed, never mind two more,' he said moving closer to me.

I stayed in a slumber mode and did not allow myself to wake up fully. I was wondering if Granny believed me after all and had been too scared to stay in her own bed and got into Uncle Franks bed too. I woke with a jolt.

The sunlight was peeping through the dishevelled curtains on Uncle Frank's bedroom window. I raised my head and peeped over his rugged face and open mouth. His snoring gave way to intermittent snorts. I could see the back of a small head face down on the mattress on the other side of Uncle Frank. I stretched up a little further in the bed and smiled, it was Mattie.

'Will you leave the child alone, and funnily enough I am missing a hen, so maybe there is another one of those wild things with white fur around the place,' Granny half heartedly scolded Uncle Frank when he gibed me at the breakfast about, 'Wildcat Ghosts and red hens.'

Mattie glanced at me and shook his head slightly.

'I did see a wildcat ghost, its fur was white and spiked and it had a hen its mouth,' I said softly with tears welling in my eyes looking into my bowl of porridge.

'Did the wildcat go boooo, I'm a ghost?' Mattie asked moving close to my ear.

'You believed me,' I said to Mattie looking for support for my vision the previous night.

'No I didn't,' he protested.

'Then why did you get into Uncle Frank's bed too?' I asked turning to him.

I saw Mattie blushing as he said dismissively, 'Because I was cold, that's why.'

Uncle Frank and I laughed at his lame excuse for joining us in the bed as Granny tried to conceal a wide grin and changed the subject with a question, 'By the way did ye have a nice chat with Mister Byrne, a great man for the stories, mind you, you mustn't have stayed very long?'

'No we didn't like to, he said that he was tired but he did say that you were the best cook in Ireland,' Mattie answered with his head bent over his porridge bowl.

Granny's smile of pride broadened before going into the scullery where she called back, 'I have a few extra scones here ye might bring over to Stephen before ye start cutting the hay.'

'For heaven's sake mother we won't have anything left for ourselves the way you are going,' Uncle Frank said getting up from the table.

'Now don't be long,' Granny said leaving a basket covered with a tea towel on the table in front of me.

'Let's get this over with as soon as we can,' Mattie whispered going out the front door,' he took a quick look back and added in a whisper, 'it's sweetie time.'

'You can go on your own to the shop,' I muttered in protest realising his intentions.

'That's the thanks I get for saving you again,' Mattie snubbed.

My confused look forced him to give an explanation.

'What about Granny's missing hen, if it hadn't got caught in the net that you put up in the sally tree maybe the wildcat wouldn't have been able to catch it, and did I rat on you...no.' Mattie somehow was convincing himself that he had done a good deed.

As we walked through the fields towards Stephen and Agnes's house I knew that I shouldn't feel guilty about the hen but I did. Mattie took the basket from me as we manoeuvred our way through the small collapsed gate to the farmyard. Stephen was bending over a metal bath beside the half whitewashed wall at the gable end of the house. He stopped midstream raising the stubby bristled whitewash brush from the bath.

'I hope you are doing as good a job on the walls as you did on the ground over there,' Mattie called pointing to large white dollop splatters on the ground near the cottage window.

'How are ye doing?' Stephen greeted moving cautiously towards us.

The whitewash brush dribbled a trail behind him.

'Ah that,' Stephen gave recognition to Mattie's statement and chuckled as he pointed, 'no, you can't blame me for that,' his chuckling brought on a cough which made him clear his throat, 'I'll give ye a good laugh about that,' he said reaching for the basket, 'from your Granny I'll bet, a heart of gold that woman.'

We followed him towards the door as he spoke, 'Anaways as I was saying, you remember that wildcat yoke you saw in my yard the last time ye were here?' We both nodded anxious to hear his wildcat story.

'Well yesterday I had just started my whitewashing and had left the bath-full of whitewash over there,' he pointed again to the splattered area, 'when low and behold if the wild yoke didn't come into the yard like lightening, squealing and buck lepping he was, turning and twisting.' My jaw was dropping on his every word as we entered the kitchen, 'and the next thing—'splash'— straight head over heels into my bath full of whitewash, well the sight of him trying to wriggle himself out of the bath.'

He was still giggling and chuckling putting the basket on the table, 'And then it gave another bucklep out of the bath, white as a ghost it was, and off with him, over the wall and down through the field, like the hammers of hell,' he took a deep breath, 'I don't know how it knew where it was going 'cause that whitewash, if it doesn't blind ya, it would burn your eyes red,' he concluded with a gasp putting the last scone on the table.

Agnes was snuggled in the same chair as she had been the last time I saw her.

Mattie raised his hands to his head and shrieked as he called out what I was privately thinking, 'The ghost, the white wildcat ghost with the red eyes, your ghost Finn.' He did a sporadic dance in the middle of the kitchen before spurting out the door.

'Ye're gas buckeens,' Stephen said with a bewildered look before tossing one of the scones to the cowering dog behind Agnes's chair.

I coyly replaced the tea towel in the empty basket. I lifted it and was on my way out the door when I heard a moan from near the fireplace.

'Well don't tell me they are back again,' Agnes sighed and turned sideways in her armchair.

I tried to catch up with Mattie but apart from his head start on me, his desire to spread the news that solved the mystery of the 'wildcat ghost' got him to Granny's house well before I did.

'The ghost mystery has been solved I hear,' Uncle Frank called from the far side of the horse he was harnessing to the mower in the yard.

'Granny says that it is the funniest story she has ever heard,' Mattie shouted coming out the front door into the yard and then added, 'oh, Uncle Frank, Granny said that she needs potatoes.'

'Does she want them now?' Uncle Frank asked with a frown.

'No, Granny's okay for today she said but she will need them for tomorrow's dinner,' Mattie replied handing the bucket to Uncle Frank.

'That woman will meet herself coming back she's so far ahead of herself,' he muttered dropping the bucket between his legs on the mower.

Uncle Frank tossed the bucket towards the gate of the potato field as he passed. He stopped at the second meadow he had cut the previous day and tied the horse to the open gate and told us to follow him in. He gave another practical quick lesson on how to rake the hay into small cocks and waited as we each took a practice run at doing the same under his watchful eye.

'Ye're getting better so I'm splitting ye up,' he said turning to me, 'I'm trusting you to rake it into small cocks here, and Mattie you come with me.'

Mattie was hitting the rake off the ground striding behind him.

It was true for Uncle Frank we were getting better at our work but it still didn't make it any easier or less boring. I was just finishing the last row of hay to be raked into small hay cocks when I froze as a frightening thought came into my mind; the spade; Uncle Frank will need the spade to dig the potatoes.

I scaled the fence furthest from the meadow that Uncle Frank and Mattie were in and headed down the lane. The spade was still resting deep in the briars. I received a few scrapes retrieving it and made final use of it by burying the remainder of Mattie's discarded medical supplies in one of the animal trap holes that were never used. The dead hen that I'd thrown into the briars yesterday was gone. A shiver went down my spine when I think where I'd seen it last; in the mouth of the 'ghost wildcat' last night.

I cautiously scurried back up the lane to the potato field and lodged it as near as memory would permit in its previous position. When I was leaving the potato field I heard the drone of an engine coming up the road. It was a white van stopping on the road near the gate at the top of the lane and I could see a small man with glasses sliding form the driver's seat and going to the gate.

As it drove down the lane I read the sign painted on the side; 'Pat Tobin For All Your Grocery Needs.' I returned to the meadow I had been working in and finished raking the remaining hay into small cocks in double fast time before heading down the lane.

The van was parked near the wall at the gate entrance to the house as I reached the yard. Then I heard footsteps running down the lane behind me. It was Mattie at high speed with the rake bouncing and dragging behind him. I could see Uncle Frank tying the hitched horse to the gate at the potato field and silently complimented myself for having put the spade back in time. The hall door was wide open and I could hear jovial conversation coming from the house as I walked in the door.

Granny introduced me to the man as 'Mister Patrick Tobin' as I came into the kitchen. His greasy black wavy hair hung scraggily around his spectacle frames that contained the thickest lenses I had ever seen. His eyes looked bulging and distorted.

'Are you the travelling shop man?' Mattie asked rushing past me to face the small man.

'No need for introductions, Pat Tobin at your service,' he grinned pushing his spectacles back up to the bridge of his nose.

He had occupied the same chair as Sadie-Tom and the postman had used. He asked us if we were busy and if we were enjoying our holiday. I thought that they should have been two separate questions as they had no bearing on one another. I just nodded and said we were having a great time and Mattie asked him when he was opening his shop.

'After this fine dinner,' he replied pulling the plate of bacon, cabbage and potatoes closer to him.'

'Let ye start, Frank shouldn't be too long,' Granny said coming from the stove with two more full dinner plates and placing them in front of Mattie and I. I was nearly finished my dinner when I heard the horse and mower crunching through the front yard.

'How are you, Pat?'

'Great, how is yourself?'

Uncle Frank and Pat exchanged greetings as Uncle Frank walked through the kitchen carrying a bucket of freshly dug potatoes.

During the dinner Pat Tobin listened with gasps and groans as Uncle Frank relayed the story of my attack on the wildcat and the subsequent dousing in Stephen's whitewash bath. I was petrified that he was going to undo Pat's heroic image of me by telling him about my fright with the ghost but he didn't. They all think that I am very brave to have tackled the wildcat on my own but I know the real story and it's staying with me.

Pat had just started the story of Tim Herrity's sow and bonhams when Mattie butted in.

'We know about that, are you ready to open the shop now?' Mattie asked pushing his empty plate to the centre of the table.

'Have some manners,' Granny scolded placing a cup of tea in front of the travelling-shop-man.

'Thanks verra much ma'am,' Pat said with a sigh of satisfaction and then continued, 'ah sure that's right, what am I thinking about at all, I remember now, sure Tim told me when I was talking to him that it was ye who ran for help to Frank.'

Pat remained silent listening to Uncle Frank expand on his efforts to save the bonhams as he spilled four spoons of sugar into his tea and stirred vigorously.

'I hope you have a plentiful supply of sugar in stock,' Uncle Frank laughed as he nodded to Pat replacing the teaspoon in the sugar bowl.

'Supply and demand, Frank,' Pat said stretching and slapping Uncle Frank on the back.

Mattie fidgeted impatiently at the kitchen door until Pat had finished his tea and kept in step with him to the back door of the van.

Pat slid back the padlock on the van door and dropped down a small stepladder. He was securing it in place when Mattie put his knee on the floor of the van and crawled in.

'Easy cann't ya,' Pat said climbing up the steps.

The rear inside storage area of the van had well stocked shelves on both sides and also along the closed partition behind the driving seat. Mattie held out his open hand to Pat.

'One shilling's worth of sweets,' Mattie gasped handing the ill-gotten money over.

Mattie had changed his mind several times with his sweet selection choice before Pat called a halt to Mattie's exchanges with stern words.

'No more changing your mind, that's your lot now, take it or leave it.'

Granny had to step back suddenly as Mattie ran and jumped from the back of the van with a wild leap. She had a vexed face as she swung her basket at him as he slipped around the side of the van. Pat helped Granny on board with an outstretched hand and a broad smile. She placed her basket on the van floor and perused along the shelves. I felt uncomfortable when the first thing that Granny put in her basket was a packet of flour.

'What do you prefer, strawberry jam or raspberry? Granny smiled as she held a jam jar in each hand in front of me.

I had no doubt that I was going to chose strawberry because Vinny had told me stories about how his brothers used to piddle in the raspberry bucket to get more weight in it when they were out picking fruit for the farmers at home. Strawberries were safer he had told me because they were picked into punnets and would leak any liquid so you couldn't piddle in them.

I had just said, 'Strawberry, please Granny,' when the van strutted forward to the jerky sound of a chugging engine that then cut out.

I grabbed Granny's arms as she stumbled backwards. I heard the clang of glass on the floor as Pat reached and steadied my Granny by grabbing her by the shoulders to stop her imminent fall to the van floor.

I looked to the floor as she regained her balance. One pot of jam was splattered and leaking its bright red colourful contents onto the floor; the other lay nestled on the bag of flour in the basket with a label smiling up at me that read 'Farm Fresh Strawberry Jam.'

I was next to stagger as Pat pushed past me and leaped out of the van. I saw Mattie running past the back door of the van once with Pat hot on his heels. The next time Mattie came to the back of the van he was being held by the scruff of the neck. The man holding him was adjusting his glasses as he spoke, 'I think Tim Herrity's suspicions are correct, you need a bit of conduct put on ya.'

I held Granny as she fumbled her way, wheezing deeply, down the steps and into the safety of her farmyard.

'I had to leave it in gear, the handbrake is broken,' Pat explained to Uncle Frank as he rushed out the front gate to his distraught mother. The travelling shop was jammed into the wall near the gate. Granny ordered Mattie to clean up the jammy mess in the van but then when she saw he was spreading it more than cleaning it she did it herself much to the protestations of the van owner.

The damage to the front wing of the van was minimal and Pat dismissed an offer of payment for the paintwork scrapes with the reassuring words, 'Not to worry, they will match the dints on the other side.'

The farewells were formal and very much in contrast to the earlier merriment. 'What did you mean, Tim Herrity's suspicions were correct?' Granny pushed Pat Tobin on his previous statement as he was starting up the van engine.

'Ah nothing, nothing, ma'am,' he said with a wave driving away.

I was taken to the same meadow as Mattie this time. Mattie was very muted doing his raking in the field behind an angry uncle. His performance had improved immensely and apart from breaking two wooden prongs on the hay rake that were caused by him whacking down on leaping frogs, the end of the work in the meadow for that day was uneventful.

Mattie ate his two boiled eggs at tea without saying anything except 'thank you.' Granny stuck to her threat; after the tea and Rosary, Mattie was sent straight to bed. I went with Uncle Frank to collect more sheep from the hills and corral them in the sheeppen for shearing and dipping to morrow.

While Uncle Frank was milking I tried to have some fun with Toss and Shep. I threw a stick and told them to 'fetch' but when they tried to eat it as if it was food and realised that it wasn't, they just dropped it and walked away and showed no further interest in following any more sticks. I had time to think of Mattie and I felt a bit sorry for him but also relieved that he wasn't using me in any of his 'mad hatter schemes' for the time being anyway.

I saw Baba at the side of the house and it was making mock charges at the water barrel. As I got closer it gave a wild leap and did actually puck into the water barrel. The goat looked over at me and did a giddy dance shaking its head. I heard a laugh coming from the direction of the sally tree. I followed the sound of "pisst, pisst" and looked up the tree.

Mattie was sitting on a stout branch half way up the tree and when I came under it he dropped down a toffee bar wrapper on my head, 'Too late' he dribbled through a mouthful of sweets. As I waked away I noticed that the bedroom window was open to its full capacity.

'He shouldn't have left the keys in his van-shop and anyway I'm not used to those stupid gear sticks at the back of the steering wheel,' Mattie said to me as I got into bed after a supper of scones without the raisins but with strawberry jam. Mattie got neither but he appeared to be happy enough sucking a gobstopper lying back on his pillow. I lay back on my pillow too thinking of Uncle Frank's answers to my questions when we were gathering the sheep earlier, without the company of Mattie.

When I asked my uncle what age he was he said that he was between thirty and forty. I don't know why he didn't give his exact age; maybe Granny stopped giving him birthday parties when he was thirty and then he didn't bother counting after that.

I asked about my Grandfather. He seemed proud telling me that his father was an Irish Volunteer soldier but then sounded sad when he mentioned that he died when Uncle Frank was eight. I asked him if my Grandfather was shot dead in a war but when he shook his head I wasn't that interested and then went on to ask if he had a girlfriend and what's her name and where does she live.

He hesitated and then coyly said that his girl friend is called Beatrice and that she lives in America but that she comes home to her parents in Portwest every second year. He blushed when I asked him when he was getting married and after a few dry coughs he just said that he had to go to Portwest on Saturday for some farm supplies and that Mattie and I could go with him. I asked him what Beatrice worked at but he just roared at the dogs who had gone far 'too wide' before the sheep on the side of the second hill and never answered my question.

When I told Mattie the important news about going to Portwest he gave a loud choking noise and spat out the gobstopper. When he caught his breath again he was smiling.

'Portwest, great; the "flicks," sweets, chips' he said finding his gobstopper in the fold of the blanket and replacing it in his mouth. I don't know if they have a cinema or a chip shop in Portwest but I let Mattie believe that they had for now because of his chastisement from Granny.

Immediately after breakfast this morning Uncle Frank got straight into the shearing and dipping. We were dispatched to the meadow to do some more hay shaking and then raking that into small haycocks.

During the dinner he told Mattie and I that we were to release the sheep from the drying-pen after dinner and bring them back up the hill as he had to call on Myles Biggins to see what day suited him to borrow his trailer to bring in some turf.

Granny wanted to know why he couldn't have asked Myles Biggins that question after Mass last Sunday. 'And anyway,' she said strengthening her point, 'what's your hurry, sure you won't be bringing in the turf for at least another week or two.'

'Tom Moran got in before me last year and I had to wait for two more weeks for my turn,' Uncle Frank explained restraining his temper leaving the table.

I calculated our time left in Doiredrum and came to the conclusion that we would probably be back in our own home by the time Uncle Frank would be bringing in the turf so I asked Granny what it involved. She looked pleased with my interest, dropped her dish towel on the table and sat down beside me as she went on to explain.

'Well the turf has been cut out of the bog already, hence the turf sods and bog holes, I'm sure that you have seen them going up the hills for the sheep.'

I nodded and interrupted 'How was it cut?

'With the slane,' Granny pre-empted my next question and continued, 'a "slane" is like a spade with a cutting blade on the side, the sods of turf are spread around for drying and then piled into little stacks to dry further,' she took a breath, 'and in a couple of weeks we'll gather it up into creels.'

Granny moved closer to me with a broadening smile, '"Creels" are large baskets, we carry the turf in them over the soft boggy ground to the trailer or truck and then its brought home and stacked beside the house and we burn it in the stove.' She pointed to the fireplace, 'For cooking and keeping us warm.'

She folding up her dish towel and looked at me for any further questions.

'Are the creels heavy?' I asked and noticed Mattie's disapproving boring face. 'The creels themselves are made of sally wicker, but a loaded creel on either side of a donkey is a heavy enough load.'

Mattie showed interest for the first time when Granny mentioned the word, 'donkey' and Granny continued, 'A day in the bog is lovely and I can tell you now that you will never drink a nicer drop of tea as the one from a bottle—milked and sugared and kept warm by a sock—lovla tea, lovla,' Granny sighed.

Mattie cringed as he pinched his nose and mimed the word 'sock.'

'The only bad thing about "a day in the bog" is the midgets, but you'll get used to them,' Granny added standing up from the table. I glanced again at Mattie; now he was yawning.

I had never loaded up a trailer of turf in the bog before but it just had to be better than making hay. I felt that I had missed out on something that I could have bragged to Sparks and Vinny about. I was distracted from my thoughts by Mattie manoeuvring his way to the kitchen window. Uncle Frank had left his cigarettes and matches on the window ledge there. When I looked again after Mattie had walked away, the box of matches was missing.

'We must be getting good at the farming because Uncle Frank is letting us bring the sheep back up the hills on our own,' I expressed my excitement to Mattie as we went out front door.

Mattie just cringed.

Uncle Frank was peddling hard across the yard as he approached the bottom of the lane before the incline. I recognised the bicycle as the one I had seen in the Old House. So did Mattie.

'I thought that that bike was an old crock of a thing, I was going to cut rubber strips out of one of the tubes to make myself a bow—make a few arrows from the sally tree and do a bit of more hunting for wildcats,' Mattie grumbled and then smirked, 'you're a lucky man Uncle Frankie that you still have a bike to peddle.'

'And I could have made myself a catapult with what was left over of the tube,' I added without giving much thought to what I had just said.

Mattie cringed before he spoke, 'Make a catapult, are you mad, sure where did you see a decent tree growing around here?'

I looked all around me and nodded in agreement. With the exception of the Pine forest near the Dutchman's house, there wasn't much of anything growing around here, never mind a tree where I could cut a good 'catapult-fork' from.

We both looked after Uncle Frank, as he rose from the saddle to strengthen his peddling ascending the lane. He left the gate open for us and the sheep—Uncle Frank thinks ahead all the time. We strolled towards the drying-pen.

Mattie frightened the sheep so much, with his screaming and hand waving, that they leaped over one another getting out the drying-pen gate. Then he tried to coax Toss and Shep to help us bring the sheep together that were scattered in the yard at the back of the Old House. Mattie's interpretation of Uncle Frank's 'dog commands' confused the dogs, and me as well, as he roared, 'up wild before, way off up front, behind them.'

The dogs only followed us and the sheep to the bottom of the lane and then turned back, leaving Mattie and I to steer them out the gate, and hill-wards on our own. The newly sheared and marked sheep, bleated and scattered as they reunited with the other sheep on the second hill.

'Right let's go and get our bike at Teach an Doch-th-ure,' Mattie fluffed and added with a broad smile checking his pocket money, 'and then to the shop.'

I got a glimpse of the ball-bearing and a box of matches when he was replacing his pocket money in his bulging trouser pocket. He did an Indian war cry racing down the hill. I didn't even try to keep up with him and when I saw him scaling the back wall at Teach an Dochtúra I strolled around the front and met him at the gate where he was already mounted on the smelly man's bicycle.

CHAPTER 19

Fire and Pink Knickers

'WE ARE JUST GOING to leave back the bike and come back okay?' I asked in a pleading fashion sliding onto the crossbar.

'Yes,' he responded and hesitated, 'and some lemonade and a small killing mission and that's it,' Mattie grunted pushing on the peddles.

'What killing mission?' I demanded to know as we got our balance.

'Those bees are going to die,' Mattie shouted like a warrior and then giggled. 'How are you going to kill them?' I asked but didn't really want to know the answer in case his plan would involve me.

'Just wait and see,' he bent forward and whispered in my ear.

He applied the brakes too late and the front wheel of the bicycle crunched into the hedge as we came to a halt and dismounted outside the Post Office side of the building.

'Exactly where we found it,' Mattie praised himself walking away and heading for the entrance to the pub and shop. I sat on the wobbly bench propped against the Post Office wall. It was the furthest bench of the two from the wasp's nest. I could hear the crows and rooks squawking high up behind me near the church as I looked back down the road we had just travelled.

I was wondering if the smelly man was in his usual corner and maybe wake up and realise that it was Mattie who had taken his bicycle and grab him, when Mattie appeared back out the door drinking from a lemonade bottle.

'Is the smelly man there?' I asked in a whisper.

'Yes, fast asleep,' Mattie giggled sitting down beside me.

'Can I have slug?' I said in a timid voice and then realised the futility of my request.

'No, get your own with your own money, and anyway you'll only put spits in it the way you drink from a bottle,' he retorted taking another gulp.

'I'm saving my money to get presents for going home and then if there's anything left I will get myself a bottle of lemonade and you're not getting any,' I threatened staring into his face.

'Who cares?' he said draining the bottle and then emitted a pleasurable gasp.

He moved his head briskly back and over, viewing in turn the Post Office door and the main entrance door as he took big strides to the petrol pump in the forecourt. He positioned himself on the roadside of the petrol pump and out of view of anybody who might look out from either, the shop, pub or Post Office. When I saw his skinny arm reaching around for the petrol pump nozzle I knew what to expect next. He was going to do one of Vinny's 'tricks.'

Vinny discovered that if you took the petrol nozzle from the petrol pump and held it down low to the ground that the petrol that was still in the hose would pour out. We got petrol that way from Noble's petrol pump. It was the same day that we had got a few old car tyres from Noble's Yard and put them on the railway track. On Vinny's instructions, Sparks and I stacked the three tyres on top of one another. We intended lighting them to see what would happen when the train crashed into them.

When Vinny was pouring the petrol from the bottle onto the tyres, some of the petrol must have spilled on the front of his jumper because when he lit the match his jumper went into a spurt of flames and when he was taking the jumper off his hair got scorched. We all got a fright and went home. I don't know what happened when the train crashed into the stacked tyres or if it ever did but the tyres were gone when we came back the next day. Vinny's face looked red and sore but he said that he didn't want to talk about it because it annoys him so Sparks and me try not to.

Mattie put the spout of the petrol nozzle to the top of the empty lemonade bottle and lowered the bottle towards the ground as he simultaneously raised the petrol hosepipe. The petrol poured freely around the top of the bottle, over his hand and onto his wellingtons for a few seconds and then trickled and stopped as the coloured liquid settled to the height of the bottleneck. He peeped around from the petrol pump before slotting the nozzle back to the cradle holder. His eyes were trained on both doors as he strode cautiously towards the disused water pump.

He ignored a few wasps that buzzed from the spout of the rusty pump to check him out as he furiously splashed and sprinkled the contents of the bottle onto the pump and up the water pump spout. He tossed the empty bottle towards a tuft of long grass near the Post Office window but it bounced on the stony ground in front and shattered and broke against the wall with a clang. More wasps had appeared over his head as he clumsily wrenched a box of matches from his pocket. I saw a movement inside the Post Office door but then I was distracted by the sight of a fat woman on a bicycle coming down the road towards us.

She appeared to be peddling in slow motion with her head bent over the handlebars. I did a quick calculation and reckoned with her speed and weight Mattie would have carried out his mission before he would be in her view and saw no reason to warn him.

When I looked back at Mattie he had a lighted match in his hand. He flicked it in the direction of the water pump. A bouncing flame was quickly followed by a burst of black smoke. Most of the flames were jumping from the water pump but smaller tongues of fire were flickering around the wristband of Mattie's jumper and from his hand.

Maura the Postmistress came out of the Post Office screaming 'Fire, fire…help! Fire!'

Mattie was running around the forecourt slapping his hands on his trousers.

Pauric raced from the pub entrance bellowing, 'In the name of Jesus, what's going on?'

The flame around Mattie's wrist and hand was extinguished but a small flame appeared around his pocket and smaller tufts flickered on and off from his wellingtons as he galloped in a circle. Then he made a sudden change in direction and ran to the corner of the forecourt towards the roadway. The fat lady on the bicycle was peddling closer.

The collision course was imminent and even if I had roared a warning it would have been too late. Mattie thumped off the cyclist and in one continuous movement the bicycle fork jack-knifed as Mattie tumbled over the bicycle and the yelping woman.

Mattie rolled along the ground and then hurriedly stumbled to his feet. The woman lay sprawled on the roadway with her legs wide apart and her flowing frock over her head. I gasped as I came to realise that I knew who the woman was without seeing her face. The last time I had seen such abundance of pink coloured material was hanging on the line over the fireplace in Stephen and Agnes's house. I was staring aghast at Agnes's pink knickers.

Pauric emptied a bucket of water on the fire engulfed water pump as he said in a crying plea, 'My blooda new petrol pump is going to go up in smoke too.'

'I've seen it all now, a water pump on fire, no peace anywhere,' the smelly man muttered stumbling across the forecourt. He stopped in mid step and glanced at Agnes's wide robust posterior still showing pink knickers as she grappled with her flabby knees to push herself upright. Moist cow dung and scraggy bits of straw patterned her bulging underwear. Walter Delaney gave himself a speedy short cut blessing and did a second take at the bicycle stuck in the hedge. 'I must be going blind, I didn't see this morning,' he gasped changing course and pulling his returned bicycle from the hedge.

The cursing and the clanging of a rolling bucket turned my head to see Pauric running towards the door flaking at a few wasps that were buzzing and bouncing off his neck and head.

The wasps banked off at the door and returned to the sporadic flaming water pump and their kamikaze compatriots. I just stood there whinging, trying to hold back a bawling cry.

I felt a hand around my shoulder and heard a caring voice, 'There, there *a grá*,' I looked up, it was Ann.

I released the welled up fear I had retained during the last few minutes into a burst of tears. Ann hugged me closer.

'Tell me this,' Maura the Postmistress demanded calling across the road to Mattie who was sucking and licking the petrol burns on his fingers, 'are ye Frank's nephews or hers?' she asked nodding towards Agnes.

'Well I can tell you this they are nothing to do with me, nor do I want any thing to do with them,' Agnes spurted out between gasps struggling to untangle the jack-knifed bicycle fork.

'That narrows it down a bit for you,' Mattie replied after removing his red, tender fingers from his mouth.

'Granny will kill us,' I sobbed.

'Your Granny will be told nothing about it, well, not by Pauric or me anaways,' Ann consoled holding her hand gently under my chin and then directed her question towards Mattie, 'are you badly burned?'

'Burning is too good for that buckeen,' Agnes puffed parking her bicycle against the shop wall.

Ann gave a quick glance at Agnes and then called to Mattie, 'Come on over here and let me take a look at you.' She beckoned a suspicious Mattie who cautiously strode across the road to her.

She made a quick prognosis and told him to come inside to the kitchen and she would put a dressing on it. I followed them in along the hallway past the shop and pub doors to the back of the house. Mattie had finished his abbreviated version of events by the time we reached the kitchen. A baby in a playpen at the corner of the kitchen looked startled as we entered. A boy aged about four and a girl aged about three looked up from the colouring books they were filling in at the table and followed us with bemused eyes.

'That's Patrick and Mary Ellen,' Ann said nodding to the children at the table, 'and that's baby JJ,' she introduced with a loving smile and opened a cupboard.

I said a humble 'hello' and Mattie made a distorted face and stuck his tongue out at the baby who looked to be welling up for a cry ever since we came into the kitchen and now decided it was time to let it loose. I heard the familiar shop bells clanging and then Pauric joined us just in time for the first screeching bawl. 'There, there JJ,' he comforted bending down to take up the frightened baby.

The pub owner had two visibly swollen red dots on the back of his neck like the ones Mattie had on the web of his fingers yesterday after the wasp had stung him. 'I eventually got a wet sack on that blooda pump' he said with a sigh, rocking his whimpering son in his arms.

'If you had a done something about those blooda wasps when I asked you we wouldn't be in this predicament now,' Ann said sternly, wrapping a bandage over the pink ointment on Mattie's hand.

'Will you stop woman, they could have burned us all to death if that petrol pump had a gone up too,' Paurdic replied immediately hugging the baby closer with a tender kiss.

'You are very good at bandaging,' I complimented Ann with a combined Mattie red herring special.

'I should be, I was a nurse before I ended up in this blooda place,' she said cutting an end to the bandage on Mattie's hand, 'but I'm afraid I won't be able to do anything for this though,' Ann tugged on the scorched sleeve of Mattie's jumper. 'That's fine, thanks,' Mattie's expression of gratitude was barely audible.

Pauric handed the now pacified baby over to its mother as he spoke, 'I have to see to Agnes in the shop,' and strode out of the kitchen.

I gently waved goodbye to the two children who had remained staring at us throughout our visit before we followed their father into the hallway. He turned right into the shop but we kept walking.

'I wouldn't mind at all but they were my clean knickers,' a female voice uttered from inside the shop. Agnes's face looked angry as she peered through the glass in the shop door as we passed.

We just increased our pace until we reached the scene of the major incident earlier. Wasps hovered and buzzed in much lesser numbers around the steaming wet sack on the water pump examining the scene of their near total annihilation.

The smell of the scorched material from Mattie's clothing was unsavoury mingling with the sweet honey odour of the fermenting hay as we waddled our way back to Granny's house. We saw the smelly man's donkeys grazing on a hill along the road. They just glanced once at us once and lowered their heads back to the grass. Our pace had begun to wane when I turned in trepidation to investigate a puffin sound behind me. It was Agnes peddling in slow motion with her head down and within a few pedal turns behind us. I was first to burst into a quick sprint. As we neared the gate Mattie removed his jumper and turned it inside out, before putting it back on again.

He unwound the carefully dressed bandage and rolled it in a ball before forcing it into his pocket, 'No questions asked, no answers needed,' he said blowing on his superficially burned hand going down the lane.

'Your jumper is inside out.' Granny's statement of fact drew a response from Mattie as he entered the kitchen, 'I know Granny, I'm keeping it clean for going to Portwest tomorrow,' Mattie exhaled slumping into the fireside chair.

'Going to Portwest tomorrow are ye, well isn't it well for some?' Granny gave a wry smile going into the scullery.

Uncle Frank was poking the stove with the tongs and then drew a glowing piece of smouldering turf from the furnace muttering, 'I don't know what the blooda hell I did with my matches,' as he touched the cigarette in his mouth with the improvised cigarette lighter.

Mattie kept the sleeve of his jumper pulled well down on his tender hand while he was having his tea. During the Rosary he took every opportunity he could without been seen to blow soothing breath on it. He made no effort to dilly dally when Granny announced 'bed time.' I was awake until Granny turned down the oil lamp in the kitchen to a soothing glow and woke to a bright morning.

'And don't forget the batteries for O'Tooles, I haven't heard a bit of news or music for nearly a week now,' Granny called to my uncle from the scullery.

'I have them in the car already, mother,' Uncle Frank replied combing and carefully spreading his scarce blond hairs as he peered into the hallstand mirror.

Mattie was wearing a shirt without his scorched jumper standing impatiently at the car as I entered the yard behind Uncle Frank.

'Are we all set,' Uncle Frank chirped red faced as he struggled balancing two cardboard boxes on his outstretched arms.

I was about to ask what was in the boxes when Granny saved me the bother with her instructions to her son, 'Bring that butter to Fitzgeralds this time, he gives a much better price than that oul Paddy Clarke does,' she called out trough the open kitchen window.

I opened and closed the gate at the top of the lane where Shep and Toss did an about turn back down the lane as we began our journey for Portwest town.

Uncle Frank slowed the car as he approached Teach an Dochtúra. I felt Mattie's finger pressing into my back.

'I'll just make a quick check on the Doc's place,' he said pulling in beside the gate entrance.

'No need to do that, Finn and me checked it yesterday after we brought those sheep back up the hill for you,' Mattie said reaching in between Uncle Frank and I.

'Well done lads, and is every thing okay?'

'Couldn't be better,' Mattie replied immediately as Uncle Frank changed gears and drove back out onto the road and took a quick glance back at Mattie as he spoke, 'are you going to be a policeman like your father when you grow up?

'If they give the Guards guns like the cops in the gangster films, I probably will,' Mattie said nestling into the back seat.

I hope the Guards never get guns I thought to myself having considered Mattie's conditions for joining the Irish Police Force.

'I won't be a second, I just have to leave these batteries into Pauric and I'll collect the two replacements on the way back,'

Uncle Frank said pulling into the forecourt at O'Tooles Bar and Grocery.

We remained totally silent until he had gone in the door entrance carrying two radio batteries which he had removed from the car boot.

'Now we'll know if that one can keep her mouth shut,' Mattie stated with a tremor in his voice.

'I believe Ann will say nothing about yesterday,' I said trying to convince Mattie as well as myself. I was looking back at the blackened and scorched rusty water pump when Mattie gasped and pointed to the hedge, 'Look at the bike, it's the smelly man's bike, if he wakes up he'll blabber everything.'

Uncle Frank had a bland serious face coming out the door. He sat back into his car and drove a short distance before speaking, 'Ann wouldn't let me wake that Delaney fella, I wanted to give him a piece of my mind about his roaming donkeys but I'll get him again.'

Mattie and I sighed loudly with relief.

'Are ye tired or something,' Uncle Frank commented picking up on our audible expression.

We just laughed and both refuted his suggestion about tiredness as we turned left at the church and followed the road sign for Portwest.

On the way to Portwest Mattie was asking a lot of questions about Portwest and I think Uncle Frank was getting a bit annoyed until Mattie asked completely out of the blue, 'Has granny ever been further than Clunmon?'

I was startled at the question but even more surprised when Uncle Frank answered with a broad smile.

'Ah-ha, your granny did a good bit of travelling in her day, let me tell you,' he rebuked Mattie's suggestion and continued, 'sure she did her Teacher Training in Blackrock up there in Dublin and after she qualified she went to England.'

'She was a teacher in England wow?' Mattie gasped.

'No, no, she went over there to look after an elderly aunt that was ill and then she came back to Ireland after a year or so and got a teaching job in Galway and later here in Doiredrum.'

'Ah, did the aunt die?' Mattie asked with a roguish sigh.

'You know what—I don't know that,' my uncle answered pensively, oblivious to Mattie's false interest, and then added, 'funnily enough your granny never talks too much about England but she got very friendly with a nun while she was there and you know what,' he concluded with glee, 'they still write to one another.'

'Is this chip-shop in Portwest very big?' Mattie yawned.

Uncle Frank frowned but didn't answer him.

CHAPTER 20

Flicks and Chips

UNCLE FRANK HAD BEEPED his car horn and waved at several people before he reached the high cut-stone monument in the centre square in Portwest town.

'See you later on Peter,' he said lowering his window addressing the man who was standing behind a canvassed roofed stall that displayed jackets, wellingtons, trousers, boots and assorted hardware items.

'Remind me to get a hacksaw from Peter before we go home, I don't know what I did with my own, I had to use my timber saw the last day to dehorn another sheep,' Uncle Frank said scratching his head.

'You're a bit careless with your tools all right,' Mattie said with a yawn.

Uncle Frank's bemused smile turned to a frown as he looked for a parking place driving slowly around The Monument. He parked between a small red van and a horse with trap that was tethered to one of the concrete hitching posts erected all around The Monument. The badly dented van had large rust patches on it and the rear bumper was hanging down to one side and dangled only a few inches from the ground. The clock on the monument showed the time as ten past twelve and I estimated that it was correct judging by the time we had left Granny's.

'That chip shop place you were asking about, blooda foreigners,' Uncle Frank repeated the answer again to one of Mattie's many questions on the drive to Portwest, 'anaways it's down that street past the cinema,' he groaned and pointed getting out of the car and added, 'I honest to God don't know why you need to go there because you're not long after your breakfast and you'll be having your dinner when we get home.'

'After the chip shop we were thinking of going to the "flicks" and we'll thumb a lift back to Granny's, so there is no need to wait for us when you get your supplies,' Mattie said before briskly stepping out of the car and heading down the street.

'Hey you, come back here!' Uncle Frank called in a gasping roar. 'Start again,' he said curiously as he watched Mattie strolling back to him,' what's this "flicks" and "thumbing lifts" about?' Uncle Frank interrogated.

Mattie repeated his intentions of going to see an afternoon matinee after the chip shop and hitching a lift back to Granny's.

'Listen to me, no flicks, no thumbing lifts, you'll meet me here in two hours,' he pointed to The Monument clock and continued, 'and we all go home together, do you understand?'

We acknowledged Uncle Frank's orders with silent nods and stood and watched as he entered a shop with large lettering painted on the wall declaring 'Gannon's Merchant Supplies.' Mattie had a spring in his step going down the street towards the distinctive odour of cooking fat. He stopped suddenly at a grocery shop before the cinema. 'We'll have a bit of the "broken biscuits" crack with this dopey looking donkey,' Mattie nudged me to look at the man behind the shop counter.

The last time I did the 'broken biscuits' prank I was with Vinny and Sparks. We went into McConkey's shop and as usual they were selling their broken biscuits at half price. Vinny asked Maud the shop assistant if they had any broken biscuits left. Maud said yes and picked up a biscuit tin with a few crummy biscuits in the bottom and asked with a forced politeness how much would we like. She was just being mean because there were other lovely broken biscuits in another tin. Vinny said we don't want to buy any broken biscuits, we just came in to give her something to do.

'Like what?' Maud barked. 'Like fixing your broken biscuits,' Vinny said and we all ran out of the shop.

The elderly man in this shop was leaning on the counter reading a newspaper. His spectacles were balanced at the end of his exceptionally long nose. The door was wide open and he blinked his eyes over his glasses, giving a quick glance at us. I hoped that the tufts of hair growing out of his ears would prevent him from hearing Mattie's remarks.

Mattie strode into the shop and stood in front of the shopkeeper who barely acknowledged his presence as he turned a page in his newspaper. I just stood in the doorway and observed. Mattie increased the pitch of his throat clearing exercise in order to get the man's attention. He peered over his glasses again and then went back to his reading. Mattie stepped closer and spoke over the top of the newspaper and directly into the man's face, 'Would you have any broken biscuits, sir?

The man licked his finger and turned another page before speaking in a calm and calculated voice, 'If you don't get out of my shop I'll break your arse with a kick.'

'They're fierce big into breaking arses, around this part of the country,' Mattie said in a subdued tone before reaching the cinema. Mattie drooled looking at the advertising poster outside; it depicted war action in the jungle with a sash banner reminder of the Saturday 3 o'clock matinee. 'The Japs and The Yanks,' Mattie said in a low pine.

Mattie had a habit of getting into trouble in the cinema at home. He had been barred twice; once for repeatedly kicking the seat in front of him every time he saw the Indians galloping on their horses and the other time for lighting a firecracker and throwing it back at the courting couples sitting in the dearer seats.

He nearly got barred a third time for having a fight with 'Snots' Mulligan during a Cavalry and Indian film. Fred was the manager of the cinema and when he heard the commotion he ran down the isle with his torch and shone it on them fighting.

When Fred dragged the two of them out from between the seats, Mattie said that 'Snots' started the fight. 'Snots' excuse was that Mattie was annoying him by cheering for the Indians against the Cavalry but Fred didn't believe Snots and barred him from the cinema for a month.

I felt sorry for Snots because I knew that Mattie always cheered for the Indians in Cowboy films as he did for the 'Japs' and the Germans in War films. Mattie wasn't barred this time but Snots was and any time he saw Snots during his month's bar, Mattie taunted him about the great films he was missing and that they were all in Technicolor which wasn't entirely true as some were in black-and-white.

I could see into the foyer of the cinema and like Mattie I felt cheated when I saw a poster advertising two cowboy films for showing later in the week. I started reminiscing again.

I was thinking of the time I was caught out on the 'smoking lie.' I had been with Sparks and Vinny in our hideout and had taken a few puffs of Vinny's cigarette. When I went home Mammy started sniffing around me. I told her that the cigarette smoke she smelt off me must have come from the Guards smoking in the Barracks when I was there with Daddy. Mammy had no problem disseminating that I'd told a lie because it was Lent and Daddy didn't allow the Guards to smoke while he was off the cigarettes for Lent.

Because I told the lie I wasn't given any pocket money that week and hadn't any money to go the Cinema the following Saturday. It was the worst Lent ever. I was already off sweets and now no flicks. Daddy was always bossy when he was off cigarettes. I should have remembered it was Lent.

Then Vinny said that he had a plan to get me into the cinema for free. He borrowed a Ladies raincoat from his father's Ladies and Gents Outfitters shop. Vinny said that the plan better work because he had to do a lot of sneaking and ducking around his father's shop window to get the raincoat without being noticed. When questioned as to the choice he made he explained that he had chosen a Ladies raincoat because it was long but not too wide.

He also told us that he was nearly caught taking the raincoat off the dummy in the shop window. Sparks said that 'mannequin' is the correct word but we just ignored him because we had more important things to do than taking English lessons.

As soon as we slipped down the alleyway at the side of the cinema Sparks raised his hand jovially and asked, 'What's the Plan?'

Vinny shook out the raincoat he was carrying and handed it to Sparks.

Vinny put on the raincoat and buttoned it up. I crouched down and got in under it with my arms locked around his waist. I turned my head sideways as I pressed side face into his lower back. I could hear Sparks spluttering laughing and he said something about a Trojan Horse. Vinny shouted at him not to be talking about stupid things in the middle of an important mission and to check and see if either Vinny's feet or my feet could be seen under the coat.

'Not really, just a little,' Sparks muttered and then I felt the coat being pulled down nearer the ground.

Sparks was to give Vinny 'the all clear' with a thumbs-up sign, when Susie was alone at the cinema door. Susie the cinema usherette wore spectacles with thick lenses but Fred the Cinema owner was 'as sharp as a razor' as Vinny describes him.

My legs and back were getting really tired from bending when I heard Vinny say in a loud whisper, 'That's a thumbs-up from Sparks, here we go.'

I was sweating. I followed Vinny's directions to keep in step.

I could hear his muffled voice 'left, right, left, right.'

After some feet shuffling we seemed to have mastered a rhythm.

Vinny spoke in a half whisper again 'straight, straight,' then shouted out loud 'no, no, retreat, retreat.'

I heard Sparks screaming 'Abort, abort.'

I didn't know what it meant but I knew it wasn't good. I got confused. I could tell by their voices that they were panicking and I was worried.

In seconds Vinny had wrenched free from my grip on his waist. I got twisted to one side and stumbled before crashing to my knees on a cold cement step. My eyes were adjusting to the light and when they did I was looking straight into Fred's eyes. He was bending down with his hands resting on his knees and was so close that I felt sick from his smelly breath. I straightened up and didn't even try to run away. Before I turned away from the cinema door Fred said in a low threatening voice, 'Barred, one month.'

I increased my pace as I crossed the street to where Vinny and Sparks were waiting. Vinny was still wearing the coat but all the buttons were undone. The coat was dragging on the footpath as Vinny walked in circles around Sparks. We all looked in the direction of Fred's voice, 'And you two wee scuts are barred for a month as well.'

I told Mammy that I had decided not to go to the cinema for a month because it was Lent. She told me that I was a holy boy. I told the priest the whole story in confessions and he gave me an extra ten Hail Marys as penance for telling lies.

Mattie was still looking behind at the war film poster as we neared the Milano's Fish and Chip Restaurant and Take Away. Two young teenage boys were giggling and pushing one another leaving the chip shop as they tucked into their chips.

'She's yummie,' one of the youths said.

'Yes, just like the chips,' the other added slapping his pal on the back.

The chip shop had the same layout as Nicky Gunn's at home except the red formica toped tables along the walls had milk and sugar on them as well as the glass screw cap salt and vinegar dispensers.

'A plate of chips and a bottle of lemonade,' Mattie said to the young tanned skinned female assistant peering over the counter at him.

'I'll give you your drink straight away and I'll take you down your chips, if you'd like to take a seat,' she chirped in broken English prising off the cap of a lemonade bottle.

'Where are you from?' Mattie asked enthusiastically placing his half crown on the high counter.

'Milano,' she replied with a wide grin.

'Milano, I love there,' Mattie gasped, 'and I love loads of chips too,' he said taking his change and lemonade bottle with drinking straw from her as he turned and walked away.

'Yes please?' she said smiling down at me from over the counter.

'Just a lemonade please,' I answered coyly turning my blushing face towards the jukebox at the end of the counter which had a misspelled handwritten sign stuck on it; "out of orders." I took my change and did a quick calculation on how much money I would have left for presents.

Mattie was sitting at a table behind a woman with rouged cheeks and caked lipstick. She was sitting opposite a small skinny girl at the same table with the girl facing Mattie. The girl had ringlets tied with green ribbons and was wearing wire-rimmed spectacles.

'Listen Mammy,' she said making a croaking noise sucking the dregs from a lemonade bottle through a straw.

The woman slurped from a teacup and told her daughter to be quiet. A man who had been sitting on his own at the corner table near the door, stumped out his cigarette in an ash tray on the table and left.

I sat beside Mattie who was now looking at the girl through two cupped hands replicating binocular. She slowly lowered her head to the table and I had just taken my first suck through the straw when I heard a howling bawl.

'What's wrong with you now?' the angry woman barked.

'He's, he's making fun of me,' she sniffled pointing at Mattie.

The woman turned to view the accused who was now looking so innocent that even I thought he was going to cry.

'No he's not, he's a good boy,' she scolded the small girl, 'come on we're going, I have no peace with you,' she said lifting her floral coloured handbag and grabbing the girl's hand. Mattie stuck his tongue out at the sobbing girl being dragged behind the colourful female leaving the chip shop.

I had just come to the end of my lemonade when the Italian girl swaggered down the isle to our table. She just smiled placing a very large plate of chips in front of Mattie. He just gave the thumbs up sign as he pulled the fork from the bottom of the chips and dragged the salt and vinegar dispensers towards him. When I'd finished my drink I told Mattie that I was going shopping for presents for home and asked if he was coming with me.

'Off with you, I'm happy enough here,' he said squeezing another few chips into his mouth.

I went to the souvenir shop and was able to get two presents there. I got a snowy crystal ball of Portwest for Mammy and a broach for Myra. I asked for directions to a man's clothes shop and also an electrical shop. The man in the Menswear department frowned at first but then smiled broadly and obliged me by wrapping the handkerchief present I'd bought for Daddy. The man in the electrical shop said that he didn't sell screwdrivers but he directed me to a hardware shop where I got Vinny's present. Sparks present was easy to get and I got a free read of other comics in the newsagents before I picked out a 64 page war comic and a Kit Carson Dell cowboy comic. It was an economical present because I knew that I would read them before I gave them to Sparks as a present.

When I returned to the chip shop Mattie was sitting at the corner table by the door with two empty lemonade bottles in front of him and was noisily draining the last few drops from another. The formica topped table was cracked and formed a spider web pattern that spread to the empty ash tray that was on it.

'What did you buy?' Mattie asked stretching for the bag that I had combined all the presents in. I quickly moved the bag from out of his reach.

'Who cares,' he grumped wiping the vinegar and salt stained plate with a chip and tossing it into his mouth.

Two teenage boys and girls were sitting at the table where Mattie had been sitting before I went present shopping. One of the boys was holding the girls hand under the table and the other was just staring and smiling at the girl sitting opposite him. They all had lemonade bottles in front of them which they sipped periodically between chirpy bouts of giggling. The same shop assistant sped down the isle professionally carrying four plates of chips and placed them in front of the teenagers who barley acknowledged the delivery.

Mattie was stirring the sugar bowl with the straw from his bottle. With each twist in the sugar I could see small bits of black appearing and then disappearing. When the cigarette butt became visible with one of the stirs I realised what Mattie had done and just wanted to get out of there.

A gurgling sound quickly followed by a short scream drew my attention back to the teenager's table. One of the girls was holding the vinegar dispenser at arms length and gawking at it in disbelief.

'Oh look,' she whimpered, 'my chips are ruined.'

This was quickly followed by 'ah feck it' as her boyfriend pulled away the emptying salt cellar from a heap of salt on the chips in front of him.

'Look, somebody loosened the tops on the salt and vinegar yokes,' the other boy called out as he lifted the screw caps from each of the plates of chips.

'Let's go,' Mattie said pushing the cigarette butt further into the sugar before making his way to the door.

'What-a-you-do?' the Italian girl shouted her question towards the disgruntled teenagers as she rushed out from behind the counter. I grabbed my bag of presents and squeezed my way out the door past Mattie. I knew what Mattie had done. Vinny does the same thing in our chip shop at home. He loosens the caps of the salt and vinegar dispensers and when it's used the next time, the cap falls off and the contents pour out.

CHAPTER 21

The Horse and Van and Mystery Man

TWO COUPLES who were obviously tourists and whom I had seen in the souvenir shop earlier were now grouped outside on the pavement as we headed back up the street. The four were totally obese and as loud in their apparel as their American accents. With some difficulty I deciphered their cackling.

'Harry did you ask the nice lady in the store for directions to Portwest Castle?' one of the fat ladies hollered.

'Ah darn it Ethel! I forgot, hold on I'll ask these local kids' Harry said and then stood in our way as he spoke, 'excuse me guys, we are looking for directions to Portwest Castle,' he asked extending his flabby stomach.

Mattie closed one eye and looked up sideways at Harry as he spoke, 'Just keep going that way for about a mile,' Mattie pointed back towards the road we had come from Doiredrum, 'and then take the first left and you'll see it in front of you,' he concluded quivering his lips with his eye still closed.

'That sounds like one hell of a walk, maybe we should catch a cab,' Ethel suggested.

'No need for that,' Mattie advised and then added, 'if you walk there you get a free hackney service back.'

'Sounds good to me,' the others gave the result of their short debate.

Mattie waited with expectation as Harry put his hand in his pocket. Harry removed a handkerchief and repeatedly blew his nose which sounded like a dysfunctional fog horn. Mattie's "ga-ga" prank had failed again.

But I was proud of Mattie for being so helpful and knowledgeable and then realised that I hadn't seen any Castle on the way from Doiredrum to Portwest. I was going to ask him how he knew where Portwest Castle was but he had gone too far in front of me and I didn't bother.

I remembered then the day that Vinny and Sparks and I discreetly followed Mattie and Towbar out the country and we saw them moving signposts at cross roads to point in the wrong directions.

Mattie took a few sweet papers from his pocket and threw them up in the air. They blew upwards and then downwards and scattered in front of a street sweeper who stopped brushing and cursed at Mattie under his breath. Uncle Frank's car was still parked between the horse and trap and the small red van. When I got closer I looked at the clock and I realised that we still had a half an hour left to meet Uncle Frank's deadline. The boot lid of Uncle Frank's car was tied closed on two bulging sacks.

Mattie opened the small door at the rear of the horse trap and lunged onto one of the padded side seats. The horse turned his head as far as it could go with the restraining reins and with bulging eyes spluttered its objection by violent shakes of his head.

I was happy enough to sit in Uncle Frank's car and was about to move towards it when a man staggering out of a pub mumbling an incoherent ballad held my attention. He stumbled from the pavement to the road but held his balance with wild movements of his arms. Mattie was giggling watching him as the man leaned on the roof of the red van and swung the door wide open. He made two attempts to get his hand in his pocket before eventually pulling out keys and a box of matches and then dropped both. He swayed several times and then in one swoop grabbed the keys from the ground and tumbled backwards into the driver's seat.

When I looked over at Mattie he was untying the nervous

horse from his hitching post. He quickly untangled the reins and then ducked down as he moved behind the rear of the van. I had to move to the side to see what he was doing and then wished that I hadn't; the horse reins was wrapped and tied around the rear bumper of the van. The red van clanked into reverse gear with a burst of black smoke and when it cleared I could see the four recognisable tourists beginning the steep incline out of the town following Mattie's direction for Portwest Castle.

The van clanked again going into a forward gear and chugged towards Peter's stall in an anticlockwise direction with the horse and trap in tow. The horse showed signs of fretting and tried to pull to the left but the van brought him forward again as the trap slapped broadside against the stall. Peter the stall owner shouted obscenities grappling with his collapsing counter.

'Good man Barney you have an extra horsepower today,' the street cleaner hollered through a chesty laugh as the van, with a horse and trap hitched to its rear bumper, turned for the hill out of town.

A few sparks spread from the horse's metal shoes as they clanged onto the roadway matching in brightness those flying from the trailing bumper that was now dragging along the road. The exhaust silencer was definitely broken and the noise from it resounded around the square. The tourists had stopped half way up the hill and were scrambling for camera advantage points as the van, horse and trap careered past them.

'What's all the commotion about?' a man with a long white apron asked coming out the same pub door as the man in the red van had earlier.

'Ah you missed it Ciaran,' the street sweeper said moving closer and resting on his brush, 'the funniest yet, Barney Baines is heading off in his vaneen like the hammers of hell and tied to the back guess what?' He cleared a chesty cough and continued, 'Canon Dillon's horse and trap tied to the van no less.'

Two more men holding beer glasses appeared in the doorway; the small man in front had a half moon face topped by a tartan cap; the other man in the doorway was my Uncle Frank.

'Come on in and have a lemonade,' my uncle beckoned us

going back in the doorway. Mattie waited until the cavalcade which he had created had ascended the hill and gone out of sight before he followed .

'How did the Canon's horse get tangled up on Barney's van anaways? Ciaran asked going behind the counter.

'Would the Canon have been that drunk at this hour of the day to tie his horse to the back of a van?' the small man with the cap asked before taking a noisy gulp from his beer glass.

'Be jepus Willie I wouldn't put it past the same man to do something like that,' Ciaran said wiping his hands in his apron.

Mattie smiled broadly.

'Well have ye all your business done?' Uncle Frank asked sitting up on a high stool at the bar and before we could answer added, 'Ciaran, these are Tessie's lads, give them a lemonade and sure while you're there I'll have another bottle of beer.

'How are ye enjoying yer holidays?' Ciaran asked pulling the caps of three bottles in quick succession.

'Hard work but we're enjoying it,' Mattie choose to answer for both of us as he awkwardly balanced himself on the high stool beside Uncle Frank.

'Be Jepus Frank but looking at the two of ye there together,' he nodded towards Mattie, 'ye could pass for brothers,' Willie said pensively pushing his cap back to the top of his head.

'You have enough drink Willie,' Uncle Frank said with a laugh and a shake of his head.

'And that buckeen there,' he nodded towards me, 'is a ringer for the father,' Willie announced with a wide smile showing bare gums that shamelessly declared the complete absence of teeth, top or bottom.

I patiently sipped my lemonade as Uncle Frank, Ciaran and Willie talked about price rises and weather until at last Uncle Frank gasped. 'My God is that the time,' he questioned his eyesight looking at the bar clock. He raised the glass of beer to his mouth and gulped steadily until it was drained to the white froth at the bottom.

'Don't forget the hacksaw,' I reminded on the way to the car.

'Good man yourself,' Uncle Frank praised me heading to the stall.

My Uncle chatted with Peter about the Canon's horse and trap as he felt and studied the hacksaws on display and eventually bought one.

'I don't know but I could have sworn that that horse was tied to a post when I saw it earlier,' Peter said giving a glance at Mattie and me as he gave Uncle Frank his change.

As we were moving away from the stall I noticed on display the same type of screwdriver that I had bought for Vinny. It was marked at half the price that I had paid for it in the hardware shop in the town and I felt sick. Mattie gestured to me to sit in the back. I was sitting beside a container of Jeyes Fluid and two coils of barbed wire.

'What the blooda hell is going on here?' Uncle Frank exclaimed decelerating as we drove around a bend outside the town.

I looked in front between my uncle and Mattie to see a horse and trap half way up an embankment that had a high hedge. A few people were standing in a semi-circle and waving their hands in the direction of the horse. We slowed to a halt beside the scene.

The horse's reins had the rear bumper of a van attached. Mattie had his window wound down and Uncle Frank hollered through it at a man waving a jacket in front of the fretting horse. I took particular notice of the man—he only had one arm.

'Johnny, if you're wondering how that came about I can tell you,' my uncle offered an explanation.

'There's no mystery about it Frank, sure Baines nearly knocked me of my bike before the horse pulled the bumper loose from the van,' Johnny the one armed man called back as he waved a jacket in a calming fashion in front of the bewildered horse.

'I'll leave ye to it so,' Uncle Frank said slowly accelerating away.

He cursed braking hard as he rounded the next bend. Four robust people dressed in gaudy colours were walking four a breast towards us on the same side of the road. They dispersed in a waddling fashion as my uncle slowed and swerved to avoid hitting them with the car and then pursed his lips moving off.

'Did you enjoy the castle?' Mattie called leaning out the window.

I looked out the rear window to see Harry waving a clenched fist at us.

'What castle, there's no castle out this way,' Uncle Frank said changing gears with a rasping sound, 'no, I'll tell you now what they were at,' he cleared his throat and then sorted another gear. 'That crowd have been out visiting some poor family who don't have the time or the money to entertain them. Oh God but those yanks are a pain,' he shook his head and continued in a poorly mimicked American accent, 'my great grandfather was so poor and my great grandmother was so sick before they left poor old Ireland,' and added in his own accent, 'it's a pity I didn't drive into them,' he concluded and smiled at Mattie.

'Now you're talking Uncle Frank,' Mattie returned with an even broader smile.

Uncle Frank hummed and sang bits of songs until we pulled up outside O'Toole's Bar and Grocery.

'What about another lemonade, we might as well be hung for a sheep as a lamb,' Uncle Frank tittered and then pressed his finger to his lips.

'Or hung for a horse as a donkey,' Mattie muttered getting out of the car.

Uncle Frank parked behind a black Wolseley car with a GB sticker on the boot. It was at the main entrance to the bar and grocery. Three young girls were sitting gracefully on the bench outside eating ice cream. The girl in the middle started licking her ice cream profusely as she looked leeringly at Mattie and I coming towards them.

'Bring out my lemonade,' Mattie ordered quietly to me as he stopped beside the girls. I followed Uncle Frank into the bar.

The smelly man was in his usual spot snoring contentedly with his head on the counter. A man in a suit was sitting on a bar stool and banging the counter with a bawdy laugh. Pauric was laughing along with him behind the bar but then shushed his happy customer as he pointed to Walter Delaney and said in a whisper, 'Be quiet Murt or you'll disturb Walter and if you break the crust on him we'll be stunk out of it.'

Murt leaped from the stool with an outstretched hand and

strode towards Uncle Frank with long steps, 'Frank, how's-she-cuttin,'' he greeted.

'Great, how is yourself Murt,' my uncle greeted back shaking his hand.

'What are you having, what are you having,' Murt repeated slapping Uncle Frank on the back.

'A beer I suppose,' Uncle Frank responded plonking on a high-stool.

And who is this buckeen?' Murt asked looking down at me before sitting back on his bar-stool.

'This is Finn, Tessie's youngest boy, himself and his brother are staying with us for a few weeks,' Uncle Frank informed.

'Well fire it is that you, I saw you a week after you were born, I was visiting your granny and your mother was only after having you, you were born in your granny's house you know,' he spluttered a cough and continued, 'your arse was no bigger than a shirt button, would you like a lemonade?' he blabbered putting his hand inside his jacket pocket and drawing out a bulging wallet.

'I'm afraid your wrong Murt, you never met Finn before, it was probably his brother Mattie, he's outside putting chat on three lovely young girls,' Uncle Frank said winking at Pauric.

'Ah-ha ,' Murt laughed , 'they're a bit young to have notions like that yet,' he said stretching his neck to look out the bar window, 'and I suppose you better get another lemonade for your brother so,' he muttered pulling a pound note from his wallet.

'Be God Murt, things must be good abroad in London, you have the money like old hay,' Uncle Frank laughed peering into the wallet.

'Let me tell you Frank, it's hard earned, my brain is in tatters, balancing stocks and shares, day in and day out.'

'Thank you sir,' I said as he stared closer at me handing me the two bottles of lemonade.

I would have preferred something to eat than drink and was sorry now that I didn't have chips with Mattie.

'Give me another look at you,' Murt said placing his hand under my chin and studied my face as he spoke, 'well fire it, you know, he's neither like the father or the mother.'

241

Uncle Frank looked astonished as he responded to Murt's announcement.

'Above all people to comment on someone's resemblance, sure one time you even said that I would 'pass' for a brother of that blooda Dutchman, sure he's loads of years older than me.'

Pauric took the pound note from Murt and chuckled going to the till.

'You know, there's a resemblance there all right.'

'Ah will ye stop the messing and give me my drink,' my uncle bellowed.

'Does that Dutch-Buck come in for a drink these days?' Murt enquired wide-eyed.'

'Yarra not too much, thank God.' Pauric responded.

'Be japus the last time I met him here, himself and Pat Tobin nearly had a fight when William van-what's-his-name claimed that he was "Irish." Do you remember?'

'Ah that was good craic all right,' Pauric giggled as he reminisced with a poor attempt at a foreign accent, 'zer iz a nun in Enland who can prove zat my mozder vas Irish.'

'Who is this nun anyway says Tobin and. ..?' Murt tried to continue with the story but was interrupted by Pauric.

'Zat is none of your business,' the bar owner quoted with a bawdy laugh.

'I saw the blood rising in Tobin's face, be japus I thought he was going to hit the "Dutch-buck" a skelp,' Murt chuckled.

'Ah! Irish one day—with a half-Cockney, half-Yankee, half foreign accent the next day—and he has a Canadian passport, listen lads, listen, with a name like that—he's a blooda Dutchman and that's that,' my uncle roared slamming his glass on the counter.

Uncle Frank had startled me and I left the bar. I pondered on what I had heard; I'm neither like Mammy or Daddy now, and smile entering the forecourt.

'It's about time,' Mattie huffed grabbing the lemonade bottle from me.

'And have you never tasted ice cream before either?' the smaller of the three girls asked me with a pitiful look.

242

'This is Carol, this is Maura and the big one is Margaret,' Mattie introduced tactfully before I could answer. He winked at me putting the bottle to his ice-cream-stained lips. The tallest of the three girls looked heavenward and the middle sized girl clenched her fists with a disapproving look at me.

The girl that looked the youngest giggled and spoke, 'No, no, no, I'm Carol and I'm nearly six, that's Margaret,' she pointed and she's only three year older than me, and Maura is my big sister, she's eleven.'

'Good grief, how many times have you to be told our names?' Margaret asked staring angrily at Mattie.

'Margaret, tell Finn about the time you went to France, he'd love to hear all about it,' Mattie said moving away and sitting on the other bench outside the post office.

I don't know why Mattie said that but I wished that he hadn't. I was glad to be finishing my lemonade so that I could return the bottle and get away from listening to Margaret talking about places in France that I never heard of, or is ever likely to see.

'No, no, I have enough,' Murt said stepping down from his high stool.

'Ah you will, you will,' Uncle Frank was insisting holding Murt's shoulder as I placed the empty lemonade bottle on the counter.

'Well okay I'll have a brandy so,' Murt said sitting back on his stool.

'A brandy how-are-you,' Uncle Frank lilted his shock,' you'll have a beer like the rest of us.'

Pauric followed me to the end of the bar as I was leaving, 'Bring in your brother's bottle, if you know what I mean,' he whispered over the counter to me. I knew exactly what he meant; no more fires. I like Pauric and Ann for not telling about the water pump fire.

'Did you hear that, Mattie doesn't go to school because his parents can't afford the school books,' Carol called in a startled voice to her two sisters as I went back out into the fresh air. Carol was sitting beside Mattie looking puppy eyed into his face.

'Pauric's orders,' I said grabbing the empty bottle from his hand.

243

'Now don't forget what you are to ask your father when he comes out,' I heard Mattie say in a low voice to the overwhelmed girl.

I was placing the bottle on the counter when I heard a tap on the window. The smelly man grunted but didn't move. Pauric raised his hands in anticipation and then lowered them with a smile as Walter Delaney went back to his heavy snoring.

We all turned towards the source of the tapping. Margaret had her face close to the window as she spoke, 'Papa, if we have to be in Cong by five?' she pointed at her watch.

'Well fire it is that the time,' Murt exclaimed gulping his beer to the last drop. He pushed me to one side going out the door and rushed to the black Wolseley car.

'Oh Papa, Papa, this boy never tasted ice cream 'til he had a bite of Maura's and mine, will you buy him a big ice cream, oh please Papa, please,' Carol pleaded going towards her father.

'He's ever-so-poor, they live in a small hut up on the side of that mountain,' Maura added her plea, pointing to the mist covered Croke Patrick mountain.

'Oh ho, oh ho,' Murt puffed slumping in under the steering wheel.

The three girls all vanished into the back and Margaret pulled the door closed.

'Oh ho, oh ho, "poor" is it, I never met a poor sergeant's family yet,' he said before slamming the door closed.

'You're no Santa Claus, with your ho-ho-ho,' Mattie muttered as the car sped onto the road and back towards the church.

Carol waved through the rear window and I waved back. Mattie twisted his ears with his hands and stuck his tongue out. Just then Uncle Frank emerged from the front door, glassy eyed and carrying two radio batteries, but I'm sure that he didn't notice Mattie's antics.

'Don't let those spill,' Uncle Frank said shoving the two radio batteries between the coils of barbed wire and Jeyes Fluid container in the back seat beside me. The batteries looked like large rectangular milk bottles with two rubber caps on either side.

'Have ye a date with the girls, you couldn't go wrong there

boys, their father is loaded with money,' Uncle Frank smiled broadly driving out of the forecourt. 'What does he work at?' I asked with the intension of getting away from the 'girls and dates' stuff.

'Well nobody really knows the truth about what Murt works at but I can tell you this, he hadn't an arse in his pants, like the rest of us, when he left this parish about twenty years ago to go to England,' Uncle Frank replied rasping another gear.

'I know what he works at,' Mattie yawned.

'You do?' Uncle Frank chirped.

'Yes, the young girl Maura told me.'

'Her name is Carol,' I corrected Mattie.

'Ah, who cares,' Mattie said staring out the window in a huff.

'Come on, come on, what does he do?' Uncle Frank pressed showing great interest.

'He has the best job in the world,' Mattie drooled and sighed.

'Come on, come on,' my uncle ordered.

'He has a lorry and he collects scrap from garages and factories, and then what he doesn't sell to the Scrap Dealers he can keep for himself—just imagine keeping all that scrap,' Mattie concluded enviously.

'Aha, aha, well isn't that the best ever, and did she tell you anything else?' my uncle pressed.

Mattie thought for a while and then answered slowly, 'Oh yes she said that I wasn't to tell anyone what her father worked at.'

My uncle shook his head and laughed before speaking, 'Stocks and shares how–are–you, do you know...' Uncle Frank stopped mid sentence as he swerved towards the ditch to allow a jeep travelling at high speed in the opposite direction to pass on the narrow road.

'That's that blooda Dutchman, he'll kill somebody yet,' Uncle Frank said gritting his teeth as he manoeuvred his Morris Minor along the grass bank and back on the road.

One of the radio batteries was tumbling off the seat at his first swerve but I caught it just in time and only a small drop of liquid spilled from the battery and onto the seat. I was just about to wipe it with my hand when I noticed that the liquid was sizzling on the seat.

'Uncle Frank,' I called with a worried voice.

'Yes?'

I continued, 'Some water came out of the battery when you swerved and it's boiling on the seat now,' I explained moving away from the battery.

Uncle Frank braked so fast that I had to leap for the battery to stop it tumbling again, 'Water how are you, that's acid! Keep away from it!' he hollered leaping from the car just as it stopped.

He rushed to the car boot and after a short while rummaging there he returned and vigorously started rubbing the bubbling acid with an old hand-knitted sock.

'Good man Pauric, didn't bother your arse tightening the caps,' he muttered during the course of his clean up.

He repeated much the same throwing the sock over the hedge before getting back in the car. Uncle Frank didn't speak again until we reached the gates at the top of the lane and he still sounded very annoyed.

'Finn, I thought I told you to close the gate when we were coming out.'

'I did close it Uncle Frank, sure you waited on the road 'til I did,' I exonerated myself in a pleading fashion.

'Huh! sure you did,' Mattie huffed accusingly.

I slapped him on the head and in a loud burst repeated that I had closed the gates.

'Will ye stop fighting ye blooda ceolans, Mattie will you close it behind me.'

'Of course I will Uncle Frank, any job I am given to do will be done,' Mattie said and then looked back at me with a grin.

'Well ye took your time, what kept ye so long, the dinner is ruined,' Granny said in a scolding tone as we followed Uncle Frank into the kitchen.

'Who left the gate open, had you visitors?' Uncle Frank replied with a question going through to the scullery with the two radio batteries.

'No, no nobody,' Granny replied in a hesitating tone.

'That blooda Dutchman, Van Heyningen, nearly drove us over a ditch and caused one of the radio batteries to spill, nearly destroyed the blooda car seat on me,' Uncle Frank said coming back from the scullery and plonking in the fireside chair. 'Oh, oh yes he called here, here,' Granny stuttered a little, 'he, was here in the yard when I came back from Breda Fenlon's...'

'That nosey parker,' Uncle Frank muttered with gritted teeth.

I don't think my uncle is friendly with Breda Fenlon.

Granny ignored my uncle's interruption and appeared to be more flustered as she continued, 'I, I dropped Breda up the carpet-mat that, tha, that Tessie sent with the boys.'

'That blooda Dutchman must have left the gate open so, what did he want?' my uncle snapped.

'He, he ah,' Granny hesitated and slowly added as if she was deep in thought, 'he said that some of your sheep were straying around his green houses.'

'He said blooda what?' Uncle Frank replied standing up abruptly.

Granny blessed herself and retired to the scullery.

'He has some blooda cheek, my sheep go nowhere near there, blooda foreigner, with his glasshouses growing foreign vegetables,' Uncle Frank sucked heavily on his cigarette and continued in a threatening mood, 'I'll be up to see Mister van Heyningen in the morning.'

'You needn't bother, he has gone back to Holland for a few days to visit his, his...mother,' Granny sounded flustered and then added, 'he's leaving for the boat tonight.'

'That was a very cosy chat ye had after him blaming our sheep for straying,' Uncle Frank said with a raised voice flicking his cigarette ash carelessly on the floor.

Granny spoke solemnly joining us at the dinner table, 'I was hoping that we could all go to Confessions this evening.'

Mattie frowned staring at her.

'But judging by the state of you,' Granny gave a stern glance at Uncle Frank, 'we better leave it 'til next Saturday.'

Mattie smiled at the end of Granny's announcement.

'Maybe he mightn't be there himself,' Uncle Frank said with a shake of the head and went on to tell Granny about the Canon's horse being tied to the back of Barney Baines's van.

'Somebody is going to have to do something about that Barney Baines lad, he'll spend all the inheritance on drink in no time, God rest his father but he must be turning in his grave to see what's going on,' Granny sighed woefully.

'If the drink don't soak up the money, the gambling will,' Uncle Frank spoke with a slight slur in his voice.

I thought that it was a good idea to get away from the present subject and asked Uncle Frank what work he planned to do next.

'Next week, please God, we should have all the hay in from the fields and then bring the sheep and lambs back up the mountain and then bring in the turf the following week,' Uncle Frank replied taking a deep breath.

'Ah,' I said with disappointment, 'we won't be here for bringing in the turf so, because The Yank, ah, er, Mister Joyce,' I corrected myself, ' is coming here to bring us home on the Monday after next.'

'Be God you're right,' my uncle replied, 'we better get in a bit of fishing so—I'm sure your mother wont say "no" to a nice salmon'

'Don't forget to hold back a lamb too, so they can bring it back home with them also,' Granny ordered.

'I have a nice one picked out already to kill,' Uncle Frank said with a yawn.

Mattie had been waiting with his mouth open to get a chance to ask questions, 'How soon are we going fishing and when are you going to kill the lamb?' he asked staring wildly at Uncle Frank from the end of the table.

'How about a bit of fishing after I have the cows milked and the lamb can wait until the middle of the week,' he replied while wiping his mouth with the back of his hand.

'Yes, yes, yes,' Mattie voiced his excited approval.

'Don't be going anywhere until you connect up that radio

battery for me I don't know what's going on the world,' Granny ordered.

'Yes mother,' Uncle Frank replied in a subdued tone.

We helped our uncle to carry the first sack of grain from the car boot to the Old House but we dropped our end of the sack twice on the way. He carried the second sack and coil of barbed wire on his own and told me to bring the Jeyes Fluid.

CHAPTER 22

The Board that Sank

WE STAYED WITH UNCLE FRANK from the time he brought in the cows and milked them until they were turned back out to the fields in the misconstrued assumption that our presence would hasten things up.

'Where are the fishing rods,' Mattie asked sticking close to Uncle Frank as he strode towards the back of the old house.

'Fishing rods?' Uncle Frank smiled, 'follow me and I'll show you the sort of fishing rods we have in these parts.' He winked at me going towards the back door to the Old House. The wire that used to be bound around the bolt was lying on the ground so he just slid the bolt back and pushed in the door in one movement.

By the way he was talking I was convinced that he was going to take down the nets that I now know from Mattie my uncle uses in the river at night time. I was wrong. He fumbled his way towards the cartwheel beside the open hearth and forcefully pulled a tea chest to one side. It was the one that Mattie had been rummaging in.

I squinted behind the stack of old blackened pots to see if the parcel was still where I had replaced it. I couldn't see the parcel but then I remembered what Granny had said about bringing it to her friend Breda Fenlon before the Dutchman called. I'm sure that, that woman would have said something to Granny if she had noticed the mats were damaged and I feel more relaxed now that nothing was said about their condition.

'Here's our fishing rod,' Uncle Frank announced pulling his hand back down from inside the blackened chimney. He had in his hand what looked like the keel of a very small boat with loads of fishing line wrapped around it. If this is supposed to be a fishing rod it's the funniest one that I have ever seen. It's only over a foot long and under a foot wide.

'That's not a fishing rod, that's only an old board,' Mattie grumbled pulling the apparatus from Uncle Frank.

'Mind the hooks,' Uncle Frank cautioned and then added, 'that's exactly what it is, it's called, "The Board," as good as ten fishing rods and a boat.'

When we got outside in the light I examined it with Mattie. It had fly hooks attached to the fishing line and the bottom of the piece of timber had a strip of lead tacked to it.

'I'll carry that,' Uncle Frank said taking it from Mattie. 'Where are you going?' Uncle Frank called to Mattie who had gone into the field off the front farmyard. 'The river, where else?' Mattie replied turning his head back but still waking forward.

'Well have a nice time, Finn and me are going to the lake to do some fishing,' Uncle Frank called to him and then concealed a chuckle.

'Lake, what, what, lake?' Mattie spurted his excited reply running to catch up on us.

'You know the second hill where we collect the sheep for shearing?' Mattie nodded wide-eyed. 'Well in the valley between that and the next hill is a lake where you'll get as good a trout as anywhere in Ireland,' Uncle Frank replied with a wry grin. Mattie led the way based on my uncle's directions. 'He wasn't as eager going to do the hay,' Uncle Frank nodded towards Mattie and winked at me.

Mattie was wading in the shore waters as we reached the top of a boggy hill that looked down on a silver calm lake. The lake had a stony level opening to the front, was about a hundred yard long and not more than fifty yards wide with high banks on either side. Uncle Frank sat on a boulder at the water's edge and began unravelling the fishing line.

'Finn, take the end of the line and mind the hooks,' he ordered as I moved further away from The Board twirling and releasing fishing line with each step I took.

Mattie was gasping running from me to Uncle Frank like a collie dog unsure of it's master's orders to round up sheep. 'What do we do now, what do we do now?' Mattie asked through excited gasps.

'Well stop jumping around and scaring the fish for a start,' Uncle Frank ordered in a low voice leaving The Board on the ground beside his seat and then added with a sigh, 'that's the end of the line, now to straighten out the line hook.'

He bent down and moved towards me as he unravelled each of the ten pieces of fishing line that was attached about three feet apart along the main fishing line. These pieces of line varied in length from three feet to six feet and were much finer than the main line. They had imitation flies with hooks at the end. When he got as far as me he looked back at his work and gave a contented smile as he spoke, 'Well lads we're ready to launch.'

Mattie and I followed him back to where The Board was and he checked the fishing line knot on the nail protruding near the centre of it.

'Now Finn, I want you to gently take the end of the line and walk slowly over to that white rock,' he pointed towards an obvious white rock that peeped out at the beginning of the embankment on the right, 'and when I say the word "now" I want you to run along the embankment with the end of the line held tight in your hand until you come to the end of the lake and be careful because it's a sheer deep drop in the lake all along there. '

He read my bewildering look and frowned at me like an impatient teacher and said slowly, 'You will run along the bank of the lake up to the very end holding that line tightly in your hand,' he pointed and continued, 'and when I release The Board it will go out into the middle of the lake like a toy boat and the fly hooks will skip along the water from the line that you are pulling.' He stared wide-eyed at me and asked softly, 'Do you understand?' 'Yes,' I answered with my fingers crossed on my free hand. I heard Mattie giggling.

I went to my position and watched as my uncle waded into the water until the water lapped near the top of his wellingtons. He lowered The Board and held it upright in the water until the weighted lower leaded part disappeared. Mattie was so close to me that I had to yell at him that he was tripping me.

'Will you two be quiet!' Uncle Frank called over at us with a controlled roar.

As the line got tauter he called out his staggered orders in a low voice, 'Take it easy, take it easy, yes, yes, stop there,' he said in whispering gasps and raised hand. 'Now!' he called in a loud voice swiftly lowering his hand. The sudden loud roar 'now' startled me into a run along the embankment as instructed. He released his grip and pushed The Board towards the left side of the lake water.

It moved like a fish being released back into its natural habitat. The line became tight in my hand as The Board tugged at me and bobbed like a yacht in high winds struggling to make it ashore. The more I pulled and ran the more The Board tried to tug away from me. I must ask Sparks when I get home for an explanation as to how this happens. The fly lines floated precariously from the main line as I mastered a few undulations without slowing my speed. Mattie's scream of joy staggered my pace and I had to pound faster on the grass to regain my previous speed.

His first scream of joy was quickly followed by more excited yells as fish rose to the surface to take the imitation fly bait.

'Keep pulling, keep pulling!' Uncle Frank roared as he followed behind coming to the end of the lake. I kept pulling long past the lake's end and only stopped when I had tugged The Board onto dry land. Mattie seemed to be dancing in time with various sized trout that wriggled and bounced on the rushy shore. Their fly hooked lips opened and closed gulping in fresh air instead of water.

'Pull a few rushes,' Uncle Frank ordered in a happy tone as he unhooked the brown trout gasping their last.

'Not bad for the first trawl,' he said threading the rushes through the gills of the fish and out through their mouths.

'Four fish,' Mattie called out holding high the fish threaded on the rushes and then dropped them with a plea, 'please Uncle Frank can I have a go?'

'Of course,' Uncle Frank agreed, enjoying our excitement.

I wasn't happy with the way Mattie was holding the line. It looked to be too loose in his hand but I know better than tell Mattie that he's doing things wrong. Uncle Frank called out his instructions and repeated his actions as he had done with me at the other end of the lake. After Uncle Frank shouted 'now' he watched Mattie start his run and then lit up a cigarette and strolled behind us. I was given the job of carrying the fish and stayed a long way behind Mattie to follow his implicit instructions; 'I'm doing this all on my own,' he had threatened me.

Mattie was slowing his run and then going fast again as trout leaped to the same fate as the ones had done before them. Mattie was pulling and tugging and running and jumping along the bank and then the inevitable happened. I saw him disappear just after he had come to the top of an undulation. He reappeared again tumbling down the embankment and barely stopped short of touching the water. Uncle Frank pushed me to one side and ran towards Mattie. The fish dangled and bounced on the rushes in my hand as I increased my pace towards my brother.

We all stood and gawked as fly hook after fly hook bobbed under the water, pulled along by the baited fish to the centre of the lake. The main line slid slowly out of reach away from the shore, and silently slid snakelike just below the surface as if being sucked there by the listing board that gave no indication of its previous purpose other than what it looked like now; a weighted board drifting and listing in the water.

'It must have been a very, very big one, broke the line,' Mattie panted his explanation coming slowly back up the embankment and then broke into a run as Uncle Frank flicked his cigarette to the ground and gave chase to his screaming nephew.

Uncle Frank gave up the chase and slowed to a pace that I could catch up on him. I said nothing for awhile and then asked about going net fishing in the river. He just glared at me and I went silent again. Then I decided to try a different tactic to see if I could humour him.

I asked him if he ever went 'Striddeling.' I got some reaction this time; he twirled his lip and repeated the word Striddeling' in such a way that I knew he was wondering what Striddeling was; so I told him.

I explained that it didn't require fishing rods, The Board or nets; all you had to do was pull a rush or long piece of straw and kick a hole in the ground until you found a small worm and then tie it to the straw.

'Most streams in farmer's fields that drain to a river have Striddelies in them,' I explained our fishing grounds to my bemused uncle and then gave more details, 'lower the worm and straw into the stream and when the Striddely bites on the worm, just yank it out.'

When I had given him all the information and knowledge about Striddeling he just frowned and asked, 'Sure wouldn't the fish break the straw?' When I showed him the size of a Striddely by holding up my little finger he waved his hand dismissively and increased his pace.

I caught up with him and told him about the time that Sparks and Vinny and I were out Striddeling. 'Vinny fell into the stream,' I began my story to gain his attention and looked into his face for reaction as I continued, 'Sparks and I pulled him out and he was all wet and muck so we decided to bring him home,' I looked at my uncle and he appeared to be interested in my story so I continued, 'when we arrived at Vinny's house his mother was weeding the front garden and when she looked at the state of Vinny she hit him on the back with a rake and told him to go inside and sent Sparks and me home.'

I noticed a smile appearing on my uncle's face. When I had finished my story I remained silent and so did he. Then suddenly I was pleasantly surprised when he tapped me on the head and spoke, 'Well I suppose there's no point in being cross with you, it wasn't you who lost The Board in the lake.'

I felt more at ease now to ask again about how the net fishing in the river is done. 'It's not hard sums or spellings that we're talking about here,' he began as we strolled down the hill for the road, 'all you do is find a good deep hole in the river, a "salmon pool" we call it, and all you do then is tie the net, or hold it if you have enough help, from one side of the bank to the other, at one end of the pool.' He cleared his throat and continued, 'Then throw stones and make plenty of splashes at the opposite end of the pool and the salmons flee for their lives towards the net.' Uncle Frank pulled open the gate as if he had timed it to illustrate his story, 'Then pull out your net and there's your salmons, if there were any there in the first place,' he laughed going down the lane.

'And then do you kill them with the spear thing then?' I asked excitedly.

'Not at all that's a different way we fish with the spear,' he spluttered and then pressed his finger to his mouth and continued in a low voice, 'I might get a chance to show you how to do that before you go back.'

Before we entered through the small gate Uncle Frank put his hand on my shoulder and spoke solemnly, 'Don't be telling your father about the way we fish or he'll have me arrested.' I shook my head as a show of word of honour that his secret was safe.

Mattie was coyly sitting at the kitchen table nibbling a sandwich when we arrived. Uncle Frank gave a scouring look at him.

There was a familiar odour in the kitchen that I tried to name but just couldn't. Granny had her head sideways listening to the radio that was emitting Irish Ceilidh music in loud and then low wafts. I proudly held up the days catch in front of her but she just finished humming a tune and said that because we had eaten dinner so late that she had made sandwiches for us instead of doing a proper tea. I felt deflated by her disinterested attitude towards the fish I had caught and slowly walked into the scullery where I placed them in the sink. The goose that choked on the ball-bearing was sprawled 'oven ready' on a large oval Willow Pattern plate beside the sink.

When I was coming back from the scullery I got a familiar smell again was reminded of home; shoes were polished and left along the base of the dresser. I came up with the name of the odour that had evaded me since I entered the kitchen. It was shoe polish and that could only mean one thing; it meant Sunday Mass tomorrow.

It was dusk by the time we got around to saying the Rosary. Granny said that we could stay up to listen to a play on the radio. It was boring and I felt a bit sick listening to it. I fell asleep in the fireside chair about halfway through and don't know how it ended.

I wasn't that tired then when I went to bed so I began to tell Mattie as he readied himself for bed how Uncle Frank does his net fishing in the river and that he is going to show me how to fish with the spear. I know I promised Uncle Frank that I wouldn't tell Daddy, but I'm sure it's okay to tell Mattie about the different ways they do fishing in Doiredrum, and anyways Mattie knows how they fish with The Board.

Mattie sat facing me in the bed and was listening attentively. When I'd finished telling him he moved towards me and whispered in my ear, 'We could do that net fishing in the river, just the two of us.'

I immediately turned on my side away from him and emphatically declared, 'I am not going net fishing with you.'

I felt the bed clothes being wrenched from over me as he mimicked my refusal not to accompany him net fishing.

Next I felt a sharp pain on the back of my head followed by the words, 'never hit me on the head again.' It was Mattie taking his revenge on me for hitting him in the car earlier.

CHAPTER 23

Holy Mass and Cleansing Grass

THIS IS THE FIRST TIME that I awoke feeling hungry in Granny's and what a day to pick; it's Sunday morning and that meant fasting until after receiving Holy Communion at Mass. Granny had our Sunday clothes neatly separated in the wardrobe.

'We'll be late for Mass if ye don't hurry up,' Granny called pinning her hat to her hair bun standing at the mirror in the hallway.

'Ah mother stop will ya, we still have nearly an hour,' Uncle Frank called from the doorway of the bathroom with his face lathered.

Granny opened the oven door and peered in as she spoke, 'Coming on nicely, another couple of hours should do it.' Just before she clanged the oven door shut I got an appetising waft of roasting goose.

Uncle Frank combed his hair-oiled wispy blond hair in front of the mirror in the hallway before he came into the kitchen. He tore a very small piece of paper from the end of the newspaper, licked it and returned to the mirror in the hallway where he stuck it on a small nick wound on the side of his cheek.

Daddy does the same when he cuts himself shaving. Uncle Frank was wearing a brown suit, white shirt and tie. The tie was mostly purple with scattered green and red twirl patterns on it. I remembered that Daddy used to wear a tie just like it a few years ago and none of us liked it. It was one Mammy had got in parcel from America.

Mattie and I got in the back seat and Uncle Frank held the door for Granny and didn't close it until she looked well settled in the front seat. The two donkeys were at the lane gates as we approached the top of the hill and did not move until I got out of the car to do the usual job with the gate. Shep and Toss passed me out at speed and vanished with the donkeys over the hill on the roadway.

Mattie sat silently picking at the scorched area on the seat that had been caused by the radio battery acid. By the time we got to the church Mattie had picked away all the crisp scorched bits and had made a clean hole as far as the sponge seat stuffing.

A sparkling new Austin Cambridge was the only other car parked outside the walls of the church as we arrived. A few men were inside the gate talking loudly amidst bouts of laughter.

'I see Canon Dillon got his horse and trap back,' Uncle Frank nodded in the direction of a horse that was grazing in a field in front of a large house beside the church.

As we were going in the gate I noticed that the church was very small and had no spire. The church bell was situated in the church grounds between the gable end of the church and the wall along the road. It was mounted on what looked like scaffolding that was imbedded in a concrete plinth. The plinth had steps all round leading to the main body of the suspended bell. A sturdy rope with two large knots on it hung from the semi circular wheel attached to the bell.

Uncle Frank stopped to talk to some men standing on the grass verge that separated the pebbled church grounds and the adjacent graveyard. They are the same men that were talking and laughing as we came in the gate but went quite as they bade Granny good morning. They all look around the same age but maybe a few years younger than my uncle.

A small hunchbacked man was standing in the church porch beside a table with a collection box on it.

'Morning, Malachy,' Granny greeted him in an official tone. She opened her handbag and removed a purse from it. She took a half crown from the purse and displayed it before dropping it in the collection box. Malachy bowed but I don't know if it through fear or respect. Granny ushered Mattie and I in front of her and we ended up in the second seat from the front of the altar.

A few other women were scattered elsewhere around the church and I could hear their gibberish whispering prayers echoing around the church as their Rosary beads clanged on the backrest of the seats in front of them. Granny more or less pushed us into the seat first and then struggled in after us. I was sitting between Granny and Mattie in the seat. I sat up after saying a prayer but Granny made me kneel down again and say more prayers. Mattie gave the impression that he was kneeling but was actually resting on his elbows in a crouched position on the backrest of the seat in front.

The church got noisier as the seats began to fill with individual people and families jostling as if they were seeking the most advantageous seats. Just before the priest came onto the altar at the start of Mass I heard the church bell suddenly ringing outside. Mattie's elbows slipped and he hit his chin on the hard timber backrest in front of him. He was rubbing his chin furiously until Granny glared at him and he stopped and knelt down properly.

'Move up, move up to the front,' the Canon called hoarsely beckoning with his hand to the people standing at the back of the church as he walked to the foot of the altar. Seven nervous looking altar boys preceded him. I looked behind me and I could see a small bit of movement near the rear of the church but nobody came as far as our seat and there was room for at least three more people. I answered aloud the Latin responses along with the Altar boys and looked at Granny for a favourable reaction. She was too busy shuffling prayer leaflets in her prayer book and didn't appear to have been listening to me so I didn't bother anymore.

When it came to the sermon the Canon stormed onto the pulpit and after emitting several loud honks from his red and purpled blotched nose he struggled furiously to shove his handkerchief back into the sleeve of his heavy vestments. I listened to the start of his sermon about sins and hell and then my mind began to wander until he pounded the semi circular cushion on the balustrade around the top of the pulpit and bellowed, 'And the money owed for the excursion to the holy shrine at Knock will be paid for in advance this time, no hiccups like the last time or I'll plaster those who don't pay on the church notice board.' He blessed himself and scurried back down to the altar. When the Altar Boy gonged the bell at the Consecration part of the Mass my mind began to wander again and I thought about one particular morning that Vinny and I had been Serving at Mass.

Before the Mass started one of our jobs as altar boys was to put water and wine in the small glass jugs in the sacristy before they were placed at the altar. Father Neylon was late for Saying Mass that morning and Mister Doyle the sexton was outside looking to see if he was coming down from the Parochial House.

While Mister Doyle was outside Vinny kept refilling the small wine jug and drinking it. I told him to stop doing it but he just laughed at me and said that it was lovely.

When it came to the Consecration part of the Mass where Vinny was to ring the bell he just started giggling and fell on top of the bell. I moved over beside him on my knees and took the gong stick from him so I could ring the bell for him but he grabbed it back from me and started flaking the bell with it. Father Neylon was staring wide-eyed over the chalice at his lips, as wine dribbled down his chin. Then Mister Doyle came rushing out from the sacristy and grabbed Vinny by the back of his soutane and dragged him into the sacristy.

After Mass was over Father Neylon and I went into the sacristy. Mister Doyle was mopping the floor. There was a terrible smell of vomit.

Father Neylon was furious when he said to Mister Doyle, 'Don't worry I'll deal with that pup.'

Even though it wasn't a Sunday Mass and there weren't too many people in the church Vinny was still told by Father Neylon that he was never to come back and Serve at Mass ever again.

Granny, Mattie and me were among the first to come back

to our seats after receiving Holy Communion but there was a long wait before everyone else had settled back in their seats too. Mattie started playing with a Rosary beads that he had found on the prayer book shelf in front of him. By the time that Mass had ended he had carved out his initials on the back of the seat in front of him by scraping the varnished timber with the metal cross on the Rosary beads.

The church had all but emptied before Granny put away her novena booklet and allowed us to leave our seat. I'm staying with Uncle Frank the next time we go to Mass. Before Granny left the church she made us wait beside her while she prayed looking up at a statue of Saint Anthony at the back of the church just inside the door. It wasn't a very big statue but it looked big as it was on top of a table with exceptionally long wooden legs.

'This way,' she said when we eventually left the church. She was walking towards the graveyard. Half way up the pathway in the centre of the graveyard she stopped and looked sad as se spoke, 'This is your grandfather's grave, God be good to him, died a young man.' The headstone engraver must have got it wrong because it said, 'Died sixty-four years of age.

She started praying silently again and Mattie and I blessed ourselves but in a second or two Mattie moved back down the pathway. I stayed with Granny until she had finished praying but as we were moving back down the path she turned off it and spoke quietly, 'I must have a word with Johnny.' I looked over at a one-armed man standing by a grave and told her that I would see her at the car. I gulp and wonder if Johnny Byrne is as good at keeping secrets as Ann and Pauric.

Outside the church Uncle Frank was talking and laughing amongst the same men again. My uncle was oblivious to Mattie who was busying himself firing small stones up at the church bell. Mattie missed the bell each time he fired a small stone but then he got a handful of pebbles, left the church grounds and released all the pebbles at once over the wall in the direction of the high bell. A few dinged off the bell but most of the pebbles showered the stain glass window at the gable end of the church.

'Mattie,' Uncle Frank called in a gasping whisper as he turned around, 'sorry lads I have to go, I'll see you in O'Tooles in a while,' he said parting company with his friends.

The smelly man, Walter Delaney was slouched motionless against one of the peers at the church gates. Then suddenly he started wriggling his back against the cut stone edge as if he was scratching his back.

'I don't know what's wrong with Johnny Byrne,' Granny said getting into the car, ' I went over to see if he wanted a lift and all he said was, "maybe I can't afford a lift from you and the price of things," not as much as a thank you for the scones,' she huffed closing the car door.

Mattie winked at me and smiled.

'Ah Johnny can be odd sometimes,' Uncle Frank dismissed her concern and continued, 'Mother, I suppose you want to do a bit of shopping for the tea and have a chat with Pauric and Ann,' Uncle Frank chirped his suggestion starting the engine.

'No, not staying, just get the Sunday Press and none of that English trash,' Granny said with a harsh glance.

Uncle Frank opened his mouth as if to protest but she cut across him with silencing words, 'You did enough gallivanting yesterday and anyway I have to keep an eye on that goose, and there is no need to shop, we are having trout for the tea,' she said with a raised head that showed that the matter was not for further discussion.

They're the trout that I caught, I smiled to myself.

'That's a lovely new car,' Mattie said as we passed the Austin Cambridge car that had been parked outside the church when we arrived.

'I'd have two of those if I had Malachy's money,' Uncle Frank said with a laugh. 'Who's Malachy?' Mattie asked sitting upright in the back seat.

'Did you see the small maneen taking the collection at the church door?' We nodded and my uncle continued, 'He rings the bell and does all that sort of thing' Uncle Frank said with a half turn of his head.

'The hunchback man,' Mattie gasped.

'Well I suppose if that's what you want to call him,' Frank said and added 'the most contrary man that was ever born.'

263

'And can he ring that bell on his own?' Mattie asked stretching further in between the two front seats.

'Sure they had to put an extra long piece of rope on the bell so he could reach it, the little gnat.' Uncle Frank replied.

'That's enough of that sort of talk, God bless the mark' Granny scolded.

Uncle Frank hesitated but then continued, 'Do you know that as soon as he rings the bell for the start of Mass he comes back into the church and locks the doors so that if you are late you can't get in, nor will he let you leave until the Mass is well and truly finished.'

'They're the Canon's orders,' Granny butted in.

'Maybe yes, maybe no,' Uncle Frank rebuffed with a shake of his head.

'And he gets a load of money just for just doing that, so he can buy a new car, wow?' Mattie quizzed excitedly.

Granny turned with a broad smile as her son went on to explain, 'No, no, he does that for free, Malachy owns a hotel in Portwest and an Electrical shop and a Butcher's shop and has two of the best farms around these parts, he just likes the idea of authority that's why he does the voluntary church work,' Uncle Frank finished with a sigh.

'One of my earlier pupils and possibly the best I ever had was Malachy,' Granny said turning to her son.

Uncle Frank beeped his horn at his friends who were playfully pushing one another on the roads between the church and the pub.

'And they were some my last and probably the worst pupils I ever had,' Granny nodded at Uncle Franks friends and then exaggerated a look of disgust.

Uncle Frank left the engine running as he dashed into the shop and returned with the Sunday Press.

Delicious wafts of roasting goose met us as we entered the house.

'Everybody change into their old clothes,' Granny ordered in the hallway.

'I'll be alright for a while, I'm only going to feed the calves,'

Uncle Frank said going straight through to the scullery and out the back door.

After changing our clothes Mattie and I raced one another through the yard to the outhouse where the calves were. We met Uncle Frank coming out the door. He was cursing as he looked in disbelief at his heavily splattered suit.

'Blooda calf scoured all over me,' he ranted rubbing the bright green dribbling mess with a fistful of grass he yanked from the base of the outhouse.

'Granny is going to kill you,' Mattie announced with his hands stuffed deep in is pockets.

Uncle Frank looked viciously at Mattie. He is defiantly in a bad mood so I think I'll offer him some advice.

'You should do what Meme Meehan does,' I said looking up at my uncle who was still furiously rubbing the stained suit with more grass.

'Who's that or what's that?' he snapped walking briskly away in the direction of the stream.

I responded immediately, 'Don't wear any clothes when you're working with calves.'

He stopped so suddenly that I bumped into him.

'What did you say?' he peered down at me with a cringed face that demanded an immediate explanation which I gave in haste;

'You see one day Sparks and Vinny and me were coming home from the Crockan, that's the name of the river where we swim, ' I specified and took a deep breath, 'and it started to pour rain so we ran to Murphy's cowshed for shelter,' I knew Uncle Frank was interested by the way his jaw was dropping so I continued real fast, 'and when we ran in the cowshed door Meme was holding onto a calf by the tail and he had no clothes on and he told us that he didn't want to get his clothes dirty and that is why he was naked,' I gasped completing the story that would explain the reason for not wearing clothes near calves.

Uncle Frank scratched his head and then shook it as he asked, 'who is this "Me, Me"?'

I went silent as I remembered something very important; it's about a promise I'd made to Meme—but it's too late now. Mattie filled the silence.

'Ah he's an oul eejit that does a bit of work for Murphy the farmer now and again,' Mattie answered for me and then added, 'his real name is Mehaul Meehan but he gets excited when you ask him his name and all he gets out is "me,me." Towbar and me ask him his name every time we see him just for the fun of hearing him say "Me-me-me," everybody calls him "Meme,"' Mattie concluded with a laugh.

The important thing I just remember is that Sparks, Vinny and me promised Meme that we wouldn't disclose his secret way of staying clean in the cowshed to anyone. He even gave us a half crown between us to keep our promise. I'll have to tell the priest in confessions about me breaking my promise.

'I think that ye are all half mad up in that part of the country,' Uncle Frank laughed bending down at the stream, 'and mad names to match, "Sparks," "Towbar," "Meme,"' he laughed.

He moistened the stained area of his suit with water from the stream and furiously rubbed it with his handkerchief as he rounded the corner into the yard.

'Now what are we going to do?' Mattie yawned kicking a stone into the stream.

I was glad that he asked because I wanted to make a 'house name sign' for Granny for a long time but I didn't know what to use to make it so I asked Mattie.

'Follow me,' he said going towards the Old House.

I'm a little bit sorry now that I asked him. He slipped the bolt back and entered the gloomy room. Mattie went straight to the tea chest he had been rummaging in before and started pulling out old crockery, framed pictures and other bric-a-brac and dropping them on the floor. He was making a lot of noise so I told him to be quiet but he just looked at me and made even more noise than before. When the tea chest was empty he climbed awkwardly into it and started ramming his knee into the side of it. He yelped one or twice before he told me to find the toolbox and get him the hacksaw.

I opened the toolbox and reported my findings, 'Uncle Frank hasn't put in the new hacksaw yet,' I called in a whisper over to him.

'It doesn't have to be a new one just get me the old one,' he snapped and yelped again after another unsuccessful attempt to knee out a side of the tea chest.

'Mattie the old one is in bits above in Teach An Dochtúra, remember, cutting out spears, or trying to?' I refreshed his memory.

'Finn, shut up,' he spurted out just as a side of the tea chest gave way, landing it and Mattie on the floor. The sheet of plywood was a bit raggedy and split at the edges where it pulled through the tack heads.

'What are you going to do with that?' I asked as he examined with delight the sheet of plywood that once was a side of a tea chest.

'What do think dumbo, it's your sign of course,' he spurted out wrenching away the top piece of beading.

'But it's too big,' I frowned.

'Not when you cut it.'

'With what? Remember we have no saw.'

'There has to be another saw somewhere, I remember now Frank said that he had to use a different saw to cut the sheep's horns when he couldn't find the hacksaw,' Mattie muttered looking around the room.

I started looking as well and when I saw the stack of blackened pots and broken cart wheel I was reminded of the parcel we had taken with us from Clunmon. I reminded Mattie how I had fixed the tear on the parcel that he had torn when he knocked the cartwheel on it.

'I didn't tear any parcel, it was you who tore it when you started pulling it away from the cartwheel' he contradicted me as he peered up the chimney where Uncle Frank had got The Board the day before.

He looked around in various parts of the room before he declared, 'I know what we'll do, we'll make the biggest house name sign in the world, get me that sheep marker stuff and a good length of wire,' he said moving to the window where daylight shone on a Raddle container.

I peeped out the door and hastily retrieved the piece of wire on the ground that was used around the door bolt.

'That's too scittery,' he barked opening the tin of red Raddle. 'Start writing,' he ordered as he pulled a pliers from the toolbox and headed out the door.

I didn't see any paint brush so I pulled a piece of wool from the wool sacks and squeezed and rolled it into a sort of a point. It wasn't a very good improvised paintbrush and the Radle began to run. I was continually wiping off dribbles but I persevered with the task in hand until I had written the house name that I wanted. I was glad that Mattie hadn't cut the plywood, because I needed all the room I could get especially for the final word in the name.

'What the hell is that?' Mattie asked with a giggle coming in the door with a length of wire and pliers in his hands.

'Teach mo Sheanmhathair' I read from my sign.

He danced around tittering for a while and then asked, 'what does it say?'

Mattie isn't very good at Irish so I translated into English for him.

'My Grandmother's House,' I said proudly.

'I don't know if that is funny or mad, but I have the wire for it anyway,' he said straightening out the coiled wire in his hand and measuring it against the length of the detached side of the tea chest.

'Where did you get that wire?' I asked looking at a small shiny white object that seemed to join two lengths of wire.

I remembered that Sparks had found things like that in the dump at the rear of Goodwins Electrical shop at home and he called them 'insulators.'

'From a pole in the back yard,' Mattie grunted his answer to my question and squeezed tightly with the pliers until he had snipped the wire.

'You cut Granny's clothes line?' I hollered in disbelief.

'You think I'm stupid Finn, it's a piece of wire near the clothes line, she never hangs clothes on it and it just goes from the clothes line pole to the window,' he answered, rummaging in the toolbox.

He came back to the sign with a screwdriver, hacked two

holes in it at either end near the top, pushed the wire through the holes, knotting it near the white insulator.

He held up the sign, with the insulator resting on two of his fingers, as if he was showing a painting for sale.

'Right, it's presentation time,' Mattie announced walking to the door.

'No,' I screamed, 'it's a surprise present for Granny, we'll hang it on her gate the morning we are going home.'

Mattie thought for a second and then flung the newly created house–name–sign towards the fireplace. It glided gracefully at first but then spun sideways, flipped upside down and landed with a flop on top of a timber barrel in the corner.

'Excellent shot Mattie,' I said concealing a laugh.

'It's better than that, it's very good,' he responded to my false praise.

CHAPTER 24

Crossing the Line

U NCLE FRANK WAS SITTING in his fireside chair reading the newspaper when we went into the house. 'Where were ye?' he asked half-hearted and then started thumbing through the pages as if looking for something in particular, 'there's a bit in the paper about what's going on up in your part of the country, listen to this,' he said holding the paper at arms length and reading, 'a man is being questioned about smuggling cigarettes, no that's not the bit, that's nothing new up your way,' he smirked fumbling back a page and then said, 'ah, yes, yes here it is, blah, blah, blah and Gardai are searching outhouses in the local area in their continuing investigation into Lord Donaldson Barbour's stolen painting but have made no arrests to date,' he concluded and briskly went back to the Sports Page.

'It's nearly time now that these Lords and the likes of them living in Ireland put back what they robbed and looted from us in the past,' Granny uttered on her way to the scullery.

Uncle Frank raised his eyes heavenward and sighed.

'Does it give any names who the smugglers are?' I asked looking over the top of the newspaper. 'No, no, they are only been questioned at the moment, they never give names unless someone has actually been charged,' Uncle Frank said without turning the Sports page.

'And your area was mentioned on the Radio News as well,' Granny said coming back from the scullery with a two pronged fork in her hand.

'What was it about?' Mattie looked excited.

'Isn't that border crossing near you called Newtown Cross?'

'Yes, yes,' we both replied together,

'Well the Customs Post on the Northern side was blown up in the middle of the afternoon, they think that it's the IRA, we'll probably get more on the evening news' she said prodding the goose cooking in the oven.

'Wow!' Mattie exclaimed.

'Small loss,' Granny murmured softly going back to the scullery but I was still able to hear her. She must know that it is a small Customs hut when she said 'small loss,' but I don't know how she knows that, because she has said that she has never been North of the border.

Vinny and I were in that Customs hut once and it's even smaller inside than it looks from the outside. We were coming back from progging an orchard about a mile past Newtown Cross on the Northern side when two RUC constables who were standing in the doorway of the Newtown Cross Customs hut called us over.

Two black coloured bicycles were resting against the timber wall of the Customs hut. The apples were very obvious bulging out through our jumpers that were tucked into our trousers.

'Where did yiz get the apples boys?' the smaller of the two constables asked as we came to the doorway.

'The lady, ah, er, the man said that we could pick a few apples,' Vinny answered unconvincingly.

'Bring them inside,' a custom's man called from behind the two policemen.

The taller constable wrenched my jumper up and the apples tumbled out on the wooden floor of the Customs hut. The small fat constable did the same to Vinny and the same thing happened with apples tumbling and spilling all around the floor. The Customs Officer sat on one of the two chairs in the hut and began drumming his fingers beside the phone on the small desk.

'Have you your mind made up yet?' the small constables asked sticking out his chest and added, 'Was it a man or a woman told yiz to steal their apples—youz call stealing apples "progging" apples, don't yiz?' the Customs Officer interrupted and then added, 'yiz can't speak the Queens English can yiz?'

'I didn't say anything about stealing or progging,' Vinny answered bravely.

'Now listen here, don't youz boys be coming into our country and stealing our property, now away off with you back to your Free State,' the taller constable sneered taking a step closer to Vinny.

'Can we take our apples?' Vinny asked squinting one eye up at him.

The constable stepped backwards and rested his arm on a filing cabinet that had a red fire extinguisher placed on the top of it and spoke solemnly.

'Yiz can surely, aye boy,' he paused for a second or two and waited as Vinny grinned bending down towards the apples.

The constable's pause was followed with a sterner tone, 'If you are prepared to bring us back to the place where you got them to check your story out,' he said peering down at Vinny. Vinny's smile vanished.

'Ach, I wont bother, my tea is ready and anyway we have nicer apples at home in my own back garden,' Vinny answered making a move to the door.

'Keep going yiz wee Papists and don't be coming back,' the Customs man called after us as he shuffled his feet threateningly on the wooden floor.

We kept looking back as we walked towards the South. The two constables slowly mounted their bicycles and peddled and coasted behind us. We waved to Jimmy in the border shop and looked back again at the stalking policemen. As soon we got to the Border Line and crossed from a good road surface to a poorer type we knew that we were safe from further interrogation; we were back in the Free State.

Vinny and I jumped in the air and at the top of our voices shouted back the local chant at the two RUC constables; 'RUC.,

RUC., Rotten Useless Cowards' and repeated and lilted the same chant several times until we were nearly hoarse. I thought for years that the letters RUC did stand for Rotten Useless Cowards until Sparks enlightened me that RUC. actually stood for Royal Ulster Constabulary.

We stood our ground and watched as the constables dismounted their bicycles and flopped them on the grass embankment on the Northern side of the divide in the road. We were in the middle of another chant when we both stopped abruptly. The Northern Ireland policemen tossed their caps towards their bicycles and burst into a chase after us on foot. When we were running past the Customs post on the Southern side, George Kelly ran out after us and also gave chase because he obviously thought we were smuggling fireworks or butter.

The week before that Kelly nearly caught Sparks and myself smuggling fireworks but we jumped the wall near the Customs post and ran along the railway track until we came to one of our secret hiding places along the railway cuttings and he couldn't find us.

I looked behind again and the only good thing about Customs Officer Kelly chasing us was that the two constables turned back for the border when Kelly came running out of the customs hut. As we turned left into Carn Lane, Kelly was beginning to lag a bit and by the time we went onto the safety of our familiar railway tracks and slid into our hiding places along the tracks the customs man was no where to be seen.

'Those RUC are not supposed to cross to our side of the Border in their uniforms, they "crossed the line,"' Vinny spoke dogmatically stretched out in the long cutting grass of the railway track embankment.

'But they weren't wearing their caps,' I informed.

'Well the last time Sparks and me taunted them,' Vinny said sitting, 'they never followed us with or without caps, but of course now that I think about it,' Vinny sniggered, 'that time we were on our side of the river and they were on the Northern side, they didn't want to get wet.'

'They must be getting fed up with us calling them names

from our side,' I gave what I thought was a reasonable explanation for their actions that day. None the less Vinny was right, they shouldn't have 'crossed the line.'

The clanging of the oven door brought me back to today. 'You can be putting away that paper Frank, dinner is nearly ready,' Granny announced sliding out the roasting tin and filling the kitchen with the aroma of roasted goose. It was a welcome change from bacon and cabbage.

'Do you like football?' Uncle Frank asked gnawing the bone of the goose leg. 'Yes,' we answered in unison.

'Where's your football?' Mattie asked standing up from the table with excitement. 'No, no, we're not going playing football,' Uncle Frank said with a laugh, 'Mayo is playing today and it's on the radio,' he checked the clock on the mantle piece, 'in about half an hour or so.' He pushed back from the table and spoke again, 'I suppose I better switch the radio on so it can be heating up,' he said moving towards the radio mounted on a high shelf near the scullery door.

A dim yellow light barley illuminated the rustic face dial as he turned a knob underneath it. Mattie sat down again and slurped noisily at the jelly Granny had put in front of him until her disapproving stare silenced him. Uncle Frank gave a few glances over at the radio as he tucked into his bowl of jelly. He scraped at the remaining pieces of jelly at the bottom of the bowl and then cringed at the crackling radio as he spoke.

'Did you move the dial of the Radio Eirann station?' he directed his question to his mother.

'And why would I? I switched it on and got the news and then turned it off,' Granny answered emphatically picking up the empty dessert bowls.

Uncle Frank was twisting and turning the tuning knob with his ear close the radio dial. He turned the volume knob and the crackling sound got louder and more irritating and he lowered it again when Granny called from the scullery.

'Will you stop with that noise, try the other battery maybe.'

'Ah mother will you stop, there's plenty of power,' then grunted slightly turning the radio to one side and began peering around the back of it, 'unless the aerial has come out at the back,' he said tracing the aerial wire from the back of the radio as far as the scullery door. 'No it seems okay as far as here,' he muttered to himself and in a near desperate tone called, 'the aerial has hardly fallen down outside is it mother or your clothes line pole isn't blown down or any thing is it?' he clawed looking for answers.

'I put out some clothes a while ago and the clothes line pole is standing, why don't you try the other battery like I asked you,' she finished as she delved into the stack of dinner dishes in the sink.

Uncle Frank just bared his teeth, clenched his fists and shook them violently near his head. 'It's not the blooda battery,' his subdued scream was barley audible through his clenched teeth. I can tell by his expressions that he is not going to do what my granny has asked.

He delicately turned the tuning knob one way and then retraced his movements in a final vain effort to tune into the football game broadcasting. After three more searching twists along the dial the annoying crackling and irritating whistling got too much for him and he turned it off with an angry twist of a knob.

'I'll be bringing that blooda radio back to Malachy, we only have it a few years,' my uncle declared with a defeatist tone plonking back in his fireside chair.

'No better man to fix it than Malachy,' Granny boasted about her ex star pupil.

I'm feeling a bit weak as I ponder the possibilities of where Mattie could have got the wire for Granny's new house sign.

'Wouldn't the man and woman in the pub have a radio, we could listen to it there?' Mattie yawned his suggestion.

Uncle Frank smiled with a summonsing command to his nephews, 'Let's go,' he said standing with a stamp of his feet.

'Don't keep those children late,' Granny peered into the kitchen as she dried a dish at the scullery door.

CHAPTER 25

Football and Biscuits

THE TRAVELLING SHOP VAN with the driver's door slid back, a battered looking red van—minus a rear bumper, two cars, a horse-and-cart and an array of bicycles seem to clutter up the forecourt, as Uncle Frank abandoned his car in a space outside the Post Office. Raucous laughter and loud voices competing to be heard floated out the open bar window as we rushed for the door.

'Frank,' 'Good man Frank,' 'How's she cutting Frank,' 'What are you having Frank,' bounced like echoes from the crowd as those present acknowledged the arrival of my uncle. We squeezed in amongst the crowd beside our uncle.

A cumbersome semicircle seemed to have formed around the centre of the bar directly in front of the radio placed on the countertop. Barney Baines had his arm around the smelly man in the corner and they appeared to be engrossed in a deep conversation with pints and half drank pints of stout in front of them.

A solitary man looked defiant in his isolation as he sat alone at a table near the back wall but within earshot of the radio. He had bulging eyes and his non-existent chin formed part of his goitre neck. The patrons got louder as the football commentator welcomed all listeners and a rasping cheer was followed by a tumultuous, 'Up Mayo.'

I felt as if someone was staring at me as I passed a bottle of lemonade from Uncle Frank to Mattie. When I looked again there were two people staring at me from the crowd, one was Johnny Byrne the man with the one arm and the other was Tim Herrity the man who owned the sow.

They were whispering to one another and nodding towards me. I turned my back on them with the intension of informing Mattie but he had moved away and was now sitting with the isolated man at the table by the back wall. I felt uncomfortable and was wondering how I could leave without drawing attention on myself. I grasped the opportunity to make an unnoticed exodus when Mayo scored a point and the whole bar erupted with cheering and roaring and backslapping.

The men that Uncle Frank was talking to outside the church were definitely the best at shouting and roaring. I was just approaching the door that led to hallway when a man on crutches appeared in the doorway and blocked my exit.

Paddy Cassidy was resting on a crutch and buttoning his fly at the same time. His eyes looked dazed and had a mad stare as he flopped against the doorframe and raised his crutch with a bellowing roar, 'Out of the trenches and charge the enemy.'

'Shut up you oul eejit,' Pat Tobin shouted from amongst the crowd which drew a bout of laughter and then a cheer as Mayo scored another point.

Paddy Cassidy rested back on his crutch and in two hops collapsed onto a form just inside the door. Then with a loud bang on the table that rocked a beer bottle and glass in front of him he roared, 'fix bayonets.' I was relieved to get outside.

As I passed the open window I could hear my uncle's shouting from inside the pub, 'For the last time lads, I'm telling you it's not the blooda battery that's wrong with the radio.'

I made straight for the bench outside the post office and flung myself onto it. My intension was to stretch out on it and leisurely sip my lemonade, away from the madding crowd, when Mattie appeared in the forecourt and came directly over to me as he looked cautiously back at the door.

'There's a lot of enemy in there,' he said with a giggle, making room for himself on the bench.

He had a bottle of lemonade in each hand and a packet of fig roll biscuits tucked under his arm.

'Where's mine?' I enquired pointing to the bottle and the biscuits.

'He just bought for one,' Mattie said resting the two bottles on the bench before stuffing the packet of biscuits down the back of his trousers and covered them with his jumper.

'Uncle Frank wouldn't do that,' I protested.

'Who said anything about Frank, the ould fella with a head like a fish bought them for me,' Mattie answered flippantly and then added after another slug which drained the bottle, 'and he's going to join me out here at half time and we'll share the "bis-cakes," he calls "biscuits," "biscake,"' Mattie giggled, 'and he was whispering all the time he was talking and made me whisper as well, in case we'd disturb them listening to the match, so he said anyway, I think he's half mad,' Mattie explained with a titter tossing the empty bottle into the hedge beside the Post Office.

'Why would he get you biscuits and lemonade?' I quizzed.

'Because he told me that he loves fishing and I told him the way I caught the fish in the lake and how we go net fishing in the river with Frank and he wants to hear all about it, that's why.'

'But you didn't catch any fish in the lake, I caught the trout, and you never went net fishing in the river,' I objected.

'So what, I might give you some of the "biscakes," if you shut your mouth when he joins us at half-time,' Mattie burst into laughter repeating the word "biscakes" a few times.

The cheers of delight were gradually lowering as the game progressed and droned into gasps and curses as the first half commentary neared an end. Mattie was admiring a three-speed bicycle and then he sat upon it and just peddled it as far as the petrol pump. I only sat on the saddle of one of the smaller bicycles but didn't move anywhere.

'I've heard enough, useless, blooda useless, I'm going home for the spuds,' I heard a voice in the hallway; it was Pat Tobin, 'wouldn't kick shnow off a rope,' he shouted coming out the door.

He stopped suddenly, poked his thick lens spectacles back to the bridge of his nose, glared at each of us in turn and addressed us sarcastically.

'I suppose I'm lucky that my van is still here.'

Mattie slid from the saddle and rested one foot on the ground. Pat Tobin then burst into a quick step towards his van and slid into the driver's seat. He waved his fist at us as he left the forecourt in a cloud of smelly diesel fumes. I hope his fist was a threat to Mattie and not me. Some people say that I look like Mammy and some say I'm like Daddy in appearance but some people say that Mattie and I are very alike and that they can't tell the difference between us. I sincerely hope that this is not one of those occasions.

The man that likes to talk about fishing came out the door and gently waved as he approached us. 'So ye're not too fond of the football,' he said in a loud voice passing the open pub window.

Mattie shrugged his shoulders and pulled his jumper well down at the back and completely concealed the packet of biscuits. I shook my head as a gesture to repudiate his suggestion regarding my dislike of football as he squeezed in between the two of us on the bench.

'I used to play for Mayo in my heyday you know,' he began and talked about all the goals he had scored and named footballers that I had never heard of that he had taken the ball off.

He kept praising himself until the commentary on second half began and then he lowered his voice and in a near whisper said, 'So ye like fishing I hear?'

His question acted like a starters pistol for Mattie to start talking.

It was just as boring listening to Mattie talking about his imaginary fishing tales as it was listening to the man talking about his football exploits. I lost interest listening to Mattie until he started elaborating on his lies. He said that Uncle Frank catches so many fish that he sells them to people and named Pat Tobin, Stephen, Tim Herrity, Ann and Pauric and even said that the Canon was one of Uncle Frank's customers.

The man looked aghast and then his face brightened up when Mattie said that we were bringing a salmon home with us on Monday.

'Tomorrow?' the man gasped.

'No, no, the Monday after that, The Yank, that's our driver, well he's collecting us and bringing us and the fish to our home,' Mattie babbled on shaking the lemonade bottle furiously until most of the contents fizzed out the top.

'And will that be in the morning or afternoon?' the man drooled. 'About eleven in the morning' Mattie yawned and then drained the bottle. The man was now speaking with a squeak in his voice as he suggested that we open the "biscakes" and that he would get more lemonade .

Mattie shook his head woefully as he spoke, 'I can't,' he said and added quickly before the man left to get more lemonade, 'the man with the glasses that drives the shop van took them from me when he was leaving a while ago,' he said looking straight into the man's face.

'He what, what did Tobin do?' the man demanded with a gasp.

'He said that he was taking the biscuits from me because I must have stolen them from his van,' Mattie repeated his bare-faced lie and continued, 'I told him that it was the nice man sitting beside me in the bar that bought them for me but all he said then was that you must have taken them from his van.'

I think that I was even more shocked listening to Mattie's lies than the man who was innocently being accused. He was so flabbergasted that he was just able to splutter out, 'Wait 'til I meet Mister "foureyes" Tobin again,' as he raced towards the pub entrance.

'What did you say that for Mattie, he's going to fight the van man when he meets him,' I said alarmingly.

'So what, I hope he kills him, Tobin nearly choked me to death the day I started his ould van.'

I wanted to go to the toilet at this stage and as I was passing the open pub window to the doorway I could hear the accused man call in a loud voice in the bar. 'They'd steal the milk from your tea around here and then blame someone else when they're not there to defend themselves.'

As I went up the hallway towards the toilet I recognised Pauric's voice responding. 'I don't know what you're talking about Con but is it as bad as taking the bit of food from peoples mouths like you do.'

The toilet door slammed behind me and I couldn't make out the reply. I thought of a question to ask Mattie when I was in the toilet and put it to him as soon as I went outside.

'Why did you tell lies to that man,' I asked, 'it's a lamb we're bringing home to Mammy, not a salmon.'

'Who cares,' Mattie muttered and then with a sparkle in his eye added, 'the nick-name for that man is "Fishy" because he has a head like a fish,' Mattie giggled looking pleased with himself.

We just sat on the bench waiting for the man I now know as "Con" but is nicknamed "Fishy" by Mattie, to return with the lemonade. Mattie wanted me to go into the pub and tell Fishy to hurry up but I refused. I wasn't going to do something like that anyway but another reason was because Mattie opened the biscuits and only gave me one and that was the one that had fallen on the ground.

When he was finished eating the biscuits he challenged me to a race cycling around the forecourt. Anytime I was winning the race Mattie would purposely crash into the back wheel of my bicycle. I heard more or less the same comments coming from inside the pub each time I cycled past the open pub window; 'worst game ever, not worth a curse, useless, blooda useless'

We stopped cycling when Barney Baines staggered out the door and stumbled towards his van. When he was opening the door he squinted over at us and pointed a finger, 'You, you, the, the,' he belched and continued, 'talking to, to, to Peter in the stall in, in, in Portwest, the Canon, bumper ah er horse,' he slurred and then slipped down the side of the van and collapsed on the stony earth.

He remained motionless for a few seconds and I was scared but then with a wild shake of his head and startled look he crawled up the side of the van and looked over at us again. Mattie dropped his bicycle and posed like a sprinter ready to start a race but Barney just waved at us and merrily asked, 'How are ye doing lads?'

We both nodded and moved back from the scattering pebbles being sprayed from the back wheels of the red van as it sped off the forecourt and then chugged slowly along the roadway. The expression on the faces of three sheep pressed to the inside back window of the van mirrored our bewilderment. We remained silent looking after the van with two gaping holes where once a bumper was lodged until it vanished around the bend.

Stephen came out of the pub next and hopped on his bicycle with the words, 'Are ye not gone home yet?'

'Of course we're gone home, you only think you see us,' Mattie muttered cheekily and laughed.

Stephen had gone up the road when I realised that I had missed my opportunity to ask him for comic swaps because I can't go to his house after Mattie knocking his sister Agnes off her bicycle.

After another while Uncle Frank came out with his four friends. They were all shouting and clapping one another on the back.

'I'll be over to you on Friday and do the hay reek with you,' one said struggling to light a cigarette and the other three slurred their words making the same commitment.

'That will be great lads, thanks Noel, thanks Maurice, thanks Garr, thanks Emmett, see you all on Friday so,' Uncle Frank said tapping each of them in turn on the shoulder before sitting into his car. We hastily joined him. We were just about to drive off when another man ran out of the pub and slapped the roof of the car.

'Yes Myles ?' Uncle Frank said lowering the window.

'Frank you know that it's not this Monday I'm coming to you with the turf trailer, it's the following Monday, you see, Tom Moran is looking for it tomorrow.'

'I know that Myles , I'll see you Monday week, thanks,' Uncle Frank said driving away slowly and honking his horn.

Another slap on the roof startled us all, 'and I'll take a look at that radio for you when I bring you over the trailer.' It was Myles again.

'Thanks Myles,' Uncle Frank acknowledged.

'Are you sure it's not the battery?' Myles called after us with a loud laugh.

'A thorough gentleman is that Myles Biggins, do anything for you, loves the ould crack,' Uncle Frank smiled sorting a gear and then frowned, ' not like that yoke ye were talking to—oh yes, what were ye talking to Reid about anyway?

'Who's Reid?' I asked moving forward from the back seat.

'Ah that man Mattie was talking to in the pub and ye were both talking to outside, 'til I put a stop to it,' Uncle Frank gave a defiant shake of his head and added, 'told him that he had no right to be talking to my nephews without my permission. Con Reid is his name,' he concluded abruptly.

'Finn put a great nickname on him, he calls him "Fishy,"' Mattie said quickly. I was just about to object when Uncle Frank said that it was the best name for him so I said nothing and just soaked up the praise.

'He was talking terrible bullshit in the bar about stolen biscakes,' Uncle Frank slurred his words, 'he kept it up all through the second half, got as drunk as a stick, nobody knew what he was talking about or wanted to know either, anyways what was he bladdering to ye about?' my uncle finished with a sigh and rubbed his stained lips with the back of his hand.

'He was talking about "football" and how great he was during his heyday,' I answered quickly, for a very good reason; I was afraid that Mattie would mentioned about the net fishing in the river and then Uncle Frank would know that I had told Mattie his secret.

As it tuned out, Mattie didn't say anything anyway, because he was too busy winding the window up and down. Just as Uncle Frank scolded him for the third time, with the words, 'Leave the blooda winder alone, cannot ya.' Mattie chuckled, 'Uh–ho,' holding the window winder up in front of him.

'Well ya blooda ceolan you had to keep at it 'til ya broke it, didn't ya.'

These were the last words spoken until we reached the house.

The words spoken inside the house weren't much more as Granny made exceptionally loud noises taking the plates out of the oven and slapping them on the table. The once beautiful, rainbow coloured, spots on the trout were barley visible through the crispy burned fish skin.

'The demon drink,' Granny muttered pouring the tea and splashing some on Uncle Frank's saucer.

Mattie and I went straight to bed after the Rosary without having to be told.

Mattie woke me a few times during the night going to the bathroom. Each time he was getting back into bed he muttered that he hates fig-roll biscuits.

CHAPTER 26

Two Lambs to the Slaughter

'Ok lads we have a lot of hay to get in,' Uncle Frank rushed us after breakfast.

We followed as he led the collared horse up the lane. I was carrying a rope that had a wide leather band in the middle.

'What exactly are we going to do and how long will it take?' Mattie asked as Uncle Frank was shackling the horse in the meadow.

'We are going to take all the haystacks from the meadows and bring them to the field beside the barn.'

He suddenly raised his fist high and roared at the horse, 'Hold up,' and continued in a more subdued tone, 'and my pals are giving me a hand on Friday to make a reek of it.'

Uncle Frank attached the rope, which I had been carrying, to the horse collar. As he tossed the rope over the haystack and tucked the leather band part to the butt of the haystack he cheerfully called aloud, 'Let's go lads.'

The horse had to do most of the work because pulling a haystack along on the ground must be harder than pulling a hay mower. It was better fun than either, raking, turning, shaking or making haystacks.

The remnants of the old hay reek was still evident in the field where we were drawing the hay to, but my uncle said that we would be making a completely new hay reek from scratch. Uncle Frank allowed us sit on top of the haystack when it was being pulled, until Mattie slipped down between the haystack and the horse. The haystack would have been dragged over Mattie only I screamed and Uncle Frank stopped the horse in time.

Mattie got a bit of a scare and Uncle Frank told him to go the house for a rest. He took a very long rest and didn't come out again until after the dinner.

This time Uncle Frank made us walk to the side of the haystack and we just had to check that the belt and rope stayed in place.

'Oh, same as yesterday,' my uncle answered Mattie's question getting up from the breakfast.

'Another boring day,' Mattie muttered his forecast for the looming day's work ahead.

He was wrong. Just as we were going up the lane and heading for the second meadow we all stopped to the shouts of 'Frank, Frank' from the roadway.

It was the postman Dan McShane. Mattie climbed over the wall and stayed in the meadow as the postman rushed to meet Uncle Frank and me in the lane. He pulled a letter from his postbag and showed it to Uncle Frank. 'It's Special Delivery,' he panted and took a breath before speaking again, 'it must be important.'

Uncle Frank tied the horse to the meadow gate and we all headed for the house.

The postman was leaving his bicycle near the front gate but then he glanced back at Mattie who was strolling down the lane. Dan turned back and brought the postbike as far as the front door. Granny had a worried look on her face as we all entered the kitchen.

'What's wrong?' she frowned.

'It's from Tessie,' the postman declared handing the letter to Granny.

I recognised Mammy's handwriting and couldn't contain a frightened gasp that led to a whinge.

'Stop that can't you,' Granny murmured tearing at the envelope.

'Is Mammy and Daddy and Myra okay?' I said in short sobs.

Then Mattie burst out crying.

'Ah will you two stop,' Uncle Frank ordered.

'There will be plenty of time for crying when you hear the bad news,' the postman's consoling attempt defied logic.

A ten-pound-note slid from the fold of the single page letter. The news must be very urgent because even though there was writing on both sides of the page, the letter still only consisted of one page. Mammy always writes loads and loads of pages with writing to the very, very bottom of each page and with more writing along the sides.

We all stared at Granny as she murmured incoherently reading each line and then turned the page over. At the start of the second page she whispered, 'Oh my God.'

Mattie grabbed Uncle Frank by the arm. Granny's sustained a frown until the end of the back page and then turned it sideways to read the "P.S.."

'Well?' Uncle Frank took the initiative.

'Is it bad news?' the postman pressed.

Mattie moved away from Uncle Frank and cowered beside Granny his eyes welling with tears.

'The gist of it is,' Granny began, then took a second look at the wide eyed postman and added calmly, 'the man who brought you down will not be collecting you on Monday—Frank has to put you on the eleven o'clock bus in Portwest on Monday,' she left the letter on the table and added, 'your mother has enclosed the bus times and connections,' she said pointing to the letter and then quickly picked it up again when Dan McShane stretched his long neck towards it.

She folded up the ten pound note and put it in her apron pocket.

'Is that it?' the postman cringed and sat back on the chair.

'More or less,' Granny gave a sly look towards Uncle Frank who acknowledged her discretion with a glance towards the disappointed looking postman.

Mattie moved away from Granny with his head slightly bowed and left the kitchen subduing audible sobs as he went.

'Will you have a cup of tea and a cut of bread?' Granny asked the postman who was making vague movements at the table.

'No, no, nothing not a thing, thanks anyway Ma'am.'

I felt myself shivering and was unable to control it so I followed Mattie out. He was just standing in the middle of hallway staring at the floor. As I passed him on the way to the bathroom he slapped me on the head saying, 'What did you make me cry for?' I didn't hit him back because I was so relieved that there was nothing to cry about.

I went back to the kitchen and joined Mattie who was standing in the centre of the floor.

When the postman had finished his second cup of tea and had eaten four slices of bread and jam he left the house. Uncle Frank read the letter sitting in the fireside chair and seemed to go over lines a few times as if he wasn't sure of what he was reading. I was glad when the postman left because I felt that Granny hadn't given out all the details when he was there and hoped that she would now that had left.

'What else did Mammy say?' I slyly advised Granny that I knew there was more to be told.

'Nothing to worry yourself about,' she said with a comforting look.

This made me worry more and it must have shown on my face.

'Well all right, but your mother does not want me to give you too many details until the investigation is complete and there may be a way of not implicating you two, so the less you know the better okay?' she concluded touching me on the arm.

'I don't understand a word of what you said Granny,' Mattie said moving towards her.'

Granny sighed and began slowly as if trying to pacify us but also stay within the guidelines of her daughter's instructions, 'All I'm going to tell you is this, that Mister Joyce, the man you call The Yank, has been arrested.'

'For what?' Mattie exclaimed with glee.

'Mattie please stay calm and listen,' Granny continued with a stern glance at Mattie, 'the unfortunate thing is that when he committed this alleged deed it would appear you two were travelling in the car with him.'

'I still don't know what you are saying,' Mattie said scratching his head and then added, 'is The Yank in jail?'

'No he hasn't even been charged, but his brother is also implicated and as your father might say, "inquiries are continuing," now not another word about this and don't say a word to anyone, the bottom line is you will be going home next Monday.' She stood up and went into the scullery.

It was a waste of time telling us not to say anything to anyone because I don't know what The Yank is supposed to have done. We went back to the task in hand and had all the haystacks removed from the second meadow before teatime. Most of the talk over the tea was between my uncle and granny as they discussed our travelling arrangements for going back home and rearrange planned farm work.

'I was just thinking so mother if there is any point in killing a lamb now that they have to travel by bus?'

'What do you mean?' Granny frowned.

'Well carrying a lamb on a bus and then having to change to another bus wouldn't it be too awkward for them?'

'I suppose you're right.' Granny thought for a second or two and then added, 'No, go ahead and kill the lamb and I'll send her just one leg and sure maybe if that's too heavy you might catch a salmon for Tessie and the lads can bring that instead,' she suggested gathering the plates from the table.

'I'll see if there is any salmon in the river on Saturday, when I'm fixing that broken fence beside one of the salmon pools, could do with a nail or two, so I'll take a look when I'm down there,' Uncle Frank said moving from the table.

Uncle Frank let us feed the calves on our own while he did the milking. I am just getting used to farming and now we are talking of going home.

'You're doing great work with the hay Granny praised us giving Mattie and me a cup of milk after the Rosary.

'We should have it all in by tomorrow and Noel, Maurice, Gar and Emmett are helping me reek it on Friday,' Uncle Frank informed and waited for a reaction.

'If you want to depend on those bucks, so be it,' Granny sighed leaving the kitchen.

'Does that mean we can go the shops on Thursday?' Mattie asked after calculating the days on his fingers.

'No, no, Thursday is a long day, we have to bring the sheep and lambs back up the mountain,' Frank said with a wide grin.

Great I thought to myself; at last I get the chance to come across some Indians. I checked that the dagger was still under the mattress before I got into bed. I fell asleep thinking about Indians in the mountains and me carrying Vinny's dagger.

The flapping bedroom curtains eventually dragged me from my peaceful sleep this morning.

We worked hard up to dinner time today.

Uncle Frank had decided over dinner that he would kill the lamb immediately after dinner before going to the last meadow to bring in the remaining cocks of hay.

'I'm taking one of your basins, Mother,' Uncle Frank said going into the scullery. He rattled and rummaged in a drawer beside the sink and then removed a long carving knife from it. I recognised it, it was the one he had used on the goose.

He handed me the basin and gave the carving knife to Mattie. Mattie aimed and fired it like a dagger at a tree just inside the gate. It stuck and twanged in the tree trunk. Uncle Frank ran to the tree before Mattie and wrenched it out, muttering, 'blooda ceolan' and held onto the knife himself. Mattie and I kept close to his heels all the way to the sheep-pen. He made two attempts to catch the panicking lamb and when he did he just arm locked it around the middle and held it like that until we went into the barn.

'Bring that oul chair over to me,' he grunted struggling with a now terrorised lamb.

Mattie rushed to get a chair in the corner that had no back and one of the legs looked very wobbly.

'I don't think that it is a good idea to sit on it,' I advised Uncle Frank who just grabbed the chair and slung it on the ground in front of himself.

'Hold the basin there,' he directed me as he wrenched the bleating lamb on its side on the chair.

My uncle knelt with one knee on the struggling weakening body of the lamb and pushed its head towards the end of the chair seat. I was holding the basin under its head. I saw him raising the treacherous knife over the lamb's neck. What was intended next suddenly and frighteningly became obvious to me.

Before he got a chance to do any other movement, in one continuous motion I had dropped the basin and ran. I did not stop running until I reached the kitchen and just stared out the window towards the barn.

A few seconds later I saw Uncle Frank racing across the yard towards the path that leads to the well. He was carrying the basin that I had been holding. In a short while he was racing back up the steps from the well with water splashing from the basin.

'What's wrong?' Granny startled me coming into the kitchen with a bundle of clothes from the clothesline. The first thing to cross my mind was had she noticed the aerial wire missing near the clothes line because I'm nearly sure that that is where Mattie got the wire to put on the house sign. She mustn't have noticed because she repeated her question.

I got a bit of a fright when Uncle Frank was going to stab the lamb,' I answered meekly.

'Sit down and rest a while so,' she said and then added 'would you like a cup of hot milk?'

Hot milk must be the only kind of medicine they have here except for the animals and then there is loads of stuff for them. I looked out the window before I sat down and saw Uncle Frank linking Mattie across the yard towards the house.

'What's wrong now?' Granny asked as Uncle Frank and a dribbling wet Mattie staggered into the kitchen.

'Ah stop will ya Mother, two blooda ceolans, one drops the basin and runs off and the other faints just as I cut the lamb's neck, I had to throw water on him to revive him.'

'Will you stop shouting sure they're only children,' Granny scolded.

'That's all right 'til you want to make some oatmeal pudding and no lamb's blood, unless you want to soak it up from all over the floor of the barn.'

'That's enough,' Granny raised her voice and added 'we can all live without having pudding,' she said placing a saucepan of milk on the stove.

I know what Mattie is going to get. I was correct, a cup of hot milk and he spent the rest of the afternoon in bed. I spent the rest of the afternoon helping Uncle Frank on my own to bring in the rest of the hay-cocks from the last meadow to be cleared.

Mattie went back to bed after the tea and was exempted from having to say the Rosary.

'That water from the well is freezing cold,' Mattie told me for the third time, how Uncle Frank had thrown some spring water over him to wake him out of his faint. 'Cold?' I repeated, 'Who are you telling, wasn't I at the bottom of it?' I reminded Mattie of the postman's bicycle incident as I undressed for bed.

He had all my comics scattered all over the bed. I checked each of them to make sure that all the back pages were in tact before I put them back in my suitcase. All pages were present and I felt that maybe Mattie is genuinely ill.

I look at the curtains and it dawns on me the journey they have made; from America in a parcel to my sister's bedroom at home, to here. They seem to be waving triumphantly at me in the summer evening breeze.

CHAPTER 27

Up the Mountain, Down the Reek

I HAD MY SHEATH AND DAGGER on my belt before going for breakfast.

Mattie woke up and grumbled 'more hay work.'

'Not today,' I contradicted him and qualified it, 'this is going up mountain day.'

When I was eating my breakfast I saw Granny rinsing out an empty liquid coffee bottle and two empty sauce bottles and wondered what her reason was for doing this. Later it was all revealed. Granny slipped the three bottles now containing milked tea and sugar into individual socks and then placed them in a green canvas bag. This was the 'lovla bog tea' she had told me about when I had asked her about working in the bog and bringing in the turf.

The sandwiches she made were so thick with sliced cold goose that I wondered how I was going to get my mouth around them. Then she tactfully pressed on the sandwiches, which she'd wrapped in butcher's wrapping paper and squeezed them beside the tea bottles in the bag with the words, 'That should keep the "fear gorta" away.' I knew that the 'fear gorta' meant 'hunger' because Mammy had said that to me in similar situations.

'God bless ye all,' Granny said sprinkling us with a gush of holy water from an improvised lemonade bottle. A label stuck on the side of the bottle read "Knock Shrine Holy Water." I wondered was she worried about an Indian attack on us but I didn't ask. Granny slung the strap of the canvas bag over Mattie's shoulder and we followed Uncle Frank out the door.

'Are we all set?' he smiled raising his stick as if leading us to battle.

Shep and Toss worked hard rounding up the sheep and lambs on the hills. Uncle Frank sorted out the stray sheep belonging to other farmers and got the dogs to guide them back to their own flock. After about an hour on the lower hills he sent a flutter through my heart with the words, 'Let's head for the mountains.'

It was difficult at the start to keep the flock together and prevent them from trying to go into other farmer's lanes but once we reached the foothills my uncle's roared directions to his dogs, 'way off wide before them,' kept them in line for the intended destination.

'Who owns those glasshouses?' Mattie asked firing a small piece of turf at the nearest one. The clod of turf bounced off the glass roof and fell harmlessly to the ground but I thought that I saw movement in the long grass at the end of the glasshouse. The two dogs came to a sudden halt, cowered and whined.

'That blooda Dutchman owns them, trying to poison people selling them his "forced grown" tomatoes, I'd go into him now and have a word with him, about him accusing my sheep of straying, only I know that he's away in Holland for a while,' Uncle Frank spoke defiantly.'

'How does a Dutchman happen to be living here?' Mattie asked firing another clod of turf in the direction of the glasshouses.

'That's a very good question Mattie.'

Mattie looked pleased with the unintentional praise from my uncle who added in an unsure tone, 'He said that he just happened to see an advert in the local paper that Breda Fenlon had land to lease, just think about this.' He turned to Mattie with a shake of the head and expounded on the mystery that was obviously confusing him—'a foreigner just happens to read an advert in our local paper—will you answer me that?'

Mattie scratched his head as he spoke, 'If you tell me what "an advert" thing is; I might be able to answer you.'

My uncle stared at Mattie, gritted is teeth and roared at the dogs, 'way off wide before them.'

The two dogs disobeyed his order and ran instead between the glasshouses. The sheep appeared to be fretting and began scattering and bleating.

The reason for the disruption of the otherwise orderly manoeuvre became apparent with the appearance of the Doiredrum Bobcat at the far end of the glasshouses. The startled animal stared back at us with wild glassy eyes before it sprang into a run. The top half of it was still spiked with the dried whitewash but the bottom part still had its natural gingery spotted fur.

'It's not dead, it's only a half ghost, he's still half white,' Mattie jumped and danced with excitement.

Shep and Toss were in close pursuit until the wildcat stopped running and pounced back at them. Both dogs skidded to a halt and whined and yelped and moved in circles but went no closer. Uncle Frank raced towards it yielding his stick and when he came as near as the dogs were to it, it just bared its teeth, spat and raced into the deep undergrowth of the forest.

'Way off wide before them,' he roared as the dogs bounded across the rough terrain to head off the frightened and fleeing flock. 'Good dogs,' he praised them as they outwitted the sheep and got in front of them. 'They're great blooda dogs,' he said with a proud shake of the head.

At one stage when Mattie and Uncle Frank were zigzagging in pursuit of the straying sheep Mattie said in a whining voice that he had to go to the toilet. 'There's plenty of room around here for that but hold on to it as long as you can until we put some sort of shape on these sheep and maybe get back on our regular route,' Uncle Frank said dismissively and then raced after a sheep and two lambs.

It took us a long time to get some sort of order on the flock and settle them in the foothills before heading back towards the mountains.

'I got two in anyway,' Mattie hollered from a dishevelled looking wooden corral nearby. I looked to investigate his claim.

So did my uncle who raised his clenched fists as he spoke,

'Will you let those sheep out, that's the holding pen we use when we are bringing the sheep down the mountain, not when bringing them up ya blooda ceolan.'

I heard Mattie muttering 'blooda ceolan, blooda ceolan" as he released the two sheep.

The flock took their own chosen route again and we had to do a lot of meandering to stay with them. The hills got steeper and steeper as we pressed on and my legs began to ache.

'Small steps and head down,' my uncle gave us the benefit of his hill climbing experience. I took Uncle Frank's advice about keeping my head down while climbing the slopes but I got curious after an hour.

I looked back and gasped at the terrain I had covered without even having noticed it. I had passed a vast forest to my right and on my left a silver lake that nestled at the bottom of a mountain cliff. I was still gawking when Uncle Frank called back in a consoling tone, 'not too far now.'

'He said the same thing to me an hour ago,' Mattie said catching up on me. The altitude and thinning air was getting to me and I began to wane. I staggered and slipped into a narrow mountain stream but my wellingtons saved me from getting really wet. Uncle Frank looked back at me and calmly said again, 'not too far now.' This time Uncle Frank honoured his statement and within a half an hour we stopped.

'Well the sheep are on their own from here. Right Mattie, open the bag,' he said looking towards Mattie and flopping down on a white rock that jutted out on the mossy green mountain.

I looked at Mattie too and he looked back at both of us. He turned his eyes towards each of his shoulders in turn and then slowly back at both of us as he muttered incoherently, 'toilet.'

'What did he say?' Uncle Fran frowned turning to me?' Mattie answered for me. 'I must have left the bag behind me when I went to the toilet,' Mattie gulped.

'Ya blooda ceolan!' my uncle spurted out rising from his rock seat.

'It shouldn't be that hard to find,' Mattie began positively but then staggered his words as he looked back down the vast mountain space, ' It should, it's not far past, I think it's, near that, no over,' then he brightened up again, 'get the dogs to find it.'

'What?' Uncle Frank roared.

'Like, like, Lassie would find it.' 'What, what lassie, where, where's the lassie?' my uncle bellowed looking round him and then moved towards Mattie, obviously having misunderstood Mattie completely.

The chase began with just Uncle Frank running after Mattie but then the dogs joined in and were snapping at Mattie's heels, which only made him go faster and in the end my uncle gave up and collapsed back on the same rock breathing deeply as he lit up a cigarette.

No one spoke going back down the mountain as we walked three abreast guessing our original meandered route with eyes peeled for the sandwiches in the camouflaged green canvas bag. We gave special attention to certain places where we thought the allusive bag might be, but none were correct. We stayed in that formation until we neared the Dutchman's property but then we just spread out in our own way because we knew that we had passed there on the way up the mountain before Mattie had to relieve himself.

The 'fear gorta' was evident on our white drawn faces as we waddled into the kitchen. Granny broke the silence as we hacked at the remaining meat on the goose carcass scattered on the oval plate in the centre of the table. 'I know it was your father's ammunition bag, from his days in the Volunteers, God be good to him.' Granny placed her hand on my uncle's shoulder and continued, 'but sure the child didn't lose it on purpose.'

Mattie looked over at Uncle Frank for a sign of forgiveness, there wasn't any. The 'fear gorta' was completely banished as we followed up the goose pickings with a helping of ordinary tea and bread. After tea we followed my uncle up through fields.

It was more or less a silent affair as we dragged and carried the tree branches that Uncle Frank had cut around the surrounds of the farm to the field that the reek was going to be constructed. We had started the base for the new reek. He used the wheel barrow to draw stones and rocks which he emptied and spread over the branches.

'It's a damp course for the hay reek,' he answered my question precisely but added no more.

When we were finished with the foundation for the reek Uncle Frank mentioned that he was going butchering the lamb that he had killed yesterday. It could have been an offer if we wished to see how it was done but we didn't take him up on it. We played at making small dams in the stream instead and I was glad when it was Rosary time.

As I lie back on my pillow I think of the day I had; I didn't get tasting that 'lovla bog tea,' didn't have a mountain picnic and never even saw one Indian.

'If his dogs are so great why didn't he get them to "go off wide up down before them" and find the blooda, blooda sandwiches?' Mattie muttered pulling the bedcover over his head. At least I am going to sleep with a smile on my face.

I woke to laughing and shouting coming from the kitchen. I could smell a fry-up but I knew that it wasn't Sunday. By the time I got dressed and waited for Mattie to come out of the bathroom Granny was the only one left in the kitchen. She was clearing off the table.

'Did those wild bucks wake you, I'd say you would have slept longer after your long day yesterday?' Granny pitied putting a plate of bacon and eggs in front of me.

'I think so,' I said wiping my eyes and looking out the wide open kitchen window.

Three of Uncle Frank's friends, Noel, Maurice and Emmett were laughing and talking in the front yard with my uncle. Before I sat down to my breakfast I saw Garr racing down the lane on his bicycle and he headed straight for his pals who had to jump out of his way for safety.

'You'll be late for your own funeral,' Noel laughed at him as he walked back to them having thrown his bicycle against the barn wall.

'I'll tell you what lads, but I think I got a bad pint last night, I don't know if it was the eighth pint or the tenth one but be Jeepus my stomach paid for it during the night,' Garr cringed rubbing his stomach.

'I think that Pauric mixes it with slops when you're not paying attention,' Maurice winked behind Garr's back.

'Maybe it's one of Delaney's half drank pint you got,' Emmett teased him.

'Ah be jeepus stop will ye, I'm sick enough.'

'Mother has a bit of breakfast inside for you,' my Uncle Frank offered but Gar's visual reaction said a definite 'no' and my uncle continued, 'right lads the sooner we start the sooner we finish.'

Uncle Frank's announcement broke up the banter and they headed into the field that had a load of haystacks waiting to be constructed into one hay reek. Mattie yawned coming into the kitchen. I went to the bathroom and then waited for Mattie to finish his breakfast before we both went out to join the "meitheal" of men who had already began their work. Most of the haystacks that we had taken there from the meadow had been knocked and scattered.

They dragged the hay beside the proposed reek site and began the construction layer by layer and pile by pile.

'Why can't you do it the old way and bring in the hay from the meadow as we need it,' Noel asked stumbling over a haystack that Emmett had just demolished. 'Don't be afraid of change,' my uncle grunted raising a pitchfork of hay over his head and tossing it in front of him.

Mattie and I were assigned the job of compressing the hay by jumping and dancing on top of it as the men pitch forked and tumbled the hay into us. As the reek got higher two wobbly looking ladders were put against the rising hay-reek as a means of entry on and exit off. Maurice and Emmett took turns first of all at helping us stamp down the hay and then they swooped with Noel and Garr. Uncle Frank did a bit of everything. When it got back to Maurice and Emmett's turn they started throwing hay on top of me and knocking me at every opportunity. They were encouraged greatly by Mattie who also joined in the fun of trying to smother me.

In the end I got fed up and scurried down the ladder and sort of stumbled off the last wrung onto the ground. I was just getting my balance when Maurice landed beside me with a wild yell,

'Get back up on that reek you deserter.' He had slid down the side of the reek without using any ladder.

I sprinted out the gate but Maurice caught up with me and swung me over his shoulder in the fireman's lift. 'Do you know what we do with deserters around here?' he panted and continued as he ran towards the stream. 'We drown them,' he laughed bending down and lowering my head near the babbling stream waters. I could hear the laughter coming from the reek field. 'Let's find a deep spot,' Maurice grunted stepping onto a shiny sandstone in the middle of the stream.

The ground and water below me began twirling. I heard Maurice curse and then my body went rigid as the cold mountain stream water engulfed my body. I had landed flat on my back in the stream but I managed to keep my head above the water and crawled to the side. Maurice was sitting in the stream rubbing his elbow. His cursing was nearly drowned out by the wails of laughter that was now coming from the working men.

'Sorry about that Finn,' he said getting to his feet. I could see blood running down the sleeve of his shirt and I pointed it out to him.

He pulled his sleeve up and a wide gash appeared just above his elbow. 'You better go the house and get dry,' he said glancing once more at his wound and heading back to his work.

'What about your cut?' I asked.

'I'll be better before I'm married, and that gives it plenty of time to heal,' he said with a raucous laugh running towards his pals who were still in the thralls of laughter.

Granny is right; they are "wild bucks." It was hot milk and bed for me for the rest of that working day.

I lay back on the bed and began thinking of the last time I had fun with hay. Sparks, Vinny and I were out in Murphy's hayshed. When we had finished playing Paratroopers with the umbrellas Vinny lit up a cigarette and handed it to Sparks for a drag.

Sparks had just taken one drag and 'bang'; he flopped down in front of us. He didn't hurt himself because when he fainted he fell on a pile of hay just outside the hayshed opening. We got a terrible fright. We got scoops of water in our hands from the cow trough at the side of the hayshed and threw them on his face. I had seen cowboys who had been knocked out in a saloon fight getting better straight away when their partner threw water on their face so I knew what to do.

Sparks sat up after a few splashes of water but he was very, very pale. He was groaning and said that he wanted to go home. We helped Sparks to stand up but he staggered back towards the hayshed and vomited all over the place just outside the hayshed entrance.

The hayshed was burned to the ground that night. Daddy was in charge of the investigation. I heard Daddy telling Mammy at tea time that he was sure that Mister Murphy's hayshed was burned by some drunken Traveller. He explained his reason for thinking so.

'The Traveller must have got sick and must have fallen asleep with a lit cigarette in his hand,' Daddy spoke authoritatively and then added with a smirk, 'I think he had a lady friend with him, I found the burned remains of a lady's umbrella.' Daddy had spoken in a very low voice, but I still heard him. Mammy blessed herself and looked up to heaven and said it was a terrible thing to happen but at least nobody was burned to death.

Vinny and Sparks and I thought it was a terrible thing to happen too. We had no place to play Paratroopers now. Murphy's hayshed was great. You could jump from the rafters of the hayshed onto big piles of hay with just an umbrella and you wouldn't get hurt. Mammy was looking for her umbrella the following Sunday when she was getting ready to go to Mass. I couldn't remember if I had taken it home with me from Murphy's hayshed the day Sparks fainted, so I said nothing.

Mattie burst into the room and woke me hollering 'get up for your dinner.' I must have dropped off to sleep during my reminiscing. I had my dinner after Uncle Frank and his friends and Mattie had gone back to the reek building.

I returned to my room after the dinner and began reading the comics I had bought for Sparks as a present but I know he won't mind under the circumstances. I waited for the "meitheal" of men to finish their tea and then I went out to the kitchen to have mine. Mattie had dined with the rest of the men and had gone to the top of the lane with them and Uncle Frank to say their goodbyes.

I went out into the yard after the tea and strolled into the reek field. All was quiet now. I stepped around the completed reek as if doing an inspection. It looks like a very large thatched cottage constructed completely with hay but without windows or doors. I look at it as a monument erected in honour of the fruits of my labours. I heard tittering and turned to see Uncle Frank and Mattie looking in the gate at me. My uncle spoke, 'God, but you're the "cut" of your father the way you walk,' and shook his head walking away. 'You're a blooda ceolan,' Mattie giggled climbing over the gate to join me. He didn't stay long when he couldn't convince me to go to the river with him.

I hope that Uncle Frank can bring us fishing in the river tomorrow I smile and ponder lying back on my pillow. Mattie's wheezy breathing is beginning to annoy me. Doctor Walsh, our doctor at home, said that Mattie has a touch of Asthma so I don't think that working with dusty hay is good for him.

I am just dropping off to sleep when I remember that I am going to Confessions tomorrow and my eyes shoot open. I think that I will be a long time going to sleep tonight settling on the best ways to tell all my sins without getting too much blame.

CHAPTER 28

Salmon and Sins

'WAIT FOR ME,' Mattie calls running from the bathroom and following Uncle Frank and me out the door. 'Are we using the nets?' he asked tucking himself beside Uncle Frank crossing the yard.

'No, not during daylight,' Uncle Frank said dismissively and then added, 'just looking now but I'm bringing the spear just in case I see one and get a clear shot.' 'Will I get the gun?' Mattie asked with a half turn back towards the house.

'Ah will you listen to me, I said a clear shot with the spear, not a clear shot with a gun.'

Mattie and my uncle don't communicate very well. Mattie looked disappointed and was even more when my uncle told both of us to stay at the door of the Old House as he went in on his own.

He slipped the spear from behind the barrel near the fireplace and then moved back towards the window where he picked up a hammer from the ledge. I'm glad that he didn't go further than there in case he saw the house sign that was a surprise for Granny and will also be a surprise for him. He grabbed a fistful of nails from a box in the broken cupboard and shoved them in his pocket as he moved towards the door.

He reluctantly allowed Mattie carry the spear with the words, 'only as far as the river,' but when Mattie raised it and aimed it like an Indian's spear at the rooster perched on the gate peer my uncle grabbed it from him, 'do you want the blooda Bailiff to see it do you,' he snapped looking around him suspiciously. 'No we do not want the blooda bailiff to see it,' Mattie mimicked heading down the field towards the river.

We stopped at a broken part of the fence near the river and my uncle began repairing it by driving fencing nails around the net wire into the fence poles. I was surprised again when he conceded to Mattie's begging to hammer some nails. My uncle gave the nail the first few taps and then handed the hammer to Mattie to bury it. Mattie move so fast that my uncle couldn't stop him. He swung the hammer to the side and whacked the nail that just twanged through the air and bounced to the side in the grass.

'Find that,' my uncle barked grabbing the hammer back from him.

'But you have a load of nails left,' Mattie protested. 'And what if a cow or sheep was to swallow it?' Uncle Frank said between gritted teeth.

We kept looking for the nail while Uncle Frank continued with his repair work. 'What's a "Bailiff"?' I asked Mattie in a whisper.

'How should I know,' he replied calmly.

'But you gave the impression that you did,' I pressed.

'Ah, I just let on that I did, he'd only think I'm stupid if I didn't know a small word like "Bailiff,' Mattie answered and then gave a small yelp as the illusive nail pricked his finger, 'I found it Uncle Frank,' he called to my uncle who was testing a piece of the fence he had strengthened.

'Now let's see what's in the river to our liking,' my uncle said with a wink.

As we were coming close to the river Mattie pulled at my shirt and pointed out of sight of Uncle Frank. He was pointing at Micky McGinn walking in our direction along the far side of the riverbank.

'I think I have a stone in my welly,' Mattie cringed hopping on one leg.

'How would you get a stone in your wellington walking in grass?' Uncle Frank quizzed.

'Maybe it's one of you nails then, ye keep going and I'll catch up later,' Mattie answered moving to a mossy mound.

He plonked himself on top of it and went through the motions of someone about to take off a wellington. My uncle raised the spear playfully at him and shook his head. I couldn't think of any excuse not to go any further and looked back in anger at Mattie for deserting me.

He was now lying flat on the mossy mound and peeping over it as we got closer to Micky McGinn who had stopped and was obviously waiting to talk.

'How are you Micky?' 'Great Frank, how is yourself,' they greeted one another. 'Oh this is Finn, one of Tessie's lads,' my uncle introduced and I gulped.

'Well is that a fact, I thought for a moment it was one of Stephen's nephews,' he responded in a cunning tone.

He had his hand held gently to his chin as he spoke through the parted fingers that barley covered his protruding teeth. His protruding eye swivelled in its socket as he turned his head sideways and studied me. My uncle looked at me and hesitated and then tapped the spear against his wellington as he spoke, 'Anything in the river Micky?'

'Saw a nice one yesterday a couple of pools down, but it was gone this morning,' he answered my uncle and cocked the other eye at me.

'Well I'll take a look seeing as I'm this far, see you Micky,' my uncle said moving off.

'Good luck, Frank,' Micky McGinn murmured glaring at me.

'Oh Micky,' Uncle Frank stopped suddenly and turned around holding up the spear. My heart stopped as well. 'Any sign of you know who?'

'No, no thank God, not since last week anyway,' he answered with a wave.

'Who is "you know who"?' I asked with relief moving away from the uneasy situation but with no interest in the answer.

'Well you should know…' my uncle stopped mid sentence, distracted by screams coming from behind us.

We both turned together and stared aghast at what was unfolding before our eyes. Mattie was dancing and screaming as he was slapping himself on the head, face, body and legs in quick succession. We moved back towards him and the word "pismires" became audible between his sporadic screams as he jumped and slapped his way towards the river. Uncle Frank looked anxious and increased his step.

As Mattie got nearer the river he began shedding his clothes and was down to his underpants by the time he was stepping on the pebbles at the river's edge.

'What the blooda hell are you at?' Uncle Frank roared at him as he leaped from the bank into the river basin beside him.

'Pismires, pismires,' Mattie screamed throwing his underpants in the air before lying face down in the stony shallow water that ran and splashed over his thin white naked body. After a while he crawled over the watery stones and turned and looked face up as the water flushed through his hair.

My uncle looked perturbed and then turned away as he begged, 'What is he at?'

I explained to my uncle that Mattie must have pismires on him like we get sometimes near the bank of the Crocken and the only way to get rid of them is to strip off and jump in and then shake your clothes to bits. I knew by the expression on his face that he still wasn't sure what was going on so I tried again. After I explained that the Crocken was our local river for swimming and that we call "ants," "pismires," he turned back around and roared at Mattie to get dressed and go back to Granny.

I saw Micky McGinn viewing Mattie's antics with interest and then his broad smiled revealed his protruding yellow teeth as he looked heavenward and walked away. My uncle handed me the hammer as we hugged the riverbank. I looked back once more before we followed a sharp bend in the river. Mattie was scrutinising his underpants as he held them in front of his face. I knew that his intentions were to go back to Granny fully dressed.

'I think that this is the pool Micky was talking about,' my

uncle said in a whisper as we both approached a widening in the dark flowing river. Uncle Frank raised his hand in a gesture for me to stay where I was.

The water was clearer where it scooped the bank and the river bottom was just about visible. My uncle got on his knees and crawled like a raiding Apache towards a tattered whinn-bush that grew ghostlike over the water. He laid the spear to his side as he cautiously caught a branch of the bush. He slowly pressed it down towards the water and then held it in a steady position. Uncle Frank edged his head over the riverbank until he cleared the grassy bank with just his eyes and nose. I knew by the slight jerk of his head that he had been startled and he groped for the spear without looking.

My mouth went dry as he raised the spear and lunged it into the water. He rolled back raising the spear high as a whipping and wriggling salmon tumbled on the riverbank at the end of the spiked spear.

My uncle aided by the whinn-bush pushed himself away from the river to view his awesome catch.

'Don't let him jump back in,' he hollered.

I followed the orders, dropped the hammer and pulled the speared fish further inland. He stood on the salmon with both feet and yanked the spike from the neck of the salmon that still fought its captors.

'She's ten pounds if she's an ounce,' my uncle said reaching for the hammer I had discarded in the grass.

A swift thump on the salmon's head brought his struggling to an end.

'Can I, can I, bring it to Granny?' I begged.

He smiled broadly presenting it to me.

'Keep it by your side we don't want certain people to see it,' he hollered after me. I want everyone to see it I thought to myself running up through the fields. I carried the salmon at first, by hooking my finger in its gill, but after awhile my finger began paining me and was forced to lift the weighty fish by the tail end as well, for support.

I could hardly contain my excitement bursting in the scullery door and showing Granny with the prize salmon but her reaction or lack of it curbed my enthusiasm.

'Just put it in the sink like a good boy.'

I barely paid attention to what she had to say next as I strolled through the kitchen.

'Oh I gave Mattie your ironing so put it away in your wardrobe and leave your Mass clothes ready for the morning.'

When I went into the bedroom Mattie wasn't there but I could hear him with his now renowned feeding call "Chuck-chuck, chuckie-chuck." I looked out the open window and followed his voice.

He was up at the gable end of the house on the embankment. Baba was standing motionless a few feet in front of him. Although Mattie had his back to me I could still get a glimpse of the multicoloured wellington socks that he was dangling in front of the pet goat as he repeated, 'chuck, chuck chuck' and then in a tantalising tone said, 'look, much nicer than underpants.' Mattie stepped closer dangling the socks and I saw a small reaction from the bemused farmyard pet.

He was now gently swaying the socks just below his waist in a teasing fashion. It happened so fast that it was all over before Mattie could move either way. The goat sprung through the colourful socks and rammed its head up between Mattie's legs pushing him backwards and flat on the grass beside the dropped multicoloured socks. Baba then lowered its head towards the ground and poked at one of the socks that somehow lodged on its horns. This seemed to terrorise the goat more and it danced and twisted out of sight behind the gable of the house.

My burst of laughter got Mattie's attention as he cringed getting to his feet holding his hands tight between his legs.

'What are you laughing at?' Mattie whined and then added with a giggle, 'He's a mad goat, he prefers smelly underpants to lovely coloured socks.'

'I know what you did with your underpants,' I exclaimed, realising just now how Mattie had disposed of them.

'Keep your mouth shut if you know what's good for you,' Mattie threatened moving towards me at the bedroom window.

I went straight to the bathroom and locked the door for my safety. He tried the door handle a few times and attempted Uncle Franks accent as a ploy to gain entrance but his efforts were all in vain.

When I thought it was safe to come out I opened the door gently and waited. I could hear a conversation going on in the kitchen between Granny and Uncle Frank. I tiptoed down the hall and listened attentively to what Granny was saying.

'Well he never mentioned anything to me about stripping off and getting into the river to get rid of ants.' Uncle Frank's response was muffled and incoherent but Granny's voice was still clear as she continued, 'All I know Frank is, that the little lad came in here and his hair looked wet and when I asked him about it he said that he was sweating from running all the way from the river because he was afraid of seeing you killing a salmon like the way you kill baby lambs.'

I felt a sharp pain on the top of my head. Mattie was pulling me by the hair into the bedroom. We were wrestling for a while until Mattie pushed me into the wardrobe which resulted in a loud thud, which in turn resulted in a loud roar from our uncle. 'Be quiet you two.'

After dinner we went with him to repair more fences but he did all the hammering this time. Granny rushed Uncle Frank at the milking and told us that we could wear the same clothes we had on us now for going to confessions but to change into our shoes.

I noticed Pat Tobin's shop van parked outside O'Tooles. Granny must have too because she said in a mumble; 'no danger of Pat going to confessions.'

When we were going into the church Mattie said that he wouldn't bother going to confessions because he had nothing to tell.

'Just think of what happened at the river today and the lie you told me about why your hair looked wet, I'm sure that will do for a start,' Granny said blessing herself from the holy water font inside the church door.

The church was dimly lit and Malachy was the only other person sitting in the bench adjacent to the confessional box. The name "Canon J. Dillon" was written in gold lettering over the varnished half door adorned with cardinal red curtains. Granny placed us in the bench in such a sequence that would have Mattie next for Confessions after Malachy then me, then herself and Uncle Frank last.

We were there a few minutes before the Canon whisked up the side isle and in one sweep swished the curtains back and vanished inside. Malachy went into the penitent's section and clicked the door closed. Granny nudged Mattie to go into the section on the other side. Mattie slammed the door closed and opened it again to say 'sorry' and then banged it closed again. I can tell by the expression on Granny's face that she is furious with him.

I had more or less my sins in order for confessing but when Malachy came out suddenly I got a bit flustered and lost the order I had planned. I clicked the door closed behind me and knelt down in the dark cubicle. I stared at the mesh and sliding hatch that separated the penitents and the priest and rehearsed my list of sins again.

My sins were really about covering up for Mattie's lies but then I remembered about breaking my promise when I told Uncle Frank about Meme when he was naked in the cowshed with the calf. Mattie was much quicker telling his sins than I thought he would be and when the small sliding door at the mesh slid across I was startled.

The Canon was shuffling his feet on the timber floor all through the preliminaries before I got to confessing my sins. He kept saying 'Ya, ya, ya' and clearing his throat and sniffing as I was telling him about me staying silent when I knew that someone else was telling lies. I mentioned all the times that I had done that but I didn't mention that it was my brother I was talking about. I got the impression that he was getting impatient or bored with me so I decided to be brief on the sin about breaking my promise to Meme.

I was trying to think of Meme's correct name as I began but I couldn't remember it so I continued anyway, 'Meme was naked in the cowshed with a calf and I got money...' That was as far as I got with that part of the story as a puce coloured nose and face pressed against the mesh with a gasp.

'Who was naked with a calf?' the Canon asked with a subdued cry.

He was frightening me. I still couldn't think of Meme's proper name and just said with a stammer, 'Me...eh...me.'

There was a slight lull as the Canon pressed his squashing nose even closer to the mesh. I could make out the whites of his eyes rolling in their sockets.

I decided to continue, 'I promised not to tell anyone and I got money...'

I was interrupted again, 'Who gave you money?'

At last the name came to me, 'Mehaul Meehan,' I spurted out.

The Canon moved back from the mesh with an explosive sigh and returned to his interrogation point, 'But who was naked with the calf?'

I could hear his teeth grinding and I was flustered again. I could hardly remember my own name at this stage never mind remember Meme's real name so I spluttered out, 'Me...eh...me.'

'You?' he pined his question.

Now he has me totally confused—I'm thinking really fast and come to the conclusion that he must be asking again if I got money to keep my promise to Meme.

'Yes.' I answer softly.

'Five rosaries and say a very good act of contrition,' the Canon gasped and so did I.

I could see him shaking his head as he was giving me absolution and then he slid the hatch door closed with a loud thud. I was outside the confessional when I realised that I didn't get telling the full story about breaking my promise to Meme but I think I'll wait to tell my own priest when I go home.

Five Rosaries just for covering up for Mattie I thought to myself going into the back seat of the church to make a start on my unjustified penance. By the time Granny and Uncle Frank had come out of confessions I think I had either three or four decades of a Rosary said but I wasn't sure. This was going to be a problem; to say that amount of Rosaries without a Rosary beads. I was going to look for the Rosary beads Mattie used to engrave his name on the seat but I wasn't sure if they were still there and anyway it might be a sin to take them and I don't need more penance.

'Where's Mattie?' Granny asked coming towards me in the seat.

I shrugged my shoulders and was about to say that I didn't know when I heard a clanging noise coming from the choir gallery overhead. We looked up but saw nobody and then the thumping sound of footsteps coming down the stairs brought Mattie into view.

'What were you doing up there,' she scolded in a whisper.

'Saying my penance,' Mattie whispered pressing a finger to his lips.

'Mother do you want to stop and have a word with Ann?' my uncle asked blissfully starting the car.

She hesitated and then as if conceding sighed, 'Well not for long so don't be getting involved in card games and the like.'

Uncle Frank smiled changing gears and driving off at a faster speed than usual.

I could hear shouting and cheering as we neared the pub. As we got closer and the premises came into view it was obvious that a crowd had gathered outside on the forecourt and the noise was emanating from them. We all trained our heads towards the front as my uncle slowed the car down. As he stopped the car and lowered his window I could see that a crowd had concentrated around two men who were posed in fighting positions.

'Come on Pat, hit him again he's no relation,' Barney Baines hollered from the pub door as punches were exchanged.

'Come on Pat, good man Pat,' resounded around the forecourt.

'That's it Pat,' my uncle gasped making a move to get out of the car.

'Don't you dare,' Granny said grabbing Uncle Franks arm and then ordered 'drive on.'

'Come on Fishy choke him,' Mattie roared lowering his window.

'What sort of talk is that after coming from Confessions,' Granny said turning in rage to look at Mattie and looked to her front again, 'What on earth could Con Reid and Pat Tobin be fighting about, honestly, two grown men,' she said indignantly.'

'The demon drink Granny, the demon drink,' Mattie said with a sigh nesting back into his seat and winking at me.

'What are you laughing at?' Granny questioned my uncle's sudden bout of laughter.

He made a few attempts to explain his bemusement and he eventually spoke through spurts of laughter, 'I was wondering why Tobin had his glasses on while he was fighting but sure, but sure, he wouldn't be able to see Reid if he took them off.

'You're easily amused,' Granny terminated the conversation

I left my bed and checked the clock in the kitchen; it was five past two and I wasn't sure if I had said three rosaries and four decades or visa versa. I started again but this time I tip toed back into the kitchen and took Granny's Rosary beads from the hook at the mantle piece. It was twenty past four in the morning when I was replacing them fairly satisfied that I had said all my penance and happy that I had only fallen asleep twice during that time.

CHAPTER 29

Churchtrap

I AM VERY TIRED GETTING UP for Mass this morning. We are all fasting for Communion and I am just as pleased as I don't think that I have the energy to eat after what I had to endure yesterday not least that marathon penance last night.

Uncle Frank parked behind Malachy's car when we arrived at the church. Garr, Maurice, Noel and Emmett were engaged in their usual banter just inside the Church gates.

Mattie pretended that he was tying his shoelace and I waited with him until Granny went into the church. I stood beside Uncle Frank and his friends.

'You dried out verra well?' Maurice said tapping me on the head.

'What were Reid and Tobin fighting about last night?' Uncle Frank asked enthusiastically.

'Ah something about Tobin accusing Reid of stealing "biscakes" from his van, I don't know the full story,' Noel said coyly looking first at Mattie and then at his friends who shrugged their shoulders.

Mattie was standing behind Uncle Frank at first but then quietly slipped away and into the graveyard. He jumped up and grabbed onto the top of a headstone. Noel and Emmett were pushing one another, endeavouring to impress their point as to who is the best fullback on the Doiredrum team.

Two glamorously dressed young ladies walked in the gate. All interaction stopped between the men as they stared longingly. The two females just increased their step without even a glance at their obvious admirers.

When they had gone in the church door Noel slapped my uncle on the back and asked him, 'Would ya with Alice or would ya prefer Margaret, would ya, would ya?'

'Ah, he's interested in nobody but Beatrice, am I right?' Garr quizzed through a puff of cigarette smoke.

'Isn't she home from America for good at Christmas, with a load of Dollars no doubt for a posh wedding?' Maurice added to my uncle's embarrassment.

I was thinking of joining the oul choir just to get near the Flynn girls,' Emmett tittered and added, 'that Alice is great on the organ.'

Noel whispered something in Emmett's ear and they both started pushing one another in spurts of laughter. Noel stood close to my uncle and asked again what I think is a silly question.

'Would ya with either of the Flynn girls?'

'I'm sure now that Master Flynn's daughters would be bothered with any of us.'

'Ah in your mind Frank, in your mind,' Noel pressed his finger to my uncle's forehead.

'Hey Frank, I thought your mother was a cross school teacher 'til Master Flynn took over from her,' Garr frowned before adding, 'although I wouldn't mind having him as a father-in-law, if he let me marry one of his daughters.' Garr's joviality brought a laugh from his pals.

When they started reminiscing about their school days I got bored and looked around for Mattie. I couldn't see him at first but then he emerged from behind a headstone and he was cringing, holding onto his lower back with one hand. He was walking with a stoop, with an even more noticeable cringe as he passed us and went towards the church bell. Mattie was just fidgeting with the bell rope at the start but then he stretched up on his toes and grabbed the knot in the centre of the rope. I saw Agnes coming in the gate so I got behind my uncle and his friends. Just as Agnes was going up the steps to the church the bell clanged.

Talk and movement stopped all round except for Mattie. I looked in disbelief as Mattie rose in the air with a frightened, 'Ahhhh,' his skinny legs dangling and swinging for contact with the rope. Another clang marked his decent and he gave the impression that he was going to let go, but he went back up instead, timed by another bell clang. People who had gathered outside the church wall came rushing in the gate.

Malachy came running out the main church door with the collection box in his hand and bounced off Agnes putting both off course. He staggered on course again in the direction of the bell as the Canon crunched the pebbles racing along the side of the church. He had his white surplice over his head with just one arm through the lace-trimmed sleeve.

'It's not time, I'm not ready,' he bellowed at Malachy who had just grabbed the rope and was standing over Mattie who was flat on the concrete plinth.

'It wasn't me,' Malachy pined his innocence and pointed to Mattie but the Canon had turned back for the presbytery and was scowling over at us.

Uncle Frank remained static but his pals were chuckling uncontrollably subduing an outburst of laughter. I appeared through a space between my uncle's pals and caught Canon Dillon's glare.

'Huh' he said, 'show me your company and I'll tell you what you are,' shook his head and sped hastily back towards the presbytery.

Uncle Frank was taking long steps towards Mattie who was struggling to his feet. Malachy ran back to manning his collection point. I was distracted by the burly figure of Fishy rushing in the gate squinting at his watch through swollen eyes. A gash on his lower lip glowed predominantly amongst other facial marks.

Keep away from awkward situations I advised myself as I cautiously walked towards the church door. I had reached the top step when I met Malachy exiting, I presume to do the official bell ringing that would inform people of the imminent church service. I brushed past him into the back of the church and stopped behind a man who was kneeling with one knee on his cap. He had his head bowed and it took me a second glance to realise that it was Micky McGinn.

I immediately retreated backwards with my head stooped, making sure he didn't see my face. I backed into something solid that appeared to move and I did a half turn and glanced sideways. The statue of Saint Anthony was shuddering on top of its high table plinth, so in order to steady things, and without looking, I hastily grabbed where I presumed the table leg should be; I wasn't grabbing a table leg. Wild eyes glared at me from around the side of the statue as Paddy Cassidy wrenched his crutch from my hand, for a second time in as many weeks.

The church bell clanged outside. Malachy had given his warning that he was about to close the church doors. I looked around me and felt that I was trapped in 'danger zone'; Cassidy and McGinn were in close proximity and Fishy was on the way in, so I slipped past Uncle Frank, who had his hand firmly clasped on Mattie's shoulder. I squirmed my way through other males, bunched at the rear of the church, until I got a view of the rest of the congregation seated and kneeling in church benches. I was looking for a place to sit; anywhere will do just to get away from trouble.

I marched in quickstep down the isle to a spot where I saw a small seating space on one of the benches. I clambered in between a stout lady who had a broad-rimmed hat crowning her head and a small thin lady wearing a headscarf. I knelt down between them and with closed eyes devoutly raising my joined hands in prayer.

As my trembling hands moved heavenward I felt a soft spongy sensation on my fingertips initially, and then a sort of warm dampness, that brought a soft cry of, 'Oh, suffering Jesus,' from the person in front.

I opened my eyes slowly and I could see a trickle of blood mingling with yellow pus, trickling down onto the white collar of the man sitting in the bench in front of me. I whipped my joined hands away and stared. My fingernail had lanced a boil on the back of his neck.

He was turning slowly as if pivoted on the seat. I only had to see one side of the man's face, and the bulging sty now peaking on his eyelid, to confirm that I had lanced a boil on the neck of the postman, Dan McShane. He began mopping the back of his neck with a grubby handkerchief as he twisted painfully to identify the culprit.

I kept looking downward and then noticed a drop of the blood and pus mixture on the top of my finger, which made me squirm. The bottom part of the black dress on the lady sitting to my right rested in a single fold on the bench kneeler. My kneeling position lowered to a stoop and I gently kept wiping the top of my soiled finger on the dress hem until my finger was cleaned. I sat back up on the seat. Suddenly I had the feeling that somebody was staring at me and I slowly pivoted my head right.

A wrinkled female face, with a wart and single spiralling hair strand attached, came into focus and I lowered my eyes on her apparel. Sadie-Tom in her 'Sunday Best' black dress was sitting beside me. I glanced to my left and was met by heavy jowls towering over me.

'Good morning ma'am Agnes,' I whimpered pathetically sprawling back on the bench rest realising that I was now in the 'lion's den' seated between Sadie-Tom and Agnes.

'Are you the buckeen that started-up my van and crashed it?' a rasping whisper crackled in my ear from behind.

I turned slowly and saw the scary head of Pat Tobin coming into my peripheral vision. A fresh scab dangled from a wound on his temple and his nose looked badly swollen. He had a pink bandage plaster stuck on his spectacle frames, partially covering an obvious crack in one of the lenses.

'No,' I shook my head pleadingly.

'And I suppose it wasn't you either, who said I stole your "biscakes,"' he accused, pulling back from my ear.

Seven, frightened looking, altar boys preceded the Canon from the Sacristy towards the altar. They reminded me of the Seven Dwarfs marching to work, but wearing surplices and soutanes instead of their colourful costumes.

I know by the tone of Pat Tobin's voice that he doesn't believe me, and that he's mixing me up with Mattie. Maybe he will be able to tell the difference between Mattie and I when he gets new glasses, which he definitely needs now. I knelt down and prayed that my unfortunate burden was over for the day.

I was whooshed out of my self-pitying by thumping fists on the pulpit surround.

'Brethren, "the sins of the flesh" will bring you directly to the fires of hell,' Canon Dillon was shouting.

I looked around me and noticed that the rest of the congregation were sitting up on their seats except for me who was still kneeling. I peeped out one side of the postman to see if the Canon had noticed that I was kneeling instead of sitting.

The Canon was staring down in my direction so I got back in behind the postman for cover before sitting up. I sat innocuously and used the postman's position to block the Canon's view of me. The congregation seemed to be glancing and focusing in our direction as the preacher bellowed on with his sermon.

'There is no greater insult to the Lord Jesus Christ than the "sins of the flesh."'

The postman was nervously looking left and right and he appeared to be agitated. I peeped out the other side of the postman this time and noticed that the Canon still had his eyes trained in my direction, so I got back to my cover position again and listened on to the priest, 'Man's body is meant to be a temple for God, not for Satan, and remember what I say, "sins of the flesh" are steps to Satan and hell for all eternity.'

I was glad when he left the pulpit and so was the postman I think, because he appeared to be more relaxed now that the Canon was not looking in our direction. I must ask Granny what "sins of the flesh" are and hopefully she will think that I was listening to the whole sermon.

During Communion the choir were singing out of tune, trying to accompany the organ, and people started looking back up towards the gallery. The music being emitted sounded more like it was coming from bagpipes, than from a church organ. Canon Dillon hesitated giving out the Holy Communion and frowned in the direction of the choir.

'I'm sorry Canon but it was working perfectly at choir practice on Friday,' a demure female voice called as she leaned over the gallery banister and then added, 'the organ regulator is missing and that's probably the problem.'

'Don't worry about it Miss Flynn, I'll have it seen to before next Sunday,' the Canon called back respectfully and recommenced distributing Communion.

A terrifying thought came into my mind; what was Mattie doing in the gallery after Confessions last night.

As soon as Mass was over I made a move to get out fast. I didn't want any more contact with any of the people in my immediate vicinity. I had to squeeze past Agnes because she was still kneeling.

I needed a little more room. 'Excuse me ma'am,' I whispered politely as I gently pressed her chest back a little with my hands to get more space.

Her yelp made me jump and I stumbled into the isle. I looked back at a flustered Agnes who was blessing herself repeatedly as if I had punched her but I know that I had just barely pressed in her massive chest just to get that extra bit of room to get past her.

I was gulping deep intakes of breath outside the church when I saw Fishy waving frantically over at Mattie. Mattie turned his back to him and continued to yank the gear lever on a three-speed bicycle he was holding near the church wall.

'I can't talk to you now,' Mattie said with a dismissive wave of his hand and then added hastily, 'I'm shokin' busy, I have to pack, we're going home tomorrow,' he said shoving the bicycle back against the wall with a loud clang and headed for the gate.

Before I could move Fishy had cornered me and queried in a pleasant voice.

'Ah, so the hackney driver from Clunmon is coming to take you home tomorrow, is he?'

I was glad that he wasn't talking about the so called 'stolen biscakes' incident so I answered immediately and informatively.

'Yes, but not with The Yank,' I hesitated, 'Mister Joyce I mean, he can't come for us.'

Because of Granny's directive, regarding secrecy in this matter, I didn't want to give the reason why The Yank was not collecting us, so I spurted out.

'Uncle Frank is bringing us to Portwest for the eleven o'clock bus in the morning.'

I looked at his face and it appeared to light up with such a broad smile that it made the gash on his lip gape open, but he didn't seem to mind and spoke in a whisper.

'Have a pleasant journey home.'

'What sort of antics have you been up to?' Maurice laughed as he called to the postman scurrying down by the side of the church towards the presbytery.

A moist red stain was glowing on the back of his shirt collar.

'Be Jeepus the Canon never took his eyes of you talking about "sins of the flesh,"' Noel called jovially after him.

'I'm going to see Canon Dillon about that now, staring at me if you don't mind, and me, and me...' he stammered calling back over his shoulder, 'a founder member in this parish of the Christian Men's Sodality.'

Up to now I thought it had been me that the Canon was looking at during his sermon so things mightn't be too bad after all.

I saw Granny moving in my direction as she came out the church door but before she reached me, Malachy appeared from behind her and tugged at her arm. As he was speaking to her she was closing her eyes repetitively and shaking her head from side to side. I'm sure that he is telling Granny about Mattie ringing the church bell. I'll bet that Malachy was a teacher's pet and tell-tale in school.

Granny looked around the church grounds and then hastily moved towards me.

I decided to speak first in case she asked about the broken organ as well as Mattie's bell ringing episode, 'Granny what are "sins of the flesh"?'

She had her mouth open and finger pointed as if she was going to ask me something but when she heard my question she seemed to freeze and then quickly spurted out, 'A-aa-ask your father—where's your brother?'

She didn't even wait for me to answer and stormed off into the graveyard patting her chest as if gasping for air.

I don't think that I will ask Daddy about 'sins of the flesh' because they must be complicated if Granny can't explain them. The problem with asking Daddy questions is that if you don't understand his reply the first time, he gets annoyed—I think I'll ask Sparks instead.

'And you must be one of Tessie's lads,' a tall elegant lady spoke politely as she approached me, 'I'm Breda Fenlon a great friend of your Granny,' she introduced herself.

I shake her hand with relief and delight as it dawns on me who she is—it was great to meet the person that I had helped do a favour for. I know that Uncle Frank doesn't like her because I heard him calling her 'nosey' but I think that she is a lovely person.

'How do you do, I hope the carpet-mats matched your bathroom tiles,' I enquired and waited for praise for bringing the mats down to her.

Her response was a frown—it was not what I had expected. Now something else dawns on me; had I torn her carpet mat with the nail from the broken cartwheel. She shook her head gently and opened her mouth to speak but just got as far as saying 'What...' when I made my move. I didn't need any more interrogation, quickly excused myself and headed for the church gates.

On the way there I saw Uncle Frank talking to Micky McGinn. My uncle had a dour expression on his face. I went as far as the gate and started looking around for Mattie to warn him that Granny was looking for him but then I noticed Granny with her hand on Johnny Byrne's shoulder and she was shaking her head lamentably back and forth.

'Put it there,' a gruff voice jolted me from behind.

I turned around and saw the smelly man, Walter Delaney, resting against the gate peers with his hand outstretched.

'You're verra welcome to these parts,' he said with a vice-grip handshake. I wonder would he be saying that if he knew that it was my brother and I that borrowed his donkeys and his bicycle. It's time to be 'getting out of town' I think to myself walking towards my uncle's car.

I respond to the harsh voice calling behind me, 'Finn, Finn.' Uncle Frank was marching towards me.

'What were ye doing to Micky McGinn's cattle and sheep?' he asked baring his teeth as he stared down on me.

I was beginning to feel weak and with crossed fingers softly replied, 'I don't think Mattie meant to hit them with his catapult, you see...'

'Where's that Mattie fellow?' Granny cut short my pathetic explanation storming towards us. Her answer came in the sound of a car horn.

The three of us looked towards Uncle Frank's car. Mattie's head was just visible swinging from side to side in sequence to each twist of the steering wheel as he honked the car horn again.

It was as if my uncle had opened the car door and winched Mattie out on the road in one sweeping movement.

When Granny relayed to Mattie what Johnny Byrne and Malachy had told her about his escapades, he just lowered his head and gave a cowering look. He did the same when Uncle Frank was laying bare before him the embarrassing accusations of Micky McGinn.

'Now as fast as you can go and see each of those gentlemen now and apologise and,' she paused and asked, 'Have you a shilling with you?' Mattie nodded. 'Then give it back to Mister Byrne and get back to the car immediately,' Granny ordered, pinching Mattie's ear before releasing him to carry out his task.

'Frank, our "family name" is disgraced,' Granny murmured trance-like, as we waited in the car for Mattie to return from his mission of atonement.

After a while Malachy came out the gate and did a double take as he passed the rear of his car. He retraced a step or two and began frantically wiping and polishing his boot lid.

'Fuss pot,' I heard my uncle say under his breath.

'Frank, you should have taken the wireless with you so Malachy could take a look at it, another week now without news or music,' she said with a deep sigh.

'Sure I'll drop it off to him in his shop when I'm in Portwest tomorrow bringing the lads to the bus station,' he announced as he impatiently drummed the steering wheel with his fingers.

The back door opened and Granny turned to speak to Mattie as he sat back into the car. 'Have you done what I asked?

'Yes Granny,' he replied sheepishly.

'We'll call to Ann, I haven't seen her for a while,' Granny ordered settling in the car seat.

'Ah ha,' Uncle Frank chirped starting the engine, 'looking for the bit of gossip as to how Fishy and Tobin got on last night.'

'"Fishy," who or what is "Fishy"?' Granny enquired dourly.

'That's a new nickname we have on Con Reid,' her son answered with a smile.

'That's enough of that old blather out of you and for your information I have no interest whatsoever in why that skulduggery took place,' my Granny silenced Uncle Frank until we reached O'Toole's Bar and Grocery.

'Sit on your hands and don't move 'til we get back,' Granny directed turning around to Mattie and then spoke to me in a more civil tone, 'I'm sure your uncle will get you a lemonade.'

Granny went around the side of the premises and I followed my uncle towards the bar and shop entrance.

I turned to the sound of "pssst, Finn, pssst", get me one too,' Mattie called in a whisper winding the car window down fully.

'I see no sign of "the boxers." Who won anyway?' my uncle laughed going towards Pauric who was serving behind the counter.

'I'd say they're avoiding one another,' Pauric answered with a shake of his head. 'It was a draw, we'll have to have a rematch,' Barney Baines bellowed from the end of the bar.

'Bring that out to your brother, wait until he finishes it and bring back the bottle in case your granny sees it,' my uncle said handing me two bottles of lemonade.

When I went outside Mattie was stretched out on the back seat with the door wide open.

'I have to wait until you finish it,' I informed him of his uncle's orders.

'That won't take long, I'm parched,' Mattie began gulping the fizzy drink and didn't stop until he drained it. 'Ahhh,' he gasped handing me back the empty bottle and collapsing flat back on the seat.

'Malachy is a tattler, he shouldn't have told Granny about you ringing the bell,' I comforted Mattie as I rested against the car intending to keep him company.

'Not to worry, I got my own back on him,' a voice said from inside the car.

I thought for a second or two but I couldn't make sense of what Mattie had said.

I lowered my head inside the car, 'How did you get your own back?

'I wrote; "Malachy sells bad meat," on the boot lid of his car,' Mattie chuckled.

I was so alarmed at what Mattie had just told me that I unintentionally coughed, spraying a mouthful of lemonade from my mouth. Gaining my composure again I rushed my question.

'You scraped that on his new car?'

'No dumbo, I wrote it with my finger on the dust on the boot,' Mattie retorted.

'Why did you write that about him?' I followed up in wonder.

Mattie sat upright and looked all around him before speaking.

'You remember we were at Confessions last night,' I nodded and he continued, 'well Malachy was in the other confession box when I was waiting,' Mattie looked cautiously around again and added in a low voice, 'I heard Malachy mentioning, "chops" and "steak" and "liver,"' Mattie moved closer to me, 'I couldn't hear too well, but he was probably confessing sins about "meat" and he's a butcher so he's probably giving bad meat to his customers in his hotel and in his butcher shop,' Mattie nodded in agreement with himself and lay back down again.

Now it dawns on me why Malachy was wiping his boot lid after Mass this morning.

I tried to make logic out of Mattie's presumptions but couldn't so I wander back inside the pub to return Mattie's empty lemonade bottle. I sat in the corner but then Tim Herrity came back from the toilet and sat across the table from me. He was looking very dourly at me so I just kept staring into the bottle. I think he knows that we had something to do with his sow's mishap but he didn't say anything, and I certainly wasn't going to, so I moved slowly from the table and walked quietly back up the bar.

Ann appeared from the kitchen entrance behind the bar holding a crying baby in her arms. She pressed the whiskey optic and let a very small drop into the glass she was holding.

'I hope that measure is not for me,' Barney Baines laughed from the end of the bar with his arm around the smelly man, Walter Delaney.

'Not unless you're teething,' Ann answered sharply.

'Are you breast-feeding that child?' Walter Delaney roared in a slurred voice. 'Enough of that ould talk,' Pauric demanded sternly.

'Keep your hair on Pauric, I'll tell you why I'm asking, Baines here,' he slapped his drinking partner on the back but was interrupted by Ann before he could continue.

'Frank, your mother wants to go shortly, I just have to get her some ham and tomatoes from the shop, so get that beer down you fast,' she said before turning and exited for the kitchen.

'May I continue?' Walter Delaney asked sarcastically pointing his finger at Barney Baines, 'Baines here was saying that all breast-fed children grow up to be big and strong,' he cleared his throat, spat on the floor and added, 'well I can tell you that I didn't have one of those yokes in my mouth until I was nearly thirty years of age and that's when I was abroad in England, and I'm no weakling,' he concluded expanding his chest and swaying from side to side.

The distance between the smelly man and the other patrons got greater. His movements had "broken the crust" on his reeking body again.

I moved out into the fresh air. Mattie was out of the car and sitting on the bench outside the bar window hacking a hole in the soil with the heel of his shoe.

'Granny will be coming out shortly,' I cautioned him.

'I'll hear her,' he murmured.

I sat back into the car and after a short while I could hear voices coming from the gable end of the premises. At the same time Mattie raced from the bench, leaped into the car and sat on his hands.

Ann was still holding the baby and came as far as the car with Granny.

'Goodbye boys and in case I don't see ye tomorrow, there's a few chocolate bars for your journey home,' Ann said tossing a small brown paper bag into the back seat beside us.

'I don't know if they deserve them, after what they were up to, now what do you say?' Granny prompted sternly. We expressed our gratitude for the chocolate bars.

'Finn will you get your Uncle Frank please,' Granny ordered sitting into the passenger seat carrying what was obviously ham and tomatoes in a white paper bag.

'Stay where you are Finn, I'll get your uncle,' Ann offered and then turned to Granny, 'I'll call over to you one of the evenings.'

'Do that,' Granny replied as Ann waved and headed for the door.

'She's a very nice lady,' I ventured in the cutting silence.

'You can't beat the bit of breeding. Ann's mother, and her uncle, Bishop McKeown, are my first cousins,' Granny said smugly looking towards the bar door and then added dourly, 'by the way, Ann said I must have been dreaming about the rise in the cost of flour.'

Mattie glanced at me but neither of us said anything and then I remembered that I had heard Mammy talking about her relation who was a Bishop on the Foreign Missions and said coyly.

'Granny, I think that bishop is a relation of Mammy's and doesn't that mean he's a relation of me and Mattie too?'

I knew that the red herring had worked for me when I heard Granny's reply.

'That's correct, ye are both related to a Bishop,' and paused before continuing, 'God knows its hard to imagine after hearing what ye have been up to,' she concluded cocking her head high.

Granny was shuffling in her seat and I knew that she was getting impatient but just then my uncle rushed out the door wiping his mouth with the back of his hand.

'Well, are we all set?' Uncle Frank said starting the car.

'Yes,' I said and was the only one to have replied.

'Any update on the fight last night?' my uncle tried to make conversation.

'Ann says that she knows nothing more than what we saw ourselves,' Granny answered slowly as if in deep thought.

We were a mile up the road before Granny spoke again, 'You better check the doctor's place,' she said solemnly as we approached Teach an Dochtúra.

'The lads tell me that they checked it a few days ago,' Uncle Frank replied.

'Well that's good to know, at least it's not all bad they're up to,' she said turning in Mattie's direction and then to my uncle, 'check it again now just to be sure.'

My swallow was exceptionally dry and I felt nauseous.

'Granny,' Mattie said clearing his throat and protruding his head between the front seats, 'if you like, Finn and me can check it again today, after the dinner.'

Uncle Frank was slowing down and was turning for the large gates when Granny uttered slowly.

'Well I suppose it will give you something good to do, for a change.'

Mattie stuck his tongue sideways at me as a hint of a smile touched his face.

The thoughts of what Granny would have seen had she inspected Teach an Dochtúra I couldn't bear dwelling on so I think instead about the chicken we were going to have for dinner. But now I start thinking about the chicken that got caught in the net that I erected and was savaged by the Bobcat, so I'll just look forward to going home tomorrow and the fun I'll have again with my pals Vinny and Sparks.

CHAPTER 30

Hop, Step and Bath

GRANNY CHECKED THE ROASTING chicken as soon we came in the door.

'The chicken is done and as soon as I make a drop of gravy the potatoes should be boiled so go and change while you're waiting,' she addressed us all.

The chicken was just as nice as the goose we had last week but she had loads of onions in the gravy, which spoiled the dinner for me. I decided to say nothing at this stage and just pushed them to one side with the fork.

I had changed out of my good clothes but Mattie didn't bother. I was surprised that Granny hadn't noticed this either during the dinner or when we were going out the door after dinner.

When we were going up the lane Mattie pulled me to the side.

'Follow me,' he said excitedly.

I followed him over the wall and down the field at the back of the house.

'Where are we going?' I asked losing my patience.

'To finish off your job,' he said over his shoulder.

He had told me what we were about to do by the time we had reached the Old House. He explained that it was a better idea to put up Granny's surprise house-name-sign on the gate today because we wouldn't have time in the morning. Mattie has good ideas sometimes.

I could see the house-name-sign coming into view as the room slowly filled with light. I stumbled my way to the sign that still resting on the barrel. I lifted it up by the wire and admired my work. Just before I moved away with the sign I glanced into the barrel.

On top of the bric-a-brac in the barrel was a pile of crinkled up brown wrapping paper and pieces of dishevelled string. I knew where it had all come from and I thought of all the trouble I had gone to repairing the small tear in the paper and now it was all in a mess. I wonder why Granny opened the parcel; I'm thinking that maybe she had a mat for herself in the parcel and took it out before bringing the other one to her friend Breda Fenlon when I'm distracted by a tumbling sound behind me.

Mattie was under Uncle Frank's bicycle and struggling to get up.

'An ould crock of a yoke,' he muttered pulling himself out from under the bicycle. I was still admiring my work of art as Mattie emerged from the Old House.

We retraced our steps and came back out on the lane more or less where we had climbed the wall earlier without anybody seeing us. Walter Delaney's donkey's were on the road as we approached the top of the lane but I saw them turning and they had galloped away by the time we reached the gates. Mattie helped me to tie the sign to the gate and then he crossed the road and onto the embankment on the far side.

'Are you not going to check the doctor's house?' I shouted.

'What for, sure we know it's in a mess?' Mattie called back heading for the boggy hills.

'Where are you going?' I asked catching my breath walking at a fast pace beside him.

'Up the hills, to the lake for a bit of messing and to take a long look down on the most dangerous place in the world,' Mattie said increasing his pace.

'Why do you say it's the most dangerous pace in the world?' I quizzed.

'Why, I'll tell you why,' Mattie said looking surprised at my question, 'for a start there's a wild bobcat here, donkeys that are deadly dangerous, a rooster and a goose that will attack you, a so called pet goat that will gore you in the "you know what," flying ants and pismires everywhere, snakes in the streams.'

I was going to contradict him and tell him that it was only a prank about the poisonous snake in the stream but I decided to let him carry on.

'A blooda pig that won't let you pass on the road,' he stopped and took a deep breath and then moved on calling out his danger list.

'If you're having a bit of fun somebody wants to "break your arse" with a kick,' he held up his hand and pressed on his fingers as he continued.

'I have a postman and two van-men just waiting to get their hands on me.'

My frown prompted him to elaborate.

'"Four-eyes" Tobin and that drunk fella, Barney Baines,' he cringed, identifying the "Two Van-men" and babbled on.

'A Fishy man, a one-armed man, a smelly-man, a one-legged man and a hunchback-man, all out to get me.'

He threw both hands in the air and added, 'nearly smothered by hay.'

I thought it was me, at the hay reek, he was talking about at first but then I remembered the horse nearly pulling the haystack over him.

Mattie stopped and turned wide eyed.

'And a Canon when he finds out about his horse and his crock of an oul church organ will have me excumm, ah, er…'

'Excommunicated,' I prompted and then realised that Mattie had unwittingly admitted damaging the church organ on Staurday evening and I was going to enquire how he did it, but he was in full flow so I let him continue.

'A granny that would love to clatter me and an uncle that threatened to kill me over loosing a few blooda sandwiches and you ask me, "what danger,"' he concluded increasing the length of his footsteps.

I gave some thought to what he had been saying but I would swap all that danger to have come across just one Indian.

We were heading in the general direction of the lake when he suddenly stopped, looked down at his shoes and then called back to me.

'I know why I'm so fast today, I'm wearing shoes, it's those blooda wellingtons that were slowing me down,' he said changing direction.

He was heading for the bog area between the two hills where the sheep had been grazing. He skipped towards the large bog-hole that he had failed to jump on a few previous occasions.

Mattie had galloped as far as this enormous bog-hole before but lost his nerve, at the last second, each time.

'Never let it be said that I couldn't jump an oul bog-hole,' he said gritting his teeth surveying his intended jump.

It was different than the other bog holes in the sense that apart from being wider it had a high bank on one side. Mattie took another look from the high bank and moved further back.

I stayed at the lower side of the bog hole and amused myself watching the water spiders scurry across the top of the dark brown water. I could see Mattie at the corner of my eye as he crouched like a sprinter. He gulped a few deep breaths and spurted forward as he slapped his bony buttock.

I looked away from the water spiders and gave my full attention to what was unfolding before my eyes. He was raising his legs higher with each stride and the noise of the squelching boggy surface became louder as the splashes of turf sludge rose upward and outwards as he neared his intended jump. His arms were swinging to high chest level and his head was back. I judge by the velocity he is travelling and the space between himself and the bog-hole that he is at the point of no return, even if he loses his nerve again.

Mattie's final actions formed like photographic stills; hop, step, shoe stuck, head first into water. I remained rigid as a gush of water rose and spread with a splash all around. His bony knee-caps and clawing hands surfaced first and was quickly followed by a gulping bawling scream. His head was like a platter of wet turf mould and his eyes were tightly closed. He was splashing and struggling to get his feet on something solid beneath him and when he did he was moving back into deeper water.

It was only at this stage that I could get myself to move and hollered, 'Mattie, Mattie, this way,' as I moved to the edged of the bog-hole.

He still had his eyes closed but he must have followed my voice as he turned and waded pitifully towards me waving his hands in front of him. I stretched my hand as far as possible and in one of his frantic hand waving movements he touched my hand and returned to it with a vice grip hold. I put all my weight and newfound strength into a strenuous pull until my brother staggered and flopped to the boggy ground in front of me.

He turned and sat wiping his eyes as he wailed between short bouts of sobbing. I asked him if he was okay but he just struck out with his hand so I left him and collected his shoe. I sat beside him until his crying abated and I handed it to him. He held onto the soggy shoe for a while before trying to put it on.

Even though the laces weren't pulled too tightly he couldn't get it on his foot and he threw it to one side. I opened the laces and handed it back to him and after a lot of grunting he squeezed it back on his foot.

'You're right Mattie, it is a dangerous place around these parts,' I said in an attempt to pacify him but he just wailed again and told me to shut up.

He rubbed his eyes a few more times and then staggered to his feet. I saw him pointing to the water and then he screamed and started spitting repeatedly. Between his shrieks I could make out 'swallow, water spiders.' In order to stop him screaming I lied that I had seen the water spiders running away when they saw him coming. My 'fib' worked but I forgot to cross my fingers; more sins for confessions I taunt myself. I stayed in step with him all the way back to the gate.

As the turf sludge began to dry on him he looked like the "Swamp-man" in the comics but I didn't say that to him. He sobbed now and again but said nothing. I noticed that the sign on the gate had gone a bit lopsided so I straightened it and after closing the gate followed Mattie down the lane.

Uncle Frank was coming from the well with a bucket of water as we neared the end of the lane. He did a double take and lost his grip on the bucket, 'what the blooda hell...' he muttered re-gripping the bucket and moving towards us.

'I tripped into the big hole,' Mattie said with a pathetic face that was exaggerated by the now caking turf sludge.

I saw a movement at the kitchen window as we entered the farmyard.

Mattie just sniffled to my uncle's repeated question as to how he tripped into the bog-hole. Uncle Frank looked at me for more information but I just shrugged my shoulders.

I could hear water splashing and spurting in the bathroom as we entered the hall door.

'Take those filthy shoes off where you are and get in here and take those clothes off you,' Granny called with both hands on her hips standing at the bathroom door. Granny shook her head a few times and glanced at Uncle Frank who stated the obvious in a low voice, 'he fell in a bog-hole.'

Mattie held onto the doorframe as he eased his shoes off to the sound of the filling bath resounding in the background. He strode down the hall as if he was a convicted prisoner leaving death row for the gas chamber.

'I won't ask you how it happened because you'll only tell me lies,' Granny said grabbing Mattie by the shoulder and yanking him into the bathroom.

The bathroom door was open enough to see Mattie stripping but then he stopped when he got to his underpants and looked at Granny as he spoke.

'I'll do the rest myself.'

One of Granny's hands pulled down his floppy underpants and the other swung hard across his bony bum with a painful echo. I don't know if Mattie's scream was from pain or shock as Granny twisted his ear and they both vanished behind the slamming bathroom door.

I looked at Uncle Frank who had his mouth formed in a per-fect "O" but nothing came out verbally. Then he moved quickly into the kitchen and I hastily followed him to see what his plan was going to be. He grabbed his cigarettes and matches from the window ledge and brushed me aside going out the door. It looks like his plan is to make a hasty retreat.

I stayed with him as he smoked his cigarette sitting on the small wall outside the house and after a lot of pressure I told the truth because Mattie was in the middle of his punishment and nothing was going to stop it no matter what I said. After listening to the facts of Mattie's encounter with the bog hole, Uncle Frank just shook his head and softly said, 'We'll take the cows in early.'

When I was bringing the first bucket of milk to the scullery I noticed Mattie's jumper, shirt, trousers, underpants and socks out drying on the line. As I was coming back out the door I heard 'psst, Finn, psst.' I smiled turning towards our bedroom window. Mattie was hanging out the window and smiling broadly.

He was in his pyjamas and although his hair was still wet it was combed and he looked neat and clean.

'I think I'll be a deep sea diver when I'm big,' he said with a wide grin.

'Granny was very cross with you,' I stated the obvious coming closer to him.

'I know now where Mammy got her whacking power,' he said with an exaggerated cringe and then continued, 'Ah Granny will be all right when she sees her lovla sign,' Mattie mimicked his Granny's accent.

'Yes, Mattie that's what I want to ask you about,' I said looking up at the high washing-line pole, 'where did you get the wire for the sign?'

'You see there at the scullery window,' Mattie said stretching out the bedroom window and pointing, 'well I snipped it there, cut off what I wanted and tied the rest to the bottom of the clothesline pole, you'd never notice it ' he pointed again. 'But supposing Granny needs more line when she has a lot of washing?' I quizzed with a hint of anxiety.

'Will you stop worrying, she never uses that part of the line and you heard her yourself saying, that nothing was blown down.'

My frown suggested to him that I needed reminding and he added, 'The day Frank was trying to get the radio working, remember,' Mattie concluded with a mucus sniff.

I tried to put on a scary face as I pointed and spoke, 'Oh look Mattie, a water spider coming out your ear.'

Mattie slapped his ear and when he realised that I was joking he swung his leg up on the window ledge as if he was going to chase me. It wasn't his foot that came out the window first. We both watched with open mouths as the statue of the Virgin Mary came twirling out the window and somersaulted onto a large stone near the window. The statue disintegrated into pieces before our eyes.

We remained deadly silent and listened for a reaction. A weak 'woof' from one of the dogs, a duck quacking and Baba bleating was the only response and we sighed with relief.

'Gather the bits up quickly,' Mattie directed operations from the bedroom, 'and dump every bit over there.' He pointed to the hole in the hedge near the sally tree.

Mattie was very muted at the evening tea as he sat in his pyjamas. I just ate the ham, cold chicken and tomatoes and pushed the onions to one side and said nothing. This has to be the last time that I will see onions on my plate and I smile thinking about tomorrow. Granny started the Rosary before she cleared off the table.

'You can start packing and I will finish it off for you in the morning, a grá,' Granny said, gently tapping me on the head as we rose from our knees.

Mattie teased me and kept repeating 'a gra, a gra, love, love' while I was packing. I was surprised that he even knew that "a gra" meant "love." I put my presents for home to one side in the suitcase and placed the clothes that Granny had ironed all around them. I took a long lingering look at the dagger and placed it between my ironed clothes; it was exactly like the way I had got it from Vinny—I never had a reason to use it even once. Maybe there aren't any Indians here after all.

Mattie held his suitcase up to the shelf level in the wardrobe and scooped his clothes into it before sliding it along the floor to the corner. I gave into temptation and followed suit to what Mattie was doing—I eat the chocolate bars that Ann had given me.

Even though I was very tired going to bed last night, I was a long time getting to sleep with the exciting thoughts of going home. As soon as I awoke this morning I realised that I was going home today. The morning is bright as I look out the window and I feel happy but then my mood changes as it dawns on me that the statue is not on the window ledge.

CHAPTER 31

Radio Signal, Smoke Signal

I COULD HEAR AN ENGINE NOISE in the front yard and got the smell of a fry as I was going into the bathroom. Mattie was awake and lying back on his pillow with his hands behind his head. I met Granny in the hallway as I was coming out of the bathroom and we exchanged morning greetings. I notice that she is carrying Mattie's clothes from his bog-hole encounter yesterday.

'Come and have your breakfast now and stay in your pyjamas and you are not to put on these clothes until you are ready to get into the car,' Granny threatened Mattie in the bedroom.

'Are you sure it's not in your way there?' Myles Biggins was saying to Uncle Frank as I entered the kitchen. He was pointing out the kitchen window at a turf trailer in the yard.

'It's fine there, I'll have it back to you tomorrow, Wednesday at the latest,'

'No rush,' Myles said and then turned to me as he spoke, 'so ye're back to the big city today.'

I just nodded; if he wants to think that Clunmon is a big city I won't bother contradicting him.

Granny came back into the kitchen and pulled three plates from the oven, 'Sit down there Myles and have a bit of breakfast.'

'I should say no ma'am but when you smell the ould fry its hard to say no,' he said settling in at the table.

Mattie came in and slid onto the remaining seat.

'Is this the wild buckeen I'm hearing about?' Myles said stretching and ruffling Mattie's hair.

Mattie just frowned at him and pulled back.

'You don't know the half of it,' Granny said grimly pouring the tea.

'Are ye not joining us Frank,' Myles asked buttering some bread.

'No, no Mother and I ate earlier after the milking and anyway I have to disconnect this blooda radio I'm going to drop it into Malachy when I'm in Portwest,' my uncle said moving towards the radio.

'No, don't do anything with it yet 'til I take a look at it,' Myles said wiping a dribble of egg yoke from the side of his mouth and then added, 'I meant to ask you what's that blooda sign on your gate all about, I cannot read Japanese,' he concluded with a laugh.

Granny glanced blankly at Uncle Frank who frowned, 'What sign?'

Mattie and I were looking at one another for inspiration and then Mattie spoke, 'It's a surprise we have for Granny and Uncle Frank,' he said sheepishly lowering his head.

After I explained what I'd written on the sign, Uncle Frank and Myles subdued a chuckle. Myles mustn't be able to read Irish or else my writing must have dribbled.

Granny smiled patting me on the head, 'That's a verra nice idea, thank you *a grá*.'

My uncle and Myles were laughing and talking at the table and then after breakfast Uncle Frank switched on the radio and they watched tentatively as the radio dial gradually lit up.

'You're right, it's not the battery that's wrong with this wireless,' Myles murmured and then bit on his lower lip as he slowly twisted and turned the tuning knob.

The radio scraped and whistled from low tones to irritating loud pitches.

'And I take it that your aerial is not knocked down or anything,' Myles tapped the top of the radio a few times before shaking it violently.

'No, no the aerial is fine, I think so anyways,' my uncle said steadying the radio in Myles 's hands.

'It's definitely a reception problem, where does your aerial connect?' Myles asked pulling the radio to one side and looking around the back of it.

'And from there it goes out at the side of the scullery window to the clothes line pole,' my uncle informed holing up the connection end of the aerial.

'We'll trace it out the back and see if there's a break anywhere along the way,' Myles suggested slipping the aerial wire trough his hand moving into the scullery.

Mattie frowned slightly listening to the conversation concerning the aerial wire connection to the washing line pole. I gave a dry gulp as it began to dawn on me what was holding up Granny's house-name plaque.

'When you're finished your breakfast boys go and do your packing and I'll give a hand in a minute,' Granny said taking plates from the table.

I decided to move first but Mattie was still out the kitchen door before me and we raced to the bedroom. We stood in absolute silence at the bedroom window listening to the conversation that was unfolding outside in the back yard.

'In the name of God Frank, sure look, how would you have reception, your aerial stops here at the scullery window, where's the rest of it?'

There was movement in the direction of our window and we stepped to one side still listening attentively.

'Well it's not on the ground, Myles.'

'I can see that but wait a second it's still connected on top of the clothesline pole and look it finishes here at the bottom of the poll—that looks like it's tied there.'

'How the...I wouldn't mind but I asked Mother if the aerial was down and she said that it wasn't.'

'Ah be fair to her Frank, nobody would notice unless it was lying on the ground, anyways there's your problem solved.'

Another of our problems has just begun.

The voices began to fade around the gable end of the

house, 'if it was blown down Frank, it should be around here somewhere.'

'You're right it should be.'

'How are we getting along?' a voice behind us startled us both.

'Fine, Granny,' we both said in unison running to or respective suitcases.

'And why aren't you dressed?' she directed her next question to Mattie holding up two small packages wrapped in butchers paper, 'pack these it will keep the "fear gorta" away from you 'til you get home,' she said leaving them separately on either side of the bed.

'Did you find the sandwiches I lost on the mountain?' Mattie asked lifting and sniffing the sandwich package placed on my side of the bed.

Granny shook her head and chuckled leaving the room. It was the first time I had heard her laughing like that since we arrived.

I saw Mattie stuffing his screwdriver down the back of his trouser waist and pulling his jumper well down over it before we left the room. The darning work Granny had done on the sleeve of his jumper made the burn mark barely noticeable.

'Now Finn you're are responsible for that parcel and you this one,' Granny said pointing out two parcels left resting against the hallstand as we walked with suitcases in hand down the hallway. Granny had made parcels of the salmon and the leg of lamb.

The parcels were wrapped in loads of newspapers and bound with thick white hairy string. Granny had made a sort of carrying handle on the parcel by doubling up on the string and looping it a few times. Both parcels were shaped more or less the same but I earmarked the parcel that looked like it had a salmon in it which meant that Mattie would have to carry the heavier leg of lamb.

'I can't find my shoes,' Mattie murmured going into the kitchen.

'They're there,' Granny pointed at the bottom of the dresser in the kitchen. 'What's that white stuff?' Mattie asked pointing to the white rim around his polished shoes.

'That's what happens when you polish your shoes when they are still wet, that's what Daddy told me' I answered smugly.

'Well aren't you lucky to have such a clever father,' Granny said glancing at the clock. That's the first time I heard Granny praising Daddy since I came here.

She leaned out the kitchen window and called out to her son who was still talking to Myles, 'are you ready Frank,' and then waved as she added, 'thanks again Myles for the trailer.'

'Well are we all set?' Uncle Frank asked and then directed his statement to his mother.

We found the problem with the radio, the aerial is broken, probably blown down,' he puffed pulling two multicoloured socks from his pocket, 'I found these when we were looking for the missing bit of aerial.'

Mattie glanced nervously at Granny who frowned before speaking, 'I thought I had brought those socks in from the line, anyway Mattie put them in your case now.'

I was surprised to see Uncle Frank smiling broadly as I thought that he would be annoyed over the aerial. He was also in great form at the breakfast but it probably hasn't dawned on him yet that we are going home to day and that we won't be around to help him on the farm.

Granny went over our bus timetable again and then removed the 'Knock Shrine Holy Water' bottle from the cupboard. She doused Mattie and me with a heavy sprinkling as she murmured 'God speed.'

I picked up my suitcase and the parcels which I had designated for myself to mind, and went into the yard where Uncle Frank had the car boot open.

Mattie came out carrying his suitcase and parcel and spat at the rooster perched on the gate pier, 'I hate that blooda rooster,' he muttered.

Granny gave each of us a kiss on the cheek and Uncle Frank placed our suitcases in the boot. Mattie casually dropped his parcel in beside the suitcases and got into the back seat, which surprised me because he always tries to get in the front. I carefully put the parcel I was responsible for on the floor beside my seat and sat into the car.

342

I waved looking back at Granny as we drove up the lane. She acknowledged my gesture and wiped her eye with the corner of her apron. Shep and Toss scurried after the car and barked until we reached the top of the lane. The red Raddle marks on Toss's hairy coat were barley visible now.

I volunteered to do my usual gate-opening task and was getting out of the car when I noticed that the house name sign on the gate was lopsided.

'I'm dying to see this sign,' my uncle said merrily sticking his head out the car window driving out the gateway.

Then without warning his mood changed as he brought the car to a sudden halt muttering, 'What the blooda...that wire with the white insulator...that's,' he seemed to be staggering getting out of the car, 'that's my blooda aerial!' His words ended in a bellow as he walked towards the sign.

To make things worse there were bite chunks taken out along two sides of the improvised house-name-sign. My befriended donkeys were still undeterred when it came to wanton destruction. Myles was right; it did look like Japanese writing with the sign lopsided and lettering either missing or partially eaten away by the two donkeys

'Ye blooda ceoláns, the two of you,' Uncle Frank said panting in rage and then added in a calmer tone, 'come on hurry up and close the gate behind me or ye'll be late for the bus.'

As I was closing the gate I heard galloping hoofs on the road behind me and looked. Neddy and Noddy were recklessly flaking their hind legs back at Tim Herrity's dog as it chased them up the road. I smiled getting back into the car.

'Ah sure I can connect the aerial back when I get home,' my uncle said forcing himself into good humour again.

As we neared the bend before O'Tooles Bar and Grocery, Uncle Frank had to swing the car violently to the left as a large black car careered around the corner in the opposite direction.

'Blooda maniacs,' my uncle hollered straightening the car before it mounted the embankment.

'They look posh,' Mattie said sitting upright again after being jostled and added, 'they are wearing suits and ties.'

'Posh or no posh doesn't give them the right to kill people,' Uncle Frank muttered shaking his head defiantly braking hard in the forecourt of O'Toole's Bar and Grocery.

'Stay where ye are lads I won't be long, I have to get some change,' he said getting out of the car.

'I thought that he'd be crosser over the aerial,' I said trying to start a conversation with Mattie but he just yawned and muttered, 'who cares,' so I rested back in my seat and didn't push him any further for a chat.

The car door opening suddenly jolted me and I was looking at Pauric standing beside me.

'Here lads take these with you on your journey,' he said dropping a fairly heavy brown paper bag on my lap, 'it's just a little something to say thank you for causing the row between Reid and Tobin. It was the best fight we ever saw in these parts for a long time—Mum's the word,' he concluded with a pressed finger to is lips. He left as quickly as he had appeared but then stopped half way to the door holding his hands on his knees as he shook with laughter.

'What's in the bag?' Mattie asked sitting up.

'Biscakes,' I said with a chuckle peeping into the bag.

'I wonder does he mean "Mum's the word" about the biscakes or keeping it a secret about how Tobin and Fishy ended up fighting?' Mattie frowned pensively.

Uncle Frank rushed out the door wiping his mouth with the back of his hand. 'There was a News Flash on the radio about a man shot in Holland with connections to the Portwest area, the man on the radio said that they'll have an update later,' he said starting the car and then added, 'Pauric saw those blooda eejits in the black car too but they were going to fast to get the number plate.' Mattie or I didn't comment on his report so my uncle broke into whistling an Irish tune for his own amusement.

As we approached the church I saw Malachy lifting a brown box out of the boot of his car, which was parked outside the Canon's house.

'Regular as clockwork is Malachy, every Monday delivers the Canon's weekly supply of meat,' Uncle Frank said waving to Malachy before turning the corner onto the Portwest road.

I gave a quick glance back at Mattie to see what his reaction was to his now defunct theory about Malachy selling "bad meat," but he was amusing himself picking at the sponge hole he had created in the seat a few days ago and showed no concern at all.

Just before I turned to my front again I saw three small puffs of cloud rising over the same mountain that we had brought the sheared and dipped sheep to a few days ago. Seeing the fluffy drifting clouds had a calming effect on me until I emitted an uncontrollable yelp as it dawned on me that they may not be clouds at all but were possibly Indian smoke signals.

'What's wrong with ya?' my uncle reacted to my yelp of excitement.

I wrenched my head back quickly again but we had turned the corner now and the mountain and above, were blocked from my view by the thick hedgerow and towering trees in the church grounds.

'Nothing,' I responded softly to my uncle's concern.

I pondered contentedly with thoughts of Indians galloping in the mountains and informing other Braves by smoke signals that I was on my way out of Doiredrum.

Suddenly a movement in the hedgerow to my left grabbed my attention. The 'Doiredrum Bobcat,' sporting its full natural colour, with the exception of a white prickly patch of whitewash on the top of its head, scraped purposefully with extended claw nails at the Ash tree bark. I opened my mouth to say something but then changed my mind and sat comfortably back in my seat with a contented smile. The Bobcat had survived our 'lethal weapon' attack, which meant that Mattie would never have collected his bounty.

'Look at that,' Uncle Frank broke the silence pointing further up the road, 'and they say you'll never see a policeman when you want one.' I saw a man in uniform stepping out onto the main roadway. He appeared to have stepped from behind an Oak Tree, at the junction of a laneway and the road, and was raising his hand high as a signal to stop.

'Shane, the right man in the right place,' Uncle Frank spoke excitedly lowering his window and continued, ' if you're looking for two eejits in a black car, drove us off the blooda road, they were...'

'Frank, Frank, slow down, this is Official,' the Garda Sergeant said holding his two hands out in front of him in a calming gesture.

'Official is it, well okay then Sergeant Freeman, it's not me should be slowing down it's those in the...'

'Frank,' the policeman's shout silencing my uncle and he continued, 'Frank, the car you are talking about contains two detectives from Dublin Castle. In fact I should be travelling with them but I could only give them directions to Van Heyningen's place as I have to deal with this complaint first.' He exhaled, took another deep breath and spoke even more formally than before.

'I have received reliable information that you have an illegally caught salmon in your car and...'

'What illegally caught salmon?' my uncle defiantly interrupted the Sergeant and gasped, 'Information from who?'

The policeman nodded towards my side of the car and in a subdued tone gave the barely audible order, 'Mister Reid, make your allegations please'

I could see from the corner of my eye the torso of a man coming from behind the Oak Tree. My door swung open. I was looking into the face of a man with a blackened eyes and split lip.

'Where's the salmon,' Fishy ordered, his eyes bulging with a mixture of rage and excitement. I lowered my trembling hands and still entranced by his wild stare, lifted and handed him the parcel that was at my feet.

'Here's your evidence Sergeant,' Fishy said grabbing the parcel and walking towards the policeman, 'and there's the culprit, supplying illegal salmon all over the place,' he concluded nodding to my uncle as he handed the parcel to the Lawman.

'What?' my uncle roared grabbing the door handle, 'Reid if you don't want those black-eyes polished up a bit, you better take that remark back.'

'Gentlemen please,' Sergeant Freeman hollered holding the door closed on my uncle.

'Listen, Shane, ah er, Sergeant Freeman, surely we can settle this after, I have to bring my nephews to catch the half ten bus.'

'Eleven A.M. bus to be precise,' Fishy said leeringly.

I saw my uncle's knuckles whiten, gripping the steering wheel.

After a long pause the policeman spoke.

'Ah sure, I'll probably be held up with the Dutchman's investigation for the rest of the day anyway, so both of you come and see me tomorrow morning at ten sharp at Rockennedy Garda Station.'

He was about to turn away but then asked blandly, 'Is your father still stationed up in Clunmon?' I nodded in response.

My uncle was just driving off and then stopped, 'The Dutchman investigation?' he asked putting his head out the window and calling back to Sergeant Freeman, 'Is that anything to do with the news on the wireless?'

'Just covering all angles, it's early stages yet,' the Sergeant said calmly walking away.

I was shocked and silenced by the whole event. Mattie was humming contentedly in the back seat.

The next time Uncle Frank stopped the car it was so sudden that Mattie tumbled onto the car floor in the back and I was jolted forward as far as the windscreen. 'Wait a blooda minute,' my Uncle began very slowly and then his volume and intensity increased, 'how did Reid know about…what did ye tell him?' he looked at my silent telling face, 'ah ye blooda ceolans, ye told the blooda Bailiff about our fishing…ah I don't believe it,' my uncle pined holding his face in his hands.

'Uncle Frank what's a Bailiff?' Mattie asked calmly from the back seat.

Even at this stage it still hadn't dawned on Mattie that Con Reid, alias Fishy, was the Water Bailiff.

'What's a Bailiff,' Uncle Frank repeated Mattie's question lowering his hands, 'I'll tell you what a Bailiff is,' my uncle turned and in a pining voice addressed the questioner, 'the Bailiff is the man that is going to bring me to court and have me fined or maybe sent to prison, thanks to your big mouth.'

'Prison! Wow!' Mattie chirped.

Uncle Frank looked agitated and didn't speak another word until we reached Portwest. He was staring blandly in front of him and barley acknowledged those people who were waving courteously at him as we drove through the town.

We stopped outside the bus station.

My uncle sounded bewildered as he spoke, 'Bring in your stuff and we'll get the tickets.'

As soon as we went in the door we were hushed by a small crowd gathered around a radio in the corner. I looked at the clock over the vacant ticket booth and got nervous; it was two minutes past eleven.

'Did you hear Frank, one of your neighbours was shot dead in Holland by the Guards for stealing a valuable painting up in Clunmon,' a wild rugged faced man with scraggy wiry hair spurted from the crowd.

'Will you stay quiet Ryan, you have it arse about face as usual,' a lady with horn rimmed spectacles scolded and then mimicked the man she was addressing, 'the Guards in Holland, how-are-you.'

'Will ye all stay quiet!' was roared from the crowd as all hunched nearer the radio.

'To recap,' the voice on the radio announced, 'a man believed to be a resident of Doiredrum, Portwest, County Mayo but of Dutch, Canadian origin was shot dead early this morning by Dutch Police who were conducting a sting operation to recover a valuable painting believed to be the one stolen just over two weeks ago from the home of Lord Donaldson Barbour near Clunmon. Two Chief Superintendents and a Superintendent are on their way to Holland to help identify the body and the painting. The painting is believed to be in good condition except for a minute piercing to the painting itself and a small scrape to the back of the canvas which is believed to be repairable a Police spokesman said. Lord Donaldson Barbour is said to be delighted with the news that his valuable painting has been recovered and we hope to have an interview with him later this afternoon and that's the end of the news for now and here is the weather forecast.'

While the news was on I put the biscuits that Pauric had given us into my suitcase beside my sandwiches. I walked over to Mattie who was crouched behind a chair at the side of the ticket booth, which was out of view of the people present.

I bent down beside him as I spoke, 'Mattie I think that's the man who nearly drove into us the Saturday we were coming back from Portwest.'

'What man, what Saturday?' Mattie asked disinterestedly as he twisted the screwdriver.

'The man they are taking about on the radio, the man who was shot,' I snapped.

' Don't remember.'

'You do remember, remember the day Uncle Frank was angry because the gate was left open and he was cross with Granny because he thought that she had done it and then it turns out that the Dutchman had been to see Granny complaining about the sheep near his glass houses and it was probably him who left the gates open and we met him on the road coming back, do you remember now?' I barely concluded running out of breath.

'No,' Mattie said turning the screwdriver with a crunched-up face and then hastily added, 'ah yes, I remember now, I think that it was Granny who left the gate open because she said that she had delivered that mat in the parcel to her friend.'

'Mattie, I'm not talking about the parcel for Breda Fenlon, and anyway that's the parcel that you tore when you knocked the cartwheel on it.'

'I didn't tear any parcel.'

'A nail got stuck in it when you knocked the cartwheel on it.'

'Maybe, but who tore it when they were trying to free it, ha, ha,' Mattie said with a smirk and then added, 'now go away can't you see I'm busy.'

I left him even though he wasn't busy really. He was only loosening screws from the backrest of a chair.

'And that's the end of the weather forecast,' the voice on the radio concluded.

'Ah my God more blooda rain,' the man they called Ryan yelled out.

349

'In the name of God, will you listen to what is being said Ryan, it's rain in the East and dry in the West, do you know the difference between the two.'

'What's it to you whether I do or not?' Ryan grunted heading for the main entrance door.

Just as he was exiting he pushed a man back out the door who was on his way in. Mattie came from behind the chair and stood beside me in the queue at the ticket booth. He nudged me showing me three screws before slipping them into his pocket.

'Be the feck what did ye do on Ryan,' a man with a bright red face carrying a battered suitcase said, gaining entrance on his second attempt to get in the door. He panted coming toward the ticket hatch and brushed me and Mattie out of his path as he spoke to the lady with the horn rimmed glasses who was now inside the ticket booth.

'Eileen has the Dublin bus gone yet?'

'Andy,' she replied with a barking voice, 'I told you two hours ago that your bus was leaving in twenty minutes and you just fecked off back to the pub.'

Andy just stood there saying, 'be the feck, be the feck, bus gone.'

Eileen moved her head forward and continued, 'Andy your bus has left over one and a half hours ago now get out of the way and let me deal with these other people,' she concluded with a dismissive wave of her hand.

'Oh alas, alas, back to the pub,' Andy said turning with his suitcase and headed back out the door rattling the glass in it as he slammed it closed behind him. I heard a thud to the side of the ticket booth. I looked and saw the backrest of the chair that Mattie had been unscrewing, swinging from side to side suspended by one remaining screw.

My uncle came beside us and placed a ten pound note on top of the counter hatch, 'Eileen, I hope the Longford bus hasn't left.'

'It better not be Frank, I'm the driver,' a very small man said from the crowd still gathered around the radio as he flopped a dingy flattened cap on his head.

'Ah Kevin, I didn't see you there behind the small stool,' Uncle Frank said with a laugh and continued, 'this is Mister Kevin Galvin lads, he'll put ye on the right bus for Clunmon when ye get to Longford.

Uncle Frank shook our hands and gave us a half crown each as we stood near the bus.

'Get yourselves some lemonade to have with the sandwiches when ye get to Longford,' he said before lifting our suitcases to the bus steps and then added, 'have you got your tickets in a safe place?'

We nodded as we each patted the outside of our pockets. Mattie went ahead of me onto the bus with the parcel under his arm.

'I'm sorry if we got you into trouble over the salmon,' I said in a whisper boarding the bus.

'Ah, not to worry,' my uncle sighed, 'as your father says, "why worry, wait and see."'

Mattie and I put our cases and the parcel on the luggage rack over the seats and looked out the back window of the bus. As the engine revved up and the bus rumbled forward we waved back at our uncle who was barely visible in the thick diesel smoke.

We are on our way back home and I feel good.

CHAPTER 32

The Gauntlet Home

A WELL-DRESSED MAN and woman sat near the front of the bus and an elderly man was seated about half way up so Mattie and I had sat at the very back. We agreed to say nothing to Mammy or Daddy about Fishy and the Sergeant taking the salmon; well not until we would be questioned on it anyway.

I had taken some comics out of my suitcase and was standing on the seat putting my suitcase back up beside the parcel on the luggage rack when I heard an official voice calling.

'No standing on the seats and no luggage alterations while the vehicle is in motion.'

I jumped down off the seat and looked towards the front of the bus. Mister Galvin had his finger raised and was pointing it in my direction. I don't think I like him and I was glad when Mattie started unscrewing the ashtray on the back of the seat in front of us.

I had read each of the comics twice and my stomach felt very wheezy by the time we reached Longford town.

'Try and not give this one away to the first person who asks you for it,' Mattie said mockingly handing me the parcel. I felt that I had to take the parcel because I know Mattie; he would just have left it behind on the bus and take his chances later if asked about it by Mammy.

'That's the bus you want for Clunmon,' Mister Galvin said as we disembarked, 'it should be pulling out in about an hour.'

He was pointing towards a bus that had heavy muck splatters all along the side as far as the back. I followed Mattie towards a yellow brick structure with a sign that read, 'Men's Waiting Room' but then Mattie veered right and went into a small shop beside it.

The nauseating smell of sour milk in the shop made my stomach heave even worse and as soon as I had bought my bottle of lemonade and got the shopkeeper to open it I rushed back outside to get some fresh air. It felt like forever getting out of the shop door, with my parcel under my arm, holding a suitcase in one hand and an open bottle of lemonade in the other.

I waited outside for Mattie and when he came out he was carrying a paper bag full to the brim with jelly sweets. He had chocolate bars bulging out the top of his trouser pockets.

'Blooda ceolan, sold me matches but wouldn't sell me two cigarettes,' Mattie muttered.

Uncle Frank's gift money is well and truly spent. I waited a few seconds and took a few deep breaths before following him into the men's waiting room. I took a few small slugs from the lemonade bottle to see if it would settle my stomach.

As I went into the waiting room I could see Mattie's suitcase and his bag of sweets beside it on the table in the centre of the room. He was over at the dark fireplace and he had the ragged rim of the bottle cap hooked on the very edge of the wrought iron mantlepiece.

He had his balled fist held high and was aiming it at the bottle cap as he gripped the bottle tightly with the other hand. Mattie obviously hadn't got the shopkeeper to open the cap on his lemonade bottle. He made two attempts to decap the bottle by whacking the cap with the ball of his fist and on the third try the bottle cap flipped from the bottle and scurried across the floor as the fizzy lemonade gurgled down the side of the bottle and his hand.

Two elderly men were seated on benches placed along the wall. They looked in awe at Mattie repeatedly kicking the bottle cap around the linoleum-covered floor. When he eventually succeeded in kicking the bottle cap over the fender and into the open hearth the two men smiled meekly at him.

I placed my lemonade, suitcase and the parcel on the table in the centre of the room and removed my sandwich package from my suitcase. There were four rail-backed chairs around the long wooden table. Mattie sat beside me at the table and opened his suitcase. He removed his catapult and did some mock aiming around the room. When he aimed in the direction of the two men one ducked and the other just stared with a startled look until Mattie burst out laughing and the two men looked blankly back at him.

He threw the catapult back in the suitcase and took out his sandwiches. I took one bite of my sandwich, dropped it on the table and rushed with hands on mouth into the toilet.

A culmination of reading on the bus, smelling sour milk in the shop and now after biting into a piece of onion had made my stomach do a complete somersault. I stayed in the toilet until I was nearly better but then I started worrying about missing the Clunmon bus so I slowly waddled back into the waiting room without really feeling that well.

Mattie was sitting on a chair with his hands behind his head, his feet up on my chair and he was smoking. My sandwiches were gone but I didn't care.

One of the elderly gentlemen spluttered breadcrumbs as he spoke, 'Be God but you can't beat the bit of "innion" for the flavour,' he said standing up wiping his mouth as he walked bole-legged towards the door.

'Be God but you're a gas buck,' the other man said reaching for his walking stick.

The bole-legged man held the door and spoke before leaving, 'I hope ye have a great holiday in France and thanks again for the sandwich.'

'Not at all,' Mattie responded, 'and if I'm ever in Cork I'll be sure to call into you in your sweetshop,' he said with an insincere wave and then turned to me, 'you know what Finn, from now on I'm going to get Mammy to make my sandwiches without onion, they're much, much nicer.'

I looked painfully at him before asking a question and feared the response, 'were there onions in the sandwiches you opened?' 'No,' he said with a grin.

It was the answer I feared. I was about to hit him but then I realised that I am too weak to defend myself when he retaliates so I just finished off my lemonade and pondered. I was annoyed with myself for picking up the wrong sandwiches or had Granny got them mixed up; either way I was getting sicker with the thought.

Mattie was inhaling the cigarette smoke and I thought that he looked a bit pale. He had demolished half the sweets and I noticed chocolate wrapping papers strewn on the floor. 'Where did you get the cigarette?' I asked opening the biscuit bag.

'I did a deal with old "horseshoe-legs,"' he nodded in the direction where the two men had been sitting earlier. 'Well you weren't going to eat your sandwiches were you, so I swapped your sandwiches for a cigarette,' he explained the barter that had taken place between himself and the bole-legged man.

He was looking very pleased with himself but he also looked a bit paler as he stubbed out a half smoked cigarette. 'What sort of "biscakes" did Pauric give us?' he asked reaching for the bag.

'Fig Rolls,' I answered with glee as Mattie's face turned grey. He dry wretched a few times and then raced into the toilet.

I eat a few of the Fig Rolls, finished my lemonade and had everything ready to begin the second leg of our journey home by the time Mattie came back from the toilet. He slowly pulled a few chocolate bars from his pocket, put them into his half filled sweet bag and dropped it into his suitcase.

The yellow faced clock hanging on the wall over the mantlepiece said ten to eleven and I had to rush Mattie to make a move. He had his screwdriver out again and made two attempts to remove the shiny brass knob on the inside of the waiting room door but he was unable to loosen the screw. The dirty looking bus that Mister Galvin had pointed out to us earlier was rumbling and shaking amidst the smell of vile diesel fumes as we approached it in a line of other buses.

Mattie stopped at a clean bus beside it and spoke to the driver sitting inside, 'Any chance of this one going to Clunmon?'

355

'Sorry young man, this is going to Galway, that's your one there,' the bus driver pointed.

'Ah, I know that but this one is cleaner,' Mattie said putting his foot on the first step.

'Get off,' the driver said leaning towards Mattie from his seat, 'typical "Clunmon," want to look posh and not an arse in their pants.'

Mattie said nothing and walked down the side of the bus. The bus driver tentatively watched Mattie's movements in his side-view mirror. I was watching him too as he bent down beside the back wheel. He left his suitcase on the ground and cautiously removed a matchstick from a new box of matches that he must have bought in the shop earlier.

'Get away from that valve or I'll break your arse with a kick,' the driver yelled from the door.

I was startled by the roar but I don't know why Mattie looked so shocked because he's had a lot of those threats recently and you'd think that he'd be used to them by now.

Mattie had tried one of old tricks. He got in trouble at school a few times for letting the air out of his teacher's scooter by pushing a matchstick into the tube valve.

He waddled towards the Clunmon bus and barely answered to the driver's question regarding the possession of a ticket as he climbed on board with his suitcase. We took similarly placed seats as we had on the first leg of our journey and I put my suitcase and the parcel on the rack before the bus started. I didn't remove any comics from the suitcase this time. I had learned my lesson about the effect that reading had on me while riding on a bus.

There were only about six or seven people on board at any given time as the bus stopped on route to either let people on or off. We spent the time reminiscing about our holiday or just gawking out the window.

When we stopped in Edgeworthstown a woman and child-in-arms was one of four adults waiting to board the bus. She has a tartan shawl pulled around her shoulders that also partially covered the child's head. The Tinker woman's hair was black and greasy with a balding parting in the middle.

She had been arguing with the Bus Inspector who appeared to be preventing her from boarding the bus. The man in uniform wore a high cap with braid on the peak. He was small and fat but raised himself on his toes intermittently when he was arguing with the woman.

The inspector eventually conceded and let her on the bus. She sat half way up. She looked back at us and smiled but we just stared out the side window until she turned to her front again. Just before the bus pulled away the inspector hopped on and sat in a vacant seat beside the driver. After a while he got up and started asking passengers to show their tickets.

When he was about half way up I heard Mattie taking a gulp of air, 'Oh no, not that Bus Inspector.' he gasped in a whisper pushing his head down behind the seat.

'What?' I asked, 'have you lost your ticket?'

'No, I have my ticket,' he grunted pulling from his pocket, his ticket and the ashtray he had removed from the other bus.

'Hide it,' I whispered grabbing the ashtray and slipping it under the seat.

'It's not the ashtray that's worrying me, I'll tell you later,' he said twisting his jaw from side to side as he opened and closed his eyes in quick succession.

When the bus inspector came as far as the Tinker woman and child he stuck out his chest and spoke solemnly to her, 'Now Maggie, you tell me that your husband will be meeting you in Granard and will pay for your ticket this time, have I that correct?'

'You have sir, Michael Connors is a man of his word sir,' she said bringing the whimpering baby to her chest.

'He wasn't a man of his word the last time if you remember.'

'Ah sure how could he meet the bus sir and the Guards having him locked up for fighting.'

Then the baby burst into a screeching howl and the bus inspector moved towards us. He was looking a bit bemused as he stared at Mattie. I looked at Mattie; he was squinting and had his jaw twisted to one side.

'Tickets please lads,' he said scrutinising Mattie.

357

He clipped our tickets and gave them back to us and directed his question at Mattie, 'Do I know you?'

'No you don't,' Mattie answered from the side of his mouth. The bus inspector took another look back at Mattie before leaving us.

The baby was still crying and I could see it shaking its head from side to side as the mother pulled the baby's head closer to her chest. The woman's shoulders were bare now. As the bus inspector was approaching her she shouted at the baby, 'Suck it can't ya,' and then glancing up at the uniformed man and croaked, 'or I'll give it to this nice man here.' The bus inspector looked down, froze and then briskly skipped back to his seat at the front of the bus.

'Phew,' Mattie gasped rubbing and wriggling his jaw, now back to normal.

'He thinks he knows you,' I prompted.

Mattie giggled before speaking, 'Will he ever forget me,' he tittered moving close to me and spoke in a low voice, 'do you remember the heavy snow last Christmas?' he asked and I nodded, 'well yer man there, Quigley I think his name is, was standing at the Diamond waiting to inspect a bus, all dressed up like a peacock, same as he is now.' Mattie peeped over his seat, 'Anyway I bet Towbar two gobstoppers that he couldn't knock off yer mans hat with a snowball.'

'I bet you didn't pay your bet to Towbar,' I interrupted.

'No I didn't pay Towbar,' he spoke emphatically through gritted teeth, 'because Towbar missed the cap but got yer man straight in the ear,' Mattie giggled again. 'Wow,' I said with a wide smile and asked, 'and what did the bus inspector do?' 'What do you think dumbo, he ran after us of course,'

'I wouldn't say he could run very fast,' I interrupted again taking a quick peep at the small fat man.

'That's what we thought,' Mattie said peeping by the side of the seat this time, 'he ran like the hammers-of- hell after us, it was afterwards Towbar found out that he had medals for running races, anyway off with us and yer man tearing behind us, down Fermanagh Street, into Newtown Road around Eire Square.'

'And was he able to keep up with you?' I asked excitedly.

'Was he what!' Mattie said taking a deep breath, 'He was catching up on us and only we slipped through the hole in the sleeper fence there at the Gullet and onto the railway track he'd have caught us.'

'We pulled those two sleepers down in the railway fence at the Gullett,' I informed Mattie what Sparks, Vinny and I had done.

'No, not that big hole opposite Mc Cabes, he'd have been able to get through there, further up beside Seamus Geoghegans where there's only one sleeper knocked out of the fence,' Mattie contradicted me.

I took another peep over the seat at the man we had been talking about. He was looking back at us so I sat back in my seat until we reached Granard.

'Maggie, there's no sign of your husband to pay for your bus ticket,' the bus inspector called stepping off the bus.

'Ah the poor man is probably back in the 'ospital again with the bad chest,' the women shouted waddling towards the exit.

'You'll never catch me like that again Maggie,' he peeved.

'Ah catch me arse,' Maggie said with a coarse laugh stepping down off the bus.

'Will you be travelling as far as Clunmon with us Mister Quigley,' the bus driver called from his seat.

'No, no carry on Brendan, there's nobody here to get on,' he answered straightening his cap.

The bus moved off and Mattie pulled and yanked at the window until it flopped down.

He pushed his head into the opening and hollered, 'How would you like a snowball in your gob the next time.'

I raced to the back window of the bus and looked at the bus inspector throwing his cap on the ground. He looked furious with a clenched fist raised, miming curse words in our direction. I was grinning going back to my seat and lay lengthways on it for a rest.

CHAPTER 33

Back Downtown

'BE GOD BUT YE'RE GREAT MEN to sleep,' I heard in the distance and then a varied repetition became louder, 'the best sleepers I ever had on my bus, there's somebody here to meet you.'

I first focused on the bus driver through sleepy eyes and then could see the outline of a sturdy smiling man; it was Daddy.

He was wearing a sports jacket over his uniform. Mattie was yawning in the seat opposite. I looked out the window; we were back home.

'Did ye have a nice time?' Daddy asked taking our suitcases and the parcel from the luggage rack.

'Yes we had a great time,' I answered running to the front of the bus.

I think I heard Mattie say, 'Yup,' from behind me but I wasn't sure.

Sparks and Vinny were roaring, 'Yahoo' as soon as I put my foot on the first step to disembark.

'How did you know we were coming home?' I asked excitedly.

'Your mother told us,' Vinny answered and then added, 'do you know The Yank and his brother was arrested?'

'I know,' I butted in, 'sure Mattie and me met...'

'Finn,' Daddy snapped at me with wide threatening eyes.

Then I remembered Mammy's letter to Granny and said nothing more.

Daddy turned to the bus driver, 'Thanks Brendan,' Daddy said with a wave.

'No bother at all Sergeant,' the bus driver acknowledged stretching himself alighting from the bus.

Daddy handed Mattie and I our suitcases as soon as we got off the bus.

'What's this?' he asked looking bemused at the parcel wrapped in layers of newspapers.

'It's a leg of lamb, Granny sent it to you and Mammy,' I said.

He held the parcel by the makeshift handle that Granny had made with the string and held it out in the direction of Sparks and Vinny who looked at one another. Vinny eventually obeyed Daddy's silent order and took it from him.

Daddy and Mattie were walking in front of us. When I told Vinny and Sparks that I had presents for them they said that they would come to my house now and get them.

Just as we left the Diamond and entering Fermanagh Street, I heard a voice calling from behind.

'Mattie, Mattie.' We all looked; it was Towbar with his arm in a sling and a bandage wrapped around his head.

He was running to catch up with us until Daddy turned and pointed his finger at him and shouted the word, "home."

Towbar staggered to a halt and called out, 'Any crack Mattie?'

'It's wild dangerous down there,' Mattie called back and then added, 'I'll tell you all about it later.'

'No you won't,' Daddy contradicted and then I hear him mutter, 'oh no.'

He was looking at a tall spindly woman crossing Fermanagh Street from the far footpath in an obvious direction so as to meet us.

'Oh Sergeant, Sergeant they're at it again, those two corner boys, Feeney and Tighe, frightening poor Goosey,' she said approaching.

She was holding a basket up in front of her enormous breasts.

It was Missus Dixon the Vicar's wife and she was carrying her ugly Pekinese dog in her usual canine transporter; her wicker basket.

'Missus Dixon go you on down to the Barracks and make a report to Guard Brody and he'll...'

'Guard Brody, is it?' she hollered, 'I might as well tell the cat as that useless yoke,' she said in a disappointed huff crossing the street again.

Vinny and Sparks were telling me feverishly about the Northern Ireland Custom's Post being blown up one afternoon.

'The IRA blew it up in the daytime,' Vinny spurted out and then pondered before he added, 'but they let that cranky Custom's man out first.'

I wasn't sure if I knew about the explosion from Mammy's letter, in which case I was to say nothing or had Granny heard it on the radio or had Uncle Frank read it in the newspaper, so I just listened.

They were cutting across one another to tell the story concerning the aftermath of the blown up Custom's Post. Vinny and Sparks got to the scene before the RUC arrived and in the adjacent fields they found a fire extinguisher and a phone amongst the debris.

'Both items are in safe keeping in our hideout,' Sparks said wringing his hands in delight.

I laughed when they told me about Towbar falling down from the top of a tree trying to retrieve a chair that was blown up there by the explosion.

As we were nearing the end of Fermanagh Street a dishevelled looking man staggered out from Grady's Bar with his fists raised. 'I'll fight any man in this one-horse garrison town,' he was shouting.

We slowed down but my father kept walking at his usual pace with his arms swinging by his side. Mattie left Daddy's side and stepped onto the road.

The man stepped back nearer the doorway and was swaying in a boxing motion as Daddy came along side him. It all happened in a flash; I heard a splattering thump and saw the man tumble backwards into the doorway as Daddy whipped his hand into his pocket. As we passed the doorway I could see the man stretched out on his back with a smear of blood splattered from his nose to the side of his face.

When we turned at McConkey's corner a few men were standing and talking and spitting like they do there most days. When Daddy past them I saw two of them do a mock fist fight behind Daddy's back. I increased my step and caught up with Daddy and told him what the men were doing behind his back.

'Is one of them small, fat, wearing a grubby jacket and the other skinny, a head like a banana with chewed lettuce leafs for ears?'

It's great when Daddy speaks in simple language and not using complicated words; he had described the two men accurately so I just nodded my reply.

'Ah yes, Tighe and Feeney, brave men scaring an old woman and her dog.'

'Are you going to arrest them?' I asked hoping that he would especially with Vinny and Sparks watching.

My father just kept walking and spoke softly, 'Not today, but when they least expect it, they'll get their comeuppance.'

When we were crossing the road to our house an open-backed truck stopped suddenly a short distance in front of us. Daddy pointed his finger and called, 'Clerkin, I want to see a tax disc on that yoke the next time we meet.'

The driver stuck his head out the window and babbled, 'Sergeant as soon, as soon as I sell the cow the, the calf, the calf, the calf I'll do that.'

'Your last chance,' my father threatened.

I could smell the fry straight away as soon as Daddy opened the front door.

'Well how are ye a gras,' Mammy said hugging us both at the same time before we even got putting our cases down.

Vinny and Sparks stood beside me in the kitchen.

'Will ye stay for a bit of tea?' Mammy asked them before scurrying into the pantry.

They both declined with a dignified 'No thank you very much.'

I could tell by their faces that they were anxious to get their presents so I placed my suitcase on the sofa and opened it.

'And this is the leg of lamb you carried all the way for me,' Mammy responded to Mattie's false claim after he handed the parcel to her in the pantry. I was too busy to refute his claim.

I found the comics straight away in my suitcase but I had to rummage down to the bottom until I found the screwdriver.

'Wow,' Vinny uttered as I handed him the screwdriver affixed to a colourful card. I whispered to Vinny that I would give him back his dagger tomorrow. Sparks was perusing the comics as Vinny yanked free the wire that was securing the screwdriver to the cardboard.

'I read these last week,' Sparks murmured turning the pages.

'It looked bigger before I took it off the card,' Vinny complained holding the screwdriver out in front of him and then added condescendingly, 'I'm sure we'll find some use for it.'

They both said thanks as they were leaving the kitchen but I knew that they were sort of disappointed with their presents. I went to the door with them anyway.

They wanted to know if I was meeting them later to see the phone and fire extinguisher in the secret hideout but I told them that I would probably be staying in after tea to tell Mammy all the news from the West.

I saw Miss Black standing inside her gate across the road as we were discussing plans for tomorrow. The arrow that Mattie had fired into the pole in front of her house was gone. She was waving her hand gently over at me trying to attract my attention. I knew that she would be asking me questions about the weather and the farm work and the towns that I passed through so I pretended not to notice her.

After we had settled on our plans for tomorrow, Sparks and Vinny walked away. I was about to turn and go inside my house when I remembered the question that I wanted to ask Sparks. I was going to ask him earlier when we were coming down the town but when they were talking about the bombed custom's post it went out of my mind, so I shouted after him now, 'Sparks, what are "sins of the flesh"?'

I picked up on a quick movement out of the corner of my eye; Miss Black had vanished.

Sparks and Vinny stopped.

Sparks called back after a second or two as he scratched his head, 'I don't know what they are, but I'll find out.'

'Ma'am, I'll have time for my tea if you hurry, I have to see Lord Donaldson Barbour to make arrangements to get his paintings back,' Daddy was saying as I entered the kitchen.

During the tea I told Daddy that the man shot for stealing the paintings is from Doiredrum. I thought that I'd get an immediate response but Daddy finished chewing a piece of sausage before he answered and then it didn't make a bit of sense to me.

'It's all speculation at the moment,' he said in a low voice and then added, 'and I only deal with facts, now something else I want to say to you both,' Daddy said resting back on his chair.

He warned Mattie and me not to speak about our journey with The Yank or about our visit to his brother Dan Joe.

'I think Vinny and Sparks know that they were arrested,' I said trying to prompt more information from Daddy.

'Everyone knows that they were arrested for racketeering and smuggled cigarettes and illegal manufacture, sale and distribution of poiteen but what I don't want people to know is that you two were in the car with him on one of his escapades, do you understand?'

I understood some of what he said but I knew that main message was that we were to keep our mouths closed.

Mammy was refilling Daddy's teacup as she spoke, 'Your father is going to do a deal with...' Suddenly she was silenced by Daddy's raging stare and walked away in a huff without completing her chore in hand.

When Mammy had washed up after the tea I opened my suitcase again. I gave Mammy her snowy ornament, Myra her broach and Daddy his gift-wrapped handkerchief.

'Just what I wanted,' Mammy said but I think she winked at Daddy.

Myra said a hurried 'thank you,' slipping the brooch from the flimsy paper card. Daddy tore a piece of the wrapping paper peeped inside without opening it fully and murmured, 'Thanks, good boy' and left it back on the table. I think the American parcels have him spoiled.

Mattie opened up his suitcase and took out the paper bag containing assorted sweets and chocolate bars that he was not able to eat at the bus station in Longford and called out, 'presents for everyone,' as he spread them on the table

Mammy, Daddy and Myra rummaged with smiling faces as they picked their favourite sweets and chocolate. Even though Daddy had to remove his false teeth to pick off a piece of sticky jelly from his top gum plate he still said that they were lovely.

Myra was smiling clasping the broach to her ringlet but then she started whinging, 'The clasp is bent.'

'Daddy will fix it for you,' Mammy drooled on a sweet going into the pantry with a scissors where she started cutting and unravelling the string on the parcel.

Daddy was only working on the broach a few seconds when I head Myra's screeching cry.

'What's wrong with you now?' Mammy questioned from the pantry throwing newspapers to one side.

'Daddy broke my new brooch all together now,' Myra squeezed out between hysterical sobs.

'Will you take that puss of you or I'll hang the pot on it,' Mammy called back at her.

Daddy is not really great at fixing or making things but he has the best of tools.

'Where are you going to put this Mammy?' I asked holding up the snowy ornament as Mammy was nearing the end of removing the last few layers of newspapers from the parcel.

'Put it on the mantlepiece in the sitting room please,' she answered.

As I was admiring Mammy's present I just happened to look over at the small glass case in the corner of the room. There on top of the glass case was an identical snowy globe and my heart sank.

From now on I'm going to have to think seriously whether to get holiday presents or not. As I was leaving the sitting room I was pondering on this but it was put completely out of my mind when I saw what Mammy had resting on her out-stretched hands.

'That's the funniest leg of lamb I ever saw,' she said presenting a fresh salmon nestled on a white dishtowel.

A short silence was followed by, 'Yahoo,' as Mattie yelled jumping around the kitchen shouting, 'Fishy ya blooda, blooda blooda ceolan. Yahoo!'

He was still skipping and jumping and laughing until Mammy left down the salmon on the kitchen table and flicked the dish-towel at him clipping him on the side of his face.

'That's enough of that, where on earth did you hear that sort of language,' she scolded.

We are back home and no doubt about it.

The flick of the dishcloth brought Mattie back to his senses and he stared coyly around him and spoke softly, 'That's how they speak in Doiredrum.'

Daddy shrugged his shoulders and muttered, 'Well I'm off to see Lord Donaldson Barbour,' and vanished quietly out the kitchen door.

'Never in my life did I hear such language,' Mammy said lift-ing the salmon and going into the pantry.

When Mammy pressed Mattie on his outburst and antics, he cherry-picked his explanation. He said that the Bailiff was nicknamed Fishy and went on to say that he was so delighted to have got the salmon for her without being caught by Fishy the Bailiff.

'I have a feeling that there's more to it than that,' Mammy murmured cutting the head off the salmon.

I joined her in the pantry started telling her about the places we were and the people we met and eventually I got her back in good humour again. When I told her about meeting Ann and Pauric in the pub she said that Ann was a second cousin of hers and then she changed her mind and said that Ann was "five-a-kin" to her; then she thought again and finished smugly, 'her uncle Bishop McKeown is a relation of mine anyway.'

After Mammy had finished cleaning and preparing the salmon we came back into the kitchen and sat around talking. Anytime

I would mention somebody that Mattie and I had had unto-ward dealings with, Mattie would give me a worrying look and I talked about someone else.

She wanted to know why we were in the pub so often but Mattie changed the subject and started talking about the Canon and his lovely horse. After a while we ran out of news for Mammy and I was sorry that I hadn't told Sparks and Vinny that I would meet them. Mammy told us to bring our suitcases upstairs and then to come down and have our supper.

Mattie was slipping his catapult and Daddy's screwdriver under his mattress as I was leaving the bedroom.

I took the bag of fig roll biscuits downstairs with me and gave them to Mammy. She gave me two biscuits from the bag and left two more beside Mattie's mug of cocoa.

'I'll put the rest away for Sunday,' she said going into the pantry.

I smiled and said nothing as I concentrated on the fig roll biscuits beside Mattie's cocoa.

I could see Mattie's face change colours as he entered the kitchen and dwelled on his dreaded fig rolls.

He pondered for a second or two, picked up the biscuits and offered, 'Mammy I want you to have these.'

'Well I'll take one,' she said with pride looking with pride at her eldest son.

'No, no I want you to have the two,' Mattie said bringing them to her in the pantry.

Now I'm not feeling too well.

I was just finishing the last biscuit when Daddy came into the kitchen. He looked stern-faced. Mammy went into the pantry and put on the kettle. He was looking at Mattie and then me in quick succession as he sat down and nodded at us to do likewise

'Garda Brody had taken a message for me when I went back to the barracks,' my father began as he unbuttoned the top pocket of his tunic, 'it's from a Sergeant Shane Freeman, Rockennedy Garda Station,' he said with a frown watching our reaction.

'Oh isn't he who replaced you in Rockennedy?' Mammy called from the pantry door.'

Daddy raised his hand in a silencing command. Mattie looked at me with a defeatist smile as Daddy put his hand into his tunic pocket and removed his notebook.

His actions looked very official slipping a loose piece of foolscap paper from the centre pages. He replaced his notebook and opened the piece of paper.

'This is the message Garda Brody took from Sergeant Freeman over the phone, I'll read it out to you to see if it makes sense to you, because it makes very little to me,' he said giving a quick glance at us before he began to read from the note, "Message from Sergeant Freeman,' he looked at us again and continued, "I hope your sons enjoy the salmon as much as I will enjoy the filleted leg of lamb. Your brother-in-law Frank has been informed and will be in touch.'

He put the piece of paper back in his breast pocket.

'What is that all about?' he quizzed as a smile came to his face.

I tried to talk but a piece of fig roll got caught in my throat and I got a fit of coughing.

'Daddy, it's a bit hard for us to understand too but do you know who will be able to tell you,' Mattie said without flinching.

I gulped; I was sure that he was going to nominate me.

I gasped with relief when he said, 'My uncle Frank can explain anything about anything.'

I could tell by both Mammy's and Daddy's faces that they hadn't made sense of Mattie's answer and neither did I. I went to bed feeling relieved but I knew in the back of my mind that it was only a stay of execution.

Sparks and Vinny were waiting at my door when I went out after the breakfast. I gave Vinny back his dagger. I heard Sparks whispering to Vinny to make sure that he wipes the Indian's blood off it and they both started giggling. I was annoyed with them and promised myself never to mention Indians again except coming from the cinema.

When we got to our hideout I was still smarting over them laughing at me over the Indian blood on the dagger and decided to be nasty too. It worked. They were disappointed when I said that I didn't think the phone or the fire extinguisher were any good.

'Well look,' I said pointing at the phone and lifting the fire extinguisher, 'the phone is melted and this yoke is all burned on one side and what's more it's empty,' I said shaking the fire extinguisher.

'It went off accidently when Vinny was messing with it, he destroyed my jacket and trousers,' Sparks explained the empty extinguisher with a cringe. Vinny giggled but then Sparks added excitedly, 'the phone looks bad but the mechanism is okay, I've checked it and we have a plan to have our own working phone here in our hideout.'

He looked at me for a sign of support. I smiled.

CHAPTER 34

Ordinary Days and Not So

WE SETTLED BACK into our regular holiday routine at home and when we weren't at the 'flicks' or in our hideout we amused ourselves in other ways.

We netted some frogs at the sewerage water works and did some frog racing on Miss Black's galvanised coalhouse roof. Our racing came to an end when Vinny's frog hopped off the end of the roof and when he jumped down to get it, he accidentally splattered it on landing.

We took 'cock-shots' with our catapults at the bakelite insulators on top of the telegraph poles; hung around Saint Joseph's Snooker Hall when it was raining until we got barred for playing marbles on the snooker table; played 'Paratroopers' in Murphy's new hayshed but on our last jump of the day from the highest rafter, Vinny landed badly and sprained his ankle.

We had mock swordfights with sharpened sally rods resulting in Sparks having to wear an eye patch for a week; After Ivor Noble had closed for the day we did some target practice, with our bows and arrows, using his petrol pumps as the target; We broke the remaining windows in the scrapped railway carriages near the shunting line and then went on to make 'double-headed pennies' by pushing a carriage over two pennies which were placed on top of one-another on the railway line.

The three of us went bottle searching in bins for dumped 'returns' to sell them to get money for cigarettes. We didn't find any so Vinny climbed over Patsy O'Hara's back wall and took three empty lemonade bottles from the 'returns' crate and sold the bottles back to Patsy.

With the money he got we went to the shop beside our school where Vinny bought three cigarettes from 'No Scruples Daisy' and we went to the hideout for a smoke. Sparks got sick again. He might have fainted too only Vinny pushed him outside for fresh air when he saw he was about to vomit on his catapult.

We went fishing but only caught a few Perch so I told Vinny and Sparks about 'The Board' that my uncle uses for fishing. Sparks made a prototype based on my memory of what it should look like. We launched it in the Dummy's Lake yesterday but it sank so it's back to the drawing board.

We had a similar mishap with the tyres from the Vicar's field. We rolled them all the way to the Dummy's Lake because Vinny said that they would float and we could have some fun swimming out to the deep with them. Sparks disagreed with the 'floating' theory but he went along with it anyway. Spark's analysis was correct so Vinny promised that he would build a raft instead some other day.

More bad luck when we decided to test out the screwdriver that I had bought as a present for Vinny. We were in the process of taking the 'Dangerous Dog' sign off 'Grumpy' McCarney's gate when 'Grumpy,' who had been out walking his dog, managed to sneak up behind us without us hearing him or his dog. He took the screwdriver from Vinny and said that if he wanted it back he would have to bring his father with him as proof that he had permission to carry such a devise; end of screwdriver for us.

Things went wrong again when we were trying to connect the phone Vinny and Sparks got from the bombed Custom's Hut. The telegraph pole at the back of Doctor Walsh's surgery was deemed by Sparks to be the best option. We had stepped out distances, from our hideout to other telegraph poles nearby, and were satisfied that the pole at the back of the doctors surgery was the nearest to suit our needs.

There was a ladder inside the back wall of the surgery and when Vinny was trying to get over the wall to get the ladder so he could climb the telegraph pole his trousers got snagged on the low barbed wire fence located on the top of the wall. When he was un-snagging his trousers he slipped and as he was tumbling off the wall he grabbed the barbed wire and was left dangling with the spiked wire embedded in his hand.

Doctor Walsh heard him screaming and brought him into his surgery and dressed his hand.

I tried to console Vinny by telling him that we would have had to go to the dump hundreds of times to try and find enough scrap wire that would reach from the telegraph pole to our hideout and it wouldn't have been worth the effort. He agreed with that.

Vinny asked me if I would get him a pair of pliers for a present the next time so he could cut barbed wire with it. I told him that I would, because I felt sorry for him. But bearing in mind the gratitude I got from Vinny for the gift I'd bought him, I don't think I'll bother but I didn't say that out loud.

Vinny kept his word and we helped him built a raft in our hideout. It took us a long time to gather up the boards and planks required to construct it. Then we had to carry it all the way from our hideout to the Dummy's lake for the launch.

Honker McCusker and his Cara Street gang were out swimming in the lake when we arrived and asked to have a try on our raft but I knew Vinny wouldn't let them since his fight with Honker last Christmas.

The fight was over Honker sabotaging the slide we had made on the footpath on our road. We had poured the water on the footpath earlier in the evening and as the weather forecast had predicted there was a heavy frost from early evening. It was the best slide in town because it was on a hill.

Honker was doing his evening paper delivery and he asked to have a slide on it. We agreed but he came back the next day and had another slide on it. It was after he had left that Vinny was sliding down the slide when he suddenly stopped half way and tumbled forward and hopped his head on the footpath.

We examined the spot where Vinny had toppled and discovered that that part was thawing.

When Honker was coming back up the road from his paper delivery we caught him and emptied out his pockets. There was still some salt left in one of his pockets so we knew that it was he who had sprinkled some salt on our slide and caused it to thaw. We gave him a good thumping and threw the rest of his undelivered papers over Grumpy McCarney's hedge. The dog attacked the papers and flittered them.

We had a great time floating on our raft but when we came back the next day it wasn't where we had moored it. We looked around in the small woods near the lake and found a pile of cinders and charred planks. We agreed that Honker had got his revenge for not being allowed on our raft.

We met Honker and his Cara Street pals after the cinema last Saturday and challenged him and his gang to a street fight on the Fort Hill later. We always picked Fort Hill for fights because there were never any adults up there to see us fighting.

The last time we had a street fight with them I had the pellet gun that Mattie had exchanged with Ted McMahon for the roller skates with me. Honker and his pals fired a few arrows from their bows, and a few stones from their catapults, at us as we coming up the Fort Hill but when I produced the pellet gun and fired a few pellets at them they ran away.

When I went to get the pellet gun this time it wasn't there. Mattie and Towbar had gone out shooting rats at the dump and had taken the pellet gun with them. We honoured our challenge without the pellet gun and got a bad beating from Honker and his Cara Street gang.

Sparks got hit by a stone in the same eye as he had had injured in our playful sword fighting. He was lucky that he was still wearing his eye patch because the stone sort of bounced off it.

Vinny got his lip split when his catapult snapped and the ball-bearing he was using for ammo sprang sideways and whacked him in the mouth.

I was chased by 'Bibbo' Corrigan when I ran out of marble ammunition for my catapult. 'Bibbo' had fired his sharply pointed wart-stick spear at me and I tripped and fell trying to avoid it. He caught me by the hair and shoved my face into muck and took my catapult.

As we were making our way home bruised and beaten Sparks suggested that when we go back to school that we should wait by the Victoria Fountain and throw Honker's school books in the water.

'Nearly right,' Vinny said wiping the blood on his lip and then added, 'we throw Honker in first and then his books after him.'

'I'll throw the books in and you and Finn throw him in,' Sparks said being more specific about the proposed attack.

He had just beaten me to it; I had the same suggestion but with me as the one 'dumping the books.' Vinny is much better at the rough stuff than either Sparks or me.

Mattie and Towbar got in worse trouble. They took the lead off the Scrap Dealer's shed two evenings ago and tried to sell it back to Mister Faye yesterday but he recognise his roofing lead and called the Guards. Daddy had a word with Mister Faye who is a lovely man and all that happened was that Mattie was grounded for a few days and Towbar was threatened by Daddy to stay away from Mattie or else he would put him in prison.

This morning looked like it was going to be just another ordinary day but it turned out to be anything but ordinary.

Mattie was in the kitchen when I was leaving to meet Sparks and Vinny at O'Hara's shop as planned the evening before. This was Mattie's second day being kept inside for his 'roof-lead dealings' with Towbar. I was glad to be getting out of the house because Mammy was in bad form with Mattie and over the 'poor water pressure' in the tap.

The plan with my pals was to inspect the County Council dump at the outskirts of the town for anything that might suit in our hideout. As I was approaching O'Hara's shop I saw Vinny crouched down at the front wheel of a bicycle. When I got closer and noticed a front carrier on it; I knew it had to be Donald Dooley's postbike. Sparks was swatting flies with a rubber strip at the shop litterbin.

'Are you ready?' Vinny asked sitting up on the postman's bicycle.

I wasn't quite sure what Vinny's intensions were but from my past misfortune with postbikes I was about to say 'no' when suddenly Donald Dooley came out of the shop. He removed his cap and swiped it at an unsuspecting Vinny, hitting him on the side of his head.

I feel a bit sorry for Vinny because that's two day in a row that he has been whacked by an adult.

Yesterday we were sitting on Patsy O'Hara's shop windowsill reading comics when the Town Crier, 'The Corncrake,' came walking down our road. As usual he was ringing his hand-bell, and making an announcement at the top of voice. This time he was shouting 'the town water would be turned off tomorrow from ten am 'til two pm.' And as usual we heckled after him, "Ka-ke-ka-ke, Ka-ke-ka-ke," trying to make the sound of the corncrake's mating call.

He made an effort to run and catch us but we were too fast for the small elderly man and he gave up after a short distance. We were confident that we would hear his bell-ringing and his announcement coming back up the road, so unperturbed, we sat back on the windowsill and continued to read our comics.

I was engrossed in the second part of my comic when I heard a thud and yelp beside me. 'The Corncrake' had managed to sneak up on us, by not ringing his bell or making the announcement and whacked Vinny on the shoulder with his bell. Sparks and I ran away to avoid a total onslaught.

The postman hopped on his bike and merrily cycled down towards our house. The more he peddled the louder a 'clacking noise' became but he gave no indication that he was hearing anything unusual. He's obviously not wearing his hearing aid today.

'Hey! Donald Duck, your engine is "banjaxed," you need a new one of these' Vinny roared after him holding up an ice lolly stick.

I know now for definite that Vinny has jammed an ice lolly stick, near the brake-block at the fork, and in through the spokes.

He got off the bicycle at our house and made a delivery.

Vinny started swatting flies too. He didn't pay much attention to the ones he splattered on Patsy O'Hara's freshly painted wall but he showed great interest in a fly he had only injured. He picked it up between his fingers, pulled its wings off and watched it scarper along the shop windowsill.

He took the magnifying glass out of his pocket, which he got in a lucky bag yesterday and started chasing the fly with the focused sunlight beam it created, until the fly shrivelled up.

'Poo there's a terrible pong of those flies when they are frying.' Vinny commented on his game.

'That's cruelty,' Sparks huffed going into the shop.

I nodded in agreement with a cringing face.

'What are you buying me?' Vinny called after him.

'Nothing, because you're cruel,' Sparks called his answer from inside the shop.

Sparks came out of the shop and put the stick end of the ice-pop into his mouth and blew several times before he slipped the orange coloured ice-pop out of the wrapper. He offered me a lick but temptation got the better of me and I had just began sucking it when he yanked it out of my mouth. Vinny asked for a bite.

After a lot of pleading, Sparks conceded on the understanding that Vinny would stop roasting live flies.

'Hurry up and finish your ice lolly we have to go to the dump,' Vinny said as if in pain, rolling a large chunk of ice-pop around in his mouth. Suddenly he cupped his hand on a bluebottle fly that had landed on his leg. He manoeuvred the terrorised buzzing fly out between his fingers and pulled the wings off.

I was waiting to see what Sparks's reaction was going to be but just then Myra came running up the road.

'Finn, Finn,' she was shouting at the top of her voice.

'Quick, give me that fly,' Sparks said with open cupped hands going towards Vinny.

'Mammy wants to see you immed, imm, now now,' my sister panted at me.

I saw Sparks sneaking up behind my sister and in one quick movement he shoved the wingless fly down the back of her dress. Myra ran screaming in front of me as I strolled towards the house.

'Don't be long, we have work to do,' Vinny called after me.

I acknowledged with a wave.

When I went into the kitchen Mammy was sitting with her elbows resting on the table and her hands pressed to her face. Myra was standing in the corner wriggling and whinging about a fly, as she stretched her hand down the back of her dress. Mattie was sitting silently in the very corner of the sofa. I could see wide red blotches on the side of his face and a discarded dishcloth beside Mammy on the table. She looked up at me.

'Sit,' she whined and pointing at a chair beside her and then concealed her face in her hands again.

I noticed pages of a hand written letter strewn sideways on top of one another on the table and I knew straight away that Mammy had a letter from Granny. I had been praying and hoping against hope that seeing as Granny hadn't written a letter by last week, that maybe she mightn't bother writing at all regarding our activities in Doiredrum. It wasn't to be.

Granny's writing is very legible, neat and easy to read. I focused to read what was written on the pages even though most of the pages were masking one another. To make it more difficult I was reading it from an up side down position. I could read 'the horse tied' at the top of one page; I knew what that was about, I could also read ; 'the church bell' mid way down another page and I knew what that was about as I did when I saw the word 'statue.' The words 'Agnes,' 'fell' and 'bicycle' were all on one line and a quick flash came to my mind had Agnes said something to Granny about the fire at the water pump.

I could see the names Micky McGinn and Johnny Byrne and the words 'fire' and 'petrol pump' further down another page. I'm convinced now that Agnes was the informant there as I know Ann and Pauric wouldn't have told. I saw the word 'bicycle' and wondered if it was the smelly man's bicycle or the postman's; does it really matter now.

I got weaker as I realised that all these pages had writing on both sides of the paper. As I was stretching to make out what was written on a page that was sideways on the table, Mammy peered out from behind her hands and I sat back onto the chair and gulped.

She took a deep breath and gathered the pages of the letter together and began at page one, skipping what were the obvious preliminaries. Mammy read the letter slowly and clearly and gasped a few times as she glanced at either Mattie or me.

I was going to plead innocence when we were accused of destroying the doctors house and horse trap but then it dawned on me that when your only witnesses are two hairy dumb donkeys it's time to know that you are beaten so I said nothing and just listened on to more damming evidence.

When Mammy stopped reading she folded the letter and asked in a whinging tone, 'What on earth am I going to do with you two Feather Heads?'

CHAPTER 35

The *Bad* is Oft' Interred...

GRANNY'S LETTER more or less said it all. We 'took it on the chin' for the pranks we did, and were found out on, but were disgruntled about being blamed in the wrong for wrecking Teach an Dochtúra and the horse-trap; but I suppose if we hadn't corralled the donkeys in the first place they wouldn't have done the damage.

Having said that, we had some consolation in that nobody ever found out who broke the church organ or produced any proof how Tim Herrity's sow ended up in the ditch or how Baba was nearly poisoned with Mattie's underpants or where the ball-bearing came from that choked the goose, so all and all, things sort of balanced out evenly enough.

Our Summer Holidays came to an end, the episode in Doiredrum faded into insignificance and it was 'business as usual' for Sparks, Vinny and me.

The Yank and his brother Dan Joe had their day in court to answer charges of, Illicit Poiteen Distillation, Sale and Supply of same, plus an additional charge brought by Customs Officers for Cigarette Smuggling.

The case was heard before Judge McClafferty who apart from being tagged 'the hanging judge' had a bad temper and an equally bad speech impediment.

The facts of the case presented, revealed that The Yank had

smuggled cartons of cigarettes across the border and brought them in sacks to Dan Joe's home. There he swapped his smuggled cigarettes for a consignment of Poiteen from his brother. They each sold their ill-gotten goods for a small profit around their own community.

The Yank didn't divulge that Mattie and me had been travelling with him on one of his racketeering escapades and Daddy gave him an otherwise 'good character reference.' The Judge's frown of suspicion rightfully suggested that some sort of deal had been done between Daddy and The Yank.

A restrained titter rippled through the court room as Judge Mc Clafferty stammered profusely when summing up the evidence and described the criminality as, 'R-R-R-er, Redneck Ra-Ra-ra Racketeering.'

The Yank got one month's suspended sentence and a ten shillings fine.

Dan Joe however had the stubborn impression that the Judge was imitating him and in addition to uttering obscenities, roared at the Judge, "wha-wha-what, ab-bba, about the, the, the Sergeant's sons." Thankfully for Mattie and me he didn't or couldn't elaborate and with the exception of 'interested parties' nobody knew what he was talking about.

It was blatantly obvious by the Judge's facial expressions, as he listened to Dan Joe's stammering, that he had assumed that Dan Joe was mimicking him and convicted accordingly. He sentenced Dan Joe to six months imprisonment and strongly recommended that he receive psychiatric treatment during his jail term.

All National and Local Newspapers gave regular coverage and in-depth analysis concerning the story of the mysterious Dutchman who had resided in Doiredrum.

Despite the fact that William van Heyningen was in possession of Lord Donaldson Barbour's painting at the time of the fatal shooting in Utrecht, Police in either Holland or Ireland, failed in their investigation to establish, how, where or when he took possession of it.

A search of his leased accommodation in Doiredrum uncovered the address of an Orphanage in Ilford on the outskirts of London. After further enquiries at the Orphanage, detectives from Scotland

Yard learned that he had been adopted as a newborn infant by an emigrant Dutch couple, Leo and Gert van Heyningen.

The identity and history of the natural mother of the baby were not disclosed on Confidentiality Grounds, other than to say that the mother's Nationality was 'Irish.'

After completing a Public School second level education in Greater London William van Heyningen emigrated to Canada and his adopted parents, repatriated to Breukelen near Utrecht in Holland.

Enquiries by the Royal Canadian Mounted Police revealed that William van Heyningen had rented a log cabin for a number of years near Labelle at the foot of Mount Tremblant, north of Montreal.

He was known to the Labelle Police for 'intimidation activities' while a member of the Anti Hunting Lobby and 'on file' with the Montreal Police for his overt support of the Homosexual fraternity. His few friends and acquaintances described him as a very kind man and were not surprised when he "adopted" an orphaned Bobcat cub.

It also came light that he ran a small Art Gallery in Montreal. The Serious Crime Squad sought to interview him in relation to the sale of forged masterpieces, but he had vacated both his business premises, and home, before they could do so.

When the Orphanage was pressed by The Press for more information concerning William van Heyningen, they were informed that apart from the occasional, casual and general correspondence received from him over the years, they had no other contact with him.

William van Heyningen was buried in the cemetery at Breukelen.

We were only two weeks back at school after the Summer Holidays when we received the sad news of my granny's death. She had failed to recover from a fatal asthma attack. The whole family went to the funeral and we were taken there by The Yank, but without stopping at his brother's house this time.

There was standing room only in the church, and the congregation outside spilled onto the roadway. The Canon's homily had nothing but praise for Granny. 'Her devotion to the Blessed Mother was matched only by her devotion to her family and to her pupils,' Canon Dillon concluded and Mammy proudly wiped a tear from her eye.

Granny was interred with her Irish Volunteer husband in Doiredrum Church Graveyard.

After the burial Service we were joined by other mourners at Granny's house, where an impressive spread was 'laid on' by her loving friends and neighbours.

While I was at the kitchen table, prodding and peeping in sandwiches to determine which ones were without onions, I overheard a conversation between Daddy and my uncle Frank who were standing by the stove.

He told Daddy that Granny had 'gone down hill a lot' after we left, but what he found very strange was the fact that Granny was very upset over the death of the Dutchman.

'She even gave me twenty pounds to give to Canon Dillon to say a load of Masses for the Dutchman, what do you make of that?' my uncle said with a wild shake of his head. He held Daddy by the arm and glanced quickly around him before continuing.

'She insisted, that I immediately post a letter, for her, to her friend, a Sister Bernadette in England, ah, they have been writing to one another for as far back as I can remember, but anaways, here's the damdist thing.'

My uncle looked around him again, sipped some whiskey, and cautiously added in a whisper, 'Mother put newspaper cuttings about the Dutchman's investigation, in with the letter.'

Daddy frowned and sipped from his glass too.

I was listening attentively as I took a bite of a sandwich, but suddenly had to race to the bathroom—I'd bitten into an onion. I covered my mouth and nose with my hand, in case I would vomit on the way, and was about to open the bathroom door when Sady Tom came out. I still had my hand over my mouth and nose.

She glared at me and muttered, 'impenitent brat.'

I don't know what she meant and I wasn't waiting to ask her. I slammed the door closed behind me and spat the nauseating sandwich bite into the toilet.

'Yakee, yak, I'm glad to get rid of that,' I mutter leaving the bathroom and walked straight into Agnes who was dourly waiting outside. Her face cringed, as her jowls quivered over me.

'You again,' she muttered storming into the bathroom.

I skipped down the hallway and met Dan McShane, in full postman's uniform, coming in the front door. Neither of us spoke and I followed him into the kitchen.

He grabbed a handful of sandwiches from the table and with frantic head gestures beckoned Uncle Frank to come over to him. My uncle topped up my father's whiskey glass first, and then waddled over to the postman.

Mammy busied herself between groups of people making sure that all were being looked after. Myra kept following her from the kitchen to the scullery and back, offering to help her, but I knew by the way Mammy was looking at Myra that she was really in her way.

I haven't seen Mattie since I saw him slipping into Uncle Frank's bedroom after we came back from the graveyard. He is probably feeling tired from the journey and is gone for a nap.

I picked my spot back at the table so that I would be able to hear the conversation between Uncle Frank and the postman. Dan McShane bungled two sandwiches into his mouth and wiped his hand on the side of his trousers before rummaging in his postbag. He made an attempt to speak but had to swallow before he could do so.

'This came in today, it's Registered Post," he splattered and wiped his mouth.

He had handed my uncle a heavily sealed envelope, and placed a slip of paper and pencil on the table.

'Judging from the handwriting it's from that nun in England, it's addressed to your mother of course, God be good to her, but sure under the circumstances, I suppose there is nothing wrong with you signing for it and opening it.'

'The nun doesn't know that mother is dead,' Uncle Frank responded shaking his head mournfully, 'wouldn't you think somebody would have told her,' he added, unwittingly admitting his own remiss

384

He looked over at Daddy as if requesting permission to open it.

'It's Registered Post—it must be very important,' the postman announced.

'And very private,' my uncle responded.

His prolonged stare at Daddy sought an immediate directive. My father strolled over as he drained his glass and spoke authoritaitvely, 'Okay Frank, open it up.'

Suddenly—BANG—a deafening blast noise, that resounded from the direction of the front yard, rasped its way through the kitchen. I was first of the startled crowd to make it out the front door and froze on the top doorstep as I looked down in front of me.

Mattie was sprawled face-up, his head resting on the cemented surrounds at the base of the house. A smoking shotgun lay ominously on the ground between himself and the front gate.

The curious excited crowd pushed me from behind and I stumbled and landed on my knees beside the dangerous weapon. I knew straight away that it was my uncle's shotgun. Uncle Frank's bedroom window gaped wide open as the curtains flopped to and fro in the twirling breeze. A pungent sulphur odour contaminated the otherwise fresh country air.

Small light feathers swirled and floated in the wind and drifted down around the gate pier. A tail-less rooster raced and hopped around the yard making vain attempts at 'take-off' to clear the 'danger zone.'

Mattie slowly sat up, gently rubbed the back of his head and then cringed grabbing at his right shoulder. He blinked a few times before violently twisting his index finger in his right ear. He shook his head and looked dazed as he spoke.

'Phew! nearly missed him.'

From a kneeling position I looked up and kept my eyes focused on my father storming his way towards Mattie. I paid little attention to the rest of the audience who were still scrambling to get out the door but then I noticed my bewildered mother, with bawling daughter in arms, burrowing her way to the front of the crowd.

She stopped on the doorstep, glared first at Mattie, then me and pined, 'Feather Heads.'

'Up!' Daddy ordered, helping Mattie to his feet, but I got up of my own accord. Uncle Frank, still with the unopened Registered

Post in his hand, gently moved my mother aside and stepped from the front line of the crowd. He quickly made his way to the shotgun, scooped it up from the ground and wiggled his way back through the crowd at the door, without saying a word.

'Get back inside you,' Mammy ordered Mattie.

I don't know if Mattie misunderstood Mammy's command, or if he was avoiding a walk through the 'gauntlet' at the front door, because he took long strides towards the open bedroom window. He had just put his hands on the window sill, had one leg cocked, when two voices simultaneously called aloud.

'Get out,' Uncle Frank shouted from inside his bedroom window.

'Get in,' Daddy ordered pointing towards the front door.

Mattie walked with a stoop passing Mammy in the doorway with his hands raised around his head for protection. Myra was now standing and sobbing beside Mammy, and wriggled her finger threatening, as Mattie increased his pace and skipped untouched past everyone to sanctuary, behind a locked bathroom door.

All had settled back in the kitchen before my uncle returned from his bedroom. I presume the delay was caused by him trying to find a new and better hiding place for his shotgun.

I was standing beside Daddy at the same spot near the table, as I had been before the excited exodus, a few minutes earlier. The Registered Post Receipt and pencil were still on the table where the postman had left them. As soon as Uncle Frank had joined Daddy, the postman approached them and pointed to the envelope in my uncle's hand as he spoke.

'I suppose you better open it, Frank.'

'Dan, go over there to Tessie and get yourself a cup of tea,' Uncle Frank ordered nodding towards the scullery before scribbling his signature on the receipt. He handed the receipt and pencil to the displeased postman who reluctantly obeyed.

My uncle fumbled tearing at the white envelope and eventually pulled out a card. It looked like a Birthday card at first but then I saw two lines of bold lettering on the front:

With Sincere Sympathy

He cautiously and slowly opened the card outwards and read. His lips quivered as he read it for a second time. The envelope fell from his hand and floated zigzag towards the floor coming to rest under a chair. He exhaled with a pant and rested a hand on the table.

Daddy took the card and squinted, reading it, but then fumbled in his jacket pocket before he eventually found what he was looking for and removed his spectacles from the case. He settled himself and read it again. His glazed eyes gradually widened to a startled glare and looked distorted through the spectacle lenses as he muttered in a whispering gasp.

'Good God no, God no...Lord Donaldson Barbour's painting...my sons brought...oh no.'

'You're probably right about that,' Uncle Frank said in a weakening voice, 'but there can be no doubt about the other.'

'The other what?' Mammy asked coming in on the end of the conversation.

Daddy lowered the Mass Card to his side and looked at my uncle—this time it was Daddy looking for guidance. 'Tessie has to know, she has a right to know,' my uncle responded in a soft pleading voice.

Daddy gently shook his head, as a gesture that it was not the decision he wanted to hear.

'Mac, what are ye talking about, what's going on?' Mammy apprehensively addressed her husband.

Daddy looked over at my uncle again, hoping for a change in his decision.

'Give it to her Mac, give it to her,' Uncle Frank nodded pursing his lips.

Daddy slowly parted with the Mass Card and consolingly placed his hand on Mammy's shoulder. After a few meek gasps Mammy lowered the card from her tearful eyes. The Mass Card eased its way from her limp hand and toppled and flapped from the table to the floor.

Mammy, Daddy and Uncle Frank looked at one another in silence with a countenance of disbelief.

I crouched under the table, sat on the kitchen floor and picked up the Mass Card. I read:—

The Holy Sacrifice of the Mass

will be offered

for the repose of the soul of

your darling son William.

at the request of

your dear friend in Christ
Bernadette.

THE END